AFFILIATION

ANDREW GREVILLE WATTS

 FriesenPress

One Printers Way
Altona, MB R0G 0B0
Canada

www.friesenpress.com

Copyright © 2023 by Andrew Greville Watts
First Edition — 2023

All rights reserved.

No part of this publication may be reproduced in any form, or by any means, electronic or mechanical, including photocopying, recording, or any information browsing, storage, or retrieval system, without permission in writing from FriesenPress.

ISBN
978-1-03-917857-1 (Hardcover)
978-1-03-917856-4 (Paperback)
978-1-03-917858-8 (eBook)

1. FICTION, THRILLERS, MEDICAL

Distributed to the trade by The Ingram Book Company

To the Summers Family

I hope you enjoy the book

AG. Watts

PROLOGUE

"YOU CAN'T keep something like this a secret forever; you can't keep it locked away behind some steel door in the basement."

Slater just stared at Bhergosian. "You don't mind if we continue to try, do you? I mean, we've been doing it since the early sixties, and only a few have found out. We've taken care of everyone without any breach of security. Our track record is pretty good."

"How many people already know?"

Slater smirked. "As I said, our security has been excellent."

"Oh, come on. I found out. I broke through your firewall, and I'm only a computer geek. A computer genius must have gotten through before me. You can't possibly hope to control every variable."

"Spoken like a true scientist. I only control what I can. But in truth, there have been a few who have discovered what you did, but we have been able to keep them quiet, one way or another."

"What do you mean by that? Have they been killed?"

"Regrettably so. But not everyone has. Understand this: we do not want to kill anyone. When we don't have to, we don't, but sometimes it's necessary. But once we've been able to explain how important it is to keep our secret as such, most of those who have stumbled onto things have been persuaded to stay quiet."

"Someone will talk. Knowing what they know, what I know, someone will talk. Secrets always find a way out."

"Come on, Doctor. We've been able to keep something as innocuous as PLPD quiet from the public since its inception in the mid-nineties. And there are how many industry people who know all about that?"

Dr. Bhergosian knew something about PLPD from his time with Matthews. It was a prescription-data collection service that nearly every pharmaceutical company bought to better direct their marketing efforts to doctors.

"But that is a relatively minor secret. What we're talking about is huge. It will get out."

"Really? How many presidents of the United States have there been? Forty-three, forty-four?"

"I don't get it."

"Those men have all been exposed to the country's top secrets, huge secrets, our most guarded secrets: military; commercial; societal; secrets about covert operations; authorized assassinations. They know everything or nearly *everything*. How many tell-all books have been written exposing even the most innocuous of secrets after these men left office? The books that are written are simple diatribes about life in the White House or what it's like to spend the weekend at Camp David. And I'm not taking into account the other world leaders, men and women, throughout time. No one has talked. And you know how gossipy politicians are. No, it is precisely because of the nature of our secret, as you called it, that people won't talk."

"I still don't—"

"They don't talk because they know what would happen if they did talk. If they were to reveal what they know, then society would face turmoil if not complete collapse. It would not just be that secrets could not trusted to be kept as such; the very secret itself would shake society to its core. They stay silent because to do otherwise would destabilize our way of life, and those leaders only protect a country. We are protecting an entire world. If this got out, it would be a scandal on steroids. No one will talk. You can bank on that."

Bhergosian just stared at Slater. He couldn't believe what he was hearing. Ever since he had stumbled onto what was in the bunker's computer system, he'd had a burning desire to get it out to the public. That's why he had created the USB.

Bhergosian wanted to keep him talking. "If you are the one in control, and it seems that you are, then why don't you make the decision to release what you've got down there? Society would adjust."

Slater was clearly quite exasperated. A man of Bhergosian's intelligence should be able to grasp the concept of secrecy and why this needed to stay secret. Hadn't he just explained it? "If we released everything we had, the ensuing chaos would be catastrophic. The societal upheaval would be epic. We have a mission to protect what we have so carefully accumulated."

"Your mission!? Your mission is killing people!"

Slater whirled around. "Doctor, I take offence to that. We do not kill people. We preserve millions of lives. We extend lifetimes. We keep people living longer, healthier lives. The ones we've had to kill have been unfortunate but necessary. It just depends on your point of view."

Just then, the cell phone in Slater's pocket rang. "Slater here... No, no, he's still here. Where else would he be? ... You're coming now? ... Very well."

Slater turned his back to Bhergosian and spoke in hushed tones to the person on the other end of the line. During this time, Bhergosian was able to look around. He was sitting on a chair about twenty feet from the office door. There was a coffee table to his right in front of a plush leather sofa. There was a desk to his left covered in the paraphernalia you'd expect: a pen holder; a coffee cup; business card holder. There were also lots of pictures of Slater with various dignitaries: presidents, prime ministers, Nobel winners, several Hollywood celebrities. *It's interesting,* thought Bhergosian, *that there are none of his family.* While surveying the shrine, he came upon a crystal plaque set in a silver base. Bhergosian read the inscription: 'William Slater, CEO of the Year.' He was close enough to it that, if he moved quickly enough, he could grab it and use it as a weapon. The irony of hitting Slater with his own award was not lost on him. Also, sitting right beside the award was the USB stick.

Slater turned back to the doctor. "Dr. Bhergosian, they'll be here in a—" As he finished his turn towards him, Bhergosian grabbed the award with his left hand, sprang from his chair, and swung it at Slater's head. The award glanced off of Slater's right shoulder, cutting down its velocity, but it still connected with a wallop. Slater lurched to his left, crashing into the coffee table with his shins. This sent him sprawling towards the sofa, where he bounced his chest off the arm before spinning to the floor on his back. Bhergosian hesitated slightly, looking down at Slater, lying on the floor groaning and holding his head. *Thank God, I didn't kill him,* he thought. He reached down and grabbed the USB stick and ran to the door. He hid off to one side as he knew the guard outside would surely have heard the commotion and would be coming through it right away. Sure enough, the door burst open, and the guard ran into the office and quickly made his way over to the stunned CEO. Bhergosian took this opportunity to slip quietly out of the office. He ran through the outer office and into the hallway.

Back in the office, the guard reached Slater and began pulling him to his feet. "Mister Slater, what happened?" It was then the guard realized that the other man, who had gone into the office with Slater some fifteen minutes before, was nowhere to be seen. Slater was now on his knees, rubbing the side of his head. The guard still had him under the armpits and was pulling him up when Slater cut in, "Don't worry about me, you idiot! Get that asshole. Find him. Don't let him out of the building."

Slater grabbed his cell phone and punched in a number. "He got away. He hit me with my award and ran out the door when your shit-for-brains guard ran in to check." Slater suddenly looked down. "Fuck, I think he broke my award... What? What? No, he's on the loose inside the building. Find him. Lock the building down, and don't let him out. I mean, what the hell does he think he can do at this point…" Slater's voice trailed off as he looked at this desk. "Oh shit. He has the stick. He has the fucking stick. Get your men to the exits now. Get that stick back."

Dr. Bhergosian had no intention of trying to leave the building. In fact, he was counting on his pursuers thinking that's what he wanted to do. What he wanted was to find an isolated office with a computer. If he could get a mass mailing out, then someone would surely open the attachment and know what he knew. It had to get out. Someone would talk.

CHAPTER 1

YESTERDAY HAD been easy. It had been fun. Not that Derek didn't like his job nearly every day. He set his own hours. He was his own boss, and he answered to no one. Who wouldn't like that? Even with the thought of getting caught ever-present in the back of his mind, he liked his job. So, while each day usually brought a smile to his face, yesterday had been especially rewarding.

It was summer in Boston. The sun was shining. The temperature hovered in the low nineties, and the crowds flooded the downtown. The Common was packed. Quincy Market and Faneuil Hall strained with people. They were packed together, bumping into each other every three or four seconds. People were leaning over souvenir stands to get a better look at the cheap jewelry or the even cheaper T-shirt they'd buy and bring back to someone who'd offer up a thank you all the while thinking, *Is that it?* However, for Derek, the working conditions could not have been better. He had identified and tracked over a dozen marks. He had bumped into tourists and grabbed their wallets. He had picked up purses left ever so briefly unattended. He had even swiped a diaper bag. At the time he had thought, *What the hell!?* His hunch had paid off with a wallet full of cash tucked into the corner of the bag. Some dummy, in his rush to get back to the market carnage, had even withdrawn two hundred dollars in cash from an ATM and promptly left the cash in the machine after carefully checking his receipt and putting it back in his wallet. Derek had just happened to be near enough to see this and quietly pocketed the money. It was one of those dream days.

Derek had felt so good about himself, the day, and his luck, that while walking home, he cut through the parking lot of a medical clinic building where he spotted a nice new Ford Escape parked at the back of the lot, peeked inside, and saw a computer bag on the front seat. Given his luck that day, he quietly said to himself, "I can't pass this up." Derek's friends would have just smashed in the window and grabbed the bag, but he took more pride in his work than that. He had the tools to get inside. In a matter of seconds, he had the bag and was on his way with very minimal damage to the car.

Sitting on his couch at ten in the morning the next day, Derek looked over his haul from his dream day. He had pulled in over two thousand dollars in cash. He had a bunch of assorted jewelry, watches, cell phones, an iPad, some weird lighters, and the computer bag. Derek had gone through the bag several times. Aside from a very nice, new IBM laptop, it had a bunch of glossy, ringed booklets with thick pages and colorful charts and graphs inside. As well, there were some documents that looked like brochures with titles like *The New England Journal of Medicine* and *The Lancet*. Derek spent a few minutes trying to figure out what a "Lancet" was but had soon given up. As near as he could figure out, the charts and graphs were about some sort of drug for high blood pressure. What did he care about high blood pressure? He was only twenty-one years old. The computer, though, was another matter. It was an IBM T420 laptop, top of the line. It had two labels on it. One read "Property of Matthews Pharmaceuticals" and the other read "Stephanie Beachom." They'd be coming off right away. He had already talked to a buddy of his who was a computer genius.

DEREK'S FRIEND would hack into it, then strip it down so just the operating software remained. He'd then then sell it on the street. His buddy had said that they'd get at least six hundred dollars for it. They always split these deals fifty-fifty. *I might take the next couple days off.* He had laughed to himself.

The knock on the door came as Derek was putting the laptop back on the coffee table. He went to the front door and peeked through the peep hole. A FedEx agent was on the other side, holding up a package. "Package for you," he said nonchalantly.

Derek opened the door but kept the chain on. "A package for me? I wasn't expecting a package."

"Absolutely it's for you." The agent smiled. "As long as you're Derek Bolen, it's for you. You just have to sign for it to take delivery, and I'll be on my way."

Derek closed the door slightly to unhook the chain.

The fake FedEx agent in the hall, and his companion hiding out of Derek's sight, had been thorough in checking this floor of the apartment building. Using the FedEx box as a ruse, they had knocked on every door to see if anyone was on the floor. The only other person they had found at home was a little old lady on the other side of the floor. She was hard of hearing and played her TV loud to compensate. This job would be a piece of cake. The fake FedEx agent had remarked to his companion after leaving the old lady, "Poor bastard. He has no idea."

Just as Derek was sliding the chain along its track to unhook it, the kick came. It was an explosive blast that blew the door into him, knocking him onto his back, knocking the wind out of him, making him slide down his hallway and stop in front of his living room. The chain attachment ripped from its moorings, and the door jamb splintered apart where the chain attachment had been.

Derek lay on his back, struggling to breathe. He glanced up to see the FedEx agent walking towards him, followed by another guy dressed in a suit and tie. The suit quickly and quietly closed the door behind them.

"What the fuck?" Derek squeezed the words out of his mouth.

In the next instant, the FedEx agent picked him up and pushed him into his living room, landing him on the couch.

"Sit there, and don't say a thing, you dumb ass wipe, unless we ask you to say something." The force of their entry, the strength of his grip, the conviction in his voice, and Derek's own troubles to regain his wind would have been more than enough for him to comply, he thought. The handgun pointed at his head seemed over the top.

THE MAN in the suit walked calmly and slowly into the living room and looked around. Noticing the many items that made up the previous day's haul, he asked, "You a thief? A pickpocket?"

"Yeah," Derek answered, his breath now returning. "I have plans to go to college, but I need more money, you know?"

The FedEx agent leaned in on him. "Ever thought of a job?" Derek shrugged.

The man in the suit fixed his gaze on the laptop. "Here it is," he said as he picked it up. "You open this?"

"No, n-no way," stammered Derek. "I didn't do anything to it. You can have it. You can have anything you want; just leave me alone."

The man in the suit looked down at Derek, who was clearly terrified. "Well," he said, "we got what we came for, so we'll be on our way."

Derek's sense of relief was so great, he almost wet himself as the feeling washed over him. Then he saw the sneer develop on the FedEx agent's face as he leveled the gun at Derek. He threw his hands up, but the three bullets just smashed through them, slamming into and then through Derek's forehead. In the instant before death, Derek did not relive his life. Family and friends did not materialize, nor did great memories reveal themselves. The only thought that jumped into his diminishing brain was, *How the hell did they find me?*

THE MAN in the suit jumped back as the FedEx agent shot Derek. "Why the hell did you do that, Ben? We only had authorization to kill if we were met with deadly force."

"Oops."

"I don't know how this is going to play back at the store."

"Relax, Colin. What's in this box is all we need to make this look right." Ben ripped open the box and dumped a wide array of illegal drugs on the table, the floor, the couch, and Derek. A drug deal gone bad: that's what the cops would think.

They left the apartment, being careful to leave the door partially open. They wanted to lure someone in to find the body. In this heat and humidity, the smell would be bad within hours, and both men thought the apartment building smelled bad enough already.

CHAPTER 2

THE BASEMENT of Matthews Pharmaceuticals was dedicated to the company's Business Technology department. It was filled with computer stations, various screens, and equipment manned by technical support people. The people in the room monitored everything about the company. One whole section was directed at helping sales representatives, sales managers, and medical support people in the field. If they had any kind of technical problem with their laptops, cell phones, iPads, or the computer software they used, they would call these people to get it resolved. Given that there were around eight thousand people in the field in the US for Matthews, the tech support people were kept very busy. If they happened to not be fielding calls, they performed routine system checks or they monitored equipment, checked the mainframe for glitches, and pushed downloads to every computer in the company when they were directed to do so. These downloads involved new processes, anti-viral programs, Physician Level Prescribing Data, sales data ... basically anything the company told them to download.

There was another section on the floor dedicated to monitoring and auditing any and all computers and equipment the company had out in the field. Technicians in this section would be constantly looking to see if anyone had been using their equipment in contravention of company policy. Had someone sent an email that was inappropriate or that included foul and/or abusive language? The company's keystroke spyware would root that out, the monitoring station would instantly pick it up, and the person would be flagged. Had someone downloaded unauthorized software, either from the internet or with an external USB? That would be picked up the moment the computer was synchronized with the mainframe. The monitoring station would pick it up, and the person would be flagged. Was the company's equipment being used for too much personal business? The company's threshold spyware would gauge the ratio of personal business to company business. The monitoring station would pick it up, and the person would be flagged. Was the computer trying to access websites banned by the company? That would be detected by the monitoring station, and the person would be flagged. Had the computer not been synchronized with the mainframe often enough as per company policy? The monitoring station would pick that up, and the person would be flagged. Had a computer virus infected any of the company's laptops? The monitoring station would pick that up, the infected computer would be quarantined, and the virus would be eradicated.

The monitoring station was dedicated to the overall technical health of the company and keeping tight checks and balances on personnel in the field. In cases where a computer had been inappropriately used and the person flagged for it, they would be contacted. Usually, the offences were minor, and a friendly email would be sent reminding the offending individual of the company policy they had broken, and that was that. In most cases, it was enough for the flagged person to find out that they were being monitored for them to change their behavior. More serious breaches of company policy were dealt with in an ever-escalating manner up to and including dismissal. The company actually had a term for this: "Progressive Discipline Policy."

One function of the monitoring station that was not used as much as the basic watchdog was the ability of the software to detect where the company's equipment was at any given moment or where it had been in the previous thirty days. Every piece of company equipment had a GPS device embedded in it. This included laptops, iPhones, iPads, and cars. If the piece of equipment already had a GPS in it, then Matthews did nothing, but if it did not have a GPS, one was added before it went to the employee. The technology was accurate enough to pinpoint the exact location of any piece of equipment at any time. If a manager suspected a sales rep was not working, he or she could ask the monitoring station to track the employee's cell phone movements and whereabouts in a specified period of time. These movements and locations could then be checked against what the rep had entered into their computer regarding where they had been. If the GPS data did not match what the rep had entered, then the rep was confronted and usually fired. In the past, managers had needed to obtain the actual cell phone records and spend hours comparing the locations of the calls, both incoming and outgoing, against what the rep had recorded as their locations. If the rep had entered in their computer that they had been in San Antonio for four days straight, and their cell phone records had them in Las Vegas, then the manager had the evidence needed for dismissal. Although some managers liked the 'CSI'-like investigative feel of this exercise, it was cumbersome and time consuming. It was much easier and quicker to have the monitoring station use the GPS data. One thing the monitoring station knew about that not many other departments did was the GPS in company cars. Matthews, like most pharma companies, had GPS units installed post-factory before the car got to the employee. If a troublesome employee thought they were smart enough to leave their phone at home and not be caught stealing company time, they invariably took their car, and the GPS data could be used against them. So, if a computer was stolen, and it contained sensitive enough data, a request was sent by the highest company authority to pinpoint its location. The technician who did the locating had no idea what the company did with the information. They just did as they were told by Matthews Pharmaceuticals. After all, the company cut their checks.

There was another part of the basement no one had seen. It was a room located behind a steel door at the very back of the basement. Only four people had ever been seen going into it. One was the CEO, William Slater. There were two other men that went in on a fairly regular basis. They were both tall, fit, and always in expensive suits. The fourth man was a short, stocky, bald fellow with no neck and less of a personality. He entered and left the room at least five times a day. When one of the technicians had attempted to joke with him about the secrecy of this room, he had simply looked at him with a stare that everyone recognized as him saying, *"Shut the fuck up, get the fuck out my way, and don't ever fucking bother me again."* The technicians in the main Business Technology section had come to call the room "The Bunker" and the man with no neck "Der Fuhrer."

It was the GPS application that had first begun to sour Miguel Bennetto on Matthews. He had joined just over a year ago. Fresh out of MIT with a degree in computer programming and systems applications, he had struggled to find a good job that fit his credentials. He had looked extensively but had come up empty over a two-month period. One weekend, he had gone to a local job fair, stopped at the booth of Matthews Pharmaceuticals Inc., and talked to their Human Resources person about jobs at the Big Pharma company. Matthews was the biggest pharmaceutical company in the world, with 135,000 employees worldwide. Miguel had talked about his education and what he wanted to do with it, and the HR person had suggested that he apply for a job in the Business Technology section. Miguel had initially thought the job was a waste of his education, but the HR person explained that the size of Matthews provided lots of opportunities to move into areas better suited to his education and career aspirations. He might have to spend some time doing basic computer fixes and the like, but the sky was the limit. Given his lack of a job and rapidly depleting resources, Miguel had applied on the spot, and after three interviews over the next four weeks, he was hired as a support help desk technician at a salary of seventy-two thousand dollars a year and a phenomenal benefits package that included full health and dental among others.

He had enjoyed his time at Matthews, even though he felt his computer talents were stagnating, and had liked the company until the disquieting incident two weeks ago when he had been with another technician, who was running a GPS check on a rep in Tulsa.

"Mig, come over here, will ya? It's time you got more exposed to what we can do around here." The technician was Stuart Hendly, a likable guy that had been in the basement for over five years. Miguel went over as he was asked. Hendly was at a station Miguel had not worked before. He was sitting in front of a computer and typing in an access code. The screen came to life with a heading of "GPS Tracking Program" and a prompt to type in a passcode. Hendly typed in a code, and he was given access to what looked like a simple company directory.

"What's so interesting about this?" Miguel asked. "I mean, I can access the company directory from any of these computers."

"Yes, you can." Hendly smirked. "But you can't do this." He then typed in a name that resulted in an employee profile being lit up on the screen. A picture of a man who looked like he was in his late forties came up. Under the picture was the name Bob Dauphin. The screen gave some basic information on his length of time with the company—seventeen years—as well as a list of awards he had won over the years, including rep of the year six times,

President's Circle nine times, and other more obscure-sounding awards. "He looks like a great employee, right?" Hendly asked, and Miguel just nodded. "He might be," continued Hendly, "yet his manager has asked us to run a jips check."

"What's that?"

"Jips stands for GPS or 'jip the company check.' Old Bob's manager thinks his model representative has been screwing the pooch of late and falsifying his activity data. I'm going to run a check on his phone and car to see where old Bob has been over the last thirty days and compare that to what he's told the computer and Matthews about where he's been. So, all I do is ask the computer to access Bob's GPS chips in his cell phone, computer, and car and give me a report of the locations of those devices each day for the past thirty days. The thing is ... the manager thinks we're just running a check on his phone and computer. We don't tell the managers about the GPS in the car. When we give them the report, we just usually just use the phone data. Only if the rep has left his phone at home do we include the car data, but we tell the district manager that we used the phone."

Miguel had not heard of this application before and was immediately disturbed by it. "How much data are we talking about here? Will you know where the equipment has been every minute of every day?"

"Pretty much." Hendly had finished typing in some commands, and a list of addresses under the heading of a succession of dates came up on the screen. "The first thing we do is get the location information for the car and the phone and compare that to what Bob has entered." The two men studied the screen and could quickly see that some of the locations on the left, the GPS data, did not match the locations on the right—the "Bob data" as Hendly referred to it. Hendly hit the print button and quickly had the printout in his hands showing them exactly what had been on the screen. Each day showed that, at various times of the day, Bob—or Bob's car and phone—was at a different location than where he had told the computer it had been. Also, there was a location that showed a pattern of Bob being at an exact location at least four times a week at the same time every day.

"You see this?" Hendly offered. "Bob seems to go to this location nearly every day of the week. The car seems to get there at around noon, and the GPS locator doesn't have it leaving the address until after four in the afternoon.

Also, Bob's phone GPS seems to match with the car, so we can guess that Bob, the phone, and the car are together. And look at this." Hendly held up the printout and pointed to the locations under the heading 'Computer.' "You see, the computer GPS only indicates one address, which is probably Bob's house, so we know he does not carry his computer with him as per company policy. Miguel, would you please use that computer to Google that address we found for the car and phone?"

Even though Miguel felt like he was prying or even spying into someone's life, he did as he was told. He typed in the address, and his screen showed that it correlated with Lucky's Casino in Tulsa, Oklahoma. Hendly looked over Miguel's shoulder. "So, old Bob has a gambling problem, does he? He likes to hit the casino at noon and on the company time."

Miguel turned to face Hendly. "Well, maybe he finishes his work early and then takes the time after that."

"I don't think so, Sparky," Hendly replied. "We don't pay Bob to sit on his Tulsa tush, gambling away his money. We pay him to see doctors and sell pills. My guess is that someone in the field has eyes on Bob's job and knew about this, so he tipped off the manager."

"What will happen to him?"

"He'll more than likely be fired. I mean, Matthews will probably give him a package, so he doesn't ask a lot of questions or kick up a fuss about the GPS track, but he's out the door. Bye-bye, Bob." There was something in Hendly's voice that struck a chord with Miguel. This was a man's life he was talking about. He could see from his profile that he was married, and he had kids. From what Miguel could tell, he had been a great employee, winning lots of awards. Maybe he had fallen on hard times, maybe there had been a traumatic event in his life. And this data had only gone back thirty days.

"Shouldn't the company help this guy versus gunning him down? I mean, doesn't he deserve some compassion? He's done a good job for us over the years. And this only goes back thirty days. How do we know this isn't something recent and an aberration of his normal behavior?" Miguel was upset at the level of cold, calculating callousness.

Hendly casually stood up, taking the printout of the car and phone location data as well as the casino location and looked at Miguel. "Not our call, my friend, not our call. That's up to his manager and Matthews. My guess is what I said. Bob's gonzo. It doesn't matter that we only have thirty days worth of data. It could be three days and that would be enough." Hendly looked at the screen one last time and shook his head. "When will these dumb bastards learn? If they lie to the computer, we will find out. Sooner or later, we will find out."

As Hendly left him, Miguel was left standing alone, wondering about Bob Dauphin and his family and what they were about to go through. He didn't like it at the time, and two weeks later, he liked it even less.

CHAPTER 3

STEVEN WILLIAMS had been a sales representative for Matthews Pharmaceuticals for slightly over ten years. In that time, he had won numerous sales awards. He had won trips to Venice, Rome, the Caribbean, Nevis, Jamaica, and Portugal.

He had started by calling on family physicians but had been promoted to a hospital-representative position five years ago. He worked in Seattle and called on specialists based in the local hospitals. He didn't have to travel that much, which he liked. He had liked his job a lot up to about four and a half years ago. At that time, a new CEO had been installed at Matthews, and he had brought in a number of changes. In the past, all reps had had a great deal of autonomy and freedom to do their jobs in a manner they thought appropriate but still within internal company guidelines for good business practices. But since William Slater had been brought in, the changes had placed an ever-tightening series of shackles on the ordinary rep. New processes had been installed in everything from expenses to how they had to report their daily activity. In Steven's mind, the company had eroded the sense of trust that had been such a cornerstone of Matthews over the first five-plus years of Steven's tenure. The company had always trusted that the rep went out the door to do their job. With over eight thousand people in the field in the US, not punching a time clock, this trust had been critical to the day-to-day functioning of the firm. There were rules that governed how they interacted with doctors, and as long as the business results had been good and no rules had been broken, the company had let people do their own thing. The pay scales had always been good, and now he was well paid with an annual salary exceeding one hundred thousand dollars. In addition, he was usually able to earn a bonus in the area of twenty thousand dollars each year. He also had a company car with a card to buy gas and make repairs. To an outsider, his recent discontent with his company and his job would seem crazy.

Steven often had downtime in his job and would sit and wonder how he could be so discontented with what appeared to be such a cushy situation. But the changes in the company—the change in its culture, the change in its treatment of people, the change in its processes, the change in its respect for people—had Steven wondering if he could continue much longer. There had also been changes industry wide that had taken a lot of the fun out of the job. Whenever a group of older reps got together, they would lament the loss of such things as being able to take a doctor golfing or to a sporting event. Representatives were no longer allowed to buy dinner for the spouse of a doctor. There were no more giveaways of any kind. They could not give out pens, calendars, sticky pads, or anything else that could be construed as a gift, no matter how small the value. Now, there was talk that soon they would not be able to buy a lunch for a doctor and their clinic staff. Despite what the media wrongly reported as pharmaceutical reps going on lavish spending sprees to buy a doctor's loyalty towards their drug, it was simply no longer true. The industry was far less fun; his company was far less fun. But he had always come back to the same conclusion: *What the hell else am I going to do that pays me like this?* So, he had soldiered on, wondering if the new industry rules/Slater experiment was just that: a brief experiment that everyone would tire of sometime soon, and then the previous culture and respect for people could be restored both at Matthews and in the industry as a whole.

Steven had just gotten home from another day in the field. Single, he lived in a small house in a nice suburb of Seattle. He had bought the place five years ago and had not gotten into the sub-prime mess he had seen some of his friends experience over the past several years. He had bought what he could afford.

The day before, Steven had logged onto his computer and received his PLPD data for the most recent fiscal quarter but had not had a chance to read it. This was one of the biggest changes to the pharmaceutical industry that had occurred in the late nineties. Nearly every pharmaceutical company bought Prescription Level Prescribing Data (PLPD) from information collection companies. This was data that the information companies purchased from pharmacies across America. The pharmacies were grouped together by adjoining and nearby zip codes to form a representative's territory. The company then went into every zip code and polled a certain number of pharmacies. The more drugstores they polled, the more accurate and more expensive the information was that they bought to then sell. The pharmacies sold information on what drugs were dispensed by the physician who wrote the prescription. The undertaking was massive. The information was purchased by therapeutic classes of drugs, and then broken down to each and every physician writing a prescription that was filled by the store. The information was then collated by doctor, and sorted into the highest-writing doctors, by therapeutic class and individual drug. So, Steven would quickly know that Dr. X had written one hundred prescriptions of his drug in the last quarter based on the polling data. This information was then used to generate Steven's 'target list' of doctors. His list included the top 120 writing physicians from his territory. And because of the size and resources of Matthews, Steven's data was from a polling of approximately seventy-five percent of the drugstores in his area. His PLPD information was highly accurate. The data even told him how many of his competitors' drugs were being written, sorted by doctor. It even told him if his prescriptions were trending down or up by quarter for the last four quarters. It even told him what percentage of prescriptions his drug represented by every therapeutic class he worked in. It was very good data. Steven would often chuckle at the stories he would invariably hear at meetings. Old representatives would describe how in the old days, a rep had to do this leg work themselves by going into the drugstores, developing a relationship with the pharmacist, and getting the information by asking. Or they could just ask their customers after they got to know them well. Steven liked his information much better as it allowed him to tailor his efforts to certain groups of doctors who were either trending up or down in prescribing his drug. This level of data collection was all very hush-hush in the industry. When asked about it by customers who might have heard a rumor, the representative was instructed to say something like, "We do get high-level information on sales trends in our territories including some prescription information. But we do not know that you wrote drug X for Mrs. Brown last week." While this response was sort of true, it was designed to mollify the questioner without revealing the whole truth. Steven had used it many times in his career, and he had never had any pushback. If a rep went further in his explanation and a supervisor found out, then the rep was severely disciplined or sometimes let go, especially if he put his interaction in writing in his call notes. It was a secret Matthews and the other purchasing companies wanted to keep very quiet. Given how many reps were running around, Steven was amazed there had never been a journalistic exposé on this issue in the drug industry.

One of the new processes Slater had introduced was the absolute requirement that every representative log on to their computer every day and connect with the mainframe to tell Matthews who they had seen that day, at what time they had seen them, and what they had talked about. Failure to do so resulted in the rep being called before their immediate supervisor to explain why they had missed a day in the past week. Steven could still remember the quote from Slater at a meeting thirteen months ago when he had personally delivered this change to the field force at meetings across the country: *"There are no exceptions to this requirement. It is a matter of compliance. And if you are not compliant every day, then you are not compliant at all."* Steven sat in front of his computer and entered in all the calls of his day. He had seen eight psychiatrists and three geriatric specialists. He dutifully entered in the call notes, being careful not to tell the company everything. He knew his customers very well, and he often talked about personal issues: their families, issues in their personal lives, etc. If he entered any of this information, he would surely be flagged for breaching a privacy law that Matthews had decided was worth adhering to. That was another of Steven's beefs about Matthews's four-and-a-half-year-old CEO. Slater was a lawyer, and before coming to Matthews six years ago, he'd had no pharmaceutical experience. He had been the legal VP for Burger King, for crying out loud. He knew nothing about the drug industry but a lot about laws and process. But from what Steven had read, Slater also knew a lot about politics and how to smooth talk his way into whatever situation benefited him the most. In fact, Steven had read in an economics magazine a while back that Slater had quietly campaigned behind the old CEO's back for months before the Matthews board had pulled the trigger and gunned the old guy down. But to make up for being let go so unceremoniously, the outgoing CEO had received a little more than two hundred million dollars.

So, Steven was compliant about what his boss called "the basic requirements of the job."

After completing his call entry but not yet connecting to the mainframe, he clicked on his email. He had gone out the door early that Friday morning, but his phone had received an odd email message on Thursday evening with a simple "You must open this!" in the subject title. Steven was always wary of such messages as they were probably viruses, but this one was different as the sender was indicated as Helmut Bhergosian. Steven knew Dr. Bhergosian was a prominent scientist who worked for Matthews. He had been lured out of a university research position to come work for Matthews and head up its research work into schizophrenia and psychosis. And Steven remembered that odd conversation he'd had with Dr. Bhergoisan only a few weeks ago at a company meeting to roll out yet another series of changes.

Steven had done a send/receive Thursday evening after looking at his phone but had not opened the attachment in the doctor's message. He had disconnected his computer from the Matthews mainframe and ran out the door to meet a friend for dinner. Early the next morning, he ran out the door for an early seven o'clock appointment with a psychiatrist at a local hospital. Now, sitting in front of his computer, he looked at Dr. Bhergosian's message more carefully. The subject bar were the only words in the email. In the body of the message was an attached file with the title "Affiliation update 2021." Steven was a touch nervous to open the message, and his finger wavered over the "delete" button on his keyboard. This looked like a virus, and if he opened it and infected his computer, he would catch shit from his IT department, his manager, and probably his manager's manager. He hit the delete button and sent the message to his deletes folder. He then went to that folder and highlighted the message, ready to send it packing into email purgatory.

"What the hell virus nerd would know that Dr. Bhergosian worked for Matthews?" he asked out loud to himself. He then clicked on the message, and it popped up in front of him. He highlighted the attachment, double clicked on it, and opened it up.

CHAPTER 4

COLIN AND Ben had been leaving Boston after disposing of Derek when they received a call from the bunker to divert to New Mexico. Their boss on the other end had told them to head to Albuquerque to kill a Matthews sales rep and make it look like an accident. They had not questioned their orders. As former black ops agents, they did as they were told, and the money they received made everything worthwhile. After New Mexico, they had been given an assignment in Dallas and then Denver, all with the same purpose. They did not know why these reps were being taken out, but the orders were specific, and the targets needed to be eliminated ASAP.

They had just finished in Denver and were about to book a flight back to New York when a call came in to head in a different direction. They went to the airport and booked a flight to Calgary, Alberta, Canada.

CHAPTER 5

"I THINK we have it covered. We took care of the people in New Mexico, Texas, and Colorado. We're moving to contain the other breaches and should have everything cleaned up within the next twenty-four hours."

Slater just looked at the stocky, bald man sitting in front of him. While he was certain this man knew his area of expertise, he was still uneasy that the loose ends had been dangling out of control for too long. They were sitting in the situation room. Slater knew the morons on the other side of the door in the IT basement referred to it as the bunker, but he didn't care. From this room, he could monitor everything about the company's and the affiliation's interests. Every project, every potential and real breach could be monitored here. It was a safe room for him and for what he protected.

"You feel the breach has been contained then?" he asked.

"It has," answered Alman. He knew Slater was a control freak and had to have his fingers in every aspect of the store, but he didn't care. He'd humor him and then go do his job. Garret Alman was an ex-CIA black ops agent who had been recruited by Slater's predecessor ten years ago to oversee the protection of property rights at Matthews Pharmaceuticals and the affiliation. The computer system in the situation room allowed him to monitor nearly everything about the company. He could track equipment, people, and research projects connected to any company in the affiliation. He had been brought in to invigorate the security monitoring of the affiliation. Although he did not know everything about what was so guarded by Slater, he knew he was responsible for the overall protection of a large volume of intellectual property. He had been asked fourteen times over the last ten years to eliminate someone, and he had done so without question. To help him out in this regard, he had brought in two former agents he could trust. This latest string of eliminations was out of the ordinary in that there were five requests in short order, and the five were company representatives, not like before. But it didn't matter; he had carried out his instructions. Alman had taken over from another ex-agent who had retired to a very nice life in the Cayman's, and that was the eventual reward Alman wanted. So, when he was told to do something, he did it without question, like the good soldier he was.

Slater turned to face Alman again. "So Bhergosian downloaded the stick last Thursday. We caught him by way of the spyware programs, but then when he got away, he managed to get to a computer and send the information on the stick out in a mass mailing." Alman listened to the recap in dispassionate silence. Slater had a habit of going over events in a manner that reaffirmed his own sense of control more than anything else. Slater continued, "So he sent out the email message to everyone in North America from the distribution list he found. We were able to run our retrieval software program and pull back virtually all of the messages before anyone could open them, except for these five." Slater held out a sheet of paper that had five names on it. "Now, we've taken care of three of these people, and we have their computers, right?" Alman nodded yes and continued to look blankly at Slater, who went on. "What about the computer that was reported stolen on Thursday in Boston?"

"We used our GPS tracking to locate the laptop and got the property back."

"WHO STOLE it and what did we do with him or her?"

"It was a petty thief, a pickpocket. I gave instructions to my team to retrieve the property but leave the thief alone as long as they did not have to use any force to get it back."

"What if the computer had been opened and hacked into?"

"There really wasn't enough time for that to happen. The computer was taken around three on Thursday afternoon in Boston, and we got it back on Friday morning around ten o'clock. We're fine. Also, I've set up the IT guys to run a companywide check of all our computers. We're calling it a virus check to keep things quiet, but we're going to see if anyone has transferred the stick to their hard drives. We're going to do that at the regional meetings happening on Wednesday through Friday of this week. If you think about it,

Dr. Bhergosian chose a good time to breach your security. We can button up all loose ends with a computer wash of everyone's equipment."

Slater ignored the shot at "his security" and focused on the reps who had opened the attachment. "We now have three of the five taken care of. When will the other two be handled?"

"By the end of the day tomorrow."

"Isn't that taking a little too long? What if they open the attachment and view what's inside? That could spell trouble."

Alman wished like hell he knew what was in the attachment and stick but simply answered the questions put to him. "Even if they get a glimpse of the information, they'll be gone before they can do anything about it. Also, our diagnostic checks have shown that the attachment wasn't even opened by anyone. We are taking care of those who didn't delete it. Our virus alert message worked well in that almost all the receivers deleted the message and sent it to their trash bin. And like I said, your IT people will catch that and permanently delete it from the computer system."

"Alright, I guess that will have to do."

With that final comment, Slater turned and left Alman in the situation room to call his team to check on their progress. They should be in Calgary by now and quite possibly had already taken care of the Canadian rep who didn't delete the attachment. Then they'd head to Seattle and take care of the Seattle rep. Before he placed the call to Colin and Ben, he ran one more diagnostic check on the girl's and the Seattle rep's computers. After the check, he changed his mind on calling his team and placed a call to Slater instead.

CHAPTER 6

JENNA BOYD was so glad she had taken this day off. She had checked the weather network, and it had told her that Monday was going to be a beautiful day in Canmore and Kananaskis Country just outside of Calgary. She had left a message with her boss that she was taking the day and didn't even wait for the okay as she knew she would have no problem with it.

She loved coming out here from her home in Calgary and had been doing it ever since she was a kid. Her parents had loved hiking through the Nordic trail system left behind by the Calgary Olympics in 1988 and had come out whenever they could until they had died in a car accident four years ago. Whenever they had come, they would bring Jenna and her sister Janine with them. Jenna had asked her sister to come this time, but she couldn't make it. Now, she was standing along a ridge line some 1500 feet up the side of a mountain looking at a view that gave her chills. In a way she also thought her parents were still coming up with her and enjoying the view. As she looked down the ridge line, she spotted a bear about two hundred yards away. Using the telescopic lens on her camera, she quickly made out that it was a grizzly just minding its own business, eating some berries.

As she turned back to head away from the bear, she heard voices then saw two men walking towards her. They were both in hiking gear and talking casually back and forth. For some reason, her radar went up. She was quite a distance from the parking lot, and there was nowhere to go if there was trouble. She didn't know why she was nervous. She had encountered hikers before along this same trail, yet this scene had her heart racing a little. As the two men got closer, they looked up at her and smiled before returning to their back-and-forth conversation. Jenna began to relax and kick herself for being paranoid.

"It's a beautiful day, isn't it?" asked one of the men.

Jenna relaxed some more. "It is a great day to be out here. I come whenever I can. I love it out here. But be careful as you go along. There's a grizzly bear eating berries about two hundred yards down the ridge line." Jenna swept her gaze around and came back upon the two men who were now standing just a few feet away. She was relaxing even more when she looked down and her calm turned to fear once again.

The men were both wearing shiny, black dress shoes: shoes men wore with suits, not hiking gear. Now she was much more nervous, and this intensified as she noticed one of the men glance down at his hand at what looked like a picture and then back up at Jenna.

"Are you Jenna Boyd?" the man with the picture asked.

Jenna answered yes, even though she was now in full panic mode.

"Do you work for Matthews Pharmaceuticals?"

Now completely petrified, she nodded yes. She glanced back along the pathway and remembered the bear and looked past the men to see if she could squeeze by them if she ran. From the looks of them, if she took off, they'd have her in an instant, and if she tried to get by them the other way, they'd knock her down like a tackling dummy. She quickly glanced sideways into the bush, but it was thick, and she thought they'd be on her too quickly.

Just as she thought of making a break and taking her chances with the bear, the man with the picture lunged at her with such speed that there was no time for her to get away. He grabbed her quickly and forcefully covered her mouth with his right hand while the left remained free.

The second man looked at his partner. "We have to make it look like an accident."

"Are you kidding me? This is tailor-made for us. We're in the Canadian Rockies halfway up a damn mountain, standing along a narrow path. Look down, man. We'll break her neck and toss her off this ridge just like in New Mexico."

Jenna did not struggle at all, not that she could given that her attacker's grip was rock solid. But she had come out of her panic-induced fog and was thinking. Her arms were still free but the man's grip around her neck and mouth was too strong. The man's left arm was now wrapped around her body just above her waist. She was locked up tight and could not break free. Then

Affiliation

she remembered something her dad had always drilled into her when they came out to the woods to hike. Bear spray. She always put a can of bear spray in the left pocket of her hiking vest when she came out on these hikes. She flailed around a bit to distract her attacker and as her left hand fell back, she rubbed the outside of her pocket and felt the canister. *It's there*, she thought to herself. *Now, how am I going to get it?*

The man who had her whispered into her ear, "Don't scream. I'll make this as quick and painless as can be. You should not have opened that email message." His left arm began to slide up her body. His right hand moved off her mouth and took a half nelson position on her neck. Jenna began to struggle a little more, not to get away but to distract him from noticing what her left hand was doing. The man's left arm moved over her pocket and for a frantic moment, she thought he might feel the canister inside, and she'd be dead for sure. But his arm passed over the pocket and kept inching towards her neck. As it passed over her breast, the arm stopped ever so briefly, and Jenna felt a distinct squeeze. In her revulsion, she used the pause to struggle a little more, and then slipped her hand inside her pocket. She immediately found the canister of bear spray and popped the top off to get it ready. She positioned the canister so that it was pointed backward. Jenna quickly pulled her hand out of her pocket and pointed it behind her at where she thought the man's face would be; then she pressed the button down hard. Holding it down, she moved her left hand back and forth, spraying all the while.

"Holy shit! My eyes! You dumb bitch!" His grip had loosened considerably, and Jenna twisted herself free and delivered a well-placed left elbow to the man's ribs. Her attacker stumbled away from her and fell to the ground, covering his face with his hands. She then turned her bear spray towards the other man, who was reaching into his breast pocket. She pointed the can at his face and pressed down on the spray button, hitting him with a full blast in the face and eyes.

"Fuck me! God, that hurts!" The man stumbled backward holding his hands to his eyes. Jenna then turned back to face the first man, who was on one knee wiping feverishly at his eyes.

"You bitch! If it was gonna be painless before, you're gonna hurt now!"

Jenna had regained her composure as she looked hard at him. "You first." She spat as she kicked him as hard as she could right between the legs. He let out a mighty "OOMPH!" and fell on his back.

She then turned towards the other man, who was struggling to wipe his eyes at the same time as he was trying to figure out where Jenna was. She moved quickly and quietly in front of him and delivered the same blow to him as she had to his partner. *You might as well both feel the same way.* This guy exhaled and brought his knees close together as he crumpled to the ground.

Jenna took off down the path back towards the parking lot and her car. She had run quite a distance, or so she thought, when she felt a rush of air go past her ear, and then heard the retort of the gun. She turned to look back and saw both men coming hard down the path towards her. They were struggling in their fancy black shoes. They slipped and slid as they ran, which was probably why they'd missed the first shot. She looked down to where she had to go and quickly realized that she was not going to get away if she stayed on the trail, even with their shoe disadvantage. She made the decision to duck into the forest and jump off the path. *Try to navigate this terrain in those Gucci pumps.* As she moved into the woods, a branch of a tree beside her splintered into pieces, and the gun retort soon followed. Jenna kept moving, going deeper into the woods. She was an experienced hiker and could move easily through the brush. Her pursuers were not skilled, and she could hear them fighting the dense brush, swearing, and moving clumsily and loudly. Jenna quietly moved into the woods and kept a mountain peak in her sight as the landmark that would guide her back to her car. The two would-be assassins continued to make noise as they tried to follow. After only a few minutes, they stopped, and so she stopped too and listened in on them.

"What the fuck are we doing in here, Colin? Christ, I'm from New York. If there's not a street sign or a building, then how the hell am I going to find anything?"

"Yeah, you might be right," said the man called Colin. Jenna was about twenty yards from them, crouched low and out of sight. "Maybe we should get back on the path and get back to the parking lot. We can wait for her there."

"What if she doesn't show?"

"Well, when we get back to the car, we'll call the store and have the GPS tracking system locate her car and follow it, so we'll know where she's going. Hell, that's how we tracked her here."

"Okay, that sounds fine, but he'll be pissed we didn't get her the first time."

"Screw him. He's not out here in the fucking Canadian wilderness tromping around in seven-hundred-dollar shoes. If he wants to, he can come and finish her off himself. Let's go."

"Should we stay in Calgary to finish her or go to Seattle and get that guy—what's his name? Williams? He's the guy that copied the attachment to the USB stick. We need to get that back."

"Let's consult with the store, but I say we finish her first."

Jenna had heard everything. *GPS system in the car? What the hell is that? And who is this guy in Seattle anyway? And oh, by the way,* she thought, *why the hell do these guys want to kill me!?*

CHAPTER 7

THE REGIONAL meetings of Matthews US were held twice a year in addition to a big national meeting held at the end of the calendar year somewhere in the US. The shorter regional meetings were only a day and half long. The reps flew in on the Wednesday morning, met for lunch, went to their meetings, and continued all day Thursday. Thursday night was a big blowout bash designed to get everyone drunk and show what a great company Matthews was. Matthews gave everyone the chance to sleep in on Friday, and the reps left at various times during the day.

The meetings in LA brought together all the reps from the western region, which included Washington State.

Steven arrived at LAX at ten in the morning with a bunch of Seattle and area reps. They were always met at the airport by the travel company rep and transferred to a bus to take them to the hotel. It was well coordinated, and everyone got to where they needed to go.

At the luggage carousel, Steven was talking to a friend from Nevada. He liked these meetings because he could catch up with old friends and gripe to people who felt his pain about Matthews. This friend was Robert Longhill, a psychiatry specialty rep like Steven. "Hey, Steve, nice to see you. How's it been going in Seattle?" Robert had been in the company for about fifteen years, and he and Steven had always gotten along.

"I'm doing well, Rob. Same complaints as always, I guess."

They made some more idle chitchat while waiting for their bags until Robert asked, "Did you hear about Billy Sanduvol in New Mexico? He's dead."

"Dead!" Billy was another psychiatry rep, and Steven had known him for a few years. "What the hell happened? He was my age, for crying out loud."

"Fell off a mountain on a hiking trip last weekend."

Steven was shocked. Then Rob went on. "And that's not all. Kate Weldon in Colorado—car accident. And Paul Trackins in Dallas—suicide. All dead. All died last weekend. Bad weekend for Matthews."

Steven knew Kate quite well as they had served on an internal committee together two years ago, and he had heard of Paul. "My God! That's awful news. I just can't believe it." This consumed his thoughts for the rest of the time it took to get his bag, board the bus, and get to the hotel.

When they arrived at the hotel, they were ushered off the bus and towards a series of tables strung together. This was so they could get their meeting packages and room keys. Steven went through these motions by rote as he had done them dozens of times before. After he got his package and key, he went to his room. When he opened his package, there was a bright red sheet of paper with instructions for everyone to bring their computers to the Help Center for "system upgrades." He breathed a sigh of relief that he had deleted the Bhergosian attachment from his email system after transferring the contents to the USB stick. He had already made arrangements to meet a pharmacist buddy of his on Friday to go over what he had seen on the stick. He quickly took his laptop from his computer bag and headed downstairs to drop it off. This sort of thing was done all the time at meetings. Why they couldn't do some sort of push through the mainframe was a wonder Steven never fully grasped.

CHAPTER 8

MIGUEL HAD been called into his supervisor's office on Monday morning.

"Hey, Mig, I have a plum assignment for you. We need to spread some technical guys around the country to run a computer wash. We're looking for a virus sent via email that some reps may have inadvertently opened and loaded onto their computers. The company has regional meetings coming up so we're dispatching some Business Technology people to run the wash and find out if any computers have been infected. Your assignment is in sunny LA."

Miguel stared at his supervisor. This made no sense. They could run a virus scan from the basement. They could quickly check every computer in the company for signs of a virus. There was no need to send people to meetings around the country to do this on-site. His supervisor noticed Miguel's lack of reaction.

"Well, you're welcome, my friend. I'm giving you a trip to Los Angeles to do maybe five hour's work, and you look like I've assigned you to the bunker."

Miguel snapped out of his analytical state. "No, no, it's not that I wouldn't like to go to LA; it's just that we can do that kind of virus check from here. Why the personal attention?"

"I don't know, man, I don't know. Just book your flight for tomorrow and get your ass to the LA Hilton to start on Wednesday morning."

Miguel left the office and did as he was instructed, all the while wondering what was going on.

CHAPTER 9

STEVEN AND the rest of the regional team marched into the meeting room on Thursday morning after breakfast. The breakfast buffet had been very good. Lots of choices of fresh fruit, cereals, yogurts, scrambled eggs, poached eggs, bacon, sausage, ham, hash browns, a toast station, and an omelet station if anyone wanted. All the meals at these meetings were first class.

The welcome dinner last night had been a "trip around the world" theme. There had been buffet stations set up all around the large ballroom. There was a Thai, Sushi, Italian, and American station. The food was very good, and there was lots of it. In between each food station was a bar so that people did not have to line up long to get their favorite drink. Placed neatly in front of the stations and forming an inner ring were tables to sit at and eat. Some were higher bar-type tables while others were just standard eating tables. Within this ring of tables were games of various types. There was a foosball game, a hockey game, a shuffleboard game, two pool tables, three video games, two driving video games, and even a couple of chess sets. It was all meant to relax the group and allow for maximum interaction, so people could catch up. Starting at nine thirty, after the food stations had been cleared away and a dance floor set up, a local band began playing cover tunes to get people moving. All in all, a good evening showcasing just how much money Matthews had to throw around when they wanted to do something for their people. It made Steven wonder what the Thursday evening bash would be like.

But now the day's set of meetings would begin. The Thursday morning was always a general plenary session headed by one of the executive team leaders from New York. This meeting had snagged Jeffrey Brim, the VP of finance. He usually delivered the financial health of the company, thus his nickname "The Brim Reaper," but this morning, he went through a host of issues about the company. These included the financial health, the future drug pipeline, year-to-date sales results, new policies and processes, and a greeting from the ultimate leader, William Slater.

After the meeting, the reps all filed into their respective meeting rooms with their local area sales teams to discuss the year's activities to date and plan for the rest of the year. In Steven's meeting, his regional manager began immediately by throwing out a PowerPoint presentation on the reps' physician lists and call plans.

At the beginning of every business year, each rep had to identify and log in to their computers a list of all the doctors they were going to call on for the year. They made the list using their own judgment, but they also heavily relied on their PLPD. The rep could then sort through the doctors and plan to call on the more important ones much more often than the less important ones. The only problem was that every company had this data, although it wasn't as accurate as Matthews'. But the competitors' data still identified the biggest prescribers in a given territory. All the competitors made the same sorts of doctor call plans. This made the most important doctors very popular targets for every competing company and limited their availability to the individual rep.

STEVEN WAS somewhat lucky in that his target list was all psychiatrists and the majority of them were friendly to the pharma industry and reps as well. But he still structured his list to call more on the psychiatrists that wrote the most prescriptions and then on down the line.

In his meeting, his manager threw up each rep's call plan achievement to date one by one. They were more than halfway through the year, but the data only reflected five months' worth of calls. Every rep in the room should have delivered at least 41.66 percent of the total number of calls planned for the year. This was one of the measurement tools that all pharma companies used to assess their reps. If sales were low and calls were high, then the rep had a problem. If sales were high and calls were low, the rep had a problem. If sales were on target and calls were low, the rep had a problem because if they had made more calls, their sales would be higher. Even if both the sales and calls were perfectly on target, the rep was often chastised for not "stretching" themselves enough. It was a game some managers played on a relentless basis with their teams. Steven's manager was actually pretty easygoing about it. He gave the presentation as the data had not been downloaded to the reps yet, and he just wanted to bring everyone up to speed regarding their activity level.

The rest of the day centered around what kinds of activities and events were going to be planned for the rest of the year. It was at the afternoon break that the day turned a little for Steven. He was standing in front of the tub filled with ice and Hagen Daaz bars trying to decide which one to take when a hotel employee came up to him. "Excuse me, sir, are you Steven Williams of Seattle?"

"Yes, that's me."

"Okay, that's good, then this note is for you, sir." With that, the attendant turned and strolled away.

Steven took the note, and for a reason he couldn't figure out at the time, looked around to see if anyone was watching him. He opened the note and read it. *"I really need to see you today, after the meeting breaks at four-thirty. It's about the attachment. Meet me in Kelsey's Bar down the street. I'll be at a table at the back, and I'll know you from your company picture. A friend."* He reread the note, folded it, and put it in his pocket.

CHAPTER 10

JENNA WAS still reeling from her close call as she carefully made her way back to the parking lot. While she knew the two men who attacked her would be there, the parking area was really the only way to begin to get out of this back country.

She reached the edge of the bush overlooking the lot where her car was parked. As she crept closer to get a good look at the area, she listened for voices. She heard nothing. She got to the edge and gently pushed her face through some dense bushes to get a look at the lot. Her car was still there and there was one other car: a tan Jeep that had been there when she arrived. There were no other cars in the lot.

Maybe they pulled out just to hide and have the whole place in plain sight, she thought to herself. *Maybe they're just waiting for me to come into what I think is an empty lot and then get me.* It was at that moment that the enormity of what had just happened hit her hard. The thought of someone trying to kill her and how close she had come caused her to sit down and shake violently. This had been an experience and a half. Two men she had never met had tried to kill her. Not only that but they seemed to have targeted her specifically. They had a picture of her and had indicated that Matthews Pharmaceuticals, the drug company she worked for, seemed to be involved. This was not the movies, and she was not some character in a play. This was real. She really didn't know how to react. How would anyone? She decided to deal with the here and now and work from there.

She went over what she had heard in the woods. One of the men had said they could activate the GPS in her car and track her whereabouts—so obviously using her car to get back to Calgary was out. They had also mentioned something about going to Seattle to button things up. What was the name of the rep they had talked about? Willers? Williams? Yes, Williams, that was it. They had also mentioned a stick of some sort and the need to get it back. There was something else they had mentioned but she was having a hard time recalling it. Suddenly, she remembered. The attack on the ridge line: the man that had grabbed her had said something about making her death look just like New Mexico. So, they had killed at least one other before getting to her. The information she was processing was too surreal to imagine, but the experience she had just endured was all too real. Someone had tried to kill her. They seemed to be involved with the company she worked for, and they appeared to have killed at least one other person before the attempt on her, and they were going to try and kill someone named Williams in Seattle.

Jenna realized she had been sitting in the woods recounting her experience for quite a while. Her thoughts now turned to what to do next. She could hike her way to Canmore and tell the police, but just what would she tell them? Two men she didn't know but who seemed to know her had come out of nowhere and tried to kill her? They were nowhere to be found, and there was nothing she could show them that even remotely gave credence to her story. Jenna thought of other cases where women had told wild tales to the police to cover other problems, and she thought the cops would probably think the same of her story. They wouldn't believe her for sure. She just felt that she had to get back to Calgary. She couldn't use her car so there was the bus or hitchhiking. She looked at her car one last time and then scanned the lot and the surrounding edges for any sign of the two men. Seeing nothing, she began walking around the perimeter of the lot, staying in the bushes, so she could get to the entrance gate, the road, and then highway to hitchhike her way back to Calgary.

CHAPTER 11

MIGUEL WAS not sure that Steven Williams would show but he'd had to try. After working in the BT room and coming to suspect something weird was up, he felt honor bound to warn this person. On the way to the bar, he had thought: *Warn him of what? That he made a copy of an attachment that has apparently angered Matthews? Just what will that "anger" look like in practice? Should I tell him the computer upgrade story is a scam? Should I tell him we're really here to check if anyone has opened this attachment, and if so, what they've done with it? What about the other reps in New Mexico, Colorado, and Texas?* Miguel had hacked back into the mainframe and performed two systems checks. First, he ran a check to see if any company-wide program pushes had been run within the last few days, and there had been. A few days ago, on Sunday, a company-wide email recall had been executed by the Matthews mainframe. Miguel had even been able to identify the offending message. It was a message from a Dr. Bhergosian, and it contained an attachment. That made Monday morning's message for IT clear, as a message went out to a few people to delete the Bhergosian message as some folks did not have their computer connected to the company system on Friday night. He then ran a general diagnostic check on the entire company. He had quickly learned that, in each of the states where a rep had died, a rep had not deleted the email and had opened the email even after getting the company notice to delete the message. The New Mexico rep was dead by Saturday afternoon. The Colorado rep was dead later that day, and the Texas rep died the next day. This guy, this Williams guy, had not only not deleted the message but had made a copy to an external USB stick. As Miguel sat there and wondered, a thought occurred to him that this might be a saving grace. *If the company is behind those deaths because the reps didn't delete a darn attachment, then the contents of the attachment must be hugely sensitive and having a copy may just keep a person alive.*

Just as he finished this thought, he looked up and saw Williams walking towards the back of the bar, glancing around as he went along. Miguel stood up, caught his attention with a wave, and motioned for him to come over.

"Hello, I'm Miguel Bennetto. I sent you the note. I wasn't sure you'd show."

Steven shook Miguel's outstretched hand. "I didn't think I'd show either, but Bhergosian's message was so strange, and the attachment was so weird, I thought I'd come and see if you had any answers. I mean, I should just contact HR, tell them that I screwed up, and give everything back, right?"

"So, you really did make a copy to a USB then?"

"Uh, yeah, I made a copy. How do you know that?"

Miguel decided to jump in with both feet. He explained the level of computer surveillance all reps at Matthews were under. He went over the software download spyware, the keystroke spyware, the time-of-day spyware, and the GPS tracking devices in all cell phones, cars, and computers. He told him of his tutorial about the rep in Tulsa and how he'd probably been fired by now. He told Steven how the computer upgrade notice had just been a way of getting a hold of all the reps' computers, so they could run a thorough diagnostic to find out if anyone had done anything with that attachment other than delete it without opening the message and then delete that from the deleted folder. It was BT's job to go into the hard drive of every laptop turned in and wipe any trace of the message, the sender, and the attachment. He explained that, in doing this, the diagnostic tools had uncovered that Steven had not only opened the message but had also opened the attachment and copied the contents to a USB stick. It was at the beginning of his disclosure that the waitress came over to take their drink orders. Miguel was just getting going, and Steven ordered a pint of beer. In the middle of his explanation, she came close by, and Steven ordered a scotch. Towards the end of his disclosure, she came close by again, and he ordered another scotch. Miguel decided to lay the big one on him about the three dead reps but waited until the second scotch had arrived. Mig explained what he had uncovered about the three representatives and about how he suspected that the attachment was to blame, and that Matthews had to be involved. Steven just held his scotch glass in his hands and looked down at the table. Miguel was finished.

He held his glass and gently swirled the scotch around inside. Miguel waited. He could understand the silence. Williams either believed him or not. If he did, then the guy's world had just been turned upside down. If he didn't, then given that Williams worked in psychiatry, Miguel figured he must have been thinking about how to get away without provoking the psychotic person sitting in front of him.

Finally, he spoke but in a very hushed voice. "If what you say is true, then we should go straight to the police with everything and wash our hands of it. I mean, my career will be over and yours too, but the police will investigate and get to the bottom of this."

Miguel wanted to be as forceful but as nice as he could. "I'm not sure that's such a good idea. I mean, as you put it, all we have is you downloading some private intellectual property that you were directed to delete as a virus, and me making some unauthorized inquiries into the company directory, basically misusing company equipment. What we have is the two of us shattering company rules, and that means dismissal, and if what happened to those reps is linked to Matthews somehow, then you and I will be gone before the police can say, 'Sorry for your troubles, Matthews Pharmaceuticals.'"

Steven continued to look down, saying nothing. Miguel jumped in again. "I think you need to hang on to that stick and be very careful. I think you should go back to Seattle, and I'll go back to New York. I mean, the company knows exactly what you've done, and you're still alive, right? The company doesn't know I hacked back into the mainframe because I covered my tracks. I can go back and dig around some more."

Steven's head suddenly shot up. His gaze was piercing, and his jaw was clenched. "I don't believe any of this. I mean, who the hell are you anyway? Some guy gives me a note, and I'm stupid enough to fall for it. I mean, is this some kind of a joke? Did one of my colleagues put you up to this? This whole thing is ridiculous. I have a life back in Seattle."

Miguel just leaned in. "Yeah, this whole thing is ridiculous. Actually, it's not just ridiculous; it's unbelievable. But what I told you about the computer surveillance is true. The GPS tracking is true. The guy in Tulsa is true. And those three reps are dead. And they didn't even *open* the attachment. They just didn't delete the message. You can go back to your life in Seattle, but my guess is that, if you give back that stick, then you'll be dead very, very soon."

"But that's my point!" Steven's voice rose, and Miguel held up a hand to keep him quiet. "That's my point," he repeated in a harsh whisper. "Those other reps didn't even see what's in the attachment, so why would their deaths be connected in any way to it? Why would Matthews take them out for nothing?"

"Maybe Matthews just wanted to make sure in case their tracking software had a hole. I don't know, but it's awfully weird that the only three reps to not delete that message are dead within hours of each other. Look, give me a chance to find something ... or nothing. I'll go back to New York. I'll poke around Matthews's computer system. I'm good. I can get in and out without being caught. Whatever I find, good, bad, or nothing, I'll contact you. Give me a chance to earn your trust. In the meantime, humor me. Don't use any of the company's computers, Ipads, cell phones, nothing."

"But Matthews is a huge multi-national drug company. They don't kill people. This is not some movie script. This is real life. No, no, I can't accept this. I won't accept this. I know something of psychiatric illness, and I think you're in need of medication." With that, Steven got up and left.

Miguel just sat back. He couldn't blame him. It was a fantastical story, something out of a James Bond book. When he thought about it, he could totally understand. But something inside him told him he was right. He was no spy, no detective, and no superhero, but he was still going to dig a little more. With that, he paid the bill, went back to the hotel, to his room, and opened up his computer. A little more than an hour later, he had the bellhop deliver a message to Steven Williams's room. The bellhop confirmed the delivery but said that no one was in, so he'd slipped it under the door. Miguel looked at his watch. He had missed the bus to the gala evening.

CHAPTER 12

ALMAN HESITATED as he began to dial Slater's cell phone number. He really did not like the man. He was pompous, arrogant, and completely into himself. He could only be taken in small doses. But he paid his salary and bonuses, and there was that Cayman retirement to think about. The news he was about to relay would send Slater into a frenzied tailspin; he had no doubt about that, but it had to be done. He finished dialing the number and waited for Slater to answer.

Slater answered with the usual aloof coolness he used whenever Alman called.

Damn caller ID, Alman thought. "Mr. Slater, we may have a problem with our containment."

"What sort of a problem?"

"The rep in Seattle, the last one on our list?"

"Yes, go on. What about the Seattle rep?"

"He opened the email—"

"We know that; that's why we're taking him out." Slater was not known for patience.

"Yeah, I know we know that, but I ran a scan to check his keystrokes after he opened the email, and I found that he opened the attachment. He was the only one we know for sure who did, and then he did something else."

Slater was now feeling very queasy that someone had opened the attachment. The other reps were being taken out just to make sure they never got curious about what the attachment had meant, but this rep had *actually* opened it. "Why did he open the attachment? Didn't he get the message to delete it as a virus? And if he missed that message, didn't our email retrieval program grab the message back?"

"I guess he didn't get the virus message, and he didn't log on to his computer until after he had finished his computer entries for the day on Monday."

Slater immediately reverted to CEO mode. "But communicating only at the end of the day is against company policy. The representatives are supposed to connect to the mainframe at the beginning *and* at the end of each day. That's a compliance issue."

Alman rolled his eyes on the other end of the phone. "Well, I guess this guy forgot to be compliant for one day. The real issue here is that he made a copy of the attachment."

Slater could not understand why he was being bothered with all this. "So what? Your men will take him out, and we'll have the computer. We can then delete the message and the copy of the attachment."

Alman finally dropped the bomb. "He made a copy of the attachment to a USB stick," and for emphasis, he added, "an *external* stick."

Slater had been walking towards his office as he was talking to Alman, and he could see his secretary at the outer office door, waving some papers at him. When Alman told him of the USB stick, he stopped in his tracks, holding the phone to his ear and not saying a word. Then he slumped to his right and leaned against the wall. His secretary looked quizzically at him from twenty feet away, and Alman began shouting into the phone from his end.

"Mr. Slater?! Slater? Are you there? Are you there?"

Slater quickly regained his composure in front of his secretary and took his phone call back to his office. "What do we do now?"

"I think we wait a little bit on this. We have the regional meetings coming up where we're doing the hard drive wash. We can keep an eye on this rep there. He'll be going to the LA meetings. He can't do much there other than the meeting stuff, and we'll have his computer, so he won't be able to share anything. If he brings the USB stick with him and shares it with a friend, then we'll know when the spyware catches it. We then take him out when he gets back to Seattle."

"Why not just take him out in LA?" Slater was now anxious to put this behind him.

"Not a good idea. We don't have the USB he made. We'll have to convince him to give us the stick first, and then we'll take him out."

Slater couldn't really argue with this. They had to get the stick. Williams would be busy in LA. They could monitor his phone calls, and with the girl gone (assuming there were no more foul-ups), they'd have all the loose ends tied up by the weekend.

CHAPTER 13

STEVEN DROPPED the stick he had made into his coat pocket and left through the front door of his house. After he had opened the attachment, he had been faced with a single file folder titled "Affiliation Entities." He had opened up this file and been confronted by a series of chemical compounds and formulas under a multitude of different disease states. There was everything from Alzheimer's disease to zosters. He had no idea what they were. He'd looked at them for almost an hour and then began to wonder why Dr. Bhergosian would send them to him. He'd checked the "sent to" bar in the email and discovered that the doctor had actually sent the message to a distribution list with the heading "NA contacts." He could not figure out why the list would be headed as "Not Applicable" until it dawned on him that NA stood for North America. *Why in the world would the email be sent to the North American distribution list for Matthews Pharmaceuticals?*

He just couldn't figure out what the chemical compounds were and why the doctor had felt the need to share them. The other strange thing was that, included with each compound, was the name of the company that seemed to own it. Matthews was in the data set several times with compounds for Parkinson's, Alzheimer's, Huntington's, schizophrenia, and a few others. These were all areas that Matthews worked in and had products for on the market. But there were also many other drug company names beside various other compounds. Several of the companies were direct competitors to Matthews. Steven just couldn't understand it unless it was some sort of industrial espionage. And given the breadth of compounds on the stick, this would be industrial espionage on a massive scale. His thoughts went back to Dr. Bhergosian, and he wondered if the dinner he'd had with him several weeks ago had had anything to do with why he'd been sent the email.

Steven went over the conversation he'd had with Dr. Bhergosian four weeks ago. Matthews had pulled in the compliance-liaison reps from around the country to roll out some new procedures relating to paying expert doctors to speak to family practitioners on the company's behalf. These reps were then to go back to their respective sales teams and roll out the new procedures. Steven had been named as the compliance-liaison rep by his manager as a kind of reward. Every time they were called in, they got to go to New York to be trained on the new procedure. It usually meant a couple of days off-territory, a night in New York City at a fairly nice hotel, and a nice dinner out, all at the company's expense. Despite the fact that Steven hated all the new policies being brought in, he did not mind visiting New York, and he was piling up the Air Miles. At the last meeting, they had gone to dinner at a very nice Greek Restaurant in midtown, just off 7th Avenue. Dr. Bhergosian had joined them there, and Steven had recognized him from the company newsletter that had announced his recruitment just six weeks before. After introductions had been made during cocktails, Steven had found himself sitting next to the doctor at a long table of sixteen people.

"SO, DR. Bhergosian, why are you here?" Steven opened. "Aren't you working on your research in our New Hampshire facility?"

Bhergosian looked at Steven for a moment. It was a vacant stare. He had clearly been drinking for a while. "Our fearless leader, Mr. Slater, thought I should be the one to be here to help emphasize how important and wonderful these new rules are." Bhergosian's right hand swirled above his head. "He wanted someone of importance in the medical field to drive his new rules home." His tone was clearly sarcastic even while his speech slurred just a little.

Steven looked at him. "Well, our company tends to do that. They want to make sure we're all on board, so we sell it back to our teams."

Bhergosian had just looked at him and said nothing. But during the course of the dinner, Steven had asked him a lot about his research and what new developments were coming out of New Hampshire. Were there any new drugs about to be launched? What new drugs were in the early or mid-term pipeline? This line of questioning had really opened Bhergosian up, and he'd talked effusively during the dinner, never turning down the waiter when he offered a refill of his wine glass. By the time dessert had arrived, Bhergosian was on to his third Drambuie and quite drunk, but he was still talking.

"Actually, despite all the research money I've been given and promised by Matthews, I don't think I'll be staying around much longer." Bhergosian told Steven this as he was tracing his finger around the rim of his liqueur glass. "I don't like this company, and I don't like Slater."

Even though the man was slurring and in need of an immediate taxi home, Steven could not resist probing a little further. "Why do say that, Doctor? I mean, I can see what you mean about Slater. He's not that well liked by any of us, but what do you mean about not liking Matthews?"

At this point, Dr. Bhergosian swung his face towards Steven in a classic drunken swirl and raised his glass to use as a pointer of sorts. "Listen to me, young man. This company of yours, this *grand design,*" he waved his glass around, "has evil at its heart. It cares more about profit than people. It's hiding things ... things that should be made public."

Steven thought this guy was just grinding an axe about something to do with his research. Maybe Matthews had pulled some funding from a pet project of his. "Well, Dr. Bhergosian, the company is in the business of making money. Yes, we make money off of pharmaceuticals, but profit is not a dirty word, even in the pharma business."

Dr. Bhergosian dropped his head sharply and shook it. "No, no, no," he slurred, "you don't understand. You don't know the extent of what I know. You don't know what they hide, what they've all kept hidden for so long. It has to come out. It has to come out." At this point, the man dropped his glass and slumped down in his chair. Steven wrapped his arm around him and propped him up. He then caught the eye of one of the sales directors and motioned for him to come over. They called a cab and poured the doctor into it, giving the driver the hotel address and hoping that the good doctor got home safe.

STEVEN WAS now in his car, four weeks after the drunken musings from Dr. Bhergosian, and pulled up to the restaurant where he was meeting Nathan Cunnymore. Nathan was a buddy from university who had been a practicing pharmacist for the last eight years. Steven had called him and told him about the email and the USB he had made. Maybe Nathan could make something out of the formulas on the stick.

CHAPTER 14

JENNA HAD waited for over an hour before she felt that the two men were, indeed, gone. They had mentioned that they would go to Calgary and get her there. She had to get back, but her apartment was off-limits now. She would check in with her sister once she got back. She figured hitchhiking would be best as she was concerned one of the men could be staking out the bus terminal in Canmore. She walked towards the highway, and once there, she began walking towards Calgary, sticking her thumb out as she went. She had not hitchhiked since university, and while it was not the best way to travel, she was less afraid of that than the two men tracking her.

As she walked, she went over the whole experience again. Thinking back on it did not make it any easier to understand, and the memory, as fresh as it was, made her frightened all over again. But she had gotten away, and now she had to figure out what to do next. She went over what she had heard the men say. They had talked about New York and said something about "him" not being "happy." They'd also mentioned the tracking device in the car, and she thought that her cell phone was probably being tracked as well. She'd had no idea that GPS devices were installed in her car and cell phone, and this fact made her angry more than anything else. But what really scared her down to her core was the fact that they seemed to work for Matthews Pharmaceuticals. They had also said something about New Mexico that sounded like they had killed someone there. Finally, she remembered them mentioning the name Williams again, and then Seattle. That was who they were looking for, and Seattle seemed to be where they were going next. Jenna felt the need to warn this Williams guy, whom she assumed worked for Matthews too. But the only way to get his contact information was to use her company's address book in her Matthews computer, which was sitting on her desk in her apartment—the apartment she could not go back to. Just as she began to mull over this dilemma, a van drove by her and quickly slowed down, pulling over to offer a lift. Jenna ran up to the lowered passenger side window.

The driver looked to be in his late thirties to early forties, and he was alone in the van. "Where you headed?" he asked.

"Calgary." Jenna was uncomfortable, but she needed the lift.

"Perfect," the man said. "That's not only where I'm going; it's where I live. Hop in."

Jenna climbed in the van, thanked the man, and told a story about having had a fight with her boyfriend while hiking and him jumping into his truck and leaving her stranded. The driver seemed to buy this as he offered only his condolences on her being stranded. Jenna made sure to bring out her can of bear spray and casually twirl it in her hands, making sure the driver saw it. For the rest of the forty-five-minute drive into Calgary, they made small talk. He was a married man with three kids and was coming back from a bachelor party at a club in Banff. Jenna talked about her work, and the time passed rather quickly. When they got into Calgary, the man offered to drive her right home, but she asked if he would take her to her sister's place instead, just in case her crappy boyfriend was waiting for her at her place. He did exactly that, and after she climbed out of the van in front of her sister's condo, she thanked the man profusely. He just smiled, told her to take care of herself, waved, and drove away.

Hmm, Jenna thought, *Nice guy. After the day I've had, I deserve that.* She turned and walked up to the front door of the condo and rang the bell.

CHAPTER 15

BACK IN the situation room, Alman was confronted by Slater, who was in a foul mood.

"What the fuck are we going to do about the USB stick?"

"I think we'd better get it back," Alman said dryly. He was enjoying, just a little, seeing Slater sweat. This situation was clearly getting out of hand, and while Alman wanted to make things right, he couldn't help but bask in the moment.

"Of course, we'd better get it back!" Slater snapped. "But how are going to do that?"

"Look, my two guys are taking care of the girl in Calgary, and after they phone in, I'll send them to Seattle to take care of this guy."

"But …" there was an exasperated tone to Slater's voice, "this *guy*, as you call him, has a copy of everything on the stick! What if he shows it to someone?"

Alman thought for a moment. "Well," he began, "the regional meetings start the day after tomorrow, so he'll be unable to do anything of value until he gets back. We can even send in our team to search his place. Maybe he'll leave the USB out, and we can grab it."

Slater thought this might be doable. "Alright, we can do that. But we still need to eliminate this guy. No loose ends on this one."

Before Alman could answer, his cell phone rang. "Hello? What do you mean you didn't get her?" Alman's tone was quickly morphing into anger. "She did what? … Bear spray? And you two fuckups couldn't overcome that and catch her? She was in the woods, for fuck's sake! Alright, alright, we'll activate the GPS on her car and track her movements. You'd better hope she goes back to Calgary. Is that where you are now? … A half an hour? Okay,

Affiliation

okay, just get to her apartment and wait. I'll give you a call and let you know where she's at. Don't fuck up this time."

ON THE other end of the phone, Colin looked at Ben and sighed as he hung up. "He wasn't happy."

"Screw him," Ben said. "Like I said before, he's not the one in stupid Canada trying to get this done."

Alman turned to Slater. "The team missed getting the girl in Calgary." Alman then described what Colin had told him of the attempt on Jenna Boyd's life.

Slater just stared at Alman. "This is the team we're entrusting our entire operation to? They don't fill me with any confidence."

"WOULD YOU like me to call in another hit team? Maybe they're in the yellow pages under 'murderers for hire.'"

Slater gave Alman a look that shook him just a little. "Why would you think this girl would go right back to her apartment in Calgary? Don't you think that she'll be trying to steer clear of an address we know about?"

Slater was guessing that Jenna would assume anyone trying to kill her, who knew she was hiking, would also know where she lived. He didn't want any more slipups. He zeroed in on Alman. "Pull up the employee bio we have everyone write when they join the company. It might give us a clue as to where Ms. Boyd would go if she doesn't go back to her apartment."

Matthews, just like all the affiliate companies, had every employee write a short biography on themselves. The companies said it was to help everyone to get to know one another. They were shared on every company's internal website under some kind of "Employee Spotlight" banner to maintain the charade, but an ulterior motive for this bio was for exactly what Slater was about to do. If ever they had to track someone for any reason, they would have a composite sketch of the employee's life. They would know where their parents lived, what other family members they had, and where they were. Did they have any best friends living close by? Every affiliate company used the same template for every employee, and every employee wrote pretty much the same thing. This was information that was technically illegal to gather under freedom of information and privacy laws, but because each employee voluntarily submitted it, there was technically no breach of the law.

Alman did as he was told and pulled up Jenna's file. Her picture immediately flashed in the corner of his computer screen and the biographical information appeared below it.

"Wow," Slater said, "a very pretty woman. It's a shame she has to go."

Alman and Slater scanned Jenna's profile. She had been born and raised in Calgary. She had gone to the University of Calgary where she had obtained a degree in biochemistry. From there, she had gone to work for the university as a researcher, but she had not liked it. She had joined Matthews a little over a year ago. She loved hiking and anything to do with a back-country experience. Her parents had been killed in a car accident four years ago, and she had one sister who also lived in Calgary. Her name was Janine Boyd.

"There we go." Slater pointed when he read the text about Janine. "I'll bet she's headed there. Send your team to her sister's."

Alman agreed on this point, and after Googling Janine's name, he quickly got the address. He phoned his team, gave them the new location, and hung up.

"Okay, so after they finish her off, we'll send them to Seattle to go through this Williams guy's place and hopefully get the stick back before we eliminate Williams." Slater just nodded to Alman, turned abruptly, and walked out of the situation room.

CHAPTER 16

STEVEN WALKED into the restaurant and spotted Nathan sitting at a table near the back. He gave him a quick wave and sat down at this table.

"You sounded a touch cryptic in your message," started Nathan. "What's this all about?"

Steven leaned back in his chair and wondered where to begin. What had he heard exactly at the restaurant with Dr. Bhergosian? Did the deaths of his colleagues, people he knew, have any kind of connection to each other? Were their deaths just random? A weird string of coincidental moments? What about the tech guy he had met and his message to be aware of something going on? He began with the email and the attachment he had opened. He described the set of formulas he had found. He told Nathan about the message coming from Dr. Bhergosian and of the weird (albeit drunken) conversation he'd had with him some weeks before.

"There's also something else weird," Steven said. "When I arrived for the regional meeting, I met a friend of mine at the airport. He asked me if I had heard about these three other reps and I said, 'Heard what?' He then told me that all three had just been killed in separate incidents within the past few days, prior to our regional meeting."

"What kind of incidents?"

"Uh, one guy fell off a cliff while hiking, one was in a car accident, and the third one … the third one died of an apparent suicide."

"Well, why is that weird?" asked Nathan. "I mean, it's sad, and I feel for their families, but you know … shit happens."

"The accidents maybe. But I knew the rep who committed suicide. He was *not* the suicidal type. We both worked psychiatry, and I have to believe I would have spotted a sign of some sort."

"Perhaps, but people can fool the best of them, even real psychiatrists."

"Yeah, I know," Steven offered, "but there is also a conversation I had at the meeting with a BT guy from our company." Steven went on to tell Nathan about what Miguel had told him about the scam virus search. He went into detail about the company use of spyware to track emails and the placement of GPS tracking chips in their computers and cars. Nathan's mouth fell open as Steven described just how closely Matthews monitored their employees. He then told him how the Business Technology people had been told to search for this email and find out if anyone had opened the attachment. They had been told the attachment was a virus, and they were to delete it completely from all computers that still had it in their systems, but Miguel could tell that was a lie.

"Nathan, this fella was scared, but he was also curious as to what was happening. And he was mad."

"MAD AT who?"

"Mad at Matthews. He was going to go back to New York to start poking around the computer system there to see if he could find anything and said he'd get back to me. But he also said to not use any company property: no computers, no Ipads, no cell phones. We're going to talk on our personal phones and computers."

Steven stopped talking and looked at Nathan. He could tell Nathan was trying to process everything and come up with something to say. "Why don't you go to the police?"

"And tell them what? That I've got this USB stick that is company property? That I had a conversation about a virus, but it's not a virus according to a guy I've never met who just happened to contact me at a company meeting and tell me I'm being monitored by my own firm and that I should watch my back? Oh yeah, and there's these three people I know who just died, and I think there is a link to it all? And all this over an email? They'd just tell me to take one of the anti-psychotics I sell and give the stick back."

"Well, maybe that's what you should do. Give the stick back to Matthews and be on your way."

"Give it back," Steven said flatly. "Give it back. What if all this stuff is linked? What if the deaths of those reps are linked to this? What if the information on this stick is something important or sinister? Dr. Bhergoisan would not have sent this out for no reason. And I'm pissed off that my company feels the need to monitor what I do so thoroughly. No, I'm going to try to find out what this stuff means, and I'll also wait for Miguel to call to see if he has found anything."

Nathan just stared at his friend for a moment. "Okay, Nancy Drew. I just want to point out that this is not some spy novel you're reading. If all those events are linked, including the reps' deaths—and that's a very big if—then that means that what's on this stick is worth killing over. That means your company has killed because of the information on this stick. To be honest, I don't even know if I want to be around you. I could end up … What's that term the military uses? Collateral damage?"

"Yeah, I know. It's freaky. Believe me, I've run through a dozen different scenarios of how this can play out. But I also think that the best way for me to get through this is to hang on to this stick, and better yet, find out what's on it. I thought this Miguel guy was crazy, but now I'm beginning to believe he may be onto something."

Nathan looked at his friend again. "Okay then, let's have a look at the stick."

CHAPTER 17

JENNA'S SISTER was home, and Jenna wasted no time in telling her all that had happened. It was a recounting that shook both women. After some tough arm twisting by Janine, Jenna agreed to go to the police.

Once at the police station, they had a tough time even getting to see a detective let alone convince him of Jenna's ordeal. The cop was clearly skeptical to the point of outright disbelief of all that Jenna had to say. It just seemed so farfetched. Out of the blue, two guys had walked up, attacked her, and prepared to kill her, but she'd gotten away with a can of bear spray. Then they'd chased her through the woods, shooting at her but missing. Then they'd decided to stop chasing her, even though they obviously wanted her dead, and head back to Calgary. But first, they'd disclosed that there's a tracking system in Jenna's car, so Jenna decided to hitchhike back to Calgary. And, just to top things off, Jenna thought her company, a major pharmaceutical firm, was the real culprit. Her company wanted her dead for no apparent reason.

Jenna stared at the detective. She had to admit it sounded unbelievable. "But it's all true," she said, imploring him to believe her. "Look, can you just go get my car? Just get the car and check out the GPS chip. If it's in there, that will at least corroborate part of my story."

The cop was skeptical. It was a story so fantastic as to warrant scant attention, and he was busy with other cases. Real cases. There had been a fair number of these sorts of fabrications lately as well. It almost always came down to someone trying to get away from something they'd done that they shouldn't have, or they were just plain nuts and vying for attention. This woman didn't seem unbalanced but neither had the other people who had fabricated an abduction, a rape, a disappearance of several days without notice, etc.

"Look," said the cop, "I'll phone a buddy of mine at the Canmore RCMP detachment and see if he can run out to the lot and get your car. Why don't you both go have a seat in the waiting room, and I'll come and get you once he's gone to the lot."

Jenna and her sister felt at least a little relieved that something might get done and went to the waiting room as instructed. Once there, they occupied their time reading months-old magazines and Reader's Digests. Jenna could not help but think it was just like the doctors' offices she visited. After about twenty minutes, the detective came to the room and motioned for them to come back. They got to his desk and sat down.

"You know," he began, "making a false police report is a serious crime. I could really make it tough on you."

Both Jenna and Janine looked at each other, and Jenna spoke up. "What are you talking about? What I told you happened. What about the car?"

"THERE *IS* no car." The cop stared at them. "The car lot was—correct that—the lot *is* empty. Now, I'm not going to do anything to you, but I suggest you both go see your psychiatrist." With that, the cop turned away from them and began looking at some papers on his desk.

CHAPTER 18

IN THE bunker, Alman was staring at a screen that showed a blinking dot on a map of the area west of Calgary. He had been looking at the screen for some time and wondering why the blinking dot had not moved. He picked up the phone and called through to the main Business Technology room.

"Somers, did you activate the GPS on all of the equipment of that rep in Canada, Jenna Boyd?"

"Yes, I did. They went active two hours ago on her car, computer, and cell phone."

"Alright then."

Alman then dialed his two field agents. As soon as Colin answered, he went right into the details.

"There's something wrong. Her car has not moved since we activated the GPS chip. You said you guys took off three hours ago. Are you in Calgary yet?"

"Yeah, we're here. We're sitting in a coffee shop outside her condo. What do you want us to do?"

"Her car is still in the lot in Canmore. We think she might have overheard you guys talking and decided to stay away from her condo. I want you to go to her sister's place and wait for her there." Alman hung the phone and quickly texted the address to Colin.

CHAPTER 19

NATHAN WAS staring at the screen on Steven's personal computer. The folder containing the formulas had been opened up.

He scrolled through several pages and spent some time looking at each screen he saw.

"They look like chemical compounds," Nathan finally offered.

Steven shot him a look that seemed to ask, *"You think?"*

Nathan understood and just shrugged. "Look, I may have a pharmacy degree, but I'm not a pharmacologist or a chemical engineer. But I do know someone who might be able to help."

"Who?"

"A friend of mine works as a researcher right here in Seattle at the University of Washington. We were both in school together, but he didn't want the retail life, so he stayed and got his PharmD and specialized in research. He looks at compounds all the time." Both men agreed they'd go see him right away. Nathan got his friend on his cell phone and agreed to meet him at the university where he was still working.

"We'll be there in twenty minutes." Nathan finished the call, and they left the restaurant.

CHAPTER 20

JENNA AND Janine got back to Janine's condo after being told off by the detective. They had talked in the car about their next move. Jenna could not go back to her condo. *How long will those men wait? And just why the hell did they try to kill me? How is Matthews involved? Why is Matthews involved? How can I get myself out of this mess?* Nothing seemed to make sense to either of them. They had worked on these questions all the way back in Janine's car, similar to how they had worked on problems for school while growing up.

As they got out of the car, Janine spoke up. "Did the guys say anything at all that might lead us somewhere?"

Jenna thought back to the actual attack, and then it hit her. "The guy that had me in the choke hold, he said he would make it quick, and that I should not have opened the email."

"Email? What email?"

Jenna thought again. She got at least a dozen emails a day. Some from colleagues, some from her boss, some from head office, and some spam. She then turned her face towards her sister. "There was this one only a few days ago. It was weird. The subject heading was 'You must read this!' I initially thought it had to be a virus, but then I noticed it had come from Dr. Bhergosian, and so I opened it."

"Who's Dr. Bhergosian, and why would an email from him get you to open it?"

Jenna explained that Dr. Bhergosian was a famous research scientist. She had studied some of his work while getting her biochemistry degree. Matthews had hired him just a few weeks ago to head up some promising research linking the underlying causes of Alzheimer's disease and schizophrenia.

Suddenly, Janine looked at her sister, and her eyes opened wide. "Hey, I just read a story about that guy. It was in today's paper in the financial section. The gist of the story was questioning whether there would be a negative reaction on the street for Matthews Pharmaceuticals." Janine was a high-end financial planner/guru in Calgary. She had finished her business degree in just three years and then went on to her MBA.

"Why would there be a negative reaction on 'the street?'" Jenna made quotes with her fingers.

"Well, because he was just found dead. Apparent suicide."

Jenna went cold and slumped against the car, so Janine made her way around and propped her up. "Hey, sis, you alright?"

AFTER WHAT seemed like an eternity, Jenna looked at her sister. "Don't you think this is all linked? The email from Bhergosian, the death of Bhergosian, the dead rep in New Mexico, the guy in Seattle, me?"

Janine stayed quiet, mulling over what Jenna had said. "I don't know," she finally replied, "but let's get inside where we can continue to work this out."

"Okay, okay, but do you have anything to drink in your place because I need several stiff shots."

Janine was about to say something about alcohol impairing their ability to "work this out," but she figured they both could use some time to unwind. "I've got one of those Caesars in a can, but I think that's about it."

Jenna looked across the street at the liquor store. "I'll go get us some stuff. Why don't you go in and get some ice ready and maybe some food too."

Jenna came out of the liquor store about ten minutes later. She had some rum coolers, a nice bottle of chardonnay, a bottle of Malbec, and some beer. She went back across the street to Janine's condo. She climbed the stairs and noticed that the condo's front door wasn't closed. *Must have left it open for me*, she thought. *She knew I'd be packin'*.

CHAPTER 21

MIGUEL WAS in his apartment in Manhattan. He had been thinking about everything on the bus ride to the airport, on the plane, in the cab from the airport, and in the elevator ride to the front door. He knew that the whole story about the virus was a scam. The email message had not contained a virus. If it had, they could have handled it from the BT room. The only reason to send the BT guys to check everyone's computer was to access the hard drives and figure out if anyone had done anything with the attachment, like what Steven Williams had done: make a copy. They could do a lot from head office, but if the computer was not connected to the mainframe, they could not access the hard drive. If they could not access the hard drive, they could not wipe all traces of the email from the system. But why wipe away a harmless email? The only thing Miguel could think of was that the attachment was not harmless at all; on the contrary, it was valuable. It had to be very valuable to Matthews in some way for them to go to such lengths to keep it suppressed. Miguel also knew that, even though he had wiped Williams's hard drive clean, the keystroke spyware at Matthews would have already picked up the fact that he had made a copy of the attachment to a USB stick. Whether Williams knew it or not, Miguel thought he was in trouble. Miguel looked at his clock. It was already two in the morning. He would do some sniffing around at work tomorrow and call Williams when he got back home.

CHAPTER 22

ALMAN'S PHONE rang.

"We got her."

"How'd you do it?"

"We made it look like a B and E gone bad. Used a knife. A good clean cut across the throat. Then we trashed the place and took some minor stuff: computer, jewelry, some cash that was lying around, that sort of thing. This Canadian money is the weirdest looking stuff ... I tell ya, I don't know how these Canucks deal—"

"Are you guys sure it was her?"

"Absofuckinlutely." Colin was a tad annoyed at the interruption, as well as the doubt on the other end of the line. They knew what they were doing and had done the job right. "Yeah, the whole thing took less than three minutes after she walked in. We got there about ten minutes before she did and then waited for her. She walked in, and we finished things off."

"Did you encounter her sister?"

"No, we didn't. She must have had her own set of keys because she was alone."

"Where are you now?"

"In the car. Do you want us to go to Seattle for that other guy?"

"Yeah. Get down there but don't do anything yet. We have a slight glitch with that guy. We'll have to wait just a little bit with him. Just check into a hotel and wait for instructions."

Colin hung up, confused. "He wants us to do go to Seattle but just wait. What does that mean?"

Ben just shrugged and told Colin to drive to the Calgary International Airport.

Alman turned his attention towards his computer. He logged in to the Matthews HR website and found Jenna Boyd. He updated her information with the word 'deceased.' Then he closed his computer.

CHAPTER 23

STEVEN AND Nathan made their way from the parking lot near the pharmacy building at the University of Washington and to the building itself. They climbed the steps and pushed the large wooden door open. From there, they turned left and moved down a long hallway to the staircase at the end. They went down a flight of stairs to the basement. Steven couldn't help but think of all the hospitals he had been in, calling on doctors whose offices were spread out among different floors. The offices usually had windows and natural light, but the pharmacy was always in the basement. He thought it was cruel and ironic to put the research department for the faculty of pharmacy in the basement of the faculty of pharmacy. *I guess hospital pharmacists and researchers don't like windows,* he thought. Once in the basement, they turned down a hallway and came to an office door. They knocked, and a few seconds later, it opened.

"Nathan!" A man looking to be the same age as Nathan extended his hand and vigorously shook Nathan's, then turned to Steven and shook his hand with equal enthusiasm. He was a big guy for a researcher, or so Steven thought. Tall and muscular, with blond hair and arms that fairly bulged at the biceps. A macho researcher. Who'd have thought it?

"Seth, how are you doing?" Nathan asked. "You're looking well. The lack of sunlight down here doesn't seem to be affecting your tan. You been away or is the bronze skin artificially enhanced?"

The man Nathan had called Seth just smiled and shook his head. "No way I fake and bake, man. I just got back from Belize."

Steven watched the two men and waited. Soon, Nathan turned towards him, gesturing at him. "This is my friend Steven Williams. He's the guy with the stick full of what looks like chemical formulas. I have no idea what they are, but we thought you might."

Seth looked at Steven and then at Nathan, and what he said next took them both aback. "Where did you get them and why do you want to know what they are? I mean, is this some sort of industrial espionage thing? Will I get into major shit for looking at this stick?"

Nathan just stared at Seth, then glanced at Steven. Just how much of what had happened should they tell? It was all pretty weird, and Nathan didn't really know what to think given what Steven had told him. Maybe they were in breach of some sort of intellectual property rights law and in major shit. Although, if what Steven had said was, in fact, connected, then they were in major shit already. Again, he thought back to his first suggestion for Steven to just give the stick back.

"I received this information from a research scientist who works for my company, Matthews Pharmaceuticals." Steven decided to let Seth in on some of what had happened to convince him to look at the stick. "His name is Helmut Bhergosian, and he shipped this message out via company email to a ton of people in our company. I don't know why he would do that, and my curiosity is kind of getting the better of me, so I want to know what's on the stick. If it's just a bunch of company information, I'll leave it be, and we're done. I just can't figure out why Dr. Bhergosian would send this out if it didn't mean something." Steven finished with the stick in his hand, half holding it up for Seth and half keeping it close.

Seth surprised Steven as he reached out and took the stick, turning it over in his hands. "It's lucky you even have this thing given what happened last weekend."

"What happened last weekend?" Steven and Nathan asked in unison.

"Bhergosian. He was found dead in his apartment. Apparent suicide."

This news left the two friends cold. The coincidences, adding up in the form of dead bodies, was just too fucking scary.

"Dead?" Steven almost shouted. "How? When? What the hell?"

Seth looked at Steven, genuinely surprised by his reaction. "Yeah, he's dead. Like I just said, they found him in his apartment last Sunday. Looks like a suicide."

Nathan spoke almost in a whisper. "How did you find out?"

"A researcher buddy of mine at Harvard, Randi Thilwell, emailed me today. She thought Bhergosian should never have joined evil pharma." Seth waved his hands in the air at his turn of phrase and continued. "Randi is big on university research being kept independent from pharma, and she never would join a pharmaceutical company. She emailed me to bug me and suggest that Big Pharma must have driven Bhergosian insane."

"Why was she bugging you?" Nathan asked.

"Oh, I'm in a research study being sponsored by one of the Big Pharma companies. They're paying part of my freight and part of the palatial surroundings I work in." He then looked at Steven. "It's not Matthews." Steven just shrugged. "So, Bhergosian sent you this stick, did he?"

"No, he sent out an email with an attachment. I copied the attachment onto the USB."

Again, Seth turned the stick over in his hands, thinking and mulling. "Why would he send this out? ... Well, let's just have a look then, shall we?" He led them back into his office through a small lab that was cluttered with tubes, screens, bottles, papers, and of course, Bunsen burners. They entered an office that was equally jammed with papers and binders. A large desk was shoved into a corner and two small chairs sat in front, but they too were covered with papers to use. Seth made his way around the desk and sat down in front of his computer. He plugged the stick into the tower and proceeded to open it up. When the formulas first appeared, Seth sat back in his chair and casually scrolled through them. But he soon sat forward and began concentrating hard on what he saw on the screen. He was quickly clicking through compound after compound, occasionally sending out a whistle through pursed lips. Steven and Nathan just let him go through his sounds and gesticulations, not wanting him to stop. They wanted to know what these things were—what they *all* were—so they didn't dare stop him. Finally, Seth finished his viewing and leaned back in his chair.

"Dr. Bhergosian sent this out in an email? To a bunch of people at Matthews? How long ago did you get this?"

Steven thought back. "Uh, about a week or a week and a half ago, I think. Yeah, I think it was last Thursday or Friday, but I didn't open it until Monday morning."

"And it came from a Matthews computer?"

"Yeah, I think so, why do you ask?"

"Well, first off, some of these compounds look to be molecules that don't match Matthews's area of interest." Seth looked at the blank stares looking back at him. "I recognize some of these molecules, or rather, they seem similar to molecules that are either on the market or are in development, but they have some distinct differences. And many of them are in therapeutic areas that Matthews does not play in. Some of these are existing compounds that have an extra side chain on them. Some of them look to be combined with other chemical rings or monoclonal antibodies and stuff like that. I mean, this compound is for diabetes, but it has some elements to it that I can't get on first glance. This one looks like a biologic, similar to one that's on the market for rheumatoid arthritis, but it has some markers that I don't get. This one is for Alzheimer's, but again, it has some side chains, O-rings, that I can't figure out. This is really fascinating, guys. Say, can I make a copy of this? I'd love to study these things some more."

Ignoring Seth's initial fear of getting in major shit for even looking at the stick, and the obvious trouble of leaving behind a copy, Nathan asked, "Why would Matthews have molecules in its computer system that don't match the therapeutic areas they sell in?"

Seth looked at the two men in front of him and rubbed his chin. "I'm just spitballin' here, but maybe this *is* a case of industrial espionage. I mean, I was joking when I first mentioned it, but all these compounds in one file, all in the database of *one* company? Maybe Matthews is up to their eyeballs in spying and stealing. It makes sense that these have been stolen and stored by Matthews. I mean, in that case, they'd all be in one data set."

"Maybe they're just molecules that Matthews is investigating," Nathan offered.

"Hardly," Seth jumped in. "There are just too many here. These are molecules in diseases ranging from Alzheimer's to … well … whatever. I mean from A to Z. No drug company could afford to work in so many different areas. And that's not the way Big Pharma is going right now."

Steven cocked an eyebrow. "What do you mean by that?"

Seth looked at the screen again, as it seemed to draw him in, but then leaned back and looked at his two investigators. "Well, most big pharmaceutical companies have decided to consolidate their research efforts into four or five buckets. These buckets are really just areas they think they work well in and are positioned well for future drug discovery." Seth noticed the blank stares and proceeded further. "It used to be that drug companies let their researchers just kind of go wild and try to come up with new molecules. When they found something, they would run with it until something came of it or it was shelved. It worked to a certain extent as the industry created quite a few blockbuster drugs in many different therapeutic areas. But that model has changed in recent years to one of more focus in a few key areas. As well, the sales arms of the drug companies are getting more and more involved at an earlier and earlier stage of drug development. Now you have to provide a 'proof of concept' for your drug. That proof of concept is really the make-or-break stage for researchers, and we have to become salesmen and saleswomen to get funding. We present the concept to a board that includes pharma execs and sales execs, trying to convince them of the commercial viability of our compound. It's not so much about the pure science anymore but rather the sales potential and how big the market could be. It's about aftermarket dollars. If your proof of concept does not meet their standard for solid future revenues, then you get no money, no matter how brilliant your work is or how beneficial to mankind it could be."

Steven thought this made sense. A company could focus in areas where they had expertise and really concentrate their research dollars. "That seems to make sense to me. Successful drugs bring in more dollars for continued research that ultimately puts new and improved drugs on the market, but companies have to make a profit to do that. Profit isn't a dirty word."

Seth looked at Steven hard and then chuckled. "Yeah, profit is not a dirty word, but all these companies drone on about finding drugs that fill an unmet medical need in the world. They don't talk about the unmet financial thirst of the drug company."

The others just stared, knowing that more was coming.

"I think this whole shift in strategy is all about revenues. Just look at what Pfizer announced just a few years ago. This is one of the biggest drug companies in the world with the biggest cardiovascular product line ever. They had Lipitor for lowering cholesterol at thirteen billion dollars a year, Norvasc for high blood pressure and angina at four billion dollars, and a host of others. Their cardio products generated somewhere around twenty billion dollars a year. So, this would be their area of expertise, right? Worthy of lots of research money, right?" It was a rhetorical question, and the others waited for an answer. "Wrong. Pfizer announced they're pulling out of cardiovascular research altogether. They also announced another big portfolio, osteoarthritis, is also being abandoned. Their CEO announced that Pfizer will now play in just six areas." Seth held up his right hand, counting off items on his fingers: "Psychosis, diabetes, oncology, Alzheimer's, pain and inflammation, and vaccines."

Steven was feeling totally underwhelmed. "So what? They decided to focus research money where they think they've got good scientific programs."

Seth rolled his eyes. "Yeah, that's part of it, but the big reason is all about revenue and maintaining that revenue for the life of the product and the patient."

Nathan now jumped in. "What's wrong with that?"

"Nothing per se, it's just that they're being disingenuous at best and downright deceitful at worst." Seth looked at his students and carried on. "Why would a drug company that generates nearly twenty billion in sales in a given area pull out? Obviously, they don't think it's a profitable area moving forward. With Lipitor, Pfizer had the top-selling cholesterol drug in the world. But how much more can you lower cholesterol? And what new compound is going to be any better? Also, all these compounds come under fire from generics at some point, so the revenue stream dries up. And the patients taking these meds are Pfizer's worst enemy because they stop taking the medication at some point. Pfizer is always fighting to not only generate new prescriptions for Lipitor, but they have to spend hundreds of millions of dollars trying to convince Mom and Pop to stay on their cholesterol-lowering med or their high blood pressure med. And finally, these huge dollar medications are the first targets of generic drug companies. They go after the Lipitors of the world like a tiger to fresh meat. So, Pfizer not only spends mega millions trying to convince Mom and Dad to stay on their drug, but they also spend millions every year fighting off patent challenges from heavily funded generic drug companies."

Steven knew this was true. His own company had dozens of programs designed to keep patients on their medications for cholesterol and high blood pressure. People don't feel bad when they have either of those problems, so they end up leaving the pill bottle in the medicine cabinet. He also received many updates regarding the on-going battle to keep their medications from falling to the generics much earlier than the original patent promised.

Seth continued, sensing Steven's thought process. "They don't feel bad, so they stop taking their drug, and Pfizer suffers." Seth looked at the two of them. "The average length of time a patient takes Lipitor, supposedly a drug prescribed for life, is 351 days. That's it, less than a year, and that's even when the medication is working. Then they stop taking it, and Pfizer loses that future revenue on that patient. The patient becomes public enemy number one to the drug company because they stop taking their medication. It's not worth it to drug companies to keep developing drugs in this area because it's too hard and expensive to maintain their revenue stream. With future advances in cholesterol lowering, blood pressure lowering, or basic arthritis next to impossible, the companies are pulling up stakes and going elsewhere. Companies are putting a lot of money, time, and research efforts into developing biologics for conditions we used to treat with a pill, like high blood pressure, high cholesterol, and arthritis. We have a new biologic for lowering cholesterol, and it is insanely expensive. Also, generic companies can't create generic equivalent copies of biologics. The molecules are too complex. They've tried, but we call them biologic similar."

Steven looked away then back at Seth. "So, you're saying drug companies are not going to develop any new cardiovascular pills because they can't make any money?"

"Pretty much ... not in pill form anyway. I mean, they do (or did) make money at the start, but like I said, they also spent and spend a ton defending their turf from their patients' indifference to their own condition and the generic competition. My guess is that they're starting to say it's not worth it. A drug company wants to keep you on their medication for the entire length of a prescription, and sometimes that's the entire life of a patient. If they can't do that, their continuous revenue stream is in trouble. So, having you stay on your medication is the goal of Big Pharma. But now, let's look at the areas Pfizer is now playing in."

Seth did the finger thing again. "Psychosis: A patient has to stay on their medication for life in order to stay healthy. No drug, they relapse, and a psychotic patient is pretty visible. They know it, and their families know it, so they stay on their medication with very little prompting. In other words, very little money spent by the company. Diabetes: People know about the consequences of untreated diabetes. They have to stay on their medication or their sugars and ultimately their lives are threatened. Oncology: Would you stop taking your course of chemo if it was working? Alzheimer's: Who is going to *not* take their medication to combat a disease people list ahead of death as being something they fear the most? Pain: If someone is in constant pain, they'll take their medication forever, even if the med does not totally take away the pain. Vaccines: Governments around the world have so frightened people about the flu and Covid that people line up like sheep to get their shots. In all those areas, the patient becomes a maximum revenue generator for the company. As well, Pfizer will save hundreds of millions, maybe billions of dollars in patient-adherence campaigns and defending against generic intrusion that they can plow back into the bottom line. And these new key areas are also areas that offer hope for new scientific developments that also protect companies from generics. I mean, we already know how to lower blood pressure in many different ways, and the same goes for cholesterol. There's really nothing new to develop in these areas, and the patients and the generics will get you in the end anyway."

Steven jumped in. "The patient will get them in the end?"

"Absolutely!" Seth shouted. "Haven't you been listening? In therapeutic areas where prescription maintenance is a low priority for the patient, they turn from drug-company revenue generator to drug-company enemy because they don't stay with their therapy for as long as they are supposed to stay on it."

It was a thought that had not occurred to Steven before. Patients, or customers, become the enemy of the company supplying them the medication. It's like the company goes to war with the patient, trying to convince them to stay on a medication for a condition they can't feel. But he also had another question. "But you talked about generic competition. There are also generic drugs in psychosis, diabetes, etcetera."

"Not many. In psychosis, there are a couple, but that's also an area where the research is really exciting, and new drugs are coming that are totally different from the ones we have today, and that means more revenue. Also, the shift in psychosis is towards long-acting injectables that generics won't or can't touch. That holds true for the other areas as well. You ever hear of generic insulin? And treating diabetes is not like treating high blood pressure. The research in that area is coming out with new, novel compounds that will keep the generics at bay for a few more years. The only short-course therapy exception, if you can call it that, would be oncology where there are really no generic drugs, and that's also an area where the meds are hugely expensive—I mean profitable. Drug companies are jumping in with both feet in oncology. I mean, think about it: You may only take your cancer medication for 351 days, but the cost of that is huge."

Now Nathan chimed in. "You sound pretty cynical, Seth. Almost disdainful. Yet you're accepting drug-company research money to help 'pay your freight.'"

Seth looked up at both of them and smiled. "Cynical? Yes, I am. Disdainful? Maybe. I hadn't really thought about that. But I'm also practical. I like to eat and be able to pay my mortgage, and universities and governments have largely abandoned funding basic research, so the drug companies stepped in. They're getting into bed with more and more universities at the basic research level. They're funding programs and signing deals all the time now. The era of truly independent research is going the way of the dodo. But there's also a part of me that thinks maybe one of the compounds I'm working on will turn out to be something special, perhaps a cure even."

Steven and Nathan just looked at one another. This digression into Seth's assessment of the profit motives of drug companies had been interesting, but that's not what they were here for.

"So, back to the stick," Steven began, "any thoughts as to what these compounds are?"

Seth turned back to the computer screen and scrolled again. "Like I said, I'm not quite sure at first glance. To really give you a good answer, I'll have to make a copy and go through them in depth."

"What about the getting-in-shit part you mentioned before?" Nathan asked.

Seth just chuckled a little. "Hey, I'm a researcher. And it's like you said, Steve, curiosity has gotten the better of me as well."

Steven looked at Nathan, and they shrugged their acceptance. Seth quickly made a copy to his documents folder, safely ejected the stick, and then turned to face them, handing it back to Steven. "You wanna go for a beer?"

CHAPTER 24

THE DOWNTOWN Calgary police station was alive with activity. On any given Monday, the activity was pretty quiet, but this was no ordinary Monday. The press was camped outside, both TV and print. Inside there was an air of urgency as the communications officer talked with someone out in the field.

The police-service spokesperson was pressing for answers. "How is your investigation coming along?"

The detective was clearly not ready to be cooperative with the press. "It would move faster if you didn't have me on the phone."

"Alright, alright, but you would not believe the scene here. The press is all over the place, demanding we say something. It's not every day we get this sort of homicide."

"Granted, but we still have to do this thing right. We mess up, and the killer will go free. Has the sister given us anything?"

"No, she's pretty distraught. She keeps going on about two men who'd tried to kill her earlier today and insisting this is linked to what happened at the condo. We just can't find any evidence of a previous assault. We're thinking of bringing in a psychiatrist to see if her story is trauma induced."

"Yeah, I get your point. But let me get back to work, will ya?"

With that, the detective hung up the phone and went back to the interview room to ask a few more questions. As he opened the door, he was struck by the woman sitting at the table facing him. She was "distraught," as he had told the press secretary, but there was also a strength in her, answering everything they had thrown at her and even firing back a couple of questions of her own. He closed the door and sat down across from her.

"Ms. Boyd, can you think of anything else that might help us track down these two men you say attacked you earlier?"

By now, Jenna was numbed by everything that had happened. She had been attacked, had involved her sister in whatever was going on, and that had led to her death. She'd had nowhere else to go when she arrived in Calgary, but now she wished she had gone home instead of to Janine's. They had always counted on one another though. That's what sisters did, especially twin sisters. It was what their parents had always encouraged them to do: care for and help one another.

"No, I can't think of anything else. I just know they're linked to the company I work for, Matthews Pharmaceuticals."

The detective could not bring himself to believe that a huge multinational pharmaceutical company would so gruesomely take the life of a young woman. He had asked Jenna earlier for a reason why Matthews would do such a thing, but she could not offer him one.

"Ms. Boyd, setting that aside for the moment, this looks like a burglary gone bad. The DVD player is gone, as is some of her jewelry, some cash, and the computer, among other items. It looks like your sister walked in on the guy, or guys, and things went very bad very quickly."

Jenna was barely hanging on, but she looked at the detective and said, "I know it sounds crazy, but Matthews *is* involved somehow."

The detective just sighed and leaned back in his chair. There was really no reason to keep Jenna here any longer. "Ms. Boyd, may I call you a cab to take you home? We'll keep you completely posted as to our investigation."

Jenna just nodded and sat quietly with her head down.

The detective got up and opened the door. Turning back to Jenna, he said quietly and sincerely, "Ms. Boyd, we are all truly saddened for your loss. We're going to work our butts off to catch whoever did this. In the meantime, do you want me to put you in touch with our crisis counselors? They really can help you through this."

Jenna looked at the detective and managed a small smile but shook her head. She'd had time to think while alone in the interview room. Her attackers now thought she was dead. So, let 'em think that. That might give her some time to dig into this. Maybe she could find out something and bring it back to the police. She was no sleuth, spy, or detective, but she was determined to find out more … for her sister's sake and for her own.

CHAPTER 25

ABOUT FIVE seconds after Seth had put the stick into his computer, an alarm went off back at Matthews. Alman had seen it right away and quickly identified where it had come from. He had called Slater and was now in the situation room with him, explaining what was going on.

Anyone who accepted research money from an affiliate drug company had to agree to have a company program downloaded into their computer system. They were told it was to help in data collection, and that was partially true. But there was also very powerful spyware software loaded into the program that allowed another layer of surveillance to be handed over to the affiliation. When the USB was plugged into Seth's computer, the markers of the affiliation triggered the spyware. Seth's location had been identified seconds after the alarm went off.

"The USB was plugged into the computer of a researcher at the University of Washington. He's doing some research with another company. Our spyware picked it up right away, but that means this guy"—Alman held up a printout—"a Seth Geoghan, has not only seen the contents of the stick, but he made a copy to his computer hard drive."

Slater maintained his calm. "How long ago did the stick get loaded?"

"About five minutes ago."

"Is your team in Seattle yet?"

"They're in the air. They'll be there within the hour."

"Can they get to him right away?"

"I'll instruct them to go to the lab as soon as they land. Are they to take out this researcher?"

"Yes. Make sure it looks like an accident."

"Okay, will do."

"See to it then."

Alman could not resist any longer. "Mr. Slater, just what is on that stick anyway?"

Slater turned and looked at him before saying, "Just follow your orders and make sure your team gets Williams." With that, he left the room, and Alman picked up the phone and left a text for Colin to call him as soon as they landed.

CHAPTER 26

AFTER HE had finished with Alman, Slater took the elevator back up to his office, on the fiftieth floor, where he knew he had a visitor waiting. He entered and shook the hand of the man sitting in his armchair.

Holding up a thick document, the man waved it at Slater. "This was way too close. I thought our monitoring systems were more capable than this. I mean, we only caught on to this because of their loudmouth CEO spouted off on fucking CNN. I mean, for crying out loud!"

Slater stared back at the man and coolly responded. "The point is, Paul, we did catch it and were able to close the purchase agreement fairly quickly. The 'loudmouth CEO' you mentioned is now rich, fat, and happy, and the company's investors are happy as well."

Paul Soper was the chair of one of the larger affiliate companies. "What if someone talks again about their program?"

"That's unlikely, given the secrecy clause we stipulated in our agreement. If anyone talks, everyone has to hand back their big cheques. And even if that happens, we can go on CNN and say that the work, while promising, requires many more years of study."

"What about the scientists involved in the program?"

"Some of them have been retained at hugely rich compensation packages, so they can continue to work to their hearts content, and a few were paid just enough to guarantee they won't talk. I think we have this one covered."

"I guess so, but this could have cost billions of dollars in revenue. Maybe we need to beef up our scientific monitoring. Maybe we need to ask the board for more money."

"I've thought of that, but how much are we talking about? We're already spending a small fortune, keeping tabs on these biotechs, and there's so many of them. We can't possibly keep them all under surveillance. And governments are starting to put more money into these little guys. I think we need a two-pronged approach: We need to contact our lobbyists to put a word in governmental ears to stop funding this nonsense, and we need to press upon governments that pharma research, even biotech research, is best left to pharmaceutical companies. And that can also free up tax dollars to spend on more politically friendly projects. We also need to have all our affiliates step up their efforts to forge strategic alliances with more of these biotechs, so we can keep tabs without having to buy the little fuckers when they screw up like this."

"Doesn't this research also have to be published as per the FDA?"

"Yes, it does, but now we control where it gets submitted. The FDA mandates that all research studies be published, both good and bad. But they can't tell us which publication we submit the study to for consideration. Given the nature of this research study, we'll find some obscure, little journal to submit it to. We can also stipulate that the study has not been replicated and therefore should not be thought of as conclusive. Ownership gives us that kind of control."

"These biotech firms are only part of it. We have to continue to step into the university-based research programs, so we can monitor those."

"We're doing that. In the last five years, our level of funding at universities has increased fivefold. We're coordinating with our government lobby branch to get the word out that we are more than willing to be a good corporate citizen and help the overstretched revenue stream of government. We're doing okay here."

Soper stared at the purchase agreement in his hand. "This could have been another polio fiasco. It was just too close for me."

"Me too, my friend. Me too. We'll just have to be diligent with the surveillance systems we have in place and quick to act when we must, like we just did. Let me just go into the system and update the files for our records." Slater began typing in a password as Paul Soper looked on.

"I wish you'd change that cheesy password. It's beneath us."

"Oh, come on, Paul, it has certain pithy insouciance to it, don't you think?" Slater finished entering the password and logged on to a massive file system.

CHAPTER 27

JENNA WAS surrounded by friends and other family members at her sister's funeral. The priest had asked her to come forward and deliver the eulogy, and she had been strong throughout. She talked about how close they were, especially being identical twins. She had talked of their good times together and of how they had leaned on each other when their parents had died. After the last funeral guest had left, and she had returned to her apartment, she began to focus on what her next steps would be.

Jenna knew that a district manager would know nothing of the company supposedly ordering employees to be killed. She had to maintain a sense of normalcy to throw the people responsible off her scent. If she simply stopped entering calls and synchronizing her computer, it would raise red flags with her boss. She had to check in. She had gotten time off from Matthews, and her boss had said to take all the time she needed, so she was going to take advantage. The company policy was five days bereavement, but her manager had said to screw the policy, and she used her manager's discretion. So, Jenna was in the clear, for the foreseeable future. She knew something sinister was going on and was going to follow up. She thought about what Janine would want her to do. In the end, at the end of a long and trying day, she picked up the phone and placed a call. It was a way to start.

CHAPTER 28

"WHAT IF we were to up our political contribution arm?" Paul Soper was still fretting about their most recent scare. "Our government lobbyists could make the pitch that research funding is best left to Pharma companies, and we could pair that with a multimillion-dollar donation to the party."

Slater didn't hesitate. "You're only thinking of one element of government funding. There are multilayers of funding, and even we could not afford to pull that kind of investment together on a consistent basis. Also, we could not withstand the accounting oversight and scrutiny that kind of funding would generate. Anyway, with the funding levels we currently provide, we are in many different areas of research, and with our donations to both political parties ever increasing, we can buy a lot of favors. We are buying our way into more and more universities. Like I said, our funding of research at the university level has increased five hundred percent over the last five years. And every time we enter into an agreement, we plant our surveillance software into the university's computer system. We can even monitor research that we don't fund through our back-channel spyware. We can use the power of our numbers to continue to buy and monitor a vast array of research vehicles and biotechs. All these little biotechs are looking for venture capital funding, and we can provide a good chunk of that. As soon as we're in, we drop our surveillance software into their systems, and we're golden."

Soper nodded and added, "We need some of our CEOs to make announcements that they're expanding more and more into biotech, some sort of wave of the future shit. That should flush out quite a few smaller biotechs scrounging for funds. We can then go in and evaluate their research, and if it looks dangerous, we can snap them up."

"That's a great idea. That will scare them out of the reeds and help our surveillance efforts."

Slater and Soper then detailed a communique they would send out. Then they'd wait for replies and volunteers.

CHAPTER 29

STEVEN AND Nathan left Seth in the pub and drove to Steven's house. On the way, they discussed again the issue of just returning the USB stick, but it was now Nathan who was more on the side of keeping it. If it was as valuable as Miguel had said, then Matthews would want it back before doing anything to them.

"If this is industrial espionage as Seth said, then the more information we have before we go the 'whistle blower' route, the better," said Nathan. "We just have to avoid Matthews until we're ready."

"Oh great," Steven said. "So, we meet up with Matthews's mercenaries, and they torture us until we talk and tell them where the stick is."

Considering that the stick was in Steven's jacket pocket, it might not be a very long session.

They went back and forth until they pulled up to the house. Once inside, Steven noticed that the message light on his phone was blinking. Nathan kidded him about being the only millennial who still had a landline, but Steven just waved him off. He punched in his retrieval code and was told he had two new messages.

"Hi, my name is Jenna Boyd, and I live in Calgary, Alberta. I got your name and contact information from your LinkedIn page. I'm a rep for Matthews Pharmaceuticals, and I need to talk to you right away. It concerns an email from Dr. Bhergosian and an attachment that went with it. It's seven in the evening here right now, and I'll stay up and wait for your call. Please call me tonight. My number is 403-265-4638."

"Hi Steven, it's Miguel. I know you think I'm nuts, but I need to speak with you. I found something in a computer check that I need you to know.

It will prove that something is up, and well ... I need to speak with you. Call me tonight. I'll either wait up or wake up to take your call. Thanks."

Steven's head hurt. He had to make the calls, and he knew it, but who to call first? He asked Nathan.

"First come, first serve. Call the girl first," said Nathan. So, Steven did just that.

"Hello?" The woman sounded very young.

"Uh, hello, this is Steven Williams from Seattle, calling you back."

"Yes," Jenna said, enthusiastically. "Yes, thanks for calling me back. I'm just gonna launch right in. Did you recently receive and open an email from Dr. Bhergosian while he was still with Matthews? And the attachment in the email ... did you open it?"

"What the hell? How did you know about that? Who are you anyway?"

"Look, I know it sounds crazy, but I think there was something in that email and the attachment that was extremely valuable to Matthews. I know they don't want anyone to see it, and I know they have killed people in the last week to prevent them from seeing it or reporting it."

"Look, I don't know who you are, and I didn't think anyone could get my contact information from LinkedIn but—"

"My sister was murdered because of that email." The statement just hung there, poised on the line somewhere between Calgary and Seattle. Jenna let it hang out there, waiting for Williams's response.

"I don't know what to say to that. 'I'm sorry' springs to mind, but that seems totally inadequate. Are you sure about your sister?"

"Look, like I said, that email had something in it that Matthews doesn't want anyone to see, and they really want it back. Someone tried to kill me here in Alberta three days ago because I opened the email. I didn't even open the attachment, and they came after me. They talked about some guy dying in New Mexico, and they talked about going after you in Seattle. It may sound nuts, it may sound ludicrous, but it's real, and they're coming for you."

Steven was reeling from what this woman was saying and couldn't fully process the information. It was just coming too fast, but a question did occur to him. "Why would your sister be killed if they wanted to kill you? Did she see the email?"

Jenna got a huge lump in her throat as she began, but she persevered. "My sister was my identical twin. I was staying with her. I couldn't go back to my apartment because I heard them say they would get me there. I stepped out for a minute, and when I got back …" She just couldn't finish, but she didn't have to.

Steven listened as the woman on the other end cried, though she tried to muffle it. As he was about to speak, Nathan tapped him hard on the shoulder and motioned for him to look at the TV. "Just a minute, Jenna, hang on."

The TV was on the local news channel and the headline at the bottom of the screen said, "Breaking News." Nathan quickly turned it up.

"The fire at the university," an on-scene reporter was saying, "was contained to the Faculty of Pharmacy building and was stopped in the basement before it spread to the upper floors. The damage was extensive, however, and local officials are not saying what they will do to relocate any staff or equipment or even if any equipment can be saved."

The news anchor cut in, "Brian, do we know any more about the victim?"

"Not much, Darrin. We know he was a researcher here, and I have heard from a couple of people that his name was Seth Geoghan. He had been at the university for about five years and was considered one of the brightest minds in the department."

Nathan had still been holding the remote and snapped the TV off.

Steven stared at the darkened screen for a couple of seconds and then spoke to Jenna. "When can you get down here?"

"Why? You have something, don't you? You believe me, don't you?"

"Look, I don't know what to believe right now, but this is getting seriously frightening, and I think we need numbers, gathered together … numbers to try to figure out what to do. A friend of ours was just … he died and this … all this may have had something to do with it. When can you get down here?"

"Tomorrow. I'll fly in tomorrow."

"Good." Steven gave Jenna directions to his house from the airport, and she would let him know when her flight was coming in.

After hanging up, Steven sat down and held his head in his hands.

Nathan just looked at him. "What the hell are we going to do?"

"I have no idea, but like I said, I think we need to band together on this. I just feel we need numbers. And okay, I'm now convinced. We need to figure out what is on this stick. As long as we have it, they'll come for it … and for us."

"Are we safe as long as we have it, and they don't?" With that thought, Nathan left the room to get a drink, not waiting for an answer.

CHAPTER 30

"DID YOUR team in Seattle complete the job?"

"They did. Made it look like a fire in a chemical lab. That's not too bad."

"I suppose so. When will your team be able to finish things up?"

"They should be able to get things done tomorrow."

"Why not tonight?"

"Simple. We don't want to get the Seattle Police suspicious about multiple deaths on the same night. I think we should pick up this Williams guy and hold onto him for a day or two. Maybe we can take him somewhere outside the city and do it well away from prying eyes, police, and cameras."

"Okay, but just make sure we get him, and we need to get that stick back before we finish things."

"You're the boss."

CHAPTER 31

JENNA PUT down the phone and went to her home computer to look up flights to Seattle. There was an available seat on one leaving at 6:10 a.m., so she booked it. It was a hell of an early flight, but she needed to get going, to do something, and to find out more.

She went to her room to begin packing but instead began shaking, and the tears flowed so easily and unexpectedly that she could not stop. In truth, she did not want to stop them. The enormity of everything that had happened in the last few days hit her hard, and she allowed herself the time to bawl.

She knew she was alone. Totally alone. Her parents gone and now her sister. She had no idea what lay ahead, if she would survive another twenty-four, forty-eight, or seventy-two hours, or anything beyond that, but the drive to see it through no matter what was there.

She finished her crying, set the alarm, and collapsed into sleep.

CHAPTER 32

NATHAN CAME back into the room with his drink and mentioned to Steven that Miguel wanted him to call.

Steven nodded, picked up the phone, and dialed.

"Hello, Steven, I'm glad you called."

Call display, thought Steven. "Well, you said it was important, and we've had more crap go on here, so here I am."

"What crap?"

Steven told him about their meeting with Seth and the contents of the stick, as well as Seth making a copy. He told him about Jenna Boyd, her sister, and the fire that had apparently killed Seth.

"Miguel," Steven said, "I know I said you were crazy, and I walked out on you in L.A., but I think you might be right."

"Are you going to talk to the police about this researcher?"

"We talked about it, but what are going to say? We think a major pharmaceutical company killed him because we have a USB with a bunch of compounds on it? They'll laugh us out of the precinct and then contact Matthews about returning the stick to them. It might make Matthews think twice about killing us right away, but in the end, they'll find a way to do it. Whatever is on this USB stick is enough to kill for, and we think the only way to stay safe is to keep it and find out exactly what's on it. The more people we can include, the harder it will be for Matthews to eliminate the … uh, well … the *viewership,* for lack of a better word."

"Maybe you're right. I don't know for sure, but maybe."

"Anyway, you said you had something?"

Miguel snapped back to his reality. "Yeah, yeah, I do. There is definitely something going on. The IT techs have been asked to really ramp up our laptop surfing."

"Your what?"

"Laptop surfing. We routinely select employee computers to conduct random searches of what they've been doing. I mean, we get an alarm if you download unwanted software or if you write a message with inappropriate language or if you visit a porn site, etcetera, etcetera, but we also visit your computers to see what personal things, if any, you're using them for. If you're writing messages that don't set off our spyware alarms but are still not work related, we just tap into your computer and do a keystroke search for the last thirty days. Then we just go surfing."

Steven digested this for a second. "You guys know if we visit other sites? If we download software like a game or some music? Or if we use inappropriate language? We're monitored that much?" He was genuinely surprised.

"Oh sure. All that stuff is captured by the spyware we put in your laptops. It's dead easy. You have no idea how much you guys in the field are connected to Big Brother here in New York, not only through your computers and iPads but through your phones and cars too. But I told you all this back in L.A."

Steven had always thought it was cool the way an IT expert three thousand miles away could phone his computer and then take it over. But he thought the representative had to allow the contact.

"So, you're telling me you can get into our computers and iPads without us knowing? I thought we had to allow access like when you're doing a remote fix."

"We do handle remote fixes because you can tell us the specific problem, so we can quickly fix it. But we don't need you to allow us into your laptop. As long as your computer is on, we have a way in. And now with Wi-Fi connectivity, we can pretty much get in whenever we want."

"Holy shit. I had no idea."

Miguel went on. "Yeah, nobody does, I guess. But anyway, as I said, we have been asked to really ramp up our surfing. We've gone from three a day each to ten a day. We've been told the original message was a virus, and Matthews wants to know if it could have been forwarded to a wider set of computers. We've been told it's a security issue with wider internet implications."

"Like what?"

"Well, say someone forwarded the original attachment to their home computer. We might not pick that up right away because our spyware would not detect any inappropriate language or your computer tapping into a prohibited site. We would not get the alarm, but our surfing would pick it up, the rep would be identified, and presumably, the threat to the wider net could be stopped. That's what we've been told."

"Have you found anything?"

"No, thank God. Nothing so far. It looks as though virtually everyone just deleted the message as per company instructions. But that stick has something on it that has Matthews wigging out."

Steven turned the USB stick over in his hands. "What a nightmare."

"I'll say."

Steven suddenly sat forward. "Hey, can you do a 'surf' on a rep in Canada?"

"Yeah sure, but why?"

"Can you look up Jenna Boyd in Calgary? She's a Matthews rep in Calgary, Canada. She phoned me earlier, and we spoke. She told me that she has gotten mixed up in something involving Matthews and knew about Dr. Bhergosian and the attachment. She's on her way here to see what, if anything, she did that could have made her a target. It would confirm what she told me."

"You don't believe her?"

"Well, shit, I don't know. I do, I guess, but what if she's a plant to get me to give this thing up? I know it sounds all cloak and dagger, but it couldn't hurt, could it?"

"No, I suppose not. I'll look her up tomorrow morning first thing when I get in."

"Great, give me a call after you do."

With that, the two men hung up. Steven told Nathan about the extent of the company surveillance and what Miguel was going to do in the morning.

"Should we change houses?" Nathan asked.

It should have occurred to Steven that they were in danger given what he'd heard and seen, but he had simply been processing information, not assessing it. The question brought their situation into stark relief. They packed up some of Steven's things and left for Nathan's house. Matthews had no connection to him, so they'd be safe there.

"I'll call Jenna and let her know of the change of address," Steven said as they left. They used a taxi to make the trip, leaving Steven's car and phone behind.

CHAPTER 33

COLIN AND Ben had easily slipped away from the university after taking care of the researcher, renting a car and checking into a hotel. With the researcher out of the way, they could take a little time to finish off Williams and get this stick back. They planned to eat breakfast and then head over to Williams's house. The last few days had been good. Most of the time they spent their days and weeks setting up residences in nice locations for people they'd never met. Aside from being able to visit some beautiful and—most of the time—sunny locations, they did not do too much. There were the follow-up visits to make sure the "clients" were still in the original location and living up to whatever agreement they had signed—no inappropriate outside phone contact, no illicit research work, no email trails to previous colleagues, etc. Basically, they administered a witness-protection-like program for their employer, Matthews Pharmaceuticals. They did not ask any questions and were paid very well for their work and their discretion. It was an all-cash—no-tax situation for them.

However, occasionally, they were asked to do real mercenary work and take someone out. Over the last several days, they had taken out six people, and now, though they'd never even been to Canada before, let alone Calgary, they were looking forward to cleaning up the final loose end and getting back to New York.

As they were about to go down for breakfast, Colin's cell phone rang. It was Alman. "Did you grab Williams yet?"

"No, we wanted to make sure everything went alright with the researcher, so we stuck around while the fire and police showed up and then slipped away. We checked into a hotel. We're just going down for breakfast, and then we'll head over to his house."

"Why are you taking so long?"

"There's no rush, right? With the researcher out of the way, this Williams guy is just sitting around. I mean, he's still in Seattle, right? You turned on his tracking devices, right?"

"His car GPS says he's still at his house. The same goes for his computer and his cell phone, so yeah, I assume he's at his house. But I'd like it done sooner rather than later."

"Okay, but we need something to eat. It won't take long. If his trackers show he's moving, call us, and we'll break off right away and go get him."

Since there was very little Alman could do to move his two men, he agreed and went back to monitoring Williams through his phone, car, and computer.

Colin hung up and looked at Ben. "He's got his knickers in a knot because we're not moving on Williams right now."

"Screw him. I'm hungry."

CHAPTER 34

JENNA ARRIVED in Seattle right on time. She quickly moved through the airport and found the taxi stand where an attendant was hailing cabs for people. Jenna had always thought this was a strange custom unique to American airports. Here was an airport employee ready to hail your cab, take your destination, give it to the cab driver, and happily receive a tip. In Canada, at most airports, passengers found the cab line and waited in line for the next one to show: Self-serve.

Anyway, she went through the American cab-procurement procedure and climbed in. Steven had called her late last night to tell her the new address. He had filled her in on the sort of surveillance Mathews's reps could be put through. She'd known about the car GPS from the attempt on her life, and she apologized to Steven for not telling him about it. The phone GPS made perfect sense, so she had left her phone at home and cabbed it to the airport. Hopefully, Matthews still thought she was dead. Not having a cell phone felt weird. People were so tied to their cell phones that not having one made her feel especially vulnerable. She did not have the time to get a personal one, so she found herself constantly looking around for any sign of danger. She wanted to get to Nathan's house as soon as possible, both for the comfort of more people and stupidly, she thought, to be reconnected to a phone of any sort.

It didn't take long for the cab to get to her destination. *Nice neighborhood,* Jenna thought. A tree-lined street, cute single-family homes, and very, very green. She walked up to the front door and rang the bell. The door opened and a fairly tall, athletic-looking guy with thick brown hair stood in front of her.

"Steven?"

"Yes, that's me. Jenna? Come in, come in."

Jenna stepped in, and Steven closed the door. Another young guy was standing in the living room. This one was shorter with a thicker build, blond hair cut very short, and glasses. *But a nice face,* Jenna thought. *Kind.*

He stepped toward her and held out his hand to shake hers. "Hi, Jenna, I'm Nathan, Stevens's pharmacist friend."

Jenna shook Nathan's hand and stood to the side so she could face both men. The three of them just stood there in an awkward isosceles triangle of silence. Finally, Steven spoke. "This is all too weird. I have no idea what we're supposed to do, or where we're supposed to go. I mean, what the heck are we doing?" It was more of a plea than a rallying cry and did not instill confidence.

"You say your sister was murdered because you opened the email from Dr. Bhergosian?" Nathan asked.

"Yes, I believe so. After they tried to take me out in K-country, they tracked me to my sister's home and killed her thinking she was me. We're identical twins. We even cut our hair the same way."

"What's K-country?" asked Nathan.

Jenna explained that K-country was the local term used by Albertans to identify Kananaskis Provincial Park and surrounding area. It was a beautiful chunk of land the size of Switzerland that a previous provincial government had set aside for environmental protection, camping, hiking, skiing, hotels, and golf. She went into further detail about the attempt made to kill her. She told the two men how she had first suspected something was wrong because of the shoes being out of whack with the hiking wear, how she had used the bear spray to disable them, followed by well-placed kicks to the men's groins. She told them how she had run into the bush, about the shots they had fired, and how she had followed them to the parking lot and listened to their conversation. As she went through her ordeal, Steven had a good, long look at her. She was fairly short at about five-foot-two or three. She had short brown hair styled very well. She seemed to be very fit. Her eyes looked to be brownish green. She was a very pretty woman who obviously had a tough streak to her, given how she had gotten away and what she had gone through after the K-country attack. *I'd better pull it together,* he thought, *no more whiny outbursts.* Jenna finished her tale and just stopped talking.

Steven then spoke. "Again, I am so sorry about your sister. If this USB stick is the root cause of everything going on, then we have to find some way to neutralize the threat. I know that's stating the bloody obvious, but there has to be a way out of this mess."

"Thanks. About my sister, I mean. I'm determined to get justice for her by getting to the bottom of this. You said something last night about what's on that thing. What was that about?"

"Well," Steven started, "it's got a bunch of chemical formulas on it. We went to see a friend of Nathan's. He's a pharmacology expert." Steven didn't realize he had referred to Seth in the present tense. "Seth said that some of them resembled compounds currently on the market but with different side chains attached to them, different chemical rings, etcetera. Some of them were brand new to him. He'd never seen anything like them. And they ran the gamut from A to Z in disease states, Alzheimer's to zosters."

Now Nathan joined in. "Yeah, but he also made the point that there were so many compounds on it, in areas that Matthews did *not* play in or market drugs in. It didn't make sense ... uh ... doesn't make sense for Matthews to have the intellectual property of so many other drug companies. We're thinking this could be a case of massive industrial espionage."

"Did he make a copy of the stick?" Jenna asked.

"Yes, he did but—"

JENNA CUT him off. "Let's go back and see him. Maybe he's made some progress in deciphering them."

Steven put his hand up to stop her. "We can't. Seth died last night in a fire in his lab."

Jenna nearly fell backwards. "My God! That was the friend you mentioned on the phone? It has *got* to be connected. How the hell would anyone know he made a copy?"

It was a question the two men should have asked themselves, so when Jenna brought it up, they stared open-mouthed at each other. How would Matthews have known he made a copy? Maybe the fire had just been a horrible coincidence.

Jenna moved to the couch to sit and think. Nathan and Steven just watched. Just as Jenna looked up to speak, she glanced out the front window and spotted Colin sitting in a car in front of the house. *Oh shit. We have to go, now.* She quickly moved from the couch, grabbing the arms of Steven and Nathan, pushing and pulling them away from the window.

"What's going on?" both men asked.

"The two guys who came after me are here, in front of your house. We have to leave. We have to leave now."

CHAPTER 35

ABOUT AN hour before Jenna arrived at Nathan's house, Colin and Ben arrived at Steven's house to finish him off. They parked up the street from his house and walked casually up to the front door. Ben looked around to see if anyone was watching them. Seeing no one, he motioned for Colin to knock again. They waited a few more seconds, and then went around to the back of the house. Using some tools that they always carried, they opened the locked door and quietly went inside. After going up a few stairs, they entered the kitchen. The house was dark, no lights were on, and it was utterly silent.

"I thought this guy was supposed to be home," Colin wondered aloud.

The two men moved into the living room, and then down the bungalow's hallway, checking each room as they went. Then they doubled back and went down to the basement and made a good search there. Back upstairs, they again stopped in the kitchen.

Ben asked, "Are you sure his trackers have him here?"

"That's what Alman said. His phone, computer, and car are all here. Maybe he went out for a walk, and we should just wait."

"Yeah, maybe, but give Alman a call anyway and have him check this guy's profile. It might give us something if he is gone."

Colin called and had Alman pull up Steven's profile, the one that he—like all reps—had written when he'd joined the company.

Alman was going through it. "It says some generic stuff about his life in Seattle, time in the industry, favorite sports and activities, and—wait, wait, here's something. He has a best friend, a Nathan Cunnymore, a pharmacist in Seattle. Says here they're as close as brothers. Maybe he went there."

"Why would he go there?" asked Colin. "Does he know we're coming for him? Because if he does, it's gonna be much tougher."

"Well, look," Alman started, "if he has suspected something and has the stick, it might make sense that he would show his best friend. That seems a logical assumption to me. What about you?"

"Do you have an address?"

Alman had already googled Nathan's name and given Colin the address. An hour later, Colin and Ben were walking up Nathan's front steps and knocking on the door.

CHAPTER 36

"WHO'S THERE?"

"Mail call."

Miguel opened his office door and took the mail being offered. "Have a good day," he said and went back to his desk.

He went right back to his computer, clicked into a personnel program, and typed in "Jenna Boyd." The computer pulled up four Jenna Boyds who worked for Matthews, but only one from Canada. He read her HR file which offered the particulars about her start date, current salary, vacation entitlement, etc., and noted an update at the end: "DECEASED." So, all that was true. Matthews really thought she was dead. He now wanted to run a keystroke program on her computer. He hoped it had not been collected yet and deactivated. Miguel ran his program and surfed for Jenna's computer. Using his backdoor software, he tried to get into her computer, and to his relief, it was still active and obviously still connected to Wi-Fi. He quickly ran the program and found that she had, in fact, opened Bhergosian's original message. His spyware did not indicate that she had opened the attachment, but she had opened the message and at least had read it. *That's why they went after her,* he thought. They went after her and found her twin sister, killed her, and put it down as Jenna. But Steven had told him that this had all happened at her sister's home, not Jenna's. How could Matthews have not known she had a twin sister? Miguel went back to his personnel file on Jenna and pulled up her profile.

It went into all the things Jenna liked about Calgary and Matthews. Jenna had written about her family, how her parents were deceased, and that her best friend was her sister, but she had not written that it was her identical twin sister. Either Jenna had forgotten to write this fact or thought she had when she hadn't. But this omission had obviously saved her life, at least for the moment. He thought it through a little more. Matthews must have looked up her profile after the attack in the park. Whoever was directing traffic had sent the killers to her sister's home when Jenna did not turn up at her own home. Her sister had truly been in the wrong place at the wrong time. But if they'd gotten Jenna's sister's address from what Jenna wrote, then Steven probably had similar stuff on his profile.

He turned off Jenna's profile and quickly brought up Steven's. His address was a no brainer, but had he written anything regarding his best friend in Seattle? Sure enough, Nathan was written into his profile, complete with what he did for a living and his last name: Cunnymore. Shit. He had to call Steven right away.

Back in Steven's house, his cell phone rang and rang and rang. And Colin and Ben now knew Steven was not home and probably where they could find him.

CHAPTER 37

"WE NOW think Williams has brought in a friend of his in Seattle to at least see the stick." Alman was giving a briefing to four pharmaceutical executives, including Slater, in Slater's office.

"Why do you say that?" It wasn't Slater asking but another of the four, one that Alman had not seen before.

"Because when our team went to Williams's house this morning, he wasn't there, but all his company equipment was there, including his car. According to Williams's profile, he doesn't own a motorcycle or another car, so he's getting around some other way. And in his profile, he listed a Nathan Cunnymore as his best friend who lives in Seattle. This best friend is also a pharmacist. Also, I ran background checks on Cunnymore and the researcher who made a copy of the file on the stick. They went to the same pharmacy school during the same four-year period. It makes sense to me that it was Cunnymore who contacted the researcher, and that Williams went along. They're obviously trying to find out what's on the stick." It made sense to all four of the executives as well.

"Have you finished the job?" asked another man Alman did not know.

"We're nearly there. Our team should be at Cunnymore's house right about now. I should be getting an update very shortly."

"Okay, you can go." Slater waved his hand at Alman.

"Gentlemen," Alman finished, "what's on the stick?"

Four blank stares answered back.

CHAPTER 38

THE NATIONAL sales director for Matthews Canada sat at his desk, staring at the phone. *I really hate doing this,* he thought, although in truth, he'd only had to do it a couple of times. *I didn't know this Boyd woman that well. I only met her at meetings. She seemed nice and very competent, but I really did not know her. But all leaders must stay in touch with their people and show empathy when necessary, blah, blah, blah.* He picked up the phone to call Stephanie Debart in Vancouver. Stephanie was Jenna's district manager.

"Hello, Steph? It's Alec."

"Alec, what's up?"

"I'm just calling to say how sorry I am and express my condolences. Do you need any time away?"

"How sorry you …? Condolences? What are you talking about?"

"I'm calling about Jenna Boyd. HR phoned me to tell me that she was killed a few days ago in Calgary. Some sort of break and enter gone wrong. Come to think of it, why in the world didn't you call me?"

Stephanie answered, "Uh, that's because Jenna isn't dead. It was her sister that was killed in the break in."

"Her sister?" Alec sat back in his chair.

"Yes, her sister. It was her twin sister. Jenna is obviously severely broken up, and I told her to take all the time that she needs. I was going to let you know at our call on Monday."

"Oh my God. Her sister. That's really strange. HR has her listed as deceased. It's on her profile already. We've stopped her pay and everything."

"But why? I didn't phone anything in. HR should not have done anything until they were in contact with me."

"I agree. But they called me to tell me. I assumed you'd called them. This is quite the screw up."

"Well, we better get all that corrected. Jenna will want to keep getting paid."

"Agreed. I'll call them myself. I want to find out why they acted when they had not talked to you. I'm really sorry about this, Steph."

"That's okay, but I still don't get it. Will you call me after you speak with HR?"

"Sure thing. Pass along my condolences to Jenna when you talk to her next."

"Will do."

With that, Alec hung up and dialed down to HR. Someone was going to explain and someone was going to reconnect Ms. Boyd to the Matthews grid.

CHAPTER 39

JENNA, STEVEN, and Nathan quickly made their way out of the house using the back door. They ran through the backyard and into Nathan's garage. The three of them climbed into his car and started it before they opened the garage door. Once the door was up, they pulled out slowly and turned left down the back lane. Out on the street, they drove away.

"You're positive those were the two guys who tried to kill you?" Dumb question.

"Steven, those were the two guys. I will never forget them. But how the hell did they find us? And that brings up something that's bugged me since my sister was killed. How did they know where my sister lived or even the fact that I had a sister?"

"And going back to your original question," said Nathan from the driver's seat, "how did they know we went to see Seth? Let alone the fact that he made a copy of the USB, if in fact, they do know he made a copy."

Steven continued, "They had to know he made a copy because otherwise why was he killed? Or maybe the fire really was just a terrible coincidence."

Jenna looked sideways at Steven. "They tried to kill me, and I only opened the email and read the message body, not the attachment. All they knew was that you two went to *see* this poor guy, and he was killed. The fire was no accident." Steven nodded. He knew she was right. But now they were running.

Nathan spoke up. "You don't suppose they know about my car, do you? I mean, how could they?"

When the Bluetooth phone rang in the car, the three of them just about hit their heads on the roof from jumping so high. After the initial scare, Nathan answered.

"Hello?"

"Nathan? This is Miguel. Do you have Steven and Jenna with you?"

"We're all together, Miguel."

"Steven, are you at your house or Nathan's?"

"Neither. We're driving, but we really don't know where to—"

"Good, don't go back to your house, Steven, and don't go to Nathan's."

"We just left Nathan's." Before Steven could go, on Miguel waded back in.

"GOOD, DON'T go back there. I truly believe the three of you are in terrible danger. I think Matthews is looking for you, so that they can kill you. I ran Jenna's profile this morning, and the company has her listed as dead. But I think she—you, Jenna—are alive because you missed writing one thing in your company profile."

Jenna jumped in. "My company profile? You mean that fluff piece we all had to write when we joined? Answering questions about our lives, our likes, our families, our hobbies, etcetera?"

"Yes, that's exactly it. In your piece, you wrote all about that *and* that you had a sister, Janine Boyd. But you didn't say she was your *twin* sister."

"Yes, I did." Jenna sounded a touch affronted that Miguel would accuse her of not fully answering the company's questions, fluff piece or not. She was meticulous by nature.

"No, you didn't mention she was your twin. Maybe you were just thinking along those lines. Maybe, because you were both so attached, you just thought you put it in. In any case, I think that's why you're still alive. The killers looked at your sister and thought they had you."

Jenna had assumed that already. But she had forgotten about that fluff piece until now.

"And," Miguel went on, "I went into your profile, Steven, and you listed a Nathan Cunnymore as your best friend, so I'm sure they will track you there if you go, so don't. I mean, that's how I got Nathan's cell number, just knowing his last name. His address is a quick search and find."

Steven and Jenna looked at each other, and Nathan glanced back in his mirror. "They already did track us there," said Steven. "After what you told us about company surveillance, Nathan and I packed up and went there last night. This morning, a little after Jenna arrived, two guys showed up at his house. We ducked out the back way and now are in Nathan's car driving nowhere in particular."

"Okay, that's good. Keep driving. Don't go anywhere you normally would. There's no telling how these people will find out. Also, I ran a check on your researcher friend and correlated it with a search on Nathan. It came up very quickly that the two of you went to the same pharmacy school together. If I found that out, then so have they. They probably know you and Steven are together now, and that you've seen the stick, Nathan. I don't think they know about you, Jenna, because your profile still lists you as deceased."

Miguel was thinking of what their next move should be when he glanced at his computer screen. He still had Jenna's profile up in a split screen format with Steven's. He noticed a refresh of the screen coming through and let out a thin, silent whistle.

"Jenna," Miguel said, "I think we have another problem."

"WHAT PROBLEM?" Jenna asked.

"Your profile has just been updated to show that you are alive and well, living in Calgary."

"Shit." Jenna slumped a little in the back seat.

CHAPTER 40

COLIN AND Ben knocked on the front door, all the while looking around to make sure no one was watching or that no cars or pedestrians were coming down the street. No one was coming to the door, so Ben tried the knob. It opened.

"Uh, unlocked. Trusting people here in Seattle," noted Ben. They went inside.

The house was very quiet, and the two men immediately began looking around. They could tell nobody was home, but Colin trotted downstairs to make sure. He also checked the backyard and found the garage door up and no car on the pad. As he came back into the living room, his cell phone rang. It was Alman.

"She's not dead!" an excited and exasperated Alman said.

"Who's not dead?"

"The woman, Boyd, in Calgary. She's not dead."

"Of course, she's dead. Ben cut her throat to make sure. Believe me, she's dead."

"No, you killed her sister, Boyd. Her *twin* sister, Janine. Not Jenna."

"Oh. Well, we can't help that. She was identical to the woman we found hiking. Even the hair color and style were the same. Didn't you know she had a twin sister?"

"Her profile indicated she had a sister, not a twin sister."

"Again, we can't help that. How do you want to handle this one?"

"Are you on your way to Cunnymore's house?"

"We're in, but they're not home."

Ben had been looking around while Colin was on the phone, and he noticed a bag on the coffee table with the logo of the Seattle airport on it. He picked it up and found a water bottle and candy bar inside with a receipt. He took one look at the receipt and smiled broadly. He showed the receipt to Colin, who also smiled and cut into Alman's rant.

"She's here. Jenna Boyd came to Seattle to meet up with this Williams guy and his friend."

"How do you know that?" snapped Alman.

"We have a credit card receipt with her name on it from a store at the Seattle airport. It was generated this morning. But how are we going to find them? I mean, they must have seen us coming and taken off. They have a car we can't track. Why don't you check Williams's profile? Maybe he put down some favorite haunts or family members in Seattle or elsewhere. They may go there."

Alman thought about this for a few seconds. "If they saw you, and the Boyd girl was with them, then you've been made, and they're on the run. And she will have told them everything about herself, so they now know they're in danger. I don't think they'll go to the police, because in truth, their story would sound fantastical and probably wouldn't be believed. Anyway, if they were going to go to the police, I think they'd have done it by now. They want to know more about that stick because they showed it to the researcher. But right now, they'll most likely be wondering how we knew about Cunnymore. At the very least, they'll figure not to go to other familiar places, or at least, I wouldn't if I was in their shoes. But something else bugs me."

Colin asked, "What else?"

"Well, you said you went to Williams's house, and everything was there. His cell phone, his computer, his iPad, and his car. How would he know not to take any of these things with him? Okay, I can see the computer and iPad, he wouldn't have much need if he thought Matthews was after him. And his phone I can understand. All iPhones have a GPS locator in them, and you can't turn ours off like you can with ordinary retail phones. But why did he not take his car? We don't tell the reps that we plant GPS chips in their company cars. How did he know not to take it? Does he know about the GPS chip? And if so, *how* does he know?" Alman was thinking through his questions.

"Maybe he just guessed," Colin ventured.

"It's not something I would guess. I mean, the only ones that know are executives, myself, you two, I suppose, and the IT boys we use to activate them when we need to run a jips check on a rep. We don't even tell the district managers about them. How did he know?"

Colin came to the same conclusion as Alman but voiced it quicker. "Someone tipped him off. Maybe it was the Boyd girl."

"Maybe, but I don't know if that would be the first thing she would bring up given all the trauma she's been through. What if it wasn't her?" Alman had been standing but now sat down. "Someone tipped him off," he said, repeating Colin's conclusion. "Someone else tipped him off. That has to be it. They have someone else helping them out, probably from inside Matthews."

Colin pursued their original agenda. "Okay, someone's helping them, but how are we going to find them? We can't track them."

"I'll call our contact in Homeland Security to start pinging Cunnymore's phone. We'll track them that way." Alman had never questioned how Matthews had these kinds of contacts. But he was very glad they did.

CHAPTER 41

BACK IN Nathan's car, the conversation with Miguel had turned to trying to find out more about the extent and reach of Matthews in terms of tracking them down. There were no GPS chips to worry about, but they still felt tremendous unease.

Miguel chimed in, "Look, Matthews can't track you without a GPS, and they can't access Nathan's phone. I'd go to a hotel and check in there and wait. I'm going to dig around a little bit here."

"Dig around? How?" Steven asked,

In a joking, sarcastic tone, Miguel answered, "I'm going to put some of my superior computer skills to the test, if you must know, and see if I can hack into the mainframe. You said the info on the USB referred to something called the Affiliation? Well, I'll use that as a starting off point to see if there are any strange encryptions embedded here. I might just be able to find out something more. In the meantime, just try to stay out of sight."

"Okay," started Nathan, "but I'm also thinking we should get the hell out of Seattle. The farther away we are from those two guys, the better off I think we'll be."

CHAPTER 42

MIGUEL HAD been combing through the Matthews computer system all morning. He was alone in a small office that was only used for video conferencing. He had checked the booking log to make sure it was not booked at all that day. Earlier, he had told his boss he didn't feel well and had checked out to go home. Despite his earlier sarcasm with Steven, Miguel was an exceptional computer programmer and amateur hacker. He had gotten into a little trouble in high school by hacking into the school's system. He hadn't done anything other than look at students' grades and a few salaries, but he was caught because he'd been so engrossed in his work that he hadn't heard the janitor open the door behind him.

He had been successful at getting into the Matthews systems, though he had used his Matthews computer to do it. This greatly enhanced his chances of getting caught, but it also gave him instant access to the Matthews system via their in-house hardware. He had set up five diversionary loops through the internet, so that if anyone at Matthews got wind of his spying, they'd be led away from his third-floor office and hopefully give him the time he wanted.

He had hacked into the HR system and peeked at the salaries of some of his colleagues and bosses. He had gotten into a security system that controlled a lockdown function for the building and disabled it. He had hacked into sales analytics where he'd found an interesting directive whereby the company would stop allocating sales to territories as soon as the company had hit 102 percent of its yearly sales target. This usually occurred with twenty to thirty days left in any fiscal year. This meant that many representatives would be shortchanged on their sales efforts and get a reduced bonus, but the executives would top out on theirs. The sales bonus for top executives was set to begin paying out at ninety percent and max out at 102 percent. The bonuses of virtually everyone else were set to begin paying out at ninety percent but would not max out until they hit 120 percent of their yearly sales target. He had hacked into the financial reporting program and spent a little time digesting the size of Matthews. In the last fiscal year, they had generated a little over 184 billion dollars in sales. This was generally reported to the public, but he had found that the company based a great deal of their emphasis on a per-head-count dollar productivity metric. He had read that Canada was one of the most productive countries in the Matthews world, with a per-head dollar figure of $2476, and that many countries in the EU were the worst. France was dead last at only $567 per head. All this had been interesting, and he had done it to familiarize himself with the internal workings of the system. When he was ready to launch his hack using 'Affiliation' as a keyword, he could draw on his previous successes to guide him.

Miguel typed in 'Affiliation' in his backdoor backyard, and it led him to a program or system that appeared to be directly linked to the CEO's office. He had tried several backdoors and tricks but could not get in. He had tried to trick the system into giving up its password but got nowhere. He was about to give up when he remembered a password he had once uncovered in university. The program he had hacked into had used an anagram of a keyword related to its title and function. So, he went back into the Matthews system and tried using several different anagrams of 'Affiliation' using his own iPhone to access an anagram-solver website. He tried anagrams that were derived from a word or phrase, not necessarily containing all the letters from the original word.

Let's see ... there are literally hundreds of different possibilities. I could use the entire word or just portions of it. There are solutions using ten letters all the way down to two letters. Miguel looked at and tried dozens of words that could be formed from 'Affiliation' and got nothing.

How am I ever going to find this? Why don't I just type in 'grizzle gump ferdash.' This is hopeless, he thought.

Then another thought popped up: *What if I try another word that links both Matthews and 'Affiliation.'* Miguel looked at the words 'corporate,' 'drug company,' 'president,' 'chief executive officer,' 'chemicals,' and many others, but the list seemed endless. One word he had not tried was 'pharmaceutical.' When Miguel plugged this word into his anagram-solver website, a word formation jumped off the page at him. *It wouldn't be that cheesy, would it?* He began to type.

CHAPTER 43

"OKAY, THANKS. Can you just keep sending the GPS locations to my system here in New York? ... That's great, thanks again. Oh, just one other thing. Can you pinpoint where his incoming calls originated from, especially from today? ... You can? Great. How many did he receive and where did it or they come from? ... Only one? Really? How specific can you get the location? ... Really, right here in Manhattan? ... No, no, you don't need to give me anything other than that. I think I know where it came from. Many thanks."

Alman put the phone down. His contact in Homeland had set his workstation up to receive the GPS data from Nathan's phone, so Alman could call Colin and Ben and relay the whereabouts of his three targets. He'd have them very quickly. Slater should give him a bonus. But the other pertinent information he got was the fact that Cunnymore had gotten a call this morning from a phone in Manhattan. So, they were getting help. And he guessed the helper was in the Matthews building. And if he knew about the GPS trackers in the car, then he was probably familiar with their tracking and monitoring systems. Alman opened the door and looked out at the rows of computer stations lined up throughout the basement floor. He was met with several stares as he looked out, and he stared back with as blank a look as he could muster. As he stood there, two young men walked towards him. He was not normally approached by any of the geeks down here. He was sure they knew he was attached to the security of the company, but he did not interact with them unless it was to tell them to go away. Regardless, these two walked up to him. One was slightly older than the other.

"Uh, excuse me," said the older one, "I know you don't talk to anyone down here, and quite frankly, we're okay with that, but I also know you're attached to the security department for Matthews."

"Yeah, what about it?"

"Well, my colleague here, Stuart, found something just few minutes ago, and we were going to go right to the director, but once I saw you standing here, I thought you might be better placed to handle it."

Alman looked down at the younger one, "So … Stuart, what have you found, and why are we talking?"

The younger man stammered a little as he began but persevered. There was a genuine fear among the group regarding Alman. "Ah, yeah, yeah, I-I was doing a systems check for the HR department because their programs were running very slowly this morning, and I noticed something odd."

Alman could barely contain his impatience but remained calm and only sneered slightly. "And what did you find?"

"Right, right, I found someone, or some other computer, poking around in the system. I could tell because it was leaving a signature trail that I picked up on."

Alman stiffened and stared intently at Stuart. "You're telling me someone or some other computer hacked into our system here at Matthews?"

The older one jumped in. "Not hacked," he said. *"Hacking*. He's still in there."

"What? How long ago did you find this?"

"Ten minutes ago," Stuart and the older man said in unison.

"Show me right now," Alman said as the two men led him over to Stuart's station. Alman looked over Stuart's shoulder as he began typing away at his keyboard and quickly saw a series of numbers and other symbols appear.

"This is how I found him," said Stuart. "He's leaving behind these little bits of data as he trolls through our system. I was delving into the memory files of HR, and I noticed he was using up little bits of memory with his hacking. After HR, he went into the security system of the building and then into sales analytics. But what's odd is that he doesn't make copies of anything; he's just trolling around."

"So, he's still in the system?"

"As near as I can figure it, he is. But he's moved out of analytics."

"Can you find him again?" the older man asked.

Stuart answered, "Yeah, I can. He's still leaving behind these little bits, almost like breadcrumbs, but he's also good."

Alman jumped in. "What do you mean he's good?"

"Well, I'm having a hard time tracing his trail back to an identifiable location. He's used some diversions."

"How do you know they're diversions?"

"I can just tell. It would take too long to explain."

Alman thought about challenging this but left well enough alone. "Can you track him to his source computer?"

"Absolutely," enthused Stuart. "It will just take some time. But I won't be able to get his exact location in the building. He turned off the GPS in the computer. Like I said, he's good."

THE OLDER tech now chimed in, "Shouldn't we warn someone or shut down the system? What if he's planting a virus?"

"We can't just shut down the entire system during the day. It would mean stopping everything the company does, including taking orders, helping customers, and tracking analytics. It could be picked up by someone, and the markets could react. Does it look like this is a virus plant?" Alman directed his question at Stuart's back, and the answer came quickly.

"No, it doesn't look like a virus plant; it looks like he's just wandering around our computer systems."

Stuart's confidence actually made Alman calm.

"Well, keep at it and come knock on my door when you have a location for this son of a … this person." With that, Alman went back to the bunker to make two calls.

CHAPTER 44

IN THE car, Nathan, Jenna, and Steven tried to figure where they should go. They talked about just checking into a hotel or motel but wondered how long they should book it for. They argued about leaving Seattle and heading south, east, or even north to Canada, but the two men did not have their passports. Nathan drove around the city in loops when he began to notice something peculiar. He kept it to himself for a time but eventually had to let the others in on what he suspected.

"Excuse me, back there," he began, "I don't want to seem paranoid, but I think we're being followed."

Both Steven and Jenna whirled around in their seats to look back. All they saw was traffic—lots of traffic. Some cars were creeping up behind them and others were passing them left and right.

"I don't see anything," Jenna said. "I mean, how can you tell? There are cars everywhere."

Steven added, "Yeah, are you sure, Nathan? Maybe you *are* being paranoid. Hell, that would not be a very long walk for any of us."

Nathan was unperturbed and persisted. "No, I think we're being followed and have been for the last ten minutes. Look again, look for a grey Ford Escape about two cars back. Just watch as I make some maneuvers: lane changes, change of speeds, and such."

Nathan did as he'd said. He made a lane change to his right and then back into the center lane, and then over to his left. He sped up and passed a couple of cars and moved back into the center lane. As Jenna and Steven watched, the Grey Escape mirrored the movements of their car, all while staying about two cars back. They were being followed.

"Oh shit," spat Steven. "Who the hell, how the hell, what the hell is going on?"

"Maybe we can figure that out later," offered Nathan. "Right now, we have to try to get away from them. Jenna, can you see that far back? Is it the two guys who showed up at my house? The ones that tried to kill you?"

Jenna strained to see if she could make them out but couldn't. "No, I can't tell."

Suddenly, Steven chimed in. "Hey, what kind of vehicle did they pull up in at Nathan's house? Do you remember that?"

"Yes, it was a sedan of some sort, I didn't wait to get more than that."

"Okay, this is an Escape. So, maybe we're not being followed. Maybe it's just a coincidence." Steven continually tried to downplay any event as being sinister in nature, but Nathan was not buying this one.

"Uh, yeah, and maybe they thought we might recognize their car, returned the rental, and got a new one. Unless, of course, the killers are homegrown ... born, raised, and living in Seattle, and only use their own car," Nathan's sarcasm had made its point, and Steven relented.

"Okay, I get it, I get it. The point now being how we lose them."

"Look, I'm no race car driver, and if we suddenly take off, we're just as liable to crash, get picked up by the police, or get caught anyway. We need something cleverer than that."

Jenna had been quietly thinking of another issue that bothered her and now opened up to the others. "How did they track us down? I mean, Nathan has no GPS on his car, and we don't have any company equipment with us. How did they find us?"

Nathan shot back, "That's really immaterial right now, isn't it? They've found us, and we have to get away."

Steven spoke up. "Maybe we should just drive to a police station and park in the visitor's lot. There's no way they'd do anything to us there. In fact, maybe we should just go to the police period. This is getting nuts, or actually, it got nuts a while back, and now it's just scary as hell."

Jenna looked at Nathan and then eyed Steven carefully. "We can't turn ourselves in. No one would believe us. They didn't believe me in Calgary, and even after my sister was killed, they didn't believe me. In fact, they thought any connection between her murder and a large multi-national drug company was just ludicrous. We've talked this through already. We can't turn ourselves in."

Nathan spoke up. "Okay, agreed, but maybe going to a police station isn't a bad idea. We can wait there for a while and see if they move off."

"Okay," started Jenna, "let's say we go there, and they move away, and then we take off. Getting back to my question, how did they find us? Don't you think that, if they found us now, they'll find us again? *That's* my point. We have to figure out how they're tracking us so we can lose them for good."

Both Nathan and Steven hadn't thought through that part of the equation, and they both agreed that Jenna made a lot of sense.

The question of how they had been found lingered between the three of them as Nathan continued to drive around, occasionally glancing back to check that the Grey Escape was still tailing them.

"I suppose, if they're following us," said Nathan, "that at least means they haven't got us yet, so in a way, we're safe, right?"

The other two just nodded while each of them worked on a way to get rid of these guys for a while, at least, if not for good.

CHAPTER 45

M_A_L_P_R_A_C_T_I_C_E.

Contained within the word pharmaceutical was the word "malpractice."

After Miguel finished typing, he took a deep breath and hit "enter." His screen immediately brought him into a system with the heading "Affiliation." He was in.

Oh boy, he thought, *I'm in it now just as much as the others.* He could just close everything up and walk away. No one knew of his involvement, and he could break off contact with the others. By going forward and entering this site, there was no turning back. He paused and stared at the screen for a moment, and then clicked on the heading and entered the site.

All kinds of files appeared on his screen: 'Budget,' 'Members,' 'Surveillance,' 'Acquisitions,' 'Government Contributions,' 'Research work,' 'Entities and Compounds,' and more.

MEANWHILE, BACK in the basement, Stuart Hendly was diligently working his way through the diversionary routes Miguel had set up. He had traced four routes thus far and was working on the fifth when he leaned back in his chair and called out, "Hey, David, you'd better get over here."

The older man who had informed Alman about the breach an hour earlier came running over. "Do you have something?"

"Yes, I've gotten through four diversionary routes, and I think I'm on the final trace. I should have this guy located within a couple of minutes. You'd better go get what's-his-name."

Although David knew the importance of what they had found, and what Stuart was doing, he did not really want to go over and get what's-his-name, but he did anyway, walking over and knocking on Alman's door.

ABOUT FORTY-FIVE minutes earlier, Alman had finished talking to Ben and Colin, telling them where they could find Nathan's phone and presumably his car. Nathan appeared to be driving around Seattle using busy thoroughfares. They had agreed that Ben and Colin would turn in their rental and get a new one just in case their current rental had been seen.

He had not called Slater regarding the hacker as he had no idea what the hacker was actually looking for and did not want the hassle of trying to explain it, nor did he know if it was related in any way to the USB retrieval, although he suspected it was. He had decided to wait to see if Stuart could find anything. The knock on the door startled him out of his chain of thought, and he opened it to find the older of the two young guys standing in front of him.

"Do you have anything?"

"Yes, Stuart thinks he's very close to finding this guy. He asked me to come and get you."

The two of them walked over to Stuart's cubicle. Alman spoke first. "Stuart, do you have anything for me?"

"Yes, I do. I've gone through five different diversions to find this guy. He's good. Most amateurs wouldn't use any diversions or maybe just one or two." Stuart could feel a palpable *"get on with it"* energy coming from the man, so he cut to the chase. "What I'm saying is this hacker is very sophisticated. He thought of the diversions because he probably knew he'd be discovered fairly soon into his hacking effort. He must know something about our systems and how closely they're monitored, and he must have at least an idea of how many people might have the chance to find him."

"Are you saying you think this guy is one of you? I mean, he's a Matthews tech guy?"

"That's what I think, yeah. That's the only explanation for all this. This guy knows our system."

Alman whirled towards David. "Do you have any guys off sick today?"

David answered, "I had one guy show this morning and then book off sick. He went home."

"How do you know he went home?"

"He told me that's where he was going."

"Did you check his keycard? Do you know for certain he checked out of the building?" Every Matthews employee that worked in head office had a keycard that granted them access to the building beyond the main reception area. The key card had to be waved in front of an access pad to unlock all entry and exit doors. No one could enter Matthews without waving a keycard. No one could leave Matthews without waving a keycard. The Matthews system logged people in and logged them out. If someone opened the exit door for someone else, the card would still send a signal to the mainframe that it had left the building. If someone forgot their keycard in the building and went home, they would be stopped at the security desk as they left because their card would not send a signal that it was leaving the building. There was no way to leave without the security system knowing where a person's card was.

"No, I didn't check his keycard. But Miguel is a stand-up guy. If you think—"

"Check this guy, Miguel, right now. Check his keycard."

David ran over to his desk and typed in the access code for the keycards belonging to all the techies in the basement. When he pulled up Miguel's and let out a whistle. "Shit."

Alman heard him and ran over. "What? What did you find?"

"Miguel never checked out of the building. His keycard still reads as active within the Matthews building."

Alman didn't hesitate. He spun David around in his chair and glared at him. "I want you to check all the booking logs for meeting rooms in the building. Find out which ones are not booked for any event this morning and bring me the list. Do it now."

Alman ran back to Stuart's desk. "Do you have a location?"

"Yes, I do, and you're not going to believe this, but the hacker's signal is coming through our own routing system. He's in our building, and he's using a Matthews computer. Holy shit."

Up in the third-floor office where Miguel was working, an alarm in his computer went off. He had laid in a program that would send him an alarm if anyone had gotten through his five diversions and was tracing him to the building. *Man, these guys are better than I thought they'd be.* He'd had no time to go through the files, but he hoped he had enough time to copy it onto a stick. He inserted his USB and set the copy command to go. A progression bar appeared at the bottom of the screen, and the bar began to fill in.

In the basement, David came running over to Stuart's cubicle with a sheet of paper in his hand. Alman was already talking. "Can you pinpoint an exact location for this son of a bitch?" Clearly, he was growing more impatient and exasperated.

"No, no I can't." Exasperated, Stuart waved his hands at his screen and held them in front of it. "It doesn't work like that. I simply know he's using our router, one of our computers, and he's local … like in *our* building."

David was panting as he held out his sheet of paper. "Here's the list of all the unused rooms in the building. There's twenty-one of them."

Alman grabbed the phone from Stuart's desk and pounded in four numbers. "Security? Yes, this is Alman in the basement. We have a security breach of our computer system, a hacker, and he's still in our building. Get your teams to run in pairs and check out these unused rooms." Alman reached back and snatched the sheet form David's hands. He quickly read out the locations of the meeting rooms. "You're looking for a guy named Miguel …" What the hell was his last name? He looked back at David and repeatedly snapped his fingers.

"Benetto. Miguel Benetto."

"Miguel Benetto. We believe he's been running around in our system for about ninety minutes. He's in the building and still in the system. He probably doesn't know we're on to him. How many teams can you deploy? … Three?! … What do you *mean* we only have *six* security people on staff?! What the—" Alman stopped himself, not interested in debating the wisdom of six security people for a building that housed over five thousand, but at the end of the day, they were pharmaceutical employees, not protesters or rioters. "Okay, whatever, just get going and go now. Have your teams check in after each room they've been to and keep me informed as you go. Also, can you lock down the building so even the keycards can't open it? … Excellent. Then do it now, and … Why not? Well, turn the system back on! I don't care how long it takes, just do it!"

Alman looked at David. "The son of a bitch turned off the lockdown mechanism. He planned his escape."

THE PROGRESSION bar on Miguel's computer now read 23 percent complete.

THE FIRST security team reached the fifteenth floor of the building to check out rooms 1505 and 1509, from which they would work their way down to the eleventh floor to finish checking their assigned rooms. The third team started on the first floor with room 100 and would work up to the fifth floor, and the second team started on the sixth and would work up to the tenth floor. They were using the stairs. Each team had reached the second of their assigned floors.

THE PROGRESSION bar now read 52 percent complete.

ALMAN HAD been receiving updates on his walkie-talkie, and each "Clear" he received only made him angrier. "How fast are they moving? Are they using the stairs?"

As the teams reached the third of their assigned floors, the bar on Miguel's computer read 89 percent complete. He heard the stairwell door fly open and boots come running into the far end of the hallway. The bar read 97 percent complete.

The team on the third floor reached office 319 and pulled the door open. "Room 319 clear," they shouted into their walkies.

The bar was at 99 percent complete when Miguel heard the shout and urged the download to finish. The instant it hit 100 percent he pulled the stick out and slipped it into his pocket. He heard guards pull open another door and a moment later heard, "Room 327, clear." He opened his own door and peered down the hallway, saw the team standing in front of an office six doors away, and knew that he had to make a run for it.

CHAPTER 46

THE NERVOUS trio in the car were still wondering how to get away from their pursuers and how they'd been found.

Again, Jenna said, "We have to figure out how they found us before we try to get away, or else it's pointless."

Steven began thinking out loud. "The only way to find us is through some sort of GPS system. We ditched my company car and cell phone, and Jenna's cell is gone too, so that's out. What else do we have on us that has a GPS?"

"Maybe it was just dumb luck," Nathan offered. "Maybe they just happened to spot us."

Jenna shot that down. "They just happened to spot us after ditching their first rental and getting a new one? Ditching their first car was done to try to keep us from spotting them. They didn't change cars to go to the airport!"

"You're right. You're right, but what then?" Nathan asked.

Jenna suddenly had an idea. "Nathan, do you have your cell phone?"

"You want to make a call?"

"No, do you have it on you, as in right now? As in all the time since we left the house?"

"Yes, Miguel called us, remember? I still don't follow."

Jenna cut in. "They got the GPS or ping signal from your phone and used it to track us down. That has to be it."

Steven chimed in, "How the hell does a drug company get the GPS signal from an ordinary citizen's cell phone?"

"I don't know. Maybe they know someone in the government or law enforcement that can give it to them. But that's the only explanation."

Steven said, "Still not buying it."

Now Jenna bore down on him. "We're running from two guys who have killed several people, tried to kill me, and want to kill us, all on the orders of a so-called friendly drug company. If they can do that, don't you think they have ways of getting any information they want?"

Nathan looked at them in the rearview mirror. "She's got my vote. Should I just throw my phone out the window?"

"No." Jenna carried on, "We should try to ditch them but make them think we're still with the phone, like we should leave it where we lose these guys."

"That all sounds very James Bondish," Nathan said, "but just how in the hell are we going to do that?"

Steven had been sitting quietly, thinking of some way to accomplish what Jenna had suggested. Suddenly, he blurted out, "The casino."

Nathan sarcastically replied, "We're being tailed by two killers, and you feel the need to gamble? You have a problem."

Steven cut back in. "No, the casino in town is attached to a hotel. It's big, it's busy, it's crowded, and there's a rental car company in the main lobby. These guys haven't gotten a good look at Nathan. We drive there, and Jenna and I will lead them into the casino and lose them in there. Nathan slips into the lobby and rents a car, makes a quick call from the lobby, to allow his phone to be tracked, and then leaves it there. Hopefully, they'll think all three of us are still together, and it shouldn't be too hard to mingle and blend in with the crowd to get away. Then we meet you at the rental car and drive away. Meanwhile, probably, well ... hopefully, maybe ... these two will stay to look for us. They'll call whoever they call and be told your phone is still at the hotel. They'll continue looking as we drive away." Steven clapped his hands together and held them apart in a triumphant gesture.

Stone silence met his plan until Nathan spoke up. "That's it? Your brilliant plan? We mingle and then just drive away unseen? These guys are pros. They'll see you all the way to the rental lot and then we'll start the same game again, unless they shoot us first."

"Okay, so it's not brilliant," Jenna agreed, "but I say it's worth a shot. Otherwise, we're dead as soon as you run out of gas."

Nathan looked in the rearview mirror at both of them. "What the hell ... maybe you'll have a chance to pull on a slot machine, and we'll win big before we die. How do I get to the casino?"

CHAPTER 47

MIGUEL PEEKED outside the office he was using to see two security men open another office and jump inside. It was then he took off down the hallway and quickly headed up the stairs to the fourth floor. As the door closed behind him, he heard one of the guards shout that they had seen him, and then they started running down the hall after him. Miguel hoped they'd immediately run *down* the stairs after him. His plan was to go up to the fourth floor, head to the west side of the building, and then down the stairs at the opposite end to the main lobby. As long as the guards didn't split up and send one down and one up, he'd be fine. And as long as they didn't have time to figure out his plan and meet him at the west side door when he exited, he'd be fine. And as long as no one else heard him on the stairs and raced after him, he'd be fine. And as long as they had not overridden his override of the lockdown system, so the door would be unlocked and he could quickly get into the lobby and then out of the building onto the busy New York street, he'd be fine. Miguel almost stopped on the stairs as these thoughts raced through his mind, realizing that he had no or little idea of what the hell he was doing. All he had were a lot of ifs and hopes. He quickly moved down the hall on the fourth floor and opened the west-side stairway door. He heard nothing, so he started down the stairs.

THE TWO security guards burst through the door into the lobby and quickly scanned the area. "There's no one here. He must have exited already." They ran over to the main desk.

"Did you see anyone come through that door we just came out of and exit the building?"

"No, I didn't. There's been nobody." The two guards just looked at each other.

"He must have gone up the stairs. He's got another way out." They raced back to the stairway door.

"Uh, excuse me," the front desk guard called, "there is another set of stairs on the west side of the building. Maybe whoever you're looking for is coming out there." The guards exchanged a look and ran for the west-side stairway door.

Miguel popped out of the doorway and saw the guards heading in his direction. He took off for the nearest exit door and burst through it onto New York's busy 42nd street. He looked back to see the guards come sliding to a stop with their palms against the glass. Miguel didn't hesitate and raced down 42nd street.

I can't believe I got away, he thought. *Jason Bourne, eat your heart out.* He quickly hailed a cab, got in, and gave the driver an address.

CHAPTER 48

"WHAT THE hell was this all about?" Two members of the security detail who had been looking for Miguel were now standing in front of the computer he had used to hack into the Matthews system. They heard footsteps coming down the hallway, and a moment later, Alman entered, followed quickly by Slater and a young man they did not recognize.

Alman looked at the two guards disapprovingly. "You let him get out of the building. We traced him, and you got here while he was still in this office, and you *still* let him get out of the building."

The two guards looked at each other and back at Alman, before one offered, "Well, it was actually Scott and Spencer that got here. They chased him to the east-side stairway, but I guess he went back up, and they went down. By the time they realized he was heading to the west-side exit he … uh … got away."

Alman just looked blankly at the two guards and motioned for them to leave. Alman looked at Slater, and Slater looked at Stuart Hendly, who had come in with them, and asked, "Can you tell me what he was looking at?"

"I think so. I can run some keystroke spyware on this computer to see where he was."

Slater pulled out the chair and nodded at Stuart to sit down. "Get going."

Stuart sat at the computer and began typing. It wasn't long before he had something. "Uh, Mr. Slater, it looks like he got to an area titled 'CEO CONFIDENTIAL.' I can't tell if he made it in though as it's password protected, and even the spyware can't get by it without the password—"

Slater quickly cut in, "That's okay, Stuart, I'll take it from here. You can head back downstairs." As Stuart got up and started to leave, Slater placed his hand on his shoulder, and gave him his most convincing smile. "Thanks very much for your help today, Stuart. It was very much appreciated." Stuart left, leaving Alman and Slater alone in the office. Alman closed the door.

CHAPTER 49

JENNA, STEVEN, and Nathan pulled into the parking lot of the casino. They jumped out of their car and allowed Nathan to lead them single file into the hotel. Their "brainwave" was that the two followers would see the backs of Steven and Jenna but not get a good look at Nathan or his clothes. Anything to throw them off. Once inside, Nathan quickly cut away and moved off down a hallway connecting to the lobby and rental-car desk. Steven and Jenna stayed just outside the casino doors, waiting to see if their followers were still chasing them. Sure enough, within a couple of minutes, Colin and Ben entered the lobby area. The four briefly locked eyes, and in a surreal moment, wordlessly communicated exactly was happening between them all.

Then Colin and Ben exchanged a quick glance and raced towards them. This was an extremely public place, so they knew they could not do anything overt, but they were hoping to get them alone in a hallway or industrial-access point and grab them there. And if they had to separate to manage it, so be it.

Nathan had reached the rental-car desk, and having had his head on a swivel the whole way, was now rubbing his neck to work a kink out of it. He began the rental process, all the while glancing around, hoping not to arouse any untoward suspicion from the rental clerk.

Once inside the casino, Jenna could not believe the activity. She had never been inside any casino, so the sounds of the games, the noise of the gamblers, and the gambling itself took her by surprise. Steven noticed her hesitation and cupped her elbow, motioning for her to follow him. The three friends had agreed to allow Nathan to rent the car. If it all worked out, then Jenna and Steven would elude their chasers and make it to the rental-car parking lot where Nathan would be waiting to signal them over to his rented car where they would get in and just drive away. Simple. During the first part of the casino pursuit, Steven did not really think about what was happening, with his fight or flight response kicking in. The two of them were running on survival instinct alone.

CHAPTER 50

MIGUEL WAS sitting in a cab, still marvelling at his great escape from Matthews. He knew he could not go home, and as he recollected what he had written in his 'Welcome to Matthews's blog, he mentally checked off the places he could no longer go to.

The cab pulled up in front of the brownstone townhouse Miguel had given the driver the address to. He jumped out, ran up the stairs, and knocked on the door. A young woman about his age answered, but without allowing her to fully open the door, Miguel pushed by her into the hallway and quickly closed the door.

"You said this was an emergency. It better be, buddy boy, because I'm still not ready to see you."

"Sam, I know we had a bad breakup, but I really need you to just allow me to hang out here for a bit and think. I'm in a pickle and need a safe place."

"Okay, are you alright? You're not running from the law, are you?" It was said in a sarcastic tone because Sam knew Miguel was as straight as an arrow.

Miguel looked at his ex-girlfriend and thanked his lucky stars he had modified his Matthews blog last month, after they had broken up after a three-year relationship.

"I'm not running from the law." He smiled and then asked, "Can I use your computer?"

"Sure, you know where it is." Sam walked off towards the kitchen.

Miguel stepped into the study and sat down in front of the computer. He plugged in the memory stick and logged in to the downloaded file titled 'Affiliation.' A huge subset of files appeared on the screen. They had titles including 'Membership,' 'Revenues,' 'Political Contributions,' 'Acquisition Strategy,' 'Government Contacts,' 'International Program,' 'Monitoring,'

'Buyouts,' 'Therapeutics,' and 'Budget,' among others. He did not know where to begin. He opened the 'Membership' file, and a list of pharmaceutical companies came up. It was an extensive list, and Miguel recognized many of the names. He used the toolbar to quickly scan the sixty-two companies on the list. He opened the 'Government Contacts' file and found another list. This one was a list of names: senators, members of Congress, members of foreign parliaments, and houses of politicians from foreign governments.

He clicked on 'Monitoring Program,' and found a huge database describing, among other things, a massive attempt to monitor research work, researchers themselves, other companies, smaller biologic companies, university research arms, and government-owned research operations. It described in some detail the efforts that were taken to implant spyware, detailing hacking efforts and shortcuts into many different research systems. It also housed a huge cache of newspaper articles written on many different scientific breakthroughs. This file was massive. It highlighted a multitude of Research and Development programs in many different therapeutic areas.

There were notations indicating that the research was very promising, and even used the word 'breakthrough' several times. Beside each of these notations was a date and a footnote reading 'purchased,' terminated,' or 'forwarded.'

Miguel leaned back and thought for a minute. *Why would drug companies terminate promising research? Why would this 'Affiliation' be monitoring newspaper and other such publications for articles describing promising research?*

He clicked on a file titled 'Contribution Levels.' Each company he had seen on the membership list appeared to be here as well, except there was a dollar figure beside each one. The amounts were pretty big. They ranged from fifty million dollars beside Matthews down to 3 million dollars beside a company called 'Align Therapeutics.' *What the hell is this?*

He opened a file titled 'Buyouts,' and a simple list of names came up, each with a dollar figure beside it. Miguel scanned them but only recognized one name: Alexander Byers. He remembered him from a *Time* article written a few years earlier. The article had hailed Dr. Byers as a genius in Parkinson's disease research. Miguel remembered how it had described the work as ground-breaking and had alluded to the work being a possible cure for the condition. He remembered it quite well because his father had died of complications from Parkinson's, and he had thought about how frustrating it was that his dad had not had access to this new treatment. Though come to think of it, since the article had come out, Miguel had not heard anything else about either this scientist or his work. Beside Dr. Byers name, seven million dollars had been noted.

He then clicked on a file titled 'Termination.' This was another list of names, but instead of a dollar figure beside each one, there was just a date.

CHAPTER 51

STEVEN AND Jenna made their way deeper into the casino. They ducked around slot machines and gaming tables, all the while keeping tabs on their pursuers. Colin and Ben made their way after them, moving slowly and deliberately now. They were pros and knew that anything rushed was out of the question. Once they had the two of them, they could force them to go where they wanted, or so they hoped. Metaphorically, at least, the men rubbed their eyes and adjusted their nuts, remembering what Jenna had done to them in Kananaskis.

Steven turned to Jenna. "Let's go over to the bar."

"You want to have a drink? You *do* have a problem."

"No. It's a circular bar. We can stay on one side and keep tabs on them."

Of all the things to pop into her head, Jenna's first response was, "How do you know it's circular?"

"I've been here before."

They made their way to the bar, and Colin and Ben followed. Once around the opposite side, they looked back and saw that the two men had split up. One was coming towards Steven, and one was coming towards Jenna.

"Oh great. What now, genius?" Jenna asked.

"No, this is good," Steven answered. "It's almost two o'clock."

"What … do assassins turn into pumpkins at two o'clock?"

"No, that's happy hour here at the casino. A bell rings, and there's a stampede towards the bar. It happens every time. I think we can use that to get away to that side door over there. It opens into a hallway leading to another entrance to the lobby. If we move quickly, we can do this." Steven was genuinely excited about his revelation and plan.

"How do you know it's happy hour? How do you know a bell rings? How do you know there's a stampede? And how the hell do you know there's a side door?"

"I told you; I've been here before."

"More like worked here on the side."

Precisely after Jenna had said that, a bell rang out, and just as Steven had predicted, a flood of people hurried up to the bar and bar area. People bumped into each other with no regard for others in their way. Colin was on one side, and Ben was on the other; both were jostled, hampered, and their progress effectively stopped.

Steven waited to see the two men chasing them get ground into a mill of people, then grabbed Jenna by the arm and hurried towards the side door he had mentioned earlier. The two burst through it and raced down a hallway right into the lobby. They checked over their shoulders and saw no one behind them. Steven motioned Jenna towards another hallway with a rental-car sign over the entrance, and they ran down that one.

Back in the bar, Colin and Ben were just coming together at the other side of the bar, looking around for either Jenna or Steven and saw nothing.

"What the hell was that?" Colin shouted over the noise and crowd.

"It's happy hour," a stranger answered. "Drinks are half price if you buy them at the bar within the first fifteen minutes. Awesome, isn't it?"

The two men just looked at the happy-hour man and rolled their eyes.

"C'mon!" Ben shouted. "Let's go get them. Son of a bitch…"

The two of them quickly pushed their way through the crowd and got to the perimeter of the circular madness. They checked all around them but did not see either Jenna or Steven.

"Shit, they must have slipped back out the entrance. Let's get back there now."

Colin and Ben ran into the lobby and looked but saw no one. They ran out to the parking lot and again saw no one. Both men kept looking over the parking lot. They saw the car they had been following and jogged over to it. They looked inside and underneath and saw nothing. After getting up, Ben looked back at the hotel and nudged Colin in the ribs.

"What?"

"Look over there." Ben was pointing to the Avis car-rental sign beside the lobby's front doors.

"Well, you have to give them credit," Colin offered. "That was pretty smart."

CHAPTER 52

MIGUEL TURNED off the computer and sat back in his chair. He didn't understand much of what he'd stumbled on to, but he at least knew the enormity of it. There were, at minimum, sixty-two companies colluding on a massive scale to monitor research efforts around the world in various sites and in multiple variations. They even had a file and information on the Human Genome Project. It looked like they gave millions to political parties and individual politicians. That, in and of itself, was not strange. Politicians were bought and paid for all the time by multiple interest groups: just think NRA. But when he thought of the contributions within the overall structure of the research monitoring, the monies paid to scientists, the termination list—and what that exactly meant, he did not know—as well as other files, he knew it was all connected. It looked as though the Affiliation had a massive overall budget of some 2.6 billion dollars. But the most any one company paid was Matthews at fifty million. Given that, in 2022, Matthews had generated some 184 billion dollars in revenues, hiding fifty million would be easy. Hell, the R and D budget alone for Matthews was ten billion dollars. Their contribution was only half of one percent of that. *Easy to hide,* Miguel thought. They were buying companies and keeping research centralized. They had paid off many people, obviously ... but how and where was he supposed to proceed?

Miguel thought of the list of scientists and the one name he had recognized: Alexander Byers. He Googled the name and quickly got into a standard Wikipedia bio. He read about Dr. Byers's education, that he'd been a child prodigy, graduated from high school at fifteen, and gone on to Harvard Medical School. He had forgone any kind of clinical practice and devoted his life to research in Parkinson's disease. Like Miguel, Dr Byers's father had died of complications from the disease, and he wanted to find a cure more than anything else in his life. In 1999, he began researching the combining of current therapies with the emerging science of stem cells to see if he could make progress. In an article referenced in the Wiki bio, he'd noted that he felt he was closing in on a promising avenue and had reported to a public audience that he thought he'd had a breakthrough. He even noted that he thought this avenue of research could have applications in other diseases like MS, ALS, Alzheimer's, and psychiatric disorders. He seemed to be on the cusp of something great when, later on, he issued a public statement explaining that his work had been exhausting, and he was taking a break. He gave an assurance in his statement that his work would be carried on by his colleagues, but that he needed to take some time away to regenerate his own neurons, but that he would be back. That had been nine years ago, and Dr. Byers had never come back. In the statement, he'd specifically mentioned two other scientists and the names rang a bell with Miguel. He quickly flipped back to the memory stick, opened the 'Termination' list, and found the two names, with dates that were closest together. The Wiki bio also mentioned other colleagues of Dr. Byers, and only one name was still linked to Harvard: Dr. Randy Thilwell. Miguel thought this might be someone to contact down the road to get more information.

CHAPTER 53

ALMAN WAS sitting inside the bunker, brooding over the failure of the idiot security guards at Matthews to prevent one guy from leaving the building. As he sat in front of a bank of computers, one alarm went off and he sat forward to have a look.

He had been told by Slater several months earlier that they'd had a new protection spyware installed on their system. The CEO had said they had purchased it, but given what Alman had seen the software do, he thought it more likely that they had colluded with some level of government to "obtain it."

For lack of a better term, he called it 'Flagpole' spyware. Just like in some government departments, computer software waited for keywords to pop up on the internet, like 'terrorist,' 'bomb,' 'assassination,' and 'plot,' among others. This newer software alerted the bunker to specific names searched on the internet among the general public. The names meant very little to Alman, and this alert rarely went off. It had only done so three times since it had been installed. He had also noticed that the alert did not go off unless the name had been looked at beyond a threshold of one minute. Being curious, he had checked on the names and had found that they were scientists of one kind or another. In these instances, his instructions were clear: He was to relay the name and the circumstances surrounding the alert directly to Slater.

Alman now began looking at the name on the alert: Alexander Byers. After completing his review of the alert, he indulged his curiosity and found out that Dr. Byers was a whiz in Parkinson's research and had not been seen or heard from for many years. This alert told Alman that someone with a computer had been staying on a Wikipedia page for Dr. Byers for several minutes. His immediate thought was someone with Parkinson's was researching anything or anyone to do with better outcomes for their condition. Anyway, he compiled the report and sent a confidential email to William Slater.

CHAPTER 54

JENNA, NATHAN, and Steven had driven away from the hotel in the car Nathan had rented. It was a (hopefully) non-descript, gray Chrysler Jeep. Nathan had thought it would blend in with other cars. They had been checking behind them for several minutes but did not see another car behind them. As instructed, Nathan had left his cell phone back at the rental agency. He had put it on silent and stuffed it in a planter. Their plan seemed to have miraculously worked. Nathan had even purchased a burner phone, so they could touch base with Miguel if needed and not get noticed.

"I don't see anything or any car that looks even remotely suspicious," Jenna said.

"Neither do I," responded Steven.

Nathan suggested they drive around, well away from the hotel for a while, just to make sure, and the other two agreed.

Suddenly, Jenna cut in with a question that had been bugging her. "Steven, how did you know about all that stuff back at the casino? The circular bar, the happy-hour time, the 'stampede,' and the side door."

"I told you; I've been there before."

"But at two o'clock? And the side-door stuff was detailed. I mean, I bet there are lots of people who have 'been there before'"—Jenna made air quotes as she said this—"that don't know that stuff."

"That's because old Stevie is a T and T rep," Nathan cut in.

Jenna asked, "What's a T and T rep?"

"Tuesday to Thursday, ten till two."

"I am not a T and T rep," Steven protested. "I have been there during the week but only very infrequently."

Jenna was surprised. "You go there on workdays? During working hours?"

"Like I said, very seldom. Maybe once a month after I've made all my calls, and I'm on my way home. Sometimes, yeah, I'll get there at two or so. But I'll just stay for a bit, play a little poker or pull on the slots, and then go home." Steven leaned into the front driver's area. "I am not a T and T rep."

Nathan smiled. He knew Steven was not a slack junkie, but after all the ribbing he had taken about being 'just a pharmacist,' and 'just a pill counter,' he liked taking a shot at the pharma-rep lifestyle.

Steven looked at Jenna and realized that he did not want to disappoint her—for her to think less of him. "Look, I'm sure it's the same in Canada. We get a lot of down time in this job. Sometimes I just like to get away from it."

"You don't have to justify things to me," she answered. "I'm not your boss." Jenna knew of reps who really took advantage of the system they worked in. There were people who only worked two or three hours a day. They dropped off samples like delivery drivers and then went home or off to something else. She even knew of someone who, while working as a pharmaceutical rep, had taken the time to get his real-estate licence and then began selling houses on the side, all the while collecting his salary and benefits from his pharmaceutical-company employer. He even used his company car to drive to house showings and the company gas card to fill up the tank. This was a profession that held avenues for terrible abuses by individual representatives, although the clear majority, known to Jenna anyway, were hardworking, trustworthy, and committed to ethical practices with their companies and their healthcare customers.

Steven had been a rep for ten years. He had started at the tail end of what many now described as "the good old days." Those were the times where you could take a doctor out to dinner, and even include their spouse. The industry would pay for lavish weekends under the guise of educational opportunities. There was education that went on, but there was also a ton of partying. Back in the day, a representative could take doctors golfing during the week. He knew of reps that spent the entire summer golfing with doctors every day of the week. Companies would buy season tickets to NFL, MLB, NBA, NHL, and even some NCAA teams, and at the beginning of each season, the local reps would meet up and divvy up the games, so each rep could take advantage. It was all a widespread practice that nearly every pharmaceutical company took part in.

But in the last several years, all that had disappeared. Now a representative could bring a small lunch into a clinic and feed the doctors, but not the staff. And the controls on expenses had gotten extreme. He often thought it funny when he read in news stories about pharmaceutical company largesse when he knew it was all a complete fabrication. He had gone to see the movie "Love and Other Drugs" and had burst out laughing in the theater at the utter Hollywood fabrication they had put on film. None of any kind of lavishness went on now. Hell, a representative could not even offer a healthcare worker a pen, or even a damn post-it note, lest it be construed as a gift to "buy off" the individual and get them using your drug.

And, Steven thought, *the public doesn't even know about any of the stuff we pharma reps have to put up with.* The worst of all was the "work-with." This was a day when your boss came to visit you and followed you around and sat in on every call you made, and on every customer you saw that day. *Oh my God,* he thought, *it's awful.* Steven had often recounted to friends that his was the only industry in the world that did this. He used to compare it to anyone working in an office, so his friends could understand. A lawyer, accountant, administrator, or even a darn teacher for crying out loud ... none of these professions had to endure this practice. Imagine, he would explain, that your boss comes to where you work, sits down next you (like in a rep's car), and stares at you. You answer the phone; they listen. You meet a customer; they stare. You work on the computer; they watch. You go for coffee; they go with you. You go for lunch; they go with you. You go to the damn bathroom, and they go too, or at least wait outside for you. And when they're not watching, staring, or listening, they yammer away incessantly. It was an old and exhausting practice that Steven was convinced was still employed purely because "it has always been done this way." One rep he knew described it as having a tumor attached to your ass for the entire day. Brutal.

Steven looked up from being deep in thought. "Maybe we should just go to the cops, give them the stick, tell them everything, and go home. Once the cops contact Matthews, they'll know they have the stick and leave us alone."

"I've been thinking the same thing," Jenna offered, but she wanted to continue as well. "Maybe we should call that tech guy. What's his name? Miguel? Just to check in. Just to see if he knows anything."

"Sounds good to me," said Nathan. "At least, it can't hurt."

Nathan handed Steven the burner, and he called Miguel's number. The phone rang and rang, then went to voice mail. Steven looked at his companions and took a big chance. "Miguel, this is Steven. Just in case you're screening calls, this is a burner phone we bought. The number is 247-555-4583. Call us back if you can."

Both Jenna and Nathan looked at Steven with questioning looks. If Miguel had been taken, then he might have endangered them all. The burner phone rang.

"Hello?"

"Steve, this is Miguel. I was screening calls. I'm using a friend's phone. It's good to hear from you."

Steven quickly filled Miguel in on what had happened to them and then told him they were thinking of throwing in the towel and going to the police.

"I wouldn't do that." As Miguel began to recount his day and what he'd taken from the Matthews computer system, Steven put the phone on speaker. Miguel's voice filled the car. He told them about all the files, the Affiliation, the membership list, all the government contacts, all the research monitoring, and the list of scientists' names on both the payout list and the termination list. By this time, Nathan had pulled into a parking lot and parked so he could turn right around and listen. At the end, the three of them there in Seattle were just numb. It was enormously hard to try to comprehend the size of this.

Jenna had a look of determination on her face. "What do you think we should do, Miguel?"

"I think we should meet and compare what we've got. Maybe the four of us can make some sense of the two data sets and figure out our next logical step."

"I think you're right," said Steven. He had listened to Miguel and become strangely enraged just thinking about what this bunch of companies was doing, flying in the face of common sense and decency. These companies were up to something, and he wanted to know what. He looked at Nathan, who nodded, and then at Jenna, who gave him two thumbs up.

Miguel piped up. "Can you guys fly out here?"

"I'm not sure that's a great idea. Those guys might be watching the airport," Steven answered. "Why don't you fly here?"

"You know, I really want to stay here. There's a person I want to check out. The name was in the bio on Dr. Byers. He was listed as a colleague and fellow researcher. I googled the name afterwards, and as near as I can figure, he's still working at Harvard. I'd like to contact him and see if he'll talk about this Dr. Byers. He might have valuable information."

"Miguel," Jenna asked, "what about all the surveillance we've been subjected to? Aren't you worried about getting picked up?"

"Not really. My car isn't a company car, so there's no GPS device on it. As well, I won't use my cell phone. I'll leave it behind, much like Nathan did with his. I'll take my friend's phone." Miguel paused then, as Sam had strolled in with a bemused look on her face just in time to hear that. Cupping her phone, he whispered, "Just for a day or two. Promise." She looked skyward and walked away. "I think I'll be safe. Do you guys think you can drive out here?"

All three thought about it. Drive from one coast to another? But then all three looked at each other and nodded. "Yes," they said in unison.

"Good. Excellent. One other thing: Do you think you guys can sneak back to your homes and get your passports?"

"Why?"

"I'm not totally sure. I just think we may need to take a trip."

The three agreed to try to get Steven's and Nathan's passports. Before signing off, they committed to call in to touch base every twelve hours or so. The reception from the eastbound car might be spotty at times, but they would try to make the schedule work.

Four people on opposite sides of the country, trying to figure out a riddle without much to go on, were all thinking the exact same thing: *We're ordinary people. We just want "normal" again.*

CHAPTER 55

COLIN AND Ben got a call about five minutes after realizing that their hits had gotten away in a rental car. It was Alman telling them to break off the chase and get back to New York. Although they were disappointed not to be allowed to finish off their mission, they were thrilled to be getting out of Seattle and going home. They immediately headed to the airport and booked the first flight out they could get.

AN HOUR earlier, Alman had sent the email on Dr. Byers to Slater, and then just sat back in his chair to think. About thirty minutes into his thoughtful break, Slater called him.

"Recall your guys from Seattle. I want them back in New York."

"What?"

"I don't want our fugitives hiding out there or running somewhere else. I think we might be able to lure them in."

"How?"

"Let them think they're relatively safe. If we do nothing for a few days, they might assume things have died down and make a mistake. They've been pretty resourceful so far, so I don't want to underestimate them. They might even decide to leave the country, and if they do, we'll have them."

"Yeah, so how will that help?"

"Just leave that to me. It's done. Will you please recall your team?"

"It's done."

Slater had been sitting in his office for about an hour prior to calling Alman and ordering the recall. Staring out the window, he had been fully aware that this was a breach of a very serious nature, probably the worst since his inception as CEO and the worst since he took over the lead for the Affiliation. Like every other CEO of an Affiliation company, he knew the truth. He knew the need for secrecy. If they ever had to release what they had to the public, it would be a catastrophe of epic proportions. Companies would fall, and the entire healthcare system of many countries would be devastated. There would be widespread job loss. Health institutions would fall. Governments could fall. So, many would look for positions in other fields with no jobs. The devastation on tax revenues would be enormous. No, he knew they were right to keep this secret. This line of thinking reaffirmed his commitment. *Their* commitment—that of every person within the Affiliation who was connected to the secret. They all knew the gravity of what they guarded. And ever since the Affiliation had been created, in the wake of the polio fiasco, every member company, their representative, and their successors had kept things secret. No one had ever breathed a word. And it was not just the severance packages. The money. They did it for the greater good. They did it as a commitment to a quality society, and a sustainable society. If the public only knew of their altruism, they would understand. Perhaps. If it turned out that the four people being hunted had to be taken out, then it was a regrettable but necessary step.

He emerged from his deep thoughts and called his secretary.

"Yes, Mr. Slater?"

"Elaine, would you please put in a call to our contact at Homeland Security? Please tell him it's quite urgent, and I need to speak with him ASAP."

"Yes, sir."

A minute or two later, his phone rang. That is what paying millions in hand-outs got you.

"Hello? ... Hey, how are you? Thanks for calling me back so quickly. How are your lovely wife and kids? ... Good. Listen, I need a favor. I am going to send you the names of four of our employees. I need you to put a trace on their passports. In case they leave the country, I'd like you to contact me and let me know where they are going. Is it okay if one of these employees is a Canadian? Can you trace that passport? ... Excellent ... Serious? Perhaps. They have inadvertently gotten some sensitive company information, and we'd like to talk to them, and if necessary, get it back ... No, I don't want any law enforcement of any kind right now. I'd like to handle this as an internal matter. And please call me directly on my cell phone. Don't leave a message if I don't pick up; just call back ... Thanks so much and you take care. Bye now."

Yes, millions in contributions got you the necessary muscle exactly when you needed it.

CHAPTER 56

NATHAN, JENNA, and Steven drove around Seattle for a little while longer, just to make sure they were no longer being followed. After they were convinced that the two pursuers weren't behind them, they decided to return to the casino to get Nathan's car. They had argued a little over this, as there was still the concern that there might be some sort of tracking device on it, but they had eventually agreed that it had been Nathan's cell phone that had been used to track them down before.

Now back at the hotel parking lot, Nathan pulled slowly into a far entrance that allowed them to see the entire lot. They parked and watched to see if their two friends made an appearance. Finally, after thirty minutes, Steven offered to slip inside the hotel and casino to see if he could see them.

"What makes you think you have the ability to do that?" Nathan had a healthy level of incredulity in his voice. "I mean, one lucky escape, and you think you're 'Pharma-Man,' invisible to all those around you—"

"Look, I can keep low along the cars and go slow. They're probably not expecting us to come back here, so I imagine they're gone. This is just to make sure." Steven got out of the car.

"Be careful," his companions cautioned in unison.

Just as Steven was about to close the door, Jenna gave him a wink. "Maybe you can use your special knowledge of the place and sneak in an extra-secret side door."

Steven just smiled. *Good one.*

The wait was not long. Steven was back within fifteen minutes. "I didn't see any sign of them. I checked all over the casino floor and this parking lot, as well as the back lot that's rarely used." Jenna shot him a look, but before she could say anything, Steven emphasized, "I *told* you ... I've been here before."

"Do you think they've gone back to one of your houses?" Jenna asked.

"Maybe," Steven answered, "but we have to go and see."

They returned the rental car, climbed into Nathan's, and took off. They planned to go to Nathan's house first. Once they got there, they parked well away, and Steven and Nathan moved slowly down the street. They saw nothing. It was very quiet. The two of them went into the front yard of a house several down from Nathan's and moved towards his own. Once they got to his front yard, they stopped and looked around carefully, scouring his front lawn and looking up and down his street.

"I don't see anyone," Nathan said.

"Me either. Look, we've just got to screw up the courage and go in as quietly as we can. Let's go in the back door."

Once inside, they quickly got a hold of Nathan's passport, grabbed a few clothes, and left. They repeated the same procedure at Steven's house, and soon the three were on their way once more and beginning to think that the worst was behind them.

As they were leaving the Seattle city limits, Jenna asked, "Don't you guys have to check in with work or something? I mean, you don't want someone making up a missing person's report and getting the police looking for us."

"I did already," answered Nathan. "Told them I had a personal emergency. They said to take all the time I need."

Steven looked up. "My boss just started a two-week vacation, so I'm good. That being said, I don't think I'm returning to Matthews. There's this whole illegal, unethical, killer sort of vibe to the company now. My values don't mesh with Matthews' anymore, so screw 'em."

Both Jenna and Nathan burst out laughing, as they pulled out on I-90 and began driving east.

CHAPTER 57

MIGUEL DROVE onto the Harvard campus. The drive up from New York had been very pleasant. He almost forgot what he was driving towards and got lost in the beautiful countryside, especially as he got closer to Boston. It was one of his favorite cities. He had always enjoyed coming here. He loved Boston Common. It was smaller than Central Park, so you could easily walk around it and spend a nice summer afternoon relaxing. He had walked the Freedom Trail and visited many historical monuments. He loved the fact that you could walk around Boston so easily. He had been to Quincy Market and Faneuil Hall. He enjoyed them both. He had never been to see the Red Sox at Fenway, but he had enjoyed the atmosphere outside the ballpark on game day—it had such a wonderful festival, tailgate feel. It was too bad this trip was not for pleasure, but he still loved Boston.

He drove onto the campus and quickly found the building he was going to visit. The Clinical Sciences Building was a beautiful old Harvard campus building, just as one would expect. Two days ago, Miguel had taken very little time in finding the phone coordinates for Randy Thilwell, the colleague listed as one of Dr. Byers's closest associates. His surprise had come when he got through and a woman had answered. After stammering a little as he explained that he'd been expecting to contact a man, the woman on the other end just chuckled and said she really should go into Wikipedia and correct the spelling of her first name to end it with an 'I.' He now walked up a wonderful, old stone staircase and went inside. He checked the directory and found that Dr. Randi Thilwell was located in an office on the third floor, just as she had told him. Once he got to the office door, he knocked gently and eased the big wooden door open.

"Hello? Anyone home? I'm Miguel Benetto; we have a meeting booked."

"Hi, come on in," said a bright, cheery, young-sounding voice that both relaxed Miguel and slightly intimidated him for reasons he could not explain to himself at that moment.

Miguel pushed the door fully open, and standing up from behind a large desk was a woman who looked about thirty-five. She had short brown hair, big brownish-green eyes, and a huge smile. She was gorgeous. Another surprise Miguel had not anticipated. Without thinking, Miguel's own eyes widened, and he said, "Wow." Then he put his hand to his mouth and went on. "I am so sorry; I wasn't expecting a scientist to look … to look … to look … well, like you."

Randi half coughed, half stifled a short laugh. "That's okay. I get that reaction a fair bit at first-time meet and greets. I have come to accept it as something quite flattering."

"Well, that's how you *should* feel about it. Anyway, like I said, I'm Miguel. Thanks for agreeing to see me." Miguel held out his hand in greeting as he walked towards Dr. Thilwell. They shook hands, and she motioned for him to take a seat on the other side of her desk.

"Well, it's nice to meet you, Miguel. Ordinarily, I wouldn't meet with a stranger who called out of the blue, but you were quite convincing on the phone, and you said you wanted to talk about Dr. Byers. Alex was a mentor of mine and a good friend."

"I have to say that I was surprised so few of his colleagues were listed as associates. I would have thought that, given his work, there would be more people who would want to have their name beside his."

"That boils down to simple professional and personal umbrage. Rage even."

"I don't understand."

"When Alex dropped out, he left a lot of people high and dry. Most, if not all, the research money dried up and many people were out of work. He was the draw if you will … the genius that stirred the drink and brought in the dough. When he left, they had to either latch onto another lead researcher with good grant income or come up with their own idea and sell it to the university or some other entity and produce original work. That's tough, and so the resentment grew, and they decided not to have anything more to do with Alex."

"Why couldn't they just carry on Dr. Byers's work? I mean, he said in his farewell statement that his work would be carried on by his colleagues."

"Well, that's one of the odd things here. Besides his abrupt departure, Alex did something really weird. When a lead researcher decides to leave, they normally leave the work behind, sort of in a "best interests of science" kind of thing. But Alex didn't do that. He took everything, from his initial premise, to his initial in-vivo work, right through to his initial animal testing and early human-trial work. It's all gone."

"Ah. So, I understand why there'd be some bitterness."

"Some bitterness, Miguel? To paraphrase: 'Hell hath no fury like a researcher scorned.' You would not believe the egos that exist in the scientific world. And the politics? My god, the politics!"

"So, they all just moved on?"

"Pretty much. I mean, even I moved on to other things."

"What did you get involved in? Did you come up with your own line of research work?"

"Yeah, I did. I'm working on using genes and genetic research to see if we can identify specific genetic markers that identify links in people, or even groups of related populations, that can predict the likelihood of disease development. Even down to a specific disease."

For the second time since meeting her, Miguel said, "Wow."

Randi just smiled. "So, what's your interest in Alex anyway?"

"I just got curious about him in a sort of 'What are they doing now?' kind of way. My dad also died from complications from Parkinson's, so I have an elevated level of curiosity. I was wondering why someone with such promising research would just walk away." Miguel hoped this would satisfy Dr. Thilwell.

"Uh, okay..."

Sensing that she needed more convincing, he went on. "I mean, I work for a pharmaceutical company, in the computer department, and I see we fund all sorts of research that goes nowhere. I guess it really is a high-risk, high-reward business. It's too bad nothing came of Dr. Byers's research—"

At this point, Randi interrupted. "Now wait a minute. I mean, back the truck up. I wouldn't say nothing came of Alex's research. Just the opposite. And that just adds to the oddity of it all. Him just dropping out."

"So, his research was good? It could have led somewhere?"

"It could have led to the Holy Grail! Maybe even the cure." Seeing him about to interject, Randi held out her hand like a stop sign, palm towards him. "Possibly. I don't know. Maybe what he found was also insanely toxic it would kill thousands if administered it to a wider population. But now we'll never know."

"Why would he just stop? It doesn't make any sense."

"No, it doesn't." Randi started talking, recounting the last time she saw Alex Byers as though she were in a trance, and even periodically playing both roles of the conversation in between her own descriptive interruptions. Miguel drifted back in time with her, hanging on every word. She described how dedicated he'd been. She explained that, with his father dying of Parkinson's, Dr. Byers had been almost fanatical in his zeal to pursue the big breakthrough. He'd worked on dozens of ideas before coming up with the idea of using stem cells in combination with existing and other compounds to attack the disease. She described how it had seemed to work spectacularly in vivo. She described how things had been progressing towards full-scale human-trial work, when one day, he'd come into the lab and announced that that was it. He was dissatisfied with the results and was shutting down his lab. The entire team had been shocked. They had seen the in vivo results. They had seen the experiments in mice and rats and were thrilled with the progress.

"I went into his office and confronted him."

***

"Alex, this makes no sense. I've seen the work, *your* work, *and* the results. You can't quit."

"It's over, Randi. I can't go on. The results are bad, maybe even toxic. Deadly."

"What about Mr. Cowling?" She was shouting at him now.

"Him? Idiosyncratic response. What the religious groups would call a miracle. Probably a placebo effect. And the broader issue is one of safety. Safety for everyone … for the world."

They argued for another fifteen minutes when Randi turned to walk out.

"Randi." She turned back to face him. "Be careful as you go forward in your career. Be careful in your dealings … in where you get your funding, and how (or who) you report results to. Just ... just be careful." Alex then slumped back in his chair and rubbed his temples.

***

Randi looked up at a transfixed Miguel and smiled weakly. "I left right then and there and haven't seen him since."

Miguel just stared back at her before finally asking. "Who's Mr. Cowling?"

CHAPTER 58

JENNA WAS sitting in front of a library computer, reading articles about Alexander Byers. Ever since she had heard the name from Miguel, she had wanted to do some more research on him, his history, and his work in Parkinson's. Although she knew of him and a bit about his work, the research she was now doing gave her a better sense of what a genius he really was—or is, maybe. She didn't know. She remembered learning a little about him during her university days. He'd been held up by one of her biochemistry profs as an example of excellence. "Emulate this guy," they'd been told, "and you'll go far." But from what she was now discovering, everything excellent about Dr. Byers had stopped several years ago when he'd just up and left, seemingly taking his research with him.

"How's it going?" Steven asked nonchalantly as he approached her at the computer station. Jenna jumped at the sound of his voice, clutching a hand to her chest. "Oh, so sorry," he continued. "I guess you didn't hear me. You looked pretty engrossed."

"Don't be sorry. It is a library after all. You're supposed to be quiet."

"Okay. So, anyway, how's it going?"

"Really fascinating and really weird too." Jenna explained how Dr. Byers had seemed to be on the verge of something big and then just quit. One article she'd found hinted that he might be living on some tropical island in the Caribbean now.

"Hence the passport request from Miguel," Steven said.

"Yeah, I thought the same thing. But why would we want to go see Dr. Byers, and how is it—or he—connected to everything that's going on?" These were rhetorical questions, and she did not wait for any kind of attempt to answer. "There's something else really odd. I went into this scientific library site I belong to. It's really comprehensive. I mean, it's got thousands of articles, old and new. I ran a search for any of his scientific papers. His articles."

"Yeah."

"There's nothing. Not a single article about his work on Parkinson's. Not a single article on any area in which he worked. The whole database on Dr. Byers has been wiped clean. There's nothing listing him as the lead author."

"So, when he dropped out, he took his articles and work with him?"

"No, Steve, that's not how this works. Once you publish an article, it's out there. I mean, like … forever. It's in the public domain. It can't get erased due to scientific-knowledge infringement laws. The work stays public for others to follow and to build upon if they can. And this site I belong to buys access to all these articles. Now I remember a little about Dr. Byers from my university days. This guy was prolific. He published tons of stuff. Now, all I get are some third- and fourth-rate studies listing Dr. Byers as the fifth, sixth, seventh, or even last author, which means he was probably not even involved in the work."

"Why do you say that?"

Jenna explained that it was fairly common practice for researchers to slap a name on a study even though the scientist had done little or nothing to contribute to the work. Sometimes it was done as a favor from one researcher to another, getting their name on a published study and padding their resume a little. Or if the scientist was very well known, allowing their name to go on the list of authors might elevate the stature of the article. In this way, the study might get published in a more prestigious publication like *The New England Journal of Medicine* or *The Lancet*. This could lead to increased grant funding for the lead authors.

"That really goes on?"

"Oh sure. It may not be all that harmful. I mean, if the work is sound, then what's the issue?"

Steven immediately thought about more recent examples where some pharma companies had paid prestigious researchers to lend their name to an article even though they'd had nothing to do with the study or the writing of the article. It had been written by internal company people. Also, in this way, companies could skew results to suit their needs. Even in a simple study with three study arms—that is, three sets of patients, each using a different dose of the study drug—if the results were only positive at the higher dose, then the results could be pooled so a benefit could be shown across the dosage spectrum. And when a pharma company sponsored a research study, and the result was negative to their drug, they could use their best efforts to publish the study in the most obscure publication they could find. He had heard of one such study on one of Matthews's drugs: an antibiotic for otitis media. The results showed the Matthews drug, a newer and more expensive agent, was no better and had a few more side effects than the comparator drug, an older, very inexpensive alternative. The FDA mandates that all studies that reach a conclusion must be published. The worldwide product manager for the Matthews drug had sat on the study while he searched for a 'suitable' journal. He'd eventually found one: an obscure, nearly unknown publication in Southeast Asia. This way, the company could trumpet their commitment to complete disclosure of their results, all the while knowing that virtually no one would read the article. But he'd thought independent research was something purer.

Jenna cut into Steven's meandering thoughts. "It does go on. I mean, it's not ideal even if there's very little harm, and I know that efforts are underway to stop the practice, but it does go on."

"I guess money greases all wheels. But getting back to your original point: Dr. Byers's volume of original work is gone now?"

"Yes. All I can find are articles in the lay press, laying it on thick about how great his work was."

"Was it really that promising?"

"I'll say, at least if you believe the mainstream media. I mean, there are pictures of him with celebrity advocates for Parkinson's research standing beside him. He was big."

Steven suddenly found himself staring at Jenna, totally distracted by her. Her enthusiasm, her determination, and her intelligence all rolled up in this adorable package. He had to refocus.

"Shit, I'm overdue to check in with Miguel."

Their trip so far had gone well. They were finishing day two and hoped to be in the New York area in the next thirty-six hours. They had not been followed as far as they could tell, and they had taken turns driving while someone slept and another stayed awake, frequently watching out the rear window to see if they could pick up any followers. Now in Minneapolis, they were sure they had not been followed. They had also gotten along amazingly well. They joked that people thrown into desperate circumstances had to get along well or be toast. No *Survivor* tribal council here. They had also taken some time to share things about themselves. Nathan had offered up his love of pharmacy and of being a pharmacist. He talked about how he really strove to help his patients and be much more than just a pill counter. He attended every educational opportunity he could, and he always took the extra time to counsel his patients, even if that meant taking in fewer prescriptions. He even let it slip that he had toyed with the idea of being a jockey once, as he was only five foot five. He loved horses and going to the track.

Steven had recounted his days at university and how he had been the sports editor and editor-in-chief of the student newspaper and how he had gone into student politics to stir things up.

"You were a rabble rouser?" Jenna had asked.

"It's not as rabble rousing as you might think. I was a very conservative radical. No marches or placard waving. We went for the suit and tie look and brokered meetings with politicians and other government types to advance student causes."

"Did it work?" Jenna's question had drawn a snort from Nathan before Steven answered.

"Hardly. I ran for student-body president after my year as vice-president. I got trounced by a pot-smoking, long-haired, bearded hippie named Floyd." That had caused a good laugh.

After university, he had kind of fallen into pharmaceutical sales and was lucky that Matthews had been his first and only company for the last ten years. Turnover was huge in the industry.

Jenna had shared how she had graduated from university five years earlier with a degree in biochemistry. She'd worked as a researcher, doing work in cholesterol lowering and fatty plaques, but she hadn't really liked it. She'd wanted more interaction with people. A friend of hers who was a pharmaceutical rep had suggested looking at it as a career. She'd applied to a few firms, gotten offers from three all around the same time, and chosen Matthews. She told them how she loved calling on doctors and breaking down fairly complex scientific information into easily digestible bites for them. She told them how she loved living in Calgary and being close to the mountains. She explained that her parents had died a few years ago, and when she quickly mentioned her sister, almost forgetting what had happened, she choked up a little but stayed intact. She was determined to always view life in a positive way. That's how her parents had raised her. Life was great, and there was beauty all around, all the time. That didn't mean she was some sort of a Pollyannaish pushover. It just meant she didn't choose to dwell in the dark places.

It was during this time with Jenna that Steven realized he was becoming very attracted to her. He'd thought she was gorgeous from the moment he'd met her, but hearing her perspective on life and seeing her resolve and determination, he knew he really liked her ... a lot.

CHAPTER 59

IN THE bunker, Alman was staring at a computer screen that displayed a map of the Midwestern United States. Centered in the middle of the screen was a dot blinking in a rhythmic tone and staying stationary. There was a knock on the door. He checked his video monitor and saw that William Slater was outside. With a sigh, he got up, went over to the door, and let Slater in.

"Are they still headed east? Towards New York, or so we think?"

"Yes. They've been in Minneapolis for a couple of hours now, but I imagine they're grabbing something to eat."

"Can you zoom in on them and find out a more precise location?"

Alman complied without acknowledging and zoomed in the map of Minneapolis. The city map became larger and larger with the streets narrowing down and more detail becoming clear.

"Can you hang a tag on their GPS device?"

"Sure." Alman hung the little figure of a man on the blinking dot and then a picture came up of a parking lot next to a building.

"What is that?"

Alman used the cursor to move around the car and the parking lot to identify the building. Once he zoomed in a little more, the name on the building became clear enough to read.

Slater leaned over Alman's shoulder. "The Minneapolis Public Library. What the hell are they doing at the library?"

"No idea."

Suddenly, the tracking device began to beep with a little more urgency, and Alman clicked on another screen that showed a map with less detail. The blip on the screen was moving away from the library.

"Mr. Alman, I'm glad you had your team place this device on their car in Seattle. It's proved invaluable."

High praise indeed from the grand poohbah, thought Alman. He did not care much for Slater at the best of times, and he really did not like him sticking his nose into the business of security or hanging around like he had been doing ever since that mysterious USB stick had been made. He had been growing increasingly frustrated by Slater and by the fact that he was not being told what was on the stick.

What was so important that these lengths had to be taken to get it back? He wanted to know more.

"Look," Alman said, "why don't I just send in a strike team to get them? We can either take them out where we find them or grab them and bring them in."

"No. Absolutely not. There are now four of them working together, and we have no trace on the fourth, this Miguel Benetto. We have no idea what he downloaded, and we don't know where he is or what he's doing. We need all four together, coupled with our information, to set this straight and fully contain this breach. We need to keep them thinking they're safe."

"I don't understand that line of thought."

"Look, these people are smart and resourceful. Benetto got away here in New York. The girl got away in Calgary, and she and the other two got away in Seattle. I was right in thinking they would try to hook up to compare notes. Your device is working well. We'll get them, all four of them, in one place, at one time."

With that, Slater left Alman in the Bunker to fume a little more. In truth, the tracking device had been useful, but it was not the only way he was keeping tabs on the three miscreants. He had made a second call to his friend at Homeland Security and placed a trace on the debit and credit cards of Steven, Jenna, and Nathan. He had reports of their purchases, and like a breadcrumb trail, he had followed their trek across the country. He'd get them. And unfortunately, it looked as though they were going to be killed. It was too bad. He did not like this at all, but the industry had to be protected. The world had to remain safe. Just as he returned to his office, his cell phone rang. It was Alman.

"This is weird. The tracking device is moving through Minneapolis. And now it looks like it's heading south."

"Has it left the city?"

"No. but it's approaching the city limits, and it is absolutely heading south. It looks as though it's connecting on to I35, which is a highway heading south, away from Minneapolis."

"Well, I told you they were smart. And resourceful. It would not surprise me if they found the tracking device and stuck it on another car or truck, or something that looked like it was heading in another direction. No matter. We'll still be able to track them."

"How are we going to do that? You should have let me take them out before now. We could always have tracked this Benetto guy the old-fashioned way. I'm sure we would have found him."

"Don't worry, Mr. Alman. We'll still get them. I'm having them tracked using their credit cards." Slater probably should not have told Alman this, but he was getting a tad frustrated at Alman's lack of faith in his abilities. No, he was not a security expert, but he had enough muscle and pull to get things done and find things out. Alman needed to know that.

"How the hell did you arrange that? That information can only come from the FBI, Homeland, or other law enforcement."

"Exactly."

Just then, Slater's phone rang. It was his secretary. "Excuse me, Mr. Slater, but Mr. Denman is on line one for you."

"Put him through." Peter Denman was the CEO of Denman Pharmaceutical, the largest privately held pharmaceutical company in the world and a prominent member of the Affiliation. Many members of the Affiliation looked up to him for his smarts in running his company and his toughness in resisting the many attempts to buy out, take over, or otherwise turn his company public. His company was big, and his personality was bigger.

"Peter, what can I do for you?"

"I've called an emergency meeting of the Affiliation. I've been following our breach from your reports, and I think we need to bring everyone up to speed."

"Peter, there's no need for that. I have everything under control. Nothing has been compromised, and I'm on top of things."

"No, William. I have already called the meeting, and we need to get the logistics organized."

Although Slater was the head of the Affiliation, he knew he could not say no. Denman was too important, too powerful. "Alright, Peter, I'll get the video-conferencing system together and get the board of directors alerted."

"Wrong again. I don't mean just the board. I mean all sixty-two of us, William. We all need to get involved. We all need to know."

Slater slumped. He did not want to get the whole group together. That, in and of itself, was a security issue. But again, Peter Denman could not be denied.

"Alright again. I'll set things up here at Matthews and let the members based here in New York know so they can come in person. The rest we'll video conference in. I will get back to you with details."

"Thanks, William. I appreciate your help."

Just as he hung up, Slater got two emails that wobbled his belief that everything was under control—one more than the other.

First, he received an email from Alman that the GPS device was definitely heading south, out of Minneapolis. Then he read an email from his friend at Homeland. Steven, Jenna, and Nathan had each withdrawn a total of five thousand dollars on their debit and credit cards between yesterday and today.

"Shit. On to tracking-plan C."

CHAPTER 60

"HI, MIGUEL, it's Steven. How are you?"

"I'm good. You sound okay. Are you all okay?"

"Absolutely. We're good. I thought it was weird we got away the way we did without much fuss. I don't know how you knew, but you're brilliant. And thanks so much."

"I take it you had Nathan's car checked for a GPS device. You found one?"

"We did. Before we got to the library, we stopped by a garage and had Jenna go in. She was great. She told the mechanic she was trying to get away from a controlling boyfriend and thought he might have put a tracking device on her car to keep tabs on her. He hoisted it up on the lift and found one attached on the underside of the driver's side quarter panel. He gave it to us."

"You still have it?"

"Sort of, well, no. When we got to the library, we parked, and I put it on a car with a Texas licence plate. I figured if they're going home, they'll head south. And if they're not going home, Matthews will think we're still in Minny. Even if they head in the same direction, we'll be miles apart."

"And the credit and debit cards. Did you handle that?"

"Yeah, yeah, we did. And again thanks, I guess. We withdrew money yesterday and today. But I really don't think they can track our cards. I mean, this is a drug company not the government."

"After what I've seen on my files, I would not put anything past this group. Don't use your cards again. At least not until we absolutely have to."

"Right. Anyway, what did you find out with your visit to … to … who did you go see anyway?"

By this time, Nathan had joined the group, and they were sitting in the back of the library huddled into Jenna's computer station. Steven put the phone on speaker and turned down the volume.

"I went to see a researcher who was a colleague of Dr. Byers. Her name is Randi Thilwell."

Both Nathan and Steven looked at each other. They remembered the name from their meeting with Seth. She was the researcher who had teased Seth about accepting Big Pharma money for research work.

"You said Randi Thilwell?" Nathan asked. "I thought you were going to visit a man."

"I thought so too. Damn Wikipedia misspelling. But I did say Randi Thilwell. Do you know her?"

"No, we don't," Steven interjected, "but we've heard of her. We can tell you about that later. What happened in your meeting with her?"

Miguel went into a detailed description of his meeting with Randi and all the information he had gotten from her. He recounted how Randi had mentioned Eli Cowling, a patient Dr. Byers had recruited to take his experimental drug for Parkinson's. She described how they had argued, as it was not scientifically correct or allowed to grab some guy and give him a drug. There were protocols to be observed. A study had to be created and presented to an ethical-review board. Grabbing a guy and giving him a concoction created in a lab smacked of Dr. Frankenstein. But Alex had insisted that this first step was necessary. He did not want to enter this into the computer or report it to anyone at the university. At least not yet. And Eli Cowling was just the patient to try his treatment on. Cowling was a fifty-eight-year-old man who had been diagnosed with Parkinson's when he was thirty-five. His tremors, increasing rigidity, and bradykinesia had gotten steadily worse over the years but had been somewhat controlled and slowed with conventional medication. His meds had changed and evolved over the years, but he was still taking a heavy daily regimen and would do so for the rest of his life. His life had become filled with trips to the pharmacy for refills, new medications to try, and new side effects to deal with. Even when he was told that he could expect to live many, many more years if he stayed on his meds, he was growing increasingly unhappy at the prospect of multiple pills every day for the rest of his life. When Alex had talked to him in his office late one night, about trying this new concoction, Eli had been all in.

***

"Look, Eli, you're a family friend. I can say that because of what you and my father endured after meeting at the rehab and physiotherapy center. But this could be dangerous."

"Doc, I have had it with what I have to do just to stay alive and stay upright. Every day, just getting up is a struggle. I wake up and must focus on getting the energy to swing my legs out of bed. I grab my bar and force myself to stand. Going to the bathroom to take a dump, shave, brush my teeth, and shower is a slow-motion pain in the ass. I mean, I know these drugs I'm on are helping, but man, I'd love to see if there is something better. And the thought of having to take these drugs for the rest of my life, even if that's a long life … it's scary. I mean, I don't know what's scarier, knowing you're going to live a long time but have to take drugs or knowing that you have to take these drugs every day of your life to live a long time. If you think you have something better, I'll take the chance. I'm not married. I mean, who would want a herky-jerky guy anyway. I don't have kids, and my parents are gone. It's just me. Do you think you can help me?"

"I don't know, Eli. And I will probably lose my job, and maybe even go to jail, but I just think we have to try this out. Let's get started."

Mr. Cowling began taking Alex's concoction once a day starting on a Monday. After two weeks, he came in for his checkup. As Randi and Alex waited in Alex's office, they saw Eli come running down the hallway. He virtually vaulted over the office threshold, held his arms out wide, and gave Randi a huge hug, picking her up off the ground. He then turned his attention to Alex, who held out his hand for a handshake only to have Eli embrace him in the same bear hug he'd given Randi. At the time he had started the new drug, Eli's hands had been shaking, he shuffled his feet to walk, and it took him ten to twenty seconds to get up from a chair.

"Well, I'd say you're looking a little better than when I last saw you," said Dr. Byers in an incredible understatement.

"Doc, it's been unbelievable!" Eli shouted.

"Okay, okay." Alex's tone was cautious, and he held up his hand to try to get Eli to keep his voice down, but Randi could sense the excitement in his voice. "When did you notice things starting to change?"

"It was about three days after I started on your drug. I woke up and lay there in bed as usual, preparing myself for the ordeal of actually getting up. And as I started to try to get up, I ... I ... well, you know, Doc, it's like when you grab something you think is really heavy, and it turns out to be really light, you know? You're prepared to have to strain to pick it up, and it comes off the surface so easily, you almost throw it across the room."

"I guess so."

"That's what it was like getting out of bed. I almost threw myself across the room, everything moved so easily ... so fast."

"Then what?"

"Then I just moved around as normal. I mean, it was weird. I had to start slow because I kept expecting the tremors or the tripping, but I just didn't have any of those. There was nothing wrong with me."

"Did you continue taking the study drug?" Randi asked.

"Oh yeah, I stayed on it like just like Dr. Byers told me to. I took my fourteenth dose today."

"Okay," Alex said, "let's get your checkup going."

They put Eli through a number of tests, and he scored normal on every one of them. On this day at least, Eli Cowlings had Parkinson's without *any* symptoms.

Later, after Eli had left, Randi went into Alex's office. "You've done it! You cured him!"

"Not so fast, Randi. We've got a lot of work to do. A long way to go."

"I know, but this is fantastic! We've got to recruit more patients."

"I agree with you there. I'm going to enter this into the database, and we'll get going tomorrow."

In the next couple of days, they began the slow process of putting together a study protocol and putting out the call for some research patients. Things were progressing, and they were getting lots of interest, but then Alex had come in and pulled the plug. When Eli showed up the next day with chocolates for Alex and the entire lab staff, Randi had to tell him that Alex had left, and that the study drug was gone. Eli just slumped down into an office chair.

"What's going to happen to me?" he asked, his eyes pleading for good news.

"I don't know." That was all she could offer him.

***

The three huddled in the computer station were absolutely motionless, absolutely silent, when Miguel finished his recounting.

"Steven? Jenna? Nathan? ... Anyone there?"

"Yeah, yeah, we're here," answered Steven. "I think we're all just stunned."

"That was my reaction as well. We really need to get someone to look at what you've got on that stick."

"I guess so," said Steven, "but what happened to Mr. Cowling?"

"Randi wouldn't tell me. She just gave me his address and told me, if I really want to research Alexander Byers, I should go meet with him. I'm going to see him tomorrow."

With that, Miguel hung up. The three in the library just looked at each other, wondering what the hell was going on. What was on the stick Steven had downloaded? What was on the memory stick Miguel had downloaded? And what had become of Mr. Cowling?

CHAPTER 61

MIGUEL DROVE south from Boston towards Plymouth. It was a fairly small seaside town that housed the famous Plymouth Rock. Miguel had been to Plymouth before. He had gone when he was fourteen years old. His parents had taken him. As immigrants, his parents had always tried to instill in Miguel a sense of the history of the United States. They were so proud to have come over and become citizens. They had admired the Americans' sense of pride at their history and how, as a country, they had taken pains to preserve and display it. His parents always admired what America had achieved in its 240-plus years as a country. They always tried to pass that onto Miguel. Miguel had been to Washington and had been very impressed with how well the United States had preserved and honored their history. It gave him a sense of pride as a US citizen. When he and his family had gone to Plymouth to see "the rock," he'd been so excited. As they'd approached the area where the rock was housed, he'd gotten more and more excited, having remembered the monuments and history displayed in his other trips to the monuments of Washington: the Liberty Bell and Mount Rushmore, among others. As he and his family approached the protected area housing Plymouth Rock, he had wondered how he would feel at seeing another national treasure. What perspective would he find? When they'd gotten to the railing that protected people from falling over the edge, he'd pulled his teenage frame up and looked over the railing to the ocean shore below.

He looked at his father. "It's a rock."

"Yes, what did you expect?"

"I dunno. Maybe something more like the other sites we've seen."

"Well, Miguel," his father began, "it's what it symbolizes. A new beginning. A new start. The birth of a nation. That's what's important."

Affiliation

All Miguel could think about was that a bunch of people were looking down with amazed rapture at a fairly small, non-descript, greyish rock. It was his first feeling of disappointment at viewing an American historical monument. He went on to see a lot more of America's history and was always impressed. He loved that feeling of pride. But the sense of disappointment he'd felt at Plymouth rock had never been forgotten, and it had returned when he'd stumbled onto what Matthews and others in the industry appeared to be doing, with how illegal it appeared and its definitive air of immorality. His feelings of disappointment had grown into feelings of anger, hurt, and resentment as he uncovered more and more about what seemed to be going on. He had to uncover more if only to restore his pride in his country.

As he drove into Plymouth and navigated the streets by way of his talking GPS, Miguel knew he was in this to the end, whatever that end might turn out to be. And just maybe, the four of them together could somehow stop it.

Miguel pulled up to a bungalow. It was a pretty, Cape Cod-style house with a black roof, white siding, and black shutters on the windows. It even had a white picket fence around the front yard, which was neatly kept, and a front garden of flowers that held quite an impressive display. It was pure Americana, and to Miguel, it was beautiful. There was a man tending to the flowers, kneeling and working with his hands, digging and removing weeds and replacing soil as he went. As Miguel stopped the car and got out, he waved, smiled, and shouted, "Hello!"

"Hello, young fella. Are you Miguel Benetto?"

"Yes, how did you know that?" With everything he and his new friends had gone through, he was a touch suspicious and looked around a little nervously.

"Dr. Thilwell called and told me she had sent you down here to see me."

"You don't mind?"

"Not at all." The man strode easily across the lawn and held out his hand to shake Miguel's. "I'm Eli Cowling. What can I do for you?"

CHAPTER 62

THE AUDITORIUM at Matthews Pharmaceuticals was located on the fourteenth floor of the 42nd Street building in Manhattan. It had a private elevator from the parking lot in addition to the regular elevators that the public and/or staff took to get up to it.

On this afternoon, twenty-seven people filed into an auditorium that held four hundred. A massive screen that rivalled an IMAX screen stood at the front of the room. It was broken into thirty-five smaller screens, each with a man or a woman looking out at the people in actual attendance in the auditorium. As people filed in one by one, it was like a conclave of cardinals walking silently into the deliberation room to decide on a new pope, or perhaps something akin to the heads of the five families of Mafia lore. But in this case, they were not here to elect a pope or decide on some sort of Mafia vendetta.

Slater had worked hard to stop this meeting. He quietly seethed as he sat in the front row, watching the silent procession and the others looking out from their oversized viewing stations. He had placed many backdoor calls to the heads of the other affiliation companies, asking that they support his motion to stop or at least delay this meeting. He argued that there was not enough information, and in any case, he had the situation under control. But everyone had already been called by Peter Denman, and they would not go against the man many had already anointed as the new head of the Affiliation once Slater's five-year term was over, which was coming up fairly fast. Denman had gotten out ahead of Slater because he knew a show of leadership would hold him in good regard when the time to vote for a new lead arrived. And this time, he would not lose to Slater like he had last time. Denman had always felt vindictive towards Slater for the way he had outfoxed him last

Affiliation

time. Slater had come from a fast-food enterprise, for God's sake. He had only been at Matthews for a few months before the vote for a new Affiliation lead had taken place. But boy, he sure could play politics. He had talked to and lobbied every other Affiliation company CEO for the lead position, and he had gotten it.

Slater eyed Denman sitting among several Affiliation board members. He knew exactly what Peter was up to. It had struck him many times during his career that, no matter where you went or how high a position you achieved, there were always politics to contend with, and someone was always looking out for your job.

The CEOs of the Affiliation companies had been receiving calls from Denman starting two days earlier. He had explained that he felt this current breach was an issue of grave importance, and it was too big to leave in the hands of the board of directors alone. Every company deserved to be in the loop. He only had to hold open the spectre of a full public breach to drive home his point. That was enough.

Every CEO had quietly made plans to attend the meeting, either in person or via video conferencing. Each one had a buddy and only had to let their staff or anyone in their company know that they were going to a private meeting with just one other person: their buddy. And every three months, the buddy was switched. It had always been done this way. They were told via secure email who their new buddy was. Although full Affiliation meetings were exceedingly rare, they had to keep the rotation schedule in case they did have two or more meetings close together. If the same two CEOs were found to have multiple meetings in quick succession, things might get out. That might in turn lead to market speculation that the two represented companies were talking merger or acquisition, and that might lead to speculative buying or selling of stock. Their positions were quite public, there wasn't much they could do that did not end up in the public domain. This system even worked to protect them from leaks within their own organizations. The last full meeting had been fifteen months earlier. And like last time, the ones that personally attended arrived separately in cars that pulled quietly into the Matthews underground parking lot. They used a private entrance only accessible to the CEOs themselves. They used their own cars and drove themselves.

The private elevator was used to usher them up to the auditorium. The trick was to remain calm in the face of subterfuge.

So, they sat in the first two rows and looked to the viewing screens, waiting for the meeting to begin. Slater took note that everyone seemed to be ready, then got up and strode as confidently as he could to the podium off to the side of the stage.

"We've had some extraordinary developments over the last few days. I want to be completely transparent with all of you." All the participants had been somewhat briefed over their secure network, but Slater went over the breach again, starting with Dr. Bhergosian's email message. He went through the representatives who had opened the message and how he had acted quickly and decisively to quell this breach. He explained how Steven had made a copy and how Jenna had gotten away in Calgary and joined Steven and Nathan in Seattle. He told the group of how the three were now trekking their way towards New York, leaving out the fact that they now had no way of tracking them. Transparency had its limits.

"What we found out, subsequent to these people in Seattle, was that an employee of Matthews, based here in New York, a Miguel Benetto, hacked into our database and downloaded the files concerning the business end of the Affiliation onto some sort of external device, probably a simple memory stick, and he has, in fact, left the building. We do not know where he is."

The audience had not known this prior to the meeting, and it provoked gasps, hands rising to cover mouths, several choice expletives, and as many other hand gestures as there were attendees. Slater let this reaction go on for a moment but then held his arms up and out wide with his palms up.

"Ladies and gentlemen." He paused both to let things calm down and for effect. "What I think you should take away from this, as a bottom line, is that our surveillance systems work. We knew right away about Dr. Bhergosian. We knew right away who had opened the email. We knew right away who had gotten in and that certain information had been stolen from our system.

"Hell, we even knew that one of our Matthews computers was stolen, and we retrieved it in short order. We know who *and* what we are dealing with."

Someone attending via video screen shouted then, "But how do we know whether or not the secrets have been shared with a wider audience?"

"Or the media?" shouted someone else from the first two rows of auditorium seating.

"I think we can assume from the total lack of media activity that everything is safe. Besides, my secure site, where this Benetto fellow got his information, does not reveal the exact nature of what it is we are guarding."

The audience was still restless, and Peter Denman stood up. "I think William is correct." Denman's voice carried weight, and the murmuring subsided.

Then Slater jumped in again. "And I think you're right, Peter. I don't believe anything specific has been leaked. However, everyone has to know that we are doing everything we can to get our information back."

Now Denman grabbed the floor. "Again, I think you're right, and we certainly appreciate, somewhat, your efforts to get things under control. But I—and I think everyone here—want to know why you pulled out the team in Seattle. Surely, that is where you should have acted more boldly and taken the three individuals into some sort of custody." Denman finished and waited for Slater to begin speaking.

"We felt—"

"Because," interrupted Denman, "in that event, had you acted and grabbed the three in Seattle, we could have then isolated this Mr. Benetto without further incident." The crowd nodded in agreement.

Slater looked deadpan at Denman. "May I answer that, Peter?" Denman nodded approval. "We felt, upon sober second thought, that apprehending three people at once, including a foreign national, would raise more suspicion and subsequent publicity. Remember, we had just removed the researcher at the university. If someone had dug into these people and figured out the link, we could be in more trouble. Especially with the representative from Canada complicating things somewhat." Slater had not told anyone about Jenna's sister, and he had not told anyone about his tracking ploys having gone belly up. "We decided to track them, which is how we found out they were coming here, or at least that is what we suspect. We think the three from Seattle and Benetto have contacted one another and are working on setting up a meeting."

"A meeting? To do what?" shouted one of the attendees.

"I don't think they really know what they possess," Slater said. "I think they want to meet to compare notes and figure out a way to get out of the mess they now find themselves in."

"Are you still tracking them?" Denman asked.

"Yes, we have put a trace on their passports. If they try to leave the country, we'll know. We are tracking their credit-card purchases, so we can see their progress as they stop to gas up, grab a bite, or stay in a hotel. Once they get to New York, we will put the team on them. They can then track them, and when all four are together, we can move in and apprehend them." Everyone in the listening audience knew apprehend meant kill, but they were all businesspeople. A certain decorum had to be observed. "Once that happens, this will be over." Slater kept certain things to himself, even (or especially) from this group.

That explanation seemed to mollify the group. There were nods of approval, and the silence meant agreement, or at least it did to Slater. Not wanting to continue this any longer than necessary, he seized the moment. "We are in agreement then? We will contain this breach, settle things down, and our work will go on. And most importantly, our secret will stay within this group."

With that, screens began to go dark one by one. The people in the first two rows got up and filed to the door towards the elevator to return to their cars and go back to their offices. This meeting was, indeed, over.

CHAPTER 63

ELI COWLING showed Miguel into his home. It was well appointed but not overly so. The living room had a couch, love seat, and a chair with a reading lamp beside it. There were lots of pictures on the walls that reflected where Eli lived. Pictures of the ocean and dockside images left no doubt as to where Eli's heart was. The house looked to have all hardwood floors, big wide planks that again gave one the feeling of being in a Cape Cod-like setting. In the kitchen, Eli directed Miguel to a chair at the kitchen table. It had a tabletop that resembled the floor, all hardwood, with a big butcher block of a surface. Eli quickly made some tea and brought it over to the table.

"So, young man, you came all the way from New York to see me. How come?" There was no suspicion in Eli's tone, just curiosity.

"Well, I was investigating a story for our in-house magazine. I work for Matthews Pharmaceuticals. I wanted to show how our research efforts sometimes go awry. I wanted to show people out there that we're in a high-risk, high-reward type of business and that our research often doesn't pan out, but we still invest. We still research new compounds. We are not bad guys." Miguel did not like lying, and there was a part of him that wanted to believe what he was dishing out to Eli. He only worried that he was not a very good liar, but Eli seemed to buy it.

"So, you visited Dr. Thilwell to get a picture of Dr. Byers's work?"

Eli is a bright guy, thought Miguel. "That's right, and in the course of our conversation, she mentioned you."

"Well, what questions do you have?"

"How serious was your condition all those years ago?"

"Very. I mean, I was living, but I wasn't really alive, you know? I was managing. That's the best way I can put it."

"And then you took the new treatment Dr. Byers had come up with."

"Yes."

"How long were you on it in total?"

"I was on it for just two weeks. I have not taken it since."

"And when you went off it, did you expect your Parkinson's to return?"

"Oh my god, yes. I thought for sure it would come back. I figured that even this new drug had to be taken every day for the rest of my life or it wouldn't work. I was a nervous wreck. Every time I twitched, I'd panic. If I tripped and fell, I'd spend the next hour analyzing the fall from every conceivable angle. I became this fearful, paranoid hypochondriac."

"What happened?"

Eli explained that a friend of his had finally sat him down and said he had to relax. If his condition returned, he'd be able to deal with it, and he would not be alone. She'd help him. There were new medications coming out all the time, better meds than before, which managed Parkinson's symptoms better and maybe even helped with the disease itself. They'd manage, no matter the cost.

"As the days turned into weeks, then months, then years, I relaxed more and more. And here I am, years later."

"Have you had any symptoms return?"

"Not one. It's like my whole mind and body got a reset. Like turning off a computer that wasn't working and then rebooting it."

"So, you're cured."

"Well, we don't use the 'cured' word around here. Dr. Thilwell tells me that all the time." Eli swept his hand up and down his body. "We refer to this as an extended remission."

Miguel looked at Eli. "I don't know. If you're cancer-free for five years, they say you're cured, and you're out more than that."

"Yeah, but they cure cancer all the time. There's never been a cure for Parkinson's, just pills every day for the rest of a person's life."

Miguel continued to stare at Eli, just marvelling at the sight. "Why would Dr. Byers stop his research with a result like this? Like you?" It was a question he'd said in his head a number of times recently, and he was surprised when he heard it said out loud, even though he'd been the one to ask.

"I don't know. Dr. Thilwell has never been able to tell me. I guess she doesn't know either."

Miguel suddenly realized that Eli had referred to Randi several times. "Does Dr. Thilwell keep in touch with you?"

"She sure does. She calls me every two weeks and visits me four times a year."

"Is she just curious?"

"Not just that. She comes down here and draws blood and runs tests on it. She puts me through a neuro exam as well, and a musculoskeletal test too. She phones me later with the results. So far, everything's been great."

"Does she send the results to Dr. Byers?"

"I think she does because I always ask her if he's happy with how I'm doing, and if he's coming back. She always answers yes to the first question, and 'I'm working on it' to the second."

Randi had not told Miguel of her regular contact with Eli. She had also not said anything about contacting Dr. Byers or perhaps knowing where he was. Miguel looked at Eli again and then got up from the table. "Well, it's been so nice meeting you, Mr. Cowling."

"Call me Eli, son, and you can come back and see me anytime."

As he walked towards the front door, Miguel thought about what a nice man Eli was, and how appropriate it seemed that this random loner guy Dr. Byers had picked to be the guinea pig for his new drug was just such a nice man. His condition may have weakened him physically but not mentally. He'd been able to survive until the remission, and even if the condition came back, he thought Eli would be able to handle it.

He turned to face Eli one last time. "You mentioned that a friend gave you the strength to handle your hypochondria. I think you said 'she.' Is she still in the picture? That's a nice friend to have."

Eli chuckled. "She sure is, young man. We got married last year. She's the best thing that ever happened to me ... other than getting Dr. Byers's drug."

"Do you two have big plans for your future?"

"Nope. We'll travel some, but we like it here. We like the ocean, the town, and our garden. When you had as much trouble as I did just doing the simple things, you appreciate them all the more when you can do them again."

"That's great. Do you take any pills for your Parkinson's just in case?"

Eli burst out laughing. "No, I don't. I'm a drug company's worst nightmare, son. I don't take any pills at all."

Miguel laughed, turned, went down the front steps, and climbed back into his car. He immediately phoned Randi. When she answered, he launched right into what he had to say without even a hello.

"You didn't tell me you're still in contact with Eli and that you come down here to test him."

"That's because you didn't tell me why you *actually* came to see me. I'm not an idiot. So why don't we level with each other?"

Miguel thought for a second, and it struck him that everyone seemed to be so friggin' bright lately. "Okay, can we meet back in Boston in a couple of hours?"

"Yes." Randi gave the name of a restaurant where they could meet up.

CHAPTER 64

STEVEN ANSWERED the phone while sitting in the passenger seat. Jenna was driving. He had caught himself glancing over at her a lot over the last few hours. He had to check his glances to make sure she did not notice. He did not want to alarm her or weird her out. Nathan was sleeping in the back seat, often offering up a choice snore or mumbling something incoherent in his sleep. They'd had quite a few chuckles over the last little while. Steven had noted, though, in his many glances, how the sun would shine on Jenna and the highlights in her hair. It looked natural, no dye or coloring at all. He wondered how her eyes, or anyone's eyes for that matter, could be so clear, bright, and piercingly brown. She had an easy and familiar way that made him feel totally comfortable. When the cell phone rang, he jumped a little and glanced at the time. They had been talking non-stop for the last two hours, and it had felt like two minutes.

"Hello?"

"Hey, Steve, it's Miguel. I've just left Eli Cowling's place."

"Hang on, Mig, I'm going to put you on speaker." Steven connected to the car's Bluetooth so everyone could listen in. "Go ahead."

Miguel went on to describe his meeting with Eli, and that he now showed no signs of his Parkinson's. He told them about how Eli had taken Dr. Byers's drug for only two weeks and that nothing in the way of symptoms had come back for years.

Jenna asked, "Miguel, was his Parkinson's well controlled prior to him taking the study—I mean, Dr. Byers's drug?"

"No, not really. Eli told me he was shaking and having trouble getting up from a chair. He was having lots of trouble just doing the simple things in life. He said he was alive but not really living. Why do you ask?"

"Well, I just thought that if it was already well controlled, his remission would be slightly less remarkable."

Miguel went on to tell them of Dr. Thilwell's visits and that she might even know where Dr. Byers was now living. He told them he was going to meet up with her in the next hour or so.

"Do you think that's a clever idea?" Nathan said after having woken up to listen in.

"Is that Nathan? Yeah, I think it is. This is someone who is involved in the science and research side. She might have an idea of what I've stumbled into. She might also have an idea of what you have on that stick of ours. And … I don't know. I just trust her, that's all."

"Okay, Mig," Steven interjected. "We'll go with how you feel."

"Jenna, did you find anything out about Dr. Byers?" Miguel asked.

"Not much. But that, in and of itself, is really weird. He just dropped out of sight and so did his work. I couldn't find any papers he'd written at all. I just found some random articles where he was the fourth, fifth, sixth, or seventh listed authors, and nothing linking him to Parkinson's from a scientific standpoint. The link to Parkinson's research was stuff in the lay press. It's bizarre.

"That is odd. I'll check that out with Randi. Hey, have you guys gotten any feeling that you're being followed?

"No, not a thing," Steven answered. "Why?"

"Oh, just wondering. They've probably guessed that they're tracking the wrong car, but I bet they think you're headed here. It's logical."

"Yeah, but they don't know where, and they don't know when. If we stay off the credit-card grid and pay cash, we're invisible."

"Yes, correct. But when we meet, we should meet outside of New York, just to be safe."

"Where?"

"What about Hoboken?"

"Why Hoboken?"

"Well, it's not far from here, but it's still a little obscure. Safe, you know?"

"Okay, Mig," Steven said. "We can be in Hoboken tomorrow by four in the afternoon."

"Okay, I can as well. Let's connect tomorrow at two to set up a meeting place."

"Okay, see you tomorrow."

CHAPTER 65

MIGUEL PULLED into the parking lot of the pub restaurant Randi had recommended on the outskirts of Boston. He noticed only a few cars in the lot, and the sun lighting up the entrance. *Quaint,* he thought, *for a clandestine meeting.* He walked through the front entrance into an American version of a traditional English pub. Several tall tables on a floor raised above the bar-level floor seemed to be the main seating area. The bar itself was long and had several bar stools aligned in front of it. At the back of the raised level was another smaller section with smaller tables with regular seating. On the other side of the bar was a room with several pool tables and narrow shelves to rest a drink. There were lots of different local and international beers on tap. He went to the back of the raised level and found a table tucked into the corner and plunked himself into a chair. A server came over, and he ordered a Sam Adams draft beer. *When in Rome,* he thought. About five minutes after he had gotten his beer, Randi walked in. She saw him, gave a big wave and a huge smile, and walked towards him.

"Hi, Miguel."

"Hi, Dr. Thilwell."

"You have to call me Randi."

"Okay … *Randi.*"

When the server came over, Randi glanced at Miguel's glass and said, "Sam Adams, right? I'll have a Tennent's Lager."

"You live in Boston and don't drink Sam Adams?"

Randi just smiled and shrugged. They made small talk while waiting for Randi's beer to arrive. After she had thanked the server, Miguel told her how impressed he'd been with Eli. Randi agreed that he was amazing.

After several more seconds of silence, Miguel broke into an explanation. "Okay, I'll start. I'm going to tell you something pretty wild, but every word is true."

He then proceeded to tell her everything. The feeling of trust he had developed at their first meeting returned here, and he held nothing back. He started with the email cleanup and the meeting in Los Angeles. He told her about his meeting with Steven and his subsequent adventures. He brought in Jenna's inclusion and her arriving from Canada. He told her of the attempt on her life and the death of her sister. He went over the deaths of the Matthews representatives that had opened the email. He explained how he had hacked into the Matthews system and what he had found. He told her about the files he had copied, all the information about the membership list, the budget, the payouts, the termination list, everything. He finished by telling her how Steven had opened the email and copied the chemical formulas onto a USB stick—a stick Steven now had in his possession. Throughout it all, Randi just listened. She did not interrupt him once, or even show much emotion. She just took it all in. Miguel went on to explain why he had called her and why he had wanted to possibly track down Dr. Byers. By the time he had finished with everything, they were on to their second beer each, and there was a pause before Randi spoke.

"Is that it?"

"Is that it? Isn't that *enough?* I mean I don't think much more could be crammed into the last few days."

"No, no, Miguel. I just- I want to make sure I've heard everything."

"Yes, everything."

"So, obviously Matthews and the other companies are going to great lengths to hide something—something very big."

"Huge."

"Yes, huge. And your friends are coming here to meet you?"

"Yes, we're meeting tomorrow at four up in Hoboken."

"Hoboken? Why Hoboken?"

"I don't know. I thought we should meet outside New York City."

"Oh, okay then. Listen, can I come with you? I'd love to get a look at those chemical entities your friend has on that stick."

"Randi, people who look at that get killed. Or at least they go on a hit list. I was thinking that if you could just tell me how to get in touch with Dr. Byers, we'd call it even."

"Well, your friends are not dead. You're not dead. And I might be the kind of person who can decipher those chemical entities. And I'm sure as hell the only person who can put you in touch with Alex—ah, Dr. Byers. So, what do you say?"

Miguel nodded.

CHAPTER 66

JENNA HAD been driving for the last three hours. She was due for a break but had enjoyed the quiet time. Steven and Nathan had fallen asleep an hour or so ago, and she had not put on the radio. She had just driven and been alone with her thoughts.

She had oscillated between thinking about the events of the last several days, what they meant, and her feeling of loss. Her sister had been alive only a week ago, and now, like their parents, she was gone. Jenna and her sister had leaned on each other following their parents' deaths. They had inherited a large sum of money as well as their parents' house, which they'd sold within two months of taking possession. Neither of them wanted for money. Jenna had locked her inheritance into some rock-solid investment funds while Janine had invested some of it but had taken a chunk to finance some adventures of her own. She'd been on the last couple of weeks of her time off when she'd been killed. Now Jenna had inherited Janine's estate, but she knew she would not keep it. She had already thought of a few charities to give it to. But the feeling of being an orphan, all alone, was overwhelming at times. It was an eerie feeling.

She had come to Seattle out of anger and a need to find out more about what and who killed her sister. Meeting up with Steven and Nathan had swung her thoughts and feelings away from her orphaned state. The whole episode had been crazily therapeutic. She had not liked Steven at all after first meeting him, but she did not quite know why. She had liked Nathan a lot. He was quirky and funny and exactly what she would have wanted her brother to be if she'd had one. However, getting to know Steven better had been illuminating and easy. There was a sense of familiarity and trust with him. He was easy to talk to, and they had done so for hours on end. She had noticed him giving her looks in the car and found that quite pleasant. It was an odd time to be thinking about this sort of thing, but the quiet in the car had established its own agenda, and she just followed it.

But she did come back to their matter at hand. What *had* they discovered? There was the stick with the chemical formulas. She had recognized some of them as derivatives of existing agents, but that was it. There was Miguel's discovery of an association of drug companies that seemed to have a covert infrastructure dedicated to … to what exactly? How did it all fit together? There was Dr. Byers, who had disappeared many years ago after seemingly making a huge discovery. What had happened to his research? And now Miguel had visited Eli and seen his amazing recovery. How did it all mesh? Why the infrastructure supported by billions of dollars? Why the abandonment of promising research? Why the need to kill people? They had lots of questions but no answers. Hopefully, after they met with Miguel later today, they'd have at least a few.

CHAPTER 67

SLATER WAS sitting in his office when there was a knock at his door. Without waiting for an answer, Alman opened the door and walked in. He had a file folder with him, and he sat down in the chair opposite Slater.

"Is that the report of their movements?"

"Yes, it is. I don't know how you got this, but we have been tracking them via their E-ZPass access on various toll highways. How did you get this information?"

Slater waved his hand to dismiss further questions. "What have you got?"

"Well, after the three west coasters left Minneapolis, we tracked them through several highway tolls. As you thought, they appear to be heading towards New York State. We don't have any other credit-card transactions, but their toll information has them heading this way. They seem to be coming to meet with this Benetto guy."

"Any news on him?"

"Yeah, and it's odd." Alman furrowed his brow and rubbed his chin.

"Odd? How's that?"

"Well, this guy takes a huge risk, hacking into our system right here in the building. He plans it out well and even plans his escape. He then goes off the grid. We don't pick up anything from him until his E-ZPass info has him heading to Boston—or at least *seeming* to be heading to Boston. We couldn't figure out why he would head there, so we waited to see if he popped up anywhere else. I mean, his bio on file doesn't mention anything about him knowing anyone in Boston, so we were just guessing he was going there, but I think we were right, or at least pretty close because—and this is the weirder thing…"

Slater closed his eyes. *Boston, Alex Byers, Randi Thilwell… shit.* He leaned forward in his chair and grabbed Alman's arm. He did not want to give away anything in his facial expression. "What's the weirder thing?"

"Well, his E-ZPass recorded a toll pay on the highway heading to Plymouth."

"Plymouth? What the hell is in Plymouth?"

"We don't know. Do you?"

Slater did not know. They had buttoned up Alex Byers within days of finding out about his research work. He knew about Randi Thilwell as a close associate of Byers, and that she was still at Harvard. But why would Benetto go there? Suspecting it was getting fairly late in the evening, he glanced at his watch. It was quarter past nine. He had to go. He had work to do. Fast.

"Thanks. We're done here. You can see yourself out."

CHAPTER 68

IT WAS ten to four when Steven pulled the car into the parking lot of the pub Randi had chosen for their meeting, having taken over the driving from Jenna a few hours prior. Nathan's GPS system had neatly guided them to their meeting point.

Miguel and Randi pulled in just as Steven, Jenna, and Nathan were getting out of their car. Miguel gave a short pip on his car horn, and the three of them jumped like they had springs loaded into the soles of their shoes.

"Still a little jumpy, I guess," Miguel noted.

Randi shot him a look that said, *"Duh. Ya think?"*

After he parked, Miguel and Randi got out and walked towards the other three. He saw them staring intently at Randi and realized that he had not told them she would be coming.

"Steven," he said, extending his hand. "How are you holding up?"

"Okay, I guess. This is Jenna Boyd," he said, motioning to Jenna, "and this is Nathan."

Miguel shook Jenna's hand and said how sorry he was about her sister. Jenna said nothing but bit her lower lip. He then shook Nathan's hand and turned towards Randi.

"Everyone, this is Dr. Randi Thilwell from Harvard. She was a close associate of Dr. Byers."

Randi could sense their apprehension, but undeterred, she smiled broadly and introduced herself to the group. "Hi, everybody. It's nice to meet you all and see you in one piece. Miguel has told me about your ordeal."

Although she was new to the group and unexpected, she generated that same sense of trust Miguel had felt, immediately relaxing the group.

Affiliation

They went inside the pub and took a seat near the back where it was quiet. Once they had sat down and ordered, Miguel began. "I've told Randi everything about what we've stumbled into. She's seen the files I uh ... borrowed from Matthews Pharma." He patted his laptop. "She'll take us to see Dr. Byers once we've finished here."

The three of them looked at Randi, wide-eyed. "Yes, I know where he is, and we'll go visit him to see if he can shed any light on this, but I'm very interested to see that USB stick you've got, Steven."

"Yeah, I guess that's the next logical step." Steven reached into his jacket pocket and an immediate look of shock swept over his face. He pulled his hand out of his pocket. "It's gone!"

The others looked aghast and began to all speak at once. That's when Steven broke into a big grin and chuckled. "Here it is," he said, holding up his other hand. Everyone fell back into their chairs with a sigh.

Jenna punched Steven in the arm. "You ass!"

"Just a little levity," he said as he noticed Jenna give him an extra look and a smile.

Nathan looked at Steven with a deadpan expression and said cooly, "That was *very* little levity."

Randi took the stick and plugged it into Miguel's laptop. She quickly accessed the files and zeroed in on the Parkinson's heading. She opened it and the chemical formulation flashed up on the screen. "This is Alex's work! Here's the drug we used on Eli."

Randi then moved back to the main menu and called up the tab for a lengthy list of chronic diseases. She scrolled down Alzheimer's, amyolateral sclerosis, arthritis, bipolar disorder, colitis, depression, diabetes... On and on the list went, down through schizophrenia towards the end of the alphabet of disease names.

"There are a shitload of disease states listed here," she said.

Miguel knew better, but the others were a tad surprised by her word choice. She certainly did not fit their mold of a typical research scientist. Randi then scrolled back up and clicked on Alzheimer's, then immediately sat forward in her seat.

"I know about these two compounds. They were developed by Keith Fulman out at Stanford. I remember reading a scientific poster at a VasCog conference about six years ago. It was really cutting-edge stuff back then, and I haven't seen anything to match it since." She was clearly excited. She was focused solely on the computer screen, blotting everything else out. Her words were coming fast and furious. "He was using existing compounds that treat the symptoms of the disease and combined them with agents that target beta amyloid and tau protein to try to create plaque busters that might boost their effectiveness to create a disease-modifying agent. He was also tinkering with monoclonal antibodies and stem cells. His poster reported on a small study of sixteen Alzheimer's patients, all over sixty-five years of age, who had MMSE scores ranging from nine to thirteen. They took his compound for one month, and then he checked on them one, three, and six months later. The patients' MMSE scores improved to a range of twenty-six to thirty. It was just fantastic! I talked to him about the results, but he was being very cautious and would not disclose anything more about his research. It sounded brilliant though!" She was clearly excited as she finished and slightly out of breath.

Her head snapped up to look at her new friends then, their expressions ranging from bewilderment and confusion to sheepishness. Randi sat back and let out a loud laugh. "I've gone a little fast, haven't I? I can do that when I get going." She then explained that the current treatment for Alzheimer's consisted of drugs that simply treat the symptoms of the disease, like memory loss, loss of mental acuity and functioning, poor cognition, and some behavioral changes. They did nothing to halt its progression, nor did they change the eventual outcome: death. They did help to preserve a sufferer's personality for a while, but many patients experienced no benefit at all from the drugs. Additionally, the drugs had to be taken every day for the rest of the patient's life, and they were very expensive. Even so, the companies who sold the drugs had done a good job of convincing doctors to use them. An MMSE, or Mini Mental Status Exam, was a test widely used to assess someone's level of cognitive function. A score of thirteen and lower meant that the patient was in the severe stage of the disease and did not have that much time left. A perfect score, one that Jenna, Steven, Nathan, Miguel, and herself should get, was thirty out of thirty. Although the cause of Alzheimer's was poorly understood, a lot of research efforts were focusing on tau protein and beta amyloid, which were thought to lead to the build-up of tangles and plaques that deposit themselves in the brain and cause its deterioration. Dr.

Affiliation

Fulman's work had taken the existing drugs and built on the compounds currently being researched, as well as the monoclonal antibodies and stem cells. It looked as though he might have come up with a successful agent that could reverse the effects of the disease. What was even more fascinating, for Randi, was that after that single month of therapy, the patients stopped taking the compound yet still showed its benefits five months later. But he would not allow anyone to get a good look at his research.

"Where is he now?" Jenna asked.

"He's dead. He died in a car accident about a month after I saw him at that conference."

All five of them looked at one another. It was one of those 'My God' moments. Miguel grabbed the computer and opened his files. He went to the tab marked 'Termination List.' He scrolled down and then stopped. There was Dr. Fulman's name, complete with a date beside it.

Randi just stared at it, opened mouthed for a moment, and then said, "I can't believe this. I mean ... I just can't believe this."

"Oh my god," said Jenna. "He was killed."

"It would seem so," offered Steven, "but it just seems too surreal to imagine."

Randi was as shocked as everyone else but tried to maintain an analytical viewpoint. "Why would they kill him? Why not just pay him off like ... like Alex?" She hated the thought that Alex had accepted some big payoff and abandoned his work. "They paid off Alex and a whole host of others, as noted in Miguel's files. My only guess is that one or more of these companies wanted to exercise their control clause over the research to develop the compounds themselves. Alex and the other payoffs named a price, and then paid it. Keith must have been independently funded and dug his heels in, not agreeing to sell, and so they just killed him and took the research anyway."

"What do you mean by a control clause?" Jenna asked. "I thought Dr. Byers was independently funded."

"He was. He was funded entirely by the university for a very long time. But without any real results, the university was threatening to take away his funding and devote it to more promising research. That was many, many years ago, and that's when Alex went out and made a deal with a Big Pharma company to get funding. He had to make some sacrifices to get it though, ones that I will never make."

All four of the others just looked at Randi, willing her to continue.

"When a drug company gives money for research outside of its cozy confines, they insist you use their software for data collection, reporting purposes, etcetera. It's all linked to their mainframe. I've always seen that as an intrusion into the integrity of the work. I'll never do it, but Alex agreed. We argued about it, but he rationalized it by saying that they were just protecting their investment and intellectual-property rights."

"I'm still lost," interrupted Steven. "You mentioned a control clause and different types of funding, but I just don't get it."

Randi went into an explanation about pharma-funded research. She outlined that drug companies have their own in-house research, but that in recent years, they had been increasing their reach into university-based and other independent research projects with money. Fifteen years prior, pharma funding of independent research had been around six hundred and seventy million dollars. Now it was over six billion dollars. That increase in funding came with a price to the researcher or institution. Because pharma were all about commercialization of product, they controlled all the clinical-trial work. They set the study protocols, and when the results came in, they not only controlled the publication of the results but could also skew the findings to favor their product—and they had. She detailed how they constantly monitored the research. If data collection was too slow, they made "suggestions" on how to speed things up. This could result in sloppy methods, which could lead to mistakes or omissions that didn't reveal what researchers really needed to know about the drug being investigated. She believed that the deeper Big Pharma crept into independent research, the greater the risk was of getting a product on the market that did more harm than good.

"Just look at two examples," she said, "Vioxx from Merck and Zyprexa from Eli Lilly. Both products were in-house developments. Vioxx was for arthritis, and Zyprexa is used to treat Schizophrenia and other related disorders. Both companies hid or downplayed certain side effects from the FDA in order to win marketing approval. Merck hid the drug's negative cardiac effect, and Lilly downplayed a major effect of their drug that caused huge weight gain in people who took it. The weight gain from Zyprexa leads to a host of other problems, from diabetes to cardiovascular problems. Because both drugs were under the control of the drug company themselves, they could manipulate the data from their clinical trials to meet their own needs. Both got approved. Vioxx was pulled from the market, and Lilly has been successfully sued for hundreds of millions of dollars due to Zyprexa's weight-gain and marketing issues. But they made it to the market because the drug company controlled the information." Randi went on to state that she feared university research would also be compromised the more drug companies intruded into their independence with big money.

"Why would universities agree to accept pharma funding if it compromised their independence and integrity?" asked Jenna.

Randi sighed. "Because it takes pressure off their budgets and can reap huge financial windfalls. A university has no idea how to commercialize a product, so they use the drug-company expertise to do it for them, and it can be very lucrative."

"How lucrative?" Miguel asked.

"Well ..." Randi paused, "just look at something as innocuous as Gatorade. The University of Florida has made around one hundred million dollars since it went to market. Now imagine what a major pharmaceutical product could make and what the returns to the university would be if they commercialized a product in tandem with Big Pharma."

Miguel jumped in. "But isn't the FDA supposed to guard against sloppy data collecting or whatever, and the bad side effects?"

"That's right," Randi answered, "but they can only assess what they're given. Just remember Vioxx and Zyprexa."

"So, you're saying that drug companies hide negative data to suit their needs." It was a comment from Nathan and seemed more an assessment than a question.

"Sure, they do," Randi answered. "That's why I've stayed away from pharma drug money. I almost signed on three years ago but backed out."

"Why?" Jenna's voice was quiet. She was trying to process everything she had just heard.

"Because I remembered something Alex said to me. He told me to be very careful of how I conduct myself in research, especially where I get my funding. And a day later, he was gone."

Nathan frowned. "So, Dr. Fulman must have kept his research to himself. But now that he's dead, it must still be going on somewhere, mustn't it?"

Randi shrugged. "You know, that's something I've thought about a lot … because it's very odd."

"How so?" asked Nathan.

"Well, if Keith had kept his research away from Big Pharma and stuck to the university funding, then it would have reverted to the university after he died, but I haven't heard or seen any further results at any conference, or in online scientific share sites, or anywhere else for that matter. And what's more, I asked one of Keith's colleagues about this and was told that the research work had vanished. He thought Keith must have taken it out of the university computer system before he died and stored it somewhere else. I remember him saying how sad he was not only for Keith's death but that his paranoia and secrecy around his research had caused some real breakthrough work to disappear."

"Maybe so," Jenna said, "but it happens to be here in *this* database we've got, which means Dr. Fulman *didn't* take it out of the computer system. So, how did it vanish from the university and why isn't the research continuing?"

Randi sat back thought for a moment. "Those, my dear Jenna, are very good questions."

CHAPTER 69

JENNA LOOKED again at Randi. "The fact that Dr. Fulman's research has disappeared coincides exactly with what I discovered about Dr. Byers. All of his research work disappeared when he did. I told the guys here that I could only find references to Dr. Byers's work in the lay press. His work on Parkinson's has just vanished."

Miguel looked at Jenna. "Yeah, I guess his work has disappeared. But given the depth of what I found, it may not actually be that odd."

Randi turned to Miguel. "Mig, can you bring up those formulas again?"

"Sure." He had them up on his screen in a flash.

Randi scrolled to the amyolateral sclerosis file and opened it. "This is interesting." Sensing the group's oncoming question, she continued. "This work is using monoclonal antibodies to treat ALS. It was also used in Keith Fulman's work in Alzheimer's, and …" Her voice trailed off.

"And what?" all four asked at the same time.

"Parkinson's."

"The three conditions are linked by this formula?" Nathan asked. "By *this* work?"

"Yes. This work in ALS came out of Austria. I know these guys, or at least I know the scientists who did the work on this compound." Randi's voice could not hide her excitement. "They must have shared their work with Keith and Alex!"

Steven asked, "Where are these scientists now?"

Randi just looked at Miguel, who wore a defeated look. He did not want to look back in his 'Affiliation' file, but he opened it up anyway. He went to the 'Terminated' file and opened that up. The other four just watched as he slowly scrolled down the list of names. It was like looking at a 'killed in action' list from an armed conflict or war.

Miguel kept scrolling until Randi pointed her finger at the screen. "There they are! Those are the scientists from Austria." The names of three men were written, one after another, each with a date beside their name.

"I just don't understand," Jenna commented. "How can all these men and women, who are so big in their fields of research, up and die and there's nothing? No alarms are raised? I don't get it."

"Well, think about it," offered Randi. "These men and women are scattered all over the world. They died at very different times, and I'm guessing, in a number of different ways. Why would any of that raise a question? We're not talking about killing off a bunch of whistleblowers in close succession. Just a bunch of dumb accidents."

Everyone nodded that what she'd said made sense.

Randi jumped in again. "I think we have to go see Alex. These companies are controlling cutting-edge research and not *doing* anything with it, *and* they're killing people and getting away with it. This needs to be brought to light. I mean, these compounds could be helping millions of people around the world. We—*I* need to know why Alex just up and gave up on his research and why he took off. Once and for all … I need to know." The resolve in her voice gave the others a jolt of confidence, though none of them knew how long it would last.

"Okay," Jenna said. "So, where is he and how do we get there?"

Randi looked at them all. "We need to get to JFK. Do you all have your passports?"

CHAPTER 70

AFTER SLATER had seen Alman out of his office, he placed a call to his contact at Homeland Security. He had already told him that his four wayward employees might try to leave the country and might try it soon. The Homeland contact said that he would put out an alert for their passports, and that they would be detained. Slater told him not to do that but to let him know what country their passports were being ticketed for. He also told him that there was probably a fifth person with them at this point. He let him know that he thought the probable destination was Barbados. Now, Slater wanted to know if they'd checked in with their passports, and to confirm Barbados as their destination. If the group decided to get to Dr. Byers, then this could work out very well for Slater. The police in Barbados were loathe to attribute any tourist deaths as anything other than accidents. He could arrange for the five of them to be taken out quickly. He placed a call to Ben and Colin and told them to get themselves to Barbados as fast as they could. He explained to them that there were now five people in this group and that all five had to be taken out as fast as possible once they reached the island nation. He told them about Dr. Randi Thilwell and that she was among the five to be taken out.

"How do we know what this Thilwell person looks like?" asked Colin.

"For one thing," Slater said, rolling his eyes, "when you find the four, the fifth person with them is likely to be Dr. Thilwell, and for another thing, she is fairly well known, so why don't you just Google her and get her picture?" He shook his head. *They may be good at what they do, but man, they are not that bright.*

"Do you want us to get that stick or whatever from them?" Ben asked.

"At this point, I don't care about that. Just get them and take them out. I'm sending you some address coordinates where I'm sure you'll find them. Hell, you might even beat them there. Now get moving."

This was not the first time that Slater had engaged their services without the knowledge of Mr. Alman. It always came with a premium price point, but it had been worth it. As Denman had pointed out at their meeting, he should act boldly when the time was right, and now the time was right. He needed these people taken out either before they got to Byers or before they left after meeting with him. He'd deal with the publicity afterwards, as well as any Affiliation fall out.

Before he left his office, he checked his Cayman Island bank account, which noted forty-five million dollars on deposit. He could live on that in a non-extradition country forever if push came to shove. He left the office for home.

CHAPTER 71

THE FIVE new companions stayed in Hoboken for the night. They were confident they were not being tracked, but they did post a rotating lookout outside the two motel rooms they'd rented, just in case.

In the morning, they set off for the drive back to New York and JFK airport. They had booked five seats on a three o'clock flight to Barbados, as Randi had let them in on the fact that this was where Alex Byers had been for the past many years.

Once they got to JFK, they used valet parking to minimize any chance of meeting anyone from Matthews in the parking lot, despite the complaints from Nathan.

"This is just so expensive!"

"Nate, we are on a life-and-death mission here," Steven told him. "When you are on a life-and-death mission, you don't worry about the extra money for valet parking."

They got into the airport and made their way to the automated check-in for their airline. All went well. Once they got through security and into the departures section, they quickly found where their gate was and relaxed a little, but Steven kept looking around with his head on a swivel.

Jenna gently touched his arm. "Steven, what's wrong? What are you looking for?"

"Not so much 'what,'" he replied. "More like *who.*"

"Oh, we haven't seen them since we left Seattle. I think all our maneuvering has them stumped. I don't think they thought we would be as resourceful as we turned out to be."

"I don't know. We haven't seen them since Seattle, but I still *cannot* figure out why. Yes, we were resourceful, but I just don't buy that they're gone."

"Well, try to relax. If you're too uptight, you might actually miss something."

CHAPTER 72

AFTER BEN and Colin had hung up with Slater, they'd googled Dr. Randi Thilwell and got her picture. *What a shame,* they both thought. This was not the first time they had been asked to go on a special assignment by Slater. Previously, it had meant taking out just one person, quickly and quietly. This time was different in that they were being asked to take out five, but that was not a problem. The price went up with the urgency of the job. They had checked the flights to Barbados and only found red-eye flights.

"I really don't want to go on a red-eye," Colin had complained.

So, they'd booked a flight for three in the afternoon, leaving from JFK with direct service to Barbados.

They had left for the airport with plenty of time but had not checked any traffic updates for their route. There had been a major traffic accident, and they were sitting in traffic well away from the airport.

"What the hell are we going to do about this?" Colin asked.

"Nothing. If we miss the flight, we'll book another one. We know where they're going to be, so once we're there, we can get to the address and wait."

Just then, the phone rang, and Ben answered. "Hello?"

"It's Alman. I just got a call from Slater. The five of them are on the three o'clock to Barbados. You guys are booked on that one, right?"

"We are."

"Well, make sure you get on that flight. They'll have nowhere to go, and you can grab them right out of the airport. Quick and easy."

"Okay. We're on it." Both men went back to sitting in traffic.

After a frustratingly long delay due to the traffic accident, they got to the airport at 2:25 for their 3:00 flight. They skipped the automated check-in, ran up to a ticketing agent, and showed him their credentials.

Affiliation

"We're late for our three o'clock flight to Barbados. Can we still make it?"

"We actually close international flights one hour before departure, and it is now nearly two-thirty, so I think you've missed it. But there is another flight leaving at midnight. There'll be no extra charge for changing, as we know you can't control traffic. Do you want me to book you both on that flight?"

Colin cut in quickly. "You don't understand. We have a family member down there, and he's not well. We want to go down there and see him before he goes. He may not last until tomorrow morning."

The agent eyed them both and picked up the phone.

"Hi, it's Paul in ticketing. I have a couple of runners here who would really like to get on the three o'clock to Barbados. They have a family situation that requires them to be their tonight. Can we get them on it? Can you delay things a little?"

Colin and Ben watched as the agent stayed on the phone, nodding and mumbling the occasional "uh huh." Then he hung up.

"Well, it seems we can delay things a little for you today. We have called one of our concierge agents to come and escort you both through security and take you to the gate. You should be good to go."

Both men nodded. "Thank you."

It was 2:35 p.m.

CHAPTER 73

THE FIVE friends sat in the departures lounge waiting for the call for their flight. An attendant came over the loudspeaker, indicating that they were now ready for boarding, and the group stood up and made their way to their seating zone for their boarding sequence. They slowly made their way towards the gate agent, with Steven first in line and close to the agent's desk. He watched as an agent sitting behind the desk picked up the phone.

"What's that? A couple of runners? How long of a delay? That might be problematic because the captain has informed us that he wants to get off as quickly as possible as there's some weather closing in that could potentially really screw up this flight.... Oh, all right. We'll see what we can do." She then picked up her walkie-talkie and connected with the in-flight crew supervisor.

"We've got a couple of runners who really want to make this flight. We may have to slow things down a little and delay your departure. They should be on their way, and I was told it won't be long. Will you please inform the captain? I'll keep you posted."

Steven nervously listened in on the conversation. *What is this about?*

After they had showed their boarding passes and were on the jetway towards the plane, Jenna placed her hand on his shoulder. "What's wrong?" she whispered.

"That agent, she said that we're going to be delayed because of two late arrivals, two runners."

"So?"

"Well, our would-be assassins were a pair, weren't they?"

"Oh, Steve, come on. I think you're being overly nervous. We haven't had any signs we're being followed." Jenna's voice was comforting, but he remained nervous. They walked on the plane and went towards their seats.

It was 2:40 p.m.

CHAPTER 74

SLATER WAS driving home, convinced he had his bases covered. Everything was in motion, and he had acted boldly. He was running through scenarios of how to explain things to the Affiliation, but he thought that would be fairly easy, especially given that the threat of a breach would be over, even without the stick. The five people would be taken out in Barbados. He had given instructions for the bodies to be disposed of, so they would not be found for at least awhile. They would just disappear. Their families would fret, wonder, and file missing-person's reports. They might even go to Barbados to investigate, but that would all be a longshot. Eventually, things would quiet down, and they'd all go home. A tragic trip for those five poor souls. He had things under control.

It was 2:40 p.m.

CHAPTER 75

THE CONCIERGE ran with Colin and Ben up to the security line. It was extremely busy, but she just hurtled past dozens of disgruntled-looking passengers up to the front of the line. She quickly explained the situation to the airport security guard, and he waved them over to a scanner where they promptly came to a halt. They were waiting behind five people, and both men bounced on their toes, rocking back and forth.

"Can't we move to the front of this line?" asked Ben.

The concierge gave them a look. "We're not supposed to at this point, but I'll pop up there and see what I can do."

Once there, she spoke quickly with the agent and then waved the men up front. Both men apologized to the individuals they passed, and once they got to the head of the line, they quickly took off their shoes and belts, emptied their pockets, and walked through the security scanner. Colin went first and was waved along. Ben went right after, and a red light went off and a bell sounded.

"Excuse me, sir, but do you have any metal on you?"

"No, I don't," Ben answered honestly.

"Well, we can do a pat down, or you can step into the full body scanner for a full scan."

"I'll do the full body scan."

Ben stepped into the machine, raised his arms on cue, and the scanner whirred to life. The technician viewing the scan let it finish. The door swung open, and he gave Ben the thumbs up.

Ben quickly grabbed his belongings and bent down to put on his shoes.

"Do you really want to take the time to do that?" the concierge asked.

"Yeah, this airport carpet and floor is filthy. It will take two seconds."

Once he had his shoes back on, they took off.

It was 2:55 p.m.

CHAPTER 76

ON THE plane, Steven was becoming increasingly convinced that they were in trouble. He kept glancing at his watch, seeing the minutes tick away, and alternately glanced up towards the front door, willing it to shut. He varied those glances by looking out the seat window. He had a good view of the jetway, which was still connected to the plane. He again glanced at this watch. It was 3:05 p.m.

"Should we get off this thing? Try another flight later on?"

"Steven, we're fine," Jenna assured him. "I'm sure these latecomers are not our friends. We'll push back soon."

Just then, the captain came on the intercom. "Sorry about this delay, folks. We're waiting on two late passengers. When they make it on board, I want everyone to clap as they make their way to their seats—just to properly acknowledge that we know they held us up."

In the cockpit, the captain and the co-pilot were becoming impatient due to the delay.

The captain checked in with air traffic control. "How big is that weather system off the east coast, and how fast is it moving?"

"It's a very large system. It's moving quickly in a northeast trajectory. In another five or ten minutes, we'll have to ground you as you won't be able to skirt around it."

The captain looked at the co-pilot and said, "That's it, my call. I'm not delaying 285 people until tomorrow morning because two numbskulls couldn't get to the airport on time. Air traffic control, this is United 8375 heavy. This is my call to go. Do we have permission to push back?"

"United 8375 heavy, that's affirmative. Clear to push back."

The captain then buzzed the in-flight service director. "Yes, Captain?"

"That's it. This is my call. Runners or not, we're pushing back and getting on our way. Let's close up."

The service director put the phone down and signalled to the jetway crew that they were closing the door to push back. She then did exactly that. It was 3:10 p.m.

In his seat, Steven saw the activity and heard the front door close. So did Jenna.

"There. You see? We're on our way, and no one is attached to us or following us."

"We're haven't pushed back yet."

Just then, the plane lurched forward and began to ease backwards from its station at the gate. Steven looked out his window and noticed the jetway had been pulled back, and they were, indeed, moving backwards. He felt a wave of relief sweep over him and glanced at his watch. It was 3:12 p.m. He looked out his window again, then leaned into the glass, peering intently at the window in front of the departures lounge. Finally, he pushed back in his seat and grabbed Jenna's arm.

"What? We're on our way. What's the matter now?"

He pointed out his window, and she followed the direction of his finger towards the departures window. Then she froze as she saw Colin and Ben standing behind the window, looking at their plane. The men in the airport then turned and seemed to be yelling at a uniformed United employee with a deer-in-the-headlights look about her.

IN THE lounge, Ben was seething, and leaned in close to the concierge. "You said—you *assured us* that we would make this flight."

Just then, one of the gate agents jumped to the defense of her colleague. "Gentlemen, this was a weather-related decision. There is a big system moving up the coast. Air traffic control and the captain wanted to get going, otherwise they were going to be grounded until tomorrow morning."

The concierge looked at both men, and although oddly, she felt scared silly just looking at them, she mustered her nerve and responded. "Well, this was the captain's call. We are very sorry. I hope you understand that we did everything we could to get you on it. We can't control the weather. I would be more than happy to book you on our first available flight out in the morning. We will, of course, offer you a no-charge upgrade to business class, and we'll pay for your meals tonight and a one-night stay at the airport hotel."

Colin looked at the concierge. "Keep that offer open for another five or ten minutes please. We have to make a phone call first."

It was 3:15 p.m.

CHAPTER 77

SLATER HUNG up the phone and rolled his eyes at what he had just heard:

"We missed the three o'clock flight down to Barbados. There's another one at midnight on another airline, or we can wait and go out tomorrow morning at nine." Colin had delivered the news with as much professional stoicism as he could muster, knowing it would not be well received.

"I'm not going to engage in speculation as to how you could have missed a flight at three in the afternoon after having all day to get to the airport. Are you at the airport now or have you gone out for a nice dinner?"

Colin pulled the phone away from his ear at the sarcasm but answered calmly. "We're still here waiting for further instructions."

Slater gave him clear instructions to leave the airport and provided directions to an independent airfield. He told them to call him when they'd arrived. With that, he hung up, but his phone rang right away … before he had even finished rolling his eyes about the fiasco at the airport. He picked up the phone again.

"We got another hit on their passports." It was Homeland Security. "They were waved at the gate and boarded the plane. It's wheels up."

"Are you sure they boarded the plane?"

"Once they get waved at the jetway entrance, they cannot come off unless their passport gets waved again, having deplaned. So, yes, I'm sure they're on their way to Barbados. Are they going on a vacation?" The attempt at humor did not sit well with Slater.

"I don't think so," he deadpanned.

"Hey, how did you know going in that they'd be going to Barbados?"

"Just a lucky guess. My wife and I have taken that flight in the past."

"Well, I can have authorities waiting for them when they land. They'll be detained."

Slater did not want any further government involvement given what he had to do. "No, that's fine. I've always wanted to handle this internally. I truly believe that this has been a huge misunderstanding. If we can just connect with them, we can sort this out and bring them back to the Matthews family."

"Your call."

After hanging up, he thought for a second. *Bold moves. Decisive actions. That's what is called for. That's what the Affiliation members expect from their leader.* What he was about to do was a gamble. If it paid off, he was golden. If it didn't, there was always the Caymans. He veered his car towards the first exit and headed back towards New York, even as he placed a call.

"I won't be home tonight," he said to his wife when she answered, listening for a moment and nodding along to some minor grumbling. "I know. I'm sorry about the late notice. An emergency has come up, and I have to fly out tonight. Hopefully, it's a short trip, and I'll be home in one or two days … No, I don't need to pack anything. I left an overnight fully packed on the company plane … I know, and I'm sorry about this. Give the kids a kiss for me. I love you."

He drove towards the airstrip to which he'd directed Colin and Ben. The Matthews corporate jet was waiting. He'd call ahead, book the pilot, and give him their destination. He also made the decision to call Alman and invite him along. They may need more muscle than Colin and Ben could provide, and they certainly needed more brains. He also made the decision to let Alman in on what was on the stick—what Miguel had stolen. He had realized during this breach that he needed a right-hand man to cover for him if this ever happened again.

He, and the Affiliation, needed someone in the know who would protect their secret at a moment's notice, even if Affiliation members were not around to direct the action. He knew Alman was keenly suspicious about what was behind the computer system and why he was periodically ushered out of rooms. Alman had cornered Slater some months back and demanded to know what was going on. And he'd had a point. One doesn't hire people of Alman's background to monitor employees. People had been terminated. Bland recitations about intellectual-property rights and covert-competitive operations just did not cut it. Alman had backed off and been a good soldier after that, but it was time, and Slater was just the right leader to bring him fully into the fold. *And*, Slater thought, *having an extra ally that no one but me knows about could come in handy down the road. Plus, he'll be another person close to the secret that can be blamed if necessary and hung out to dry, thus protecting me and the Affiliation's secret.*

He turned into the airstrip and parked his car.

It was 3:50 p.m.

CHAPTER 78

THE UNITED flight touched down at quarter past seven in the evening. The captain had been keeping the passengers updated along the way, and they'd been able to make up all of the delay and then some.

The five new friends were nervous and strangely excited about being in the place where Alex Byers would hopefully meet with them. Each of them had their own entry point into this mystery. Each had their own motivation to get involved. Each had their own desire to stay in the chase. And each had their own reason to stay the course.

On the flight down, they had met at the back of the plane a couple of times to discuss things, sharing in hushed tones not only what they thought they would learn from Dr. Byers but also guesses as to what was really going on. Why the massive underground infrastructure? Why the murders? Why the payoffs? Why the monitoring? What are the chemical formulas? Could they be dangerous to people's health?

What Miguel had uncovered made them think of some CIA-like organization, but this was the pharmaceutical industry, not organized crime, even though what they had uncovered was indeed a crime.

They all felt Dr. Byers could help them. Perhaps he could even close the loop, as Nathan had put it. They also knew that Colin and Ben were back on their trail. They'd estimated they had about twelve hours or so of lead time before those two got down to Barbados. So, they had to make that enough time to get in and get out.

They were excited. They were determined. They were nervous. And they were scared.

They got off the plane and made their way into the airport. They snaked their way through customs, then immigration, and then headed out into the night air to flag a cab. However, before grabbing one, Randi dialled a number.

"Hello, Alex? ... It's me, Randi ... I'm fine. How are you? ... Good. Listen, I'm here in Barbados. I've come down to see you. It's vitally important that I meet with you, and we talk. I know you said never to come, but I'm here, and I *have* to meet with you. And I've brought some friends with me ... They're okay ... They're good, Alex. They're with me—Alex, Alex, wait. We *have* to meet with you. We can explain then. We can be at your house in less than thirty minutes ... Good, see you soon. And don't take off."

As they hailed a taxi, Jenna asked, "What did you mean, 'don't take off'?"

"Yeah, that. One of my colleagues tried to visit him two years ago. It was all set. When he showed up at Alex's house, he'd bolted. They never did meet."

Jenna frowned. "Why did he run?"

"I'm not sure. My colleague said that when he called Alex after arriving here, just like we did, Alex seemed petrified at the thought of a meeting."

"How did he sound just now?"

"Terrified." Randi's tone was deadpan, monotone, and clinical.

CHAPTER 79

ON THE Matthews corporate jet, Slater sat at the back of the plane with Alman. He was still a little dumbfounded about the short conversation he'd had with Colin and Ben as they'd all boarded the plane.

"This is nice," Ben had said. "Why don't we use this for all the jobs you send us on? It would be a lot more convenient and way less hassle. We would never a miss a flight with this thing."

"I'll say," Colin had said, jumping in, "and we wouldn't have to go through the trouble of connecting with those gun dealers every time we landed out of state. This is way better."

Alman had been the first to look away from the pair and over to Slater, who'd just shrugged and rolled his eyes, before he give them the explanation. "Well, you two, how do you think I could hide multiple uses of the Matthews corporate jet, especially given that no one who's 'technically' *from* Matthews Pharmaceuticals would be on the plane. *And,*" he stressed for added emphasis, "there really was *no* apparent *business* reason to be jetting off to the various places we have sent you in the past. Does that make sense?"

Both he and Alman had stared at Ben and Colin, who had just shrugged, after a moment of collective thought, and finished boarding the plane, though not before Colin suddenly whirled around and smugly faced Slater. "Then how are you explaining *this* little flight?"

Slater had stopped in the plane's entrance and looked at Colin with a pitying expression. "Because, dear boy, Matthews has a corporate office in Barbados for tax purposes. So, this is a business trip." At that, the two muscle men had proceeded to plunk themselves into seats at the front of the jet's interior cabin, while Slater and Alman had gone to the very back.

Alman sat looking at Slater, waiting for him to begin. He had been told to get to the airstrip and be ready to head out. Slater had explained that he was going to include Alman in some information that was very secret but that he'd decided Alman now needed to be in the know about. Slater had also hinted at having an extraordinary request that he wanted to "put out there."

"I'm glad you were able to make the flight, Mr. Alman. You know, it has just occurred to me that in the time I have known and worked with you, we have never really had a chance to just sit down and chat, quietly, just the two of us. Funny that."

Alman just looked down at his glass of scotch and then looked up and smiled ever so briefly at Slater.

"What I'm about to tell you," Slater continued, "is not shared or discussed with anyone outside of a very select group of people. The information is passed along person to person, and the chain of exclusivity has never been broken. But I realize now that we need to change this course. We need to include someone like you who can act in a proxy fashion if the time and circumstance ever arises."

"A little like this kind of time and circumstance?"

"Exactly. I'm glad you've picked up on this so quickly. But what I am going to tell you comes with a price. Once I've given you direction, I expect your undivided loyalty, and your unquestioning loyalty."

"Have I not been doing and giving that already?"

"Yes, I suppose you have, but this raises the stakes somewhat." Slater looked keenly at Alman and paused ever so briefly ... if only for effect and his own sense of occasion. "The setup back at Matthews is *not* just about monitoring people and protecting our intellectual-property rights."

Alman looked back at Slater and hoped he conveyed a bemused expression. "I figured as much. I can't think of many other companies that give instructions for people to be taken out just to protect intellectual property."

"Really?" Slater was a little surprised. "I can think of other companies that do that very thing. And governments for that matter. But I digress. The operation back at Matthews does have a lot to do with monitoring and protecting. But there's more. Much more." Slater was clearly the more nervous of the two, and both men knew it. His throat was slightly dry, and his hands were a little sweaty.

Affiliation

"So, are you going to fill me in?"

Slater took a deep breath and checked to make sure Colin and Ben were at the front of the plane. They were both there, each sipping on a beer. Like a man taking a leap of faith or a bungee jump, he nodded and dove in.

"The operation back at HQ is supported by the contributions of sixty-one other pharmaceutical companies besides Matthews. Some are very large, and some are very small. They range from traditional Big Pharma to smaller biotechs. They, or rather, *we* all support an Affiliation. This Affiliation has been around since shortly after the vaccine for Polio was invented and widely distributed. We monitor, check, and buy research, research companies, and companies as a whole that we deem to be a threat to our Affiliation. We buy people, and occasionally, we have to eliminate people. as you have been a party to over the last few years." Slater looked Alman straight in the eye. "Make no mistake, we *are* protecting our intellectual property, but we are also protecting something much greater. Perhaps it's the greatest secret, or secrets, in the history of mankind. Therefore, we must act to eliminate *when* absolutely necessary." Slater could not bring himself to say the word 'kill.'

Slater went on. "It's a secret that needs protecting in order to preserve our way of life. Not my way of life or yours, or the other people who know, but to protect a world order. If we had not been as successful as we have been in protecting this information, and if we do not continue to be successful, the result would be world calamity. A crisis of epic proportions." He stopped and stared down at his scotch glass. Alman eyed him closely but said nothing. "Only the most senior people, the CEOs of each Affiliation company, know the true nature of the operation. Even the company boards do not know. As I said, it is passed from person to person. Each outgoing CEO passes the information onto the next person. It's kind of like the meeting between the outgoing president and the incoming president, to pass along our nation's most closely guarded secrets. You'll be the first person outside of that circle to know what it is that we protect."

"This must be pretty big. I'm surprised it—whatever *it* is—has not been leaked before."

Slater sat back quickly in his chair and waved his right hand dismissively through the air. "Oh we wouldn't. No one would ever." He said this in a rushed but quiet voice. "We all know what would happen if we did. I mean, how many non-sitting presidents have revealed anything of importance after leaving office?"

"You have a point."

Slater then launched into a detailed and methodical description of the operation: the Affiliation. He again began with its creation after Jonas Salk had created a vaccine for polio. He went through the buildup. He talked of the early efforts and how laborious they had been. He described how the Affiliation had grown member by member. He went on to detail the size of the budget and how each company gave a small percentage based on their overall size and their sales volumes for a given year. Each gave an amount that was easy to hide from auditors and that wouldn't raise suspicion internally, but together, everyone's contributions made up the nearly three-billion-dollar overall budget. This money allowed the Affiliation to make smaller purchases and payoffs and run a counterintelligence operation designed to discredit research where necessary and focus prying eyes in other directions when desired.

"I thought we were the nerve center at Matthews," Alman interrupted. "There are other systems like ours?"

"Absolutely. There are not many, mind you. And Matthews is the most important as we deal with the protection and elimination aspect. But there are other affiliate companies that handle other aspects of Affiliation business. You see," he flourished, "it's all very democratic. We all share equally in the risk in order to maximize the reward. The reward, in this case, is the continued secrecy around our main purpose. And in that democratic vein, any CEO of an affiliate company can become head of the Affiliation. We nominate ourselves and then make a case before the entire membership. Each term lasts five years. I was elected four years and eight months ago."

Still without knowing everything, Alman blurted out a question. "What happens if, or when, another person is elected to lead from a different company?"

"Oh, we all have elaborate communication and computer systems. We simply have data and systems transferred to the new lead's company computer system, a system that is separate but tied into the overall computer system of the lead company."

"Tied in? So, that's how this Benetto fellow was able to hack in and get so much information. He must have broken through some firewall between Matthews and your Affiliation system."

"Yes, precisely, and that is something we will have to fix moving forward." Slater ignored the 'so much information' comment and continued, moving on to describe what they were protecting. He went through it, therapeutic area by therapeutic area, disease state by disease state. He described how Dr. Bhergosian had stumbled into their computer system. Alman knew the rest, regarding the elimination of people, and ultimately, their current pursuit of the five people and the USB stick, up ahead of them in the air somewhere.

"Do you think they know what's really on that stick? What they actually have in their possession?"

Slater sat back and tapped his front teeth with his drink's stir stick. "You know, I've thought about that a lot, obviously. I don't think they really know what they have, the full magnitude of it, I mean. Otherwise, they wouldn't be going to see Dr. Byers. I think they're still looking for answers, or at least, for confirmation."

"Who's Dr. Byers?"

Slater realized that he had omitted Alex Byers and his role—or possible role—in all of this. He explained the nature of the doctor's work on Parkinson's and explained the extent to which his work had progressed. He told Alman of how he had been tasked by the former head of the Affiliation to approach Byers and convince him to give up his research, and that failing a genial agreement to do so, Byers's research would be taken away from him. Slater finished by telling Alman of the size of Byers's payoff.

"So, it was big enough to ensure compliance."

"Yes. And there were other inducements offered to make sure Dr. Byers never talked about his research again."

"That's a ton of money to give one man."

"Miniscule compared to what it would cost our affected Affiliation and non-affiliated members if Byers's research was allowed to continue to complete fruition."

"You help non-affiliation members? That's very nice of you."

"Well, sometimes companies, unbeknownst to them, receive a corollary benefit from our vigilance."

"Why haven't any of the paid-off scientists ever talked or continued their work in secret after getting your money?"

"A few reasons. We do monitor their whereabouts, their movements, and their communications. And what would be the point of continuing work you cannot publish or recruit patients for? We'd know if something was being developed."

"Wouldn't it be cheaper to just take them out after you grab their research?"

"I agree that it would. But we are not barbarians. And we have always worried about the publicity if anyone was to link a series of deaths and start poking around. Also, I don't know if the Affiliation would ever stand for it, but lately, especially with this latest breach being so serious, I've been thinking that …"

"You're thinking it might be easier to ask for forgiveness than permission."

Slater looked at Alman, genuinely surprised that he'd anticipated what was coming. Time to act boldly. Decisively. "Exactly. How very perceptive of you."

Here comes the extraordinary request, thought Alman.

Slater stood up and reached out a hand, requesting Alman's glass. He glanced up to the front of the cabin and saw that both Ben and Colin were sleeping, then walked over to the bar and poured scotch into both glasses and plopped in a couple of ice cubes. He returned to the back then and gave Alman his glass before sitting back down.

"So, right now, we have twenty-seven scientists around the world who've been bought out. How difficult would it be to take them all out?"

Alman immediately went into his special-ops mode of thinking. "It wouldn't be that difficult at all. We would need multiple teams and a coordinated effort to get it done. One team per individual, to minimize anyone thinking beyond their own individual task. So, twenty-seven people, twenty-seven teams. Assuming the targets are where they're supposed to be, I'd say it could be done in a matter of days. And the shorter the timeframe, the better."

Slater sat forward. "Why is that?"

"Like I said, it wouldn't be difficult to take someone out, especially an unsuspecting someone. You can make it look like an accident. But if the operation extends beyond a short window, then one of the targets not yet taken might hear about a friend or friends that had been taken and not only call others but try to disappear. Then it gets dicey. Then it could end up being a real shitstorm."

"Okay, I see that. But could you pull something like that together?"

"Yeah, I could. I know enough people. It would take me about a week or two to set everything up, and then once the word is given, I'd put the wheels in motion."

Slater was very boardroom-like, and it struck Alman as odd. He could talk about this sort of thing because he'd done it, albeit in the name of God and country. But a suit like Slater, talking about this in this cold, calculating, boardroom manner? This guy was *cold*.

"We haven't talked about the cost," Alman said then. Slater just gestured with his hand for him to go on. "We'd need one million for each team. There would be travel costs, costs to purchase weapons on the black market, and then there's my fee."

"And what would that be?"

Without hesitation, without even a blink, Alman answered: "A hundred million."

Just then, the captain's voice came over the speaker. "Excuse me, guys, but we're starting our descent. We'll be touching down in twenty minutes. Please buckle in."

CHAPTER 80

THE CAB ferrying the group of five pulled up in front of a small, nondescript bungalow. It was in a quiet neighborhood and stood among rows of similar-looking bungalows on either side of the street. Each had a short stone wall framing its front yard, all of which were populated with the kind of grass always found in Caribbean areas: very green with wide, flat blades that were shortly cropped. The difference between all the other bungalows and the one they now stood in front of was the chain-link fence that attached itself to the top of the stone wall and rose above it another six to eight feet. This was completely out of character with the rest of the homes. At the center of the wall was a gate that, when opened, allowed visitors to walk up a stone pathway to the front door. As the five friends walked up to the gate, they noticed that the chain-link fence extended on both sides of the house and looked to go right around it towards the back. They also noticed a "Beware of Dog" sign on each side of the gate, as well as a security-company name sign. Randi stepped up to the front door and pressed the button on what looked like a call box, which also had a video camera peering out from the top. After hearing a buzz, they waited. Nothing happened. She pressed it again and stood back. Nothing happened.

"You shit, Alex," Randi muttered. "I can't believe you'd blow us off."

"No, someone's here. I saw the curtain move," said Nathan, standing on the path at the back of the group. He had been looking at the large front window.

Randi pressed the buzzer again and this time yelled at the house. "C'mon, Alex! Open up!"

There was a new buzz from inside the house, then a click, and the front door eased slowly open. The four behind Randi could only make out the shape of a person standing in the entranceway, but Randi immediately opened her arms wide and said, "Hello, Alex." She moved through the door's entrance and hugged the figure inside.

The remaining four moved up the steps, walked into the house, and saw a tall man who was very distinguished looking, even though he was wearing a T-shirt and Bermuda shorts. He had a shock of red hair that swept down across his forehead. Despite the Caribbean location, he was fairly pale. Not tanned at all. Randi was standing off to one side of him with her arm on his shoulder. "Alex, it's so good to see you again."

"Hello, Randi. I really wish you hadn't come. I have a life down here now. It's well away from anything in Boston, or the U.S., for that matter. I really don't know why you're here."

"Well, that's neither here nor there, is it? We're here, and we've got something to show you. And to discuss with you. These are new friends of mine. They've been through some extraordinary events over the last few days, and we think it might all be linked to what we have on a USB stick from Matthews Pharmaceuticals. It may also be linked to your work in Parkinson's research. At least, we think your work may hold a clue to unlocking what these people have found. And they've been through some hellish times actually. I just think you'll want to help us once we fill you in."

Dr. Byers smiled weakly and dropped his head just a little. He moved to the front door and pushed it closed but not before sticking his head out and giving a quick look up and down the street. Once the door clicked shut, he visibly relaxed.

"Okay, but it's late, and I've forgotten my manners. You must have had a long trip. Can I offer you anything to drink? A cold beer perhaps?"

Before anyone could say anything, Nathan quickly spoke up. "I'd love a cold beer. Thank you, Dr. Byers." He caught the startled looks from the others but was undeterred. "Hey, Dr. Byers is right. It *has* been a long trip, and I *would* love a cold beer."

He laughed out loud. "Of course, you would. Come into the kitchen."

The group followed him into the kitchen, and he got a beer for each of them. Randi looked around. "Nice place, I guess."

"It's nothing fancy, but it serves me well."

She pressed on. "I'm surprised your neighbors let you get away with that huge chain-link fence you've got wrapped around your house. It's completely out of character with the rest of the neighborhood. And why have that huge fence if the front gate is unlocked? We walked right in and up to your front door."

"Well, normally, I have the front gate locked as well, but I saw you coming from the window. I unlocked it before you got up to it. I wasn't sure right up until you got to the front door if I'd let you in. As for the entire fence set up, I have made several contributions to local neighborhood renewal. And it is a lot easier when you own the houses on either side of you."

Randi was about to take a sip of her beer when she stopped. "You bought the houses beside you? What the devil for?"

The other four were equally surprised and intrigued, and they waited for Dr. Byers to respond. He took a sip of his beer, smiled at Randi, and raised his eyebrows. "I'll show you."

He pointed to a door at the back of the kitchen and motioned for them to follow. After going through, he led them down a flight of stairs into a rec room. It had a pool table, a built-in bar, some couches and chairs, and a big-screen TV. There was also a large panel that looked like an elaborate computer-system relay hookup on the wall.

Randi took one look around. "This is it? A rec room? What ... you have big parties here and don't want to disturb your neighbors? And what's with the computer-system set up? It looks like the things we had back at the research lab."

"The computer array is for my own sense of security and connection to the outside world. I have a complete internet set up, including Wi-Fi."

"Okay," said Randi, "so you can sit in those beautiful shorts and T-shirt all day and stream to your heart's content. But that does not explain the two-houses thing."

Byers just smiled again, walked across the room, and stood in front of a door at the back of the basement. Then he flipped the cover on a small panel to reveal a keypad, into which he pressed a four-digit code. There was a large click, and then he pulled the door open. Inside was a small landing area with a door on either side.

"This door"—he pointed to his right—"leads to one house, and this door"—he pointed to his left—"leads to the other house. There is a corresponding tunnel that takes you to each house, where there is a corresponding door. Each of the interior doors to the other houses has a keypad where you must enter the four-digit code in order to gain entry. And once you're safely behind whatever door you choose, it locks, and is tamperproof. Then you're back inside and can assess your situation."

Miguel piped up first. "You connected this house to the ones on either side of you?"

"I did."

Randi looked at him open-mouthed. "You did all this? ... Again, what the devil for?"

Dr. Byers looked down at the ground and then up at all of them. "They're 'just in case' exits."

Now Jenna joined in. "Just in case of what?"

"Unwanted visitors."

Randi, paused, shook her head, and then said, "Okay, anyway, can we get back up to your main floor and go over why we came to see you?"

Dr. Byers looked a touch disappointed that they didn't want to explore his tunnel system any further. "Very well." He sighed. "Let's go back up."

They trooped through the basement and went back up the basement stairs, crossing the kitchen and moving into the living room.

"Hello, Alex," said a booming voice from a person sitting in the armchair. "It's nice to see you again. Now, I think we can all finally relax."

CHAPTER 81

BEN AND Colin stood guard outside the house but within the stone wall. Slater and Alman had arrived, found the front gate open, and proceeded up the walk and to the front door. Alman used a computer-hacking probe to quickly unlock the front door, and they were inside in seconds. They heard talking coming from downstairs and so had taken up positions in the living room to wait for everyone to return and join them. There they prepared to take control and finish this entire embarrassing episode.

"Well," Slater began, "I must admit that this has taken much longer than I thought it would and longer than I would have liked. I'm glad it's finally coming to an end. I must say that I'm quite tired of it all," he finished, rubbing his eyes in the process.

Randi spoke up first. "And what does 'coming to an end' mean, exactly?"

Slater looked at her. "Well—"

"How did you get in here so fast?" Byers demanded.

"My friend, the front gate was open, so at your kind invitation, we just walked right in."

Alex rubbed his forehead with his fingers, kicking himself for not resecuring the gate. It might have alerted them.

Slater tried again. "As I was about to say—"

"Wait a minute," Alman spat out, "where's the Filipino?"

"Oh lord." Slater rolled his eyes. "He couldn't have gotten out, could he?"

"No, I didn't," said Miguel as he emerged from the kitchen. "I thought about it, but I wouldn't leave my friends."

As if by collective telepathy, the other four all shared the same thought: *Miguel! You should have!*

"So, I guess it's back to me then, is it?" Slater asked rhetorically.

"I guess it is," said Steven. He had been sizing up the situation, trying to figure a way out.

"Well, *as* I was about to say, I'm afraid we are going to terminate this endeavor of yours and yourselves along with it." All six of them were struck by just how cold Slater sounded. He could have been talking about a sales contest.

"I don't understand," Steven complained, "we don't even know what's truly going on. We don't know what I have on this stick"—he waved it around—"and we can't make heads or tails of what Miguel has on his computer. Why does that mean we have to be … *terminated*?" He could not bring himself to say the word 'kill.'

Slater looked at each of them. "Loose ends, I suppose. You were curious enough to look up Dr. Byers and come all the way here. Alex, I can't believe you haven't told them anything."

"Well, I was about to. But I really haven't had the time. Your arrival surprised us."

"It sure did," Randi said. "How the hell did you get down here so fast?" She was also looking for a way out and thought that trying to extend the interaction seemed logical.

Slater waved his hand dismissively.

"O-Okay, okay," Nathan stammered, "if we don't know what this is all about, what all this information means, then you can just let us go back to our lives."

"No, no, no, young man. Curiosity brought you all the way here. It would surely drive you to seek answers elsewhere if we let you go back to your lives." Slater looked at Alman and nodded slightly.

"Just wait!" Jenna yelled. Everyone froze. She had tears welling in her eyes, but her look was determined, fierce, and defiant. "You killed my sister over this! You killed some company reps just because they opened an email! You tried to kill all of us!" She swept her arm around the room at the group. "So, you're going to goddam well *tell* us what this is all about, or I'll have to be the *first* one you kill because I'll be tearing out your throat if you refuse." She glared at Slater and moved an inch towards him. He flinched back, though just a little.

Steven moved to Jenna and put a hand on her shoulder, then turned to face Slater. "I still don't understand. Are those chemical formulas some sort of weird science? Are they military-grade weapons of some sort? Would they kill people en masse if you developed and released them? They must be toxic. Right?"

"My dear boy," Slater soothed, "we're in the pharmaceutical industry. We don't develop toxins. We don't work for the military. We don't *want* to kill people."

"But you don't want to cure them either." Randi's words cut the room to ribbons. They hung there, suspended, as Jenna, Nathan, Miguel, and Steven tried to process them. Slater looked surprised that she'd had the insight to figure that out. Byers looked ashamed.

Randi stepped forward towards Slater, then twirled around and faced her friends. "Don't you get it? It's exactly what we've been talking about for the past few days! Big Pharma is about revenue. Big Pharma is about profits. They need people taking drugs for the long term. They need people taking drugs for the entirety of their disease, even if that means for the rest of their lives! Actually, they hope it *does* mean for the rest of their lives. If they cure diseases, then people don't take their drugs, and they don't get the revenues!"

She whirled around to face Byers. "I'm right, aren't I, Alex? You didn't find a breakthrough in Parkinson's. You found a cure. Eli was no idiosyncratic response. He responded exactly as you'd expected, didn't he? You met him, Miguel. You saw. He took the medication for only a few days, and he's been disease-free for years!"

Slater interjected, "That, Dr. Thilwell, is the issue in a nutshell."

Nathan spoke up. "So, these compounds on this stick are cures for the diseases listed." It was a statement, not a question. He went on. "That's why Seth was so excited after he looked at them. Remember, Steve, he phoned us a little after we left the bar. He left that message saying he needed to see us. That was just before he died …" Nathan trailed off as another truth dawned on him, but then Steven spoke up.

"You had him killed, didn't you?" Slater remained silent. "But how did you know about him? How did you know he'd seen anything?"

"It's their monitoring system." Byers emerged from his shamed silence. "It's their fucking surveillance system." Slater still remained silent, amused at how everything was spilling out. Byers continued. "My guess is this that friend of yours was using research dollars from a pharma company, from an Affiliation company. Remember, Randi, I told you to be careful about your funding. That's how they got me. As soon as we accepted their funding, we had to use their computer software. They embed spyware into it to keep them abreast of the work. As soon as it detects a keyword like 'breakthrough' or 'cure,' they move in to have a closer look. If the research looks as though it might threaten their revenue streams, they take over. My guess is that, in your friend's case, the spyware detected that your stick had been inserted into his computer and its content downloaded. He'd seen way too much for their liking, so he was taken out."

Slater didn't say anything.

"I can still remember my own situation. I knew we had something special. Keith Fulman gave me his work in Alzheimer's because he could see the link to Parkinson's. I used it to further my own work. I succeeded so quickly that it amazed me. I went on and developed a compound before recording all the data in the computer of the pharma company, the computer Matthews had given me. I used some older university computers to record a bunch of work." He pointed at Slater. "That's why you didn't find out right away. That's why I was able to make a test drug before being shut down."

"So, you knew you were being monitored?" Jenna asked. "You knew you had to work outside of your shared system?" She pointed at Slater as she continued. "The system you shared with them?"

"I didn't know the extent to which I—we—were being spied on. In truth, I'm a lousy records keeper, and I used the university computer because I knew the software and how to plug everything in, so I just plowed ahead."

"Yes, you did," Slater jumped in, "and it nearly cost us dearly. Those lay-press stories were difficult to bury."

Randi was staring at Alex. "So, when you finally entered the data in the Matthews computer, and after we saw the result in Eli, they caught onto what you had."

"Pretty much." Byers answered. "I finally got around to entering the data and our research work into the … the … whatever you want to call it, the monitored computer. This was just before Eli came down to see us. Remember that visit?" Randi nodded. "I just thank the heavens I didn't enter any specific information about Eli. I'm sure that's why he's still alive. They don't know where he is. Anyway, it was the night after Eli had gone home when this guy"—he pointed at Slater now—"showed up out of nowhere in my office. He told me they'd seen the work I was doing on Parkinson's and told me how impressed they were. But they also said it was far too premature to be describing it as a breakthrough. He told me that we couldn't release anything that even remotely hinted at a cure. What was it you said, Slater? 'We can't raise expectations too high only to disappoint later.' I told him that my work would not disappoint. I explained that we were on to something monumental. That's when he brought down the hammer. That's when he explained that my work was being taken over by Matthews. He told me it was to ensure the integrity of the work was upheld. I knew it was all bullshit, and I told him it didn't matter. I knew what I had done, and I'd go elsewhere and redevelop it. It was then he told me that that would not happen. He gave me a choice: Take the money and retire or be retired permanently, as in dead." Byers shifted his gaze to Randi. "I didn't want to do it, but he, *they*, made threats against so many people who were close to me that I felt I had no other choice. I'm sorry."

Slater looked at Byers, then Randi. "Don't be too hard on him, Dr. Thilwell. He only did what many others have done before him."

Miguel had been silent up to now, trying to take everything in, but he finally spoke up. "I can't believe this. This country is supposed to be about innovation, helping people, and achieving success through hard work. That's what that stick represents. You have the cures to all these diseases, and you keep them hidden? Why?"

Slater looked at Miguel in a strangely compassionate way. "It's Miguel, isn't it? Well, Miguel, it's like Dr. Thilwell described, only much more complex." Slater had experienced something of a catharsis on the plane when he'd told everything to Alman. It had been a tremendous feeling of relief and power at the same time. Like a junkie now coming down from a high that had evaporated, he wanted that feeling again. He began to walk around to the back of the armchair he had been sitting in, clasping his hands together and mentally pressing down on his syringe.

Affiliation

"Yes, the compounds on that stick are cures. Or at least we think they are. We have cures there for Parkinson's"—he nodded towards Alex—"schizophrenia, ALS, MS, rheumatoid arthritis, Alzheimer's, among many others."

Jenna's hand flew to her face, and she gasped. "Alzheimer's? My grandmother died of Alzheimer's. We saw her deteriorate. It was heartbreaking. And she could have been cured. My god..."

"Don't be so shocked, young lady. Alois Alzheimer identified the disease that now bears his name over a hundred years ago. Did you think that, in the intervening century of study and research, all we'd come up with were a few compounds that do nothing but treat symptoms, versus halting the disease itself? Hardly, but the compounds themselves generate the revenues we need to further research in the curative compound. To study it more. They also provide a good profit for the companies and the shareholders. No, we've spent more on research into Alzheimer's than was spent sending Neil Armstrong to the moon." He waved his hand dismissively. "We discovered that cure several years ago. It was magnificent work by the way."

"Then release it," Steven spat out.

"That would be a disaster," Slater replied, before continuing, "it is, as Dr. Thilwell said, only more complex. We want to manage disease, not cure it. Unless"—he raised his hand for emphasis—"we can offer the cure in such a way that the patient has to take it for the rest of their life."

Randi jumped in. "Because that maximizes profits."

"Exactly!" Slater almost shouted, becoming that excited. He now stood behind the chair and gripped the sides at the top like an evangelical preacher at a pulpit. "After the Polio fiasco, we learned that we need to *manage* disease. We need, or we want, to keep people alive—yes, of course. But we need that to happen while they take and stay on their daily drugs. Managing disease maximizes profits. Cures kill profits. If we made the Alzheimer's compound on that stick available, we could halt it in its tracks in fourteen to twenty-eight days. It's done, over, no more Alzheimer's. But the Alzheimer's drugs we have help manage the disease and bring in five dollars per day, per patient. And those patients take the drugs for life, or at least for the rest of their lives. That's another important part of the equation. That's revenue. That's profit. Cures kill profits."

"So, the cures just stay hidden, so you can make more money?" Jenna asked.

"Certainly not." Slater sounded insulted. "Perhaps I misspoke earlier. The work goes on; it does not stop. We continue to fund the research on those compounds on the stick, on *all* of them. We want to know what the cure is and then how we can back that off a little. We want to find the pill, or the injectable, or the drink that keeps the disease at bay as long as the patient takes it every day for the rest of their lives. That's the real challenge."

"What did you mean by 'the Polio fiasco?'" Byers asked.

"Well, I wasn't around, of course, but the pharmaceutical industry of that time had been working on compounds for polio for quite some time. They were just about ready to start research trials that would offer real treatment for those afflicted. Patients would have had to take the drugs for life, but they would have remained disease-free. Think of the revenues. Then Jonas Salk came out with his vaccine and *poof.* Those forecasted revenues disappeared. The industry made a vow right then and there not to let that happen again. Our Affiliation was born. We started small with just a few members. We grew ... company by company, disease state by disease state. We began to invest more in research and development. And over the years, we've not only increased our internal investments, but we've branched out into university research and independent work. We have become very far reaching as more and more companies join the Affiliation."

Steven spoke up. "I don't understand about 'cures kill profits.' We do cure some cancers."

"A whole different area," Slater explained. "Cancer drugs are very expensive, both to develop and then to administer to patients. Patients, insurers, and governments are more willing to pay the high costs. And regulatory bodies are more willing to fast-track the newer compounds. The fast-tracking cuts down on the cost of clinical trials, and the high per-patient cost maximizes revenues. And no cancer patient stops taking their drug when it's working. They take it for the entire course of their treatment. Sometimes for the entirety of their lives."

"So?" Steven asked.

"So? Young man, are you familiar with the drug Lipitor?"

"Yes."

"It was the highest selling drug in the world at one point. But the company that marketed it had to constantly fight not only for new prescriptions, but also against their own patients who were on it, just so they would keep taking it. The average length of therapy was only 350 days. The company not only spent millions marketing the drug but also millions developing programs to keep Mom and Dad taking their medication."

Steven knew this story. *Seth was right*, he thought.

Slater continued. "People can't see high cholesterol or feel it, so they stop taking their medication. That eats into profits. But if you're diagnosed with cancer, Alzheimer's, diabetes, or Parkinson's, you'll take your medication every day to ward off the physical manifestations. If we cured those diseases with a short course of therapy, cancer excluded, we'd kill our revenues. Cures kill profits. Disease management is what we want to achieve."

The room was silent. Everyone just stared at Slater. Their thoughts ranged from numbed disbelief to rage. Time seemed to slow down.

"Why would it be a disaster to release these compounds to the world?" It was Randi. She was genuinely curious to hear the answer.

Slater almost jumped for joy. Inwardly, he did a handspring. Finally, he could explain what the Affiliation protected.

He gripped his pulpit tighter. "Dr. Thilwell, everyone..." He gazed about the room, building up tension for his sermon. "Think of it. If we released these cures, if all the people with diabetes, Parkinson's, Alzheimer's, ALS, rheumatoid arthritis, MS, etcetera, etcetera, could be easily cured, what would the millions of people who are now paid to look after them do? The need for that talent would be gone. All those jobs would be lost. I am not talking about closing an auto plant or even an automaker but a job loss of monumental proportion. No more need for caregivers, for a huge segment of the nursing profession. No more need for a huge segment of the physician population. No more researchers. No specialized areas of medicine in dozens of diseases. What would all those people do? They'd be thrown out of work and into a society that could not absorb them. The income tax revenues they generate would dry up. And the taxes we pay as companies would shrivel. The hit to the revenue line of governments all over the world would be catastrophic. They would not be able to fund anything like they do now. And think of all the other companies and industries that owe their financial health to this! To our line of work!" Slater's voice was rising with the fervor of his discord. "It would be total devastation. If those cures were released, entire industries would fail.

"The healthcare industry, in so many countries around the world, accounts for trillions in revenue. That in turn spins off into every segment of society. Just think of the consequences. Trillions of dollars in tax revenue gone. Millions upon millions of people needing another line of work. Millions of other people living well beyond their years after they are cured of their condition. What do you think that sudden bump in world population would do to the overstrained natural resources of this planet? We provide a quality of life to so many people around the world, to those who rely on us for medication, and to those who rely on us for their livelihood. My God, people, can't you all see? We protect those cures as secrets precisely because we *know* what would happen if they were released. We do it to maintain a world order, one in which all of you have survived and thrived. We know we are on a righteous path, and we will remain on the right side of history. It's not that we don't want to release those compounds to the world. It's that we know we *can't* release those compounds to the world. The social upheaval would be too much for the world to handle. I am talking about societal annihilation." Slater raised his right hand from his La-Z-Boy pulpit and slammed it into his left as if to pound his point home. He was nearly breathless. Surely the assembled would hear his message and understand.

The faces of the congregants showed incredulity. There was silence until Nathan spoke up. "You're nuts."

Slater was intensely disappointed. "Hardly," he replied. They clearly did not understand, and so now there was a job to do. He turned to Alman. "Do you want to finish it here?"

"No, let's get them back to the airstrip. We can arrange things from there." He looked at Steven. "I'll take that stick now." Steven took a look at the stick in his hand ... the one that had brought them all together—brought them all here ... and threw it at Alman.

Alman then looked at Miguel. "I'll take that computer." Miguel had been holding the laptop the entire time. He had arrived at the bungalow with it and not put it down. He contemplated his next course of action now, one he had thought of in the kitchen after his friends had been confronted in the living room. He shifted the computer into his right hand, started to gesture to Alman that he was going to toss it over to him, and then quickly pivoted it in his hand and held it like a frisbee. Before Alman could react to what he was doing, Miguel threw the laptop at Alman's chest and then followed as though he was tethered to the thing.

CHAPTER 82

THE LAPTOP hit Alman high on his chest. As he reacted to the incoming object, he leaned back and turned his head. His right hand, the one with the gun in it, reflexively pointed up at the ceiling. Miguel hit Alman like a linebacker as he stumbled backward, knocking him to the floor. Miguel followed on top of him, grabbing his right hand and hitting him with his right.

The others were frozen in place by Miguel's sudden move. They jumped at the sight and sound of the two men hitting the floor but did little else. Suddenly, Byers lunged at Slater. He grabbed him up high around his shoulders and pushed him back against the wall. "Run," he shouted at the others. "Run."

"Hurry!" Miguel grunted his agreement from the floor, "Run. This guy is strong, and I can't hold him off much longer."

"Get off me, you prick," hissed Alman.

"Alex, stop it!" Slater gasped as Byers pushed him harder against the wall. "It's no use."

Byers put his hand on Slater's face and pushed his head against the wall. "Randi," he gulped, "downstairs, the door, the code, the day I left, the day I left. Go now. Go, all of you. Hurry."

It was all happening so fast, yet their reactions seemed to convey that they had all the time in the world. The four unentangled people in the room looked at the struggling pairs of Miguel and Alman, and Byers and Slater. Then Steven suddenly snapped out if it.

"C'mon!" he shouted. "Let's go." He grabbed Jenna and pushed her towards the kitchen. Then he did the same with Randi, and then looked at Nathan, who followed after the first two. As he moved towards the kitchen, he stopped and looked back at Miguel—now being pushed over onto his

Affiliation

back by Alman, whose gun was still in his right hand. Miguel was struggling to keep it from turning inwards, towards the two of them.

"Go, Steve," Miguel said. "Go now, quickly."

Steven turned and followed the others down the stairs. He reached the group as Randi was frantically punching in numbers on the control panel beside the door at the back of the basement rec room.

"What numbers are you pressing?" Jenna asked.

"The day he left. That's what Alex said. The day he left. It was May third, 2014." Randi pressed five, three, two, zero, one, four. The keypad buzzed, and a red light came on. The door did not open. They could hear the struggle going on upstairs.

"Try day, month, year," Nathan offered. Randi pressed the keypad with the same negative result.

Suddenly, what sounded to all of them like a gunshot rang out and punctuated their panic.

"Shit," Randi muttered.

She was about to re-enter a set of numbers when Jenna stopped her. "Wait, when we came here before, Alex punched in only four numbers, not six. Try five, three, one, four.

Randi looked at her, trying to remember if she was right. A second, crisper gunshot rang out from upstairs.

"Try it," Jenna insisted.

Randi pressed the numbers. There was a click as the door unlocked. Randi beamed at Jenna and pulled the door open. The four almost fell on top of themselves as they went through the door, then swung it shut behind them and heard it lock again.

SLATER AND Alman reached the basement and found no one. Alman noticed the door at the end of the room with the keypad beside it and ran over.

"What did Byers say upstairs? The day he left? It must be the code for this door. What was the day he left?"

Slater looked at him blankly. "I have no idea."

"Shit!" Alman yelled. He pulled at the door, but nothing happened. He fired a shot beside the doorknob. Nothing. He then shot the keypad with the same result. He turned to Slater. "Let's go."

UPSTAIRS IN the living room, Byers was dead. After shooting Miguel, Alman had gone over to Byers and yanked him off Slater, quickly raised his gun, and shot him in the forehead. He then went downstairs with Slater.

Miguel was still alive but was motionless on the floor. He didn't feel any pain. He couldn't move his legs either, but he knew they were still attached to his body. Alman had finally gotten on top of him and muscled the gun into Miguel's abdomen. When the shot had gone off, Miguel felt a sharp pain as the bullet tore into and through him, ripped through his body, opening his aorta, and splitting his spinal column before exiting his back and lodging in the floor. Miguel's strength had failed him then all at once. Now he just stared at the ceiling. He'd heard his friends make it downstairs and hoped they had made their escape. Surprisingly, he felt no regret about getting involved in all of this.

He'd heard Alman go over to Byers and Slater. He'd heard the second shot, though he hadn't seen Byers go down. He'd then heard the other two men head downstairs, though the sounds were starting to seem muffled, almost as though he was underwater. He knew he was going to die very soon. His life didn't flash before his eyes. Instead, memories lapped against him in slow-moving waves: his first meaningful Christmas, his first puppy, a high school dance, a collage of family suppers. His parents moved above him. He was gasping now. It was becoming harder to breathe. He thought again of his four friends and hoped they had gotten away. He could feel his heart in his chest, struggling to keep pumping as he faded fast. He was further underwater now, the sounds growing more muffled...

He closed his eyes and thought of home.

CHAPTER 83

STATIONED OUTSIDE Byers's house by Alman, to ensure no one slipped away, Colin and Ben heard the two shots go off.

Colin nudged Ben in the ribs. "Do you think we should go in? Those were gunshots."

"No way," Ben replied.

"Okay, but I thought we were taking them back to the airfield to figure out something there."

"Maybe Alman had a change of heart. Maybe he killed that Byers guy to make it look like a break and enter gone bad. Whatever. We are staying right here ... as ordered."

Just then, Alman emerged from the front door. "Did you two see anything? Did you see them come out of the house?"

Colin looked confused. "Who?"

"Them! The four of them ... without the Filipino."

"Four?" Colin asked. "I thought there were five of them, six with the Byers guy."

Alman rolled his eyes and made himself explain. "There *were* six, but the Filipino decided to go all heroic and jumped me. Then Byers grabbed Slater, and the other four took off downstairs. I had to take both of them out. Were you two also covering the back of the house?"

"Oh," deadpanned Colin, "and yes, I mean no. I mean, we *were* covering the back of the house, and no, nobody came out. They must be still inside."

"No!" Alman shouted. "They ran downstairs and went through a door at the back of the basement. It's locked, and I couldn't get it open."

"You mean it was like an escape hatch?" Colin asked.

"I suppose. Maybe it's some sort of panic room."

Slater had now joined them on the front walkway. He was ashen gray and had vomit spittle at the corner of his mouth.

"What's wrong with him?" Ben asked, looking amused.

Alman jumped in. "He lost it when we came back upstairs. He's never seen the result of his elimination orders up close and personal before."

"Be that as it may," Slater said, recovering his composure, "what do we do now?"

"I don't know," Alman answered. "Maybe we should head back to New York and wait for them. Didn't you say you had a way of tracking their passports?"

Slater thought for a couple of seconds. "That's a good idea," he said with a brisk nod, and then pointed to the mercenaries. "But we leave these two here to see if the others come out eventually."

Alman agreed. He told Ben and Colin to get inside the house, keep the front door and all the drapes closed, and then to stay in the basement. If the locked door down there did lead to a panic room, the foursome would have to come out at some point. And in the meantime, Ben and Colin could also try to break through. He told them to give it until the next morning, and then move to the airport and watch for them there. If they did not turn up by the end of that day, they could ditch the guns and get on a commercial flight back to New York.

Colin and Ben went into the house as ordered, while Slater and Alman got into their rental car and drove away.

CHAPTER 84

IN THE house next door, to the right of Byers's bungalow from the street, the four remaining friends huddled together. Steven had been peering at the scene in Byers's courtyard through a narrow slit in the blinds.

After the "just in case" door had clunked closed behind them, they had hurried down the tunnel and ran to the door at its other end. They had heard the gunshots Alman had fired into the door and the keypad, but luckily, they didn't hear the door open or any feet coming after them. They entered the same code in the security pad beside the next door and went through it. The basement in this house was empty. They moved through the dim light of a basement window, made their way slowly upstairs, and gingerly entered the living room. The layout of this house was exactly like the other, so it made moving from room to room somewhat easy. Steven continued looking outside. The others were behind him, completely silent. Nathan was sitting with his back against a wall with his eyes closed. Randi was standing, leaning against a door jamb and staring at her phone. Jenna was sitting in the middle of the empty room with her knees bent and pulled up tight against her chest, rocking slowly back and forth. Steven turned away from the window and looked back into the room. lit only by the dim glow of streetlamps seeping through cracks in the drapes and blinds.

"Slater and that other guy just left. The other two went inside the house."

Nathan sat up, his head snapping forward. "Maybe they're going to work on the door. Maybe they're going to get it open. Then they'll find us. We've got to get out of here."

"Wait a minute, Nate," Steven said soothingly. "Byers said he designed the door to withstand any sort of tampering. I mean, they tried to shoot their way through and couldn't. I think they've gone inside to wait us out.

Maybe they think it's just another room behind it. Not many would think of a tunnel to the house next door."

"Yeah, but if they do get it open," Nathan sputtered, "then we're done for! I say we take off."

Jenna rolled her eyes. "And if they're watching the street, they'll see us leave, and then we're finished. We'll wait here for a little while. Maybe until we see them leave." This was not something she was willing to debate.

"Well, *however* we get out of here, we're hooped," Steven pointed out. "We don't have any data. All of our information is gone."

"We're not *hooped*," said Randi. She pulled herself away from the door jamb and walked towards them, holding out her phone for the others to see and glancing in the direction of Byers's bungalow. "Miguel sent the files to my phone, Steven. That's why he stayed back in the kitchen before joining us. I've got everything here: the files Miguel stole from Matthews *and* all the cures from your stick."

Randi even saying Miguel's name aloud seemed to resonate with them, and Steven came forward.

"Maybe one of us should sneak out and slip into the living room next door. Maybe he's okay, and we can get him out."

"Steven," Jenna reasoned, "I don't think that's a good idea. Not with those two over there."

"But he could be hurt. He may need help. I could slip in and get him out. We just can't leave him there." Steven sounded almost frantic.

"Steven," Randi cautioned, "you heard what these people do to others who get in their way. You heard the gunshots. I still can't believe it really, but I think Miguel and Alex are probably—"

"No," Steven said sharply, interrupted. "I know what you're about to say, and I don't want to hear it. We've got to help him somehow."

The others were quiet. Suddenly, Nathan looked up and over at Randi. "Your phone!"

"What about it."

"We can call nine-one-one, or the operator, or whoever we need to call and get the police over there. Just call and tell them you heard gunshots coming from inside the house. They'll show up fast to check it out. If Miguel needs help, or Byers for that matter, they'll get it to them. It'll also, drive those two bastards out of here."

Steven rubbed his chin. "But what if the cops come here and find *us*. We'll either be held for questioning or turned over to Slater."

"Just because they come to the front door doesn't mean we have to open it," Randi offered. "If we stay quiet, they'll assume nobody's home and leave. Then, surely, we can slip away in the confusion that will be happening at the bungalow. I think it's a good idea."

The four exchanged looks for a moment, and then Randi began to dial.

"Wait!" Steven jumped in again. "Won't the cops know that your phone made the call from this house? You know, because of GPS tracking, or cell-phone pinging, or whatever?"

"I don't think so," Randi said. "I don't think it will show up that fast, and even if it does, I think it will just show that the call came from a phone in this area. I'll just say I was walking by." Before anyone else could object Randi finished dialling and shared her planned story with the person who answered.

Then the four friends crept towards the front window and waited. Within a couple of minutes, they heard sirens in the distance, growing louder and louder. Then Steven noticed something out of the corner of his eye. Ben and Colin were scurrying out of the front door. When they hit the front walkway, they glanced up and down the street, then quickly exited the courtyard and took off into the darkness. Part two of Nathan's idea had worked. Their attention turned back to the oncoming sirens. Very soon, a police car came to a screeching halt in front of the bungalow. Then a second followed very quickly after the first. The officers got out and carefully looked at the front door of Byers's house, then slowly made their way up the front walk. The first two officers stood in front of the open door and said something the friends couldn't make out. Then they drew their guns and crept inside, followed just as slowly by the third and fourth officers. Nothing happened for what seemed like ages, though it was really only four or five minutes. Then more sirens were heard approaching.

Another police cruiser pulled up, followed closely by an ambulance. The four watched hopefully as the ambulance attendants got out of the wagon, went to the back, and opened it up. But their hopes plummeted when one of the original officers came out of the front door and waved his hand at the first ambulance attendant, following it with a shake of his head. He held up two fingers and motioned towards the house. The EMS attendant casually walked up the walkway and into the house. Within a minute, he was back outside and motioning for his partner to close up the ambulance doors.

After what looked like some shared small talk between the attendants and two of the police officers, the men climbed into their ambulance and drove away. Shortly after that, a police van pulled up with the words 'Police Forensics Unit' painted on the side. Then a Coroner's van pulled up to the front of the house.

Jenna turned away from the window and put her hand to her mouth. "Oh, God," she muttered.

Randi and Steven turned away as well. "Shit. Those bastards."

OVER THE next couple of hours, many tears were shed as they took turns watching the crime-scene investigation unfold, with multiple people moving into and out of the bungalow. At one point, they had to go completely quiet when a uniformed officer came to their front door and knocked. But after he had left, they resumed their vigil. It was Nathan who saw the two empty stretchers being brought into the house and then brought back out a short time later, each carrying a sealed body bag. He didn't say anything. They slept on and off during the night. In the morning, they were all back at the window, surreptitiously checking the crime scene. There were still two marked police cars at the house, and one unmarked car. A small group of people were gathered across the street. The front of the fence was ringed by yellow police tape. Steven pulled away and addressed the group.

"When the officers leave, we have to get out of here. We've got to move."

"Okay, that's fine," added Randi, "but where do you suggest we go?"

Just then, they heard another vehicle pull up out front. Two men jumped out of it and moved to the rear, opening the trunk and pulling out several large tools and two tool belts. One of the remaining officers motioned for the two new men to follow him into the house. After seeing the tools, Steven had an idea of what they were up to and quickly moved through their hiding house and headed downstairs. Then he went back through the door at the back of the basement and ran down the tunnel to the door at Byers's end, staying only a few seconds before sprinting back to his friends.

"We've gotta go," he said. "Now. They're making our decision for us. Those two guys are here to get that other door open. And I think they'll do it soon."

All four now recognized the need to move, and move fast. They went back to the front window and checked on the officers outside. There was no one in sight. Even the small crowd of onlookers that had gathered was gone now.

Jenna offered up a theory. "Everyone must be inside. They're waiting to get through that door. We should go right now. We have to take the chance."

"We're sure Frick and Frack aren't watching from down the street?" Randi asked.

"If they are," Jenna said, thinking out loud, "then I say we split up and go in four different directions. We agree to meet at the airport in two hours. But I don't think they'll be there."

"Done," Steven said. "And I think Jenna's right. I think those two would want to stay well away from any cops."

They opened the front door and slowly moved down the steps. Once they got to the sidewalk, they turned away from the crime scene and walked quickly away.

CHAPTER 85

AT THE airstrip, Slater and Alman were sitting on the plane but not talking. Slater had a drink in his hands, the ice cubes rattling against the glass as his hand shook. Alman was sitting across the aisle, working on Miguel's computer. He was not oblivious to the tinkling coming from Slater's glass and smiled inwardly at the hypocrisy of Slater's distress. He had been exposed at Byers's house. He'd given the kill order before, all in the name of protecting his great secret and his Affiliation. But now he'd seen the execution of that order on an individual. It was far messier than the boardroom.

Suddenly, he sat up straight, snapping to attention. "Shit."

Slater broke free of his stupor. "What?"

"He sent an email. He sent an email to Thilwell."

"Who sent an email?"

"The little Filipino. He must have sent it before he came into the living room."

"Are you sure?"

"Yes, I'm sure! I can read an Outlook account! He sent everything! Your files *and* the compounds from the stick!"

"Can you do a retrieve message? We can get it back before Thilwell opens it."

"Too late; she's got it."

"Okay, so we can contact another domestic team and get her computer from Boston."

"Yeah, fine. But she's also got it on her phone."

Slater pondered this a moment and then gave a brisque nod. "We'll have to take them here. Before we leave. They *cannot* leave this island."

Just then, the plane's captain came on the intercom. "Excuse me, Mr. Slater, but we've got two men approaching the plane. They're motioning they want to get on."

"Who are they?"

"Your two traveling companions."

Stunned, Slater and Alman looked at each other. Soon, Colin and Ben bounded up the plane's stairs and into the cabin.

"Okay," Ben said, "so we might be screwed."

CHAPTER 86

THE FOUR friends made their way down the street away from Byers's bungalow, each glancing behind them in turn to see if they were being followed. They were not. They made their way out of the neighborhood and onto a busier street, hoping to spot a taxi but stopping at the first bus stop they came across. When a bus approached, showing "Downtown" on its destination header, they got on and settled into seats near the back, staring out the windows.

"Nathan, what's wrong?" Randi asked.

His head spun around. "Huh?"

"You look puzzled."

"Yeah, I guess. I was just thinking back to something Dr. Byers said. When we came into the living room and met up with Slater and that other guy, Slater said he was surprised Byers hadn't said anything, and Byers answered that he hadn't had the time and was surprised by how fast Slater had gotten there."

"So?" Randi offered. "He didn't answer me either."

"So, how *did* he get there so fast? And more importantly, how did he know we would be there at all? At Dr. Byer's house, I mean."

The four paused a moment before Steven made a suggestion. "They probably just took a private plane ... and maybe just guessed where we were going?"

"But how did he know we were with Randi? I don't think we were followed, since if we had been, I think we would have been killed long before we ever got here. So, that means that they wouldn't have ever seen us all together. And yet, Slater either knew Randi was with us and that she would probably take us to go see Byers, or else he somehow just knew that we were traveling to Barbados and came down to get us. Either way, how did he know *any* of that?"

Again, the four were quiet. It was a good question. Nathan had a knack for pondering things that seemed fairly innocuous on the surface and finding importance in it.

Jenna posed a question of her own. "Okay. So, if we weren't followed, then what other methods could they have used to track us?"

"Well," Steven said, "there's GPS tracking, obviously. And credit-card purchases can be tracked, and maybe our passports too, but I think they'd need a government agency for that."

"And a court order as well, I'd think. Wouldn't you?" Nathan asked.

Randi jumped in then to offer some perspective. "Maybe not. Maybe spending millions of dollars on political contributions has gotten them all the favors and influence they'd ever need."

"Oh hell." Nathan breathed out. "That means they'll know where we're headed the minute we check in at the airport."

They sat in silence for a while, considering this new twist to their saga.

"Well, that settles it," Jenna said finally. "If they have a contact somewhere that will report our whereabouts and movement to them the moment we log in our passports, then we can't go home via the airport."

All four sat in silence, thinking the exact same thing: *How are we going to get home?*

Again, Nathan's memory and analytical skills came out. "Wait a second. Back at the house, Slater asked that guy - no neck, if he wanted to finish us off there. But he said no. He wanted to get us back to the airfield and go from there." The other three just stared at Nathan, urging him to continue. "He said 'airfield,' not 'airport.' They must have used a private airfield here on the island to land a private jet, which makes more sense given that we're dealing with Matthews Pharmaceuticals. So ... if *they* used a private jet, maybe we can do the same thing and take a private charter back home. Whatever contacts Matthews might have, maybe they aren't tapped into the private-charter system."

Steven reacted on instinct. "Do you know how much that will cost?!"

Nathan looked at him, dropping his arms to his sides in frustration. "Man, we're trying to stay alive here! I'll take out a second mortgage if I have to!"

"Okay, okay," Randi said, "but we don't know anything about this private airfield. How do we know it's not attached to the main airport and linked to their computer system?"

"That's a good point," Nathan said, reasonably, "but I don't think that's the case here. They were planning to grab four people, or I guess six really, and bring them back *there* to kill them. They wouldn't do that if it was a public space, or even connected to one. There'd be too many chances for us all to be seen together."

The other three gave Nathan impressed looks, which Nathan noticed. "What? I've watched cop shows, mysteries, thrillers, and stuff. It just makes sense."

"It does make sense," Jenna began, "but how are we going to even find the private airfield. And if we do find it, what if they're still there, and we stumble into them. Boom. We're done."

"Okay," Steven said. "So, first, we have to find out where this private airfield is on the island, which we should be able to find without too much difficulty, even if we just have to ask someone for directions. Then we just approach it carefully. If things look safe, we get in and start asking about chartering a flight. And if it doesn't ... we just wait until it does."

The other three nodded in agreement.

CHAPTER 87

SLATER HAD ordered the plane's captain to take off the millisecond after Ben had said, "We might be screwed."

The plane readied for take off and taxied out to the runway. The two field members let their bosses know what had happened back at the bungalow and explained how they had bolted when they'd heard the sirens. They had moved a discreet distance away and watched as the crime-scene investigation had unfolded. After the fourth police vehicle had shown up, they'd moved off and headed for the airfield.

Alman turned on the plane's satellite radio to listen to the local broadcasts. Thirty minutes into the flight, a report was aired, informing viewers of what appeared to be a double homicide in a quiet local neighborhood.

"Did you get a chance to stage a robbery scene?" Alman asked.

"No," Ben said. "We couldn't. The cops showed up too quickly."

"Shit. I should have searched them for any cell phones they might have had on them. It's the only way the police could have been contacted so fast."

"Yeah, I know," Colin said, jumping in. "But what if they turn themselves in and finger all of us?"

"I don't think they will," said Slater. "First, their story would be fantastic, outrageous, and beyond the pale. The local police wouldn't want anything to do with a grand conspiracy, nor would they readily believe it."

Slater noticed the glance Colin gave Ben at his use of the term 'grand conspiracy,' but carried on. "I think they'll try to get back to the States. 'Home,' as it were."

"Can we use your contacts to track their passports?" Alman asked. "Like we did to follow them here?"

Slater noticed the surprised expressions on both Colin's and Ben's faces at this, and shot Alman an angry look for letting something slip out that Slater did not want slipped out. Slaters' stare intensified as he looked at Alman, who quickly nodded.

Turning to Ben and Colin then, Alman cleared his throat. "Gentlemen ... why don't you two move up to the front of the plane. The bar's open. We'll take it from here."

Colin and Ben shrugged and moved forward. Even though they didn't say anything, they both knew that there had been something important behind that quick exchange. They weren't stupid.

After Ben and Colin were seated up front, Slater turned is attention back to Alman. "We don't want to let out too much, do we?"

Alman just stared back. "Yeah, whatever. Those two will only do what they're told to do and would never think to do anything more."

"Alright, but still, be careful. We have protected our Affiliation and our purpose for decades. I don't want that to unravel now." Slater was aware of Alman's disdain regarding his reaction to what had happened at the bungalow, having easily read his body language and facial expressions. Thankfully, Alman's slip of the tongue had allowed him to reassert his authority and regain a measure of control. He then grabbed his cell phone, called his contact, and set the wheels in motion to continue tracking the passports of the four remaining fugitives.

"Once we're back in the U.S., we can wait for their passports to be flagged and then move on them." Slater looked again at Alman, who nodded his agreement.

FROM THE front of the plane, Ben and Colin had been quietly observing the exchange at the back.

"How do you suppose a drug company can track passports?" Ben asked. "I thought only the government could do that. Homeland Security, or the FBI, or some other such department."

"I don't know," Colin said, "but we better start paying closer attention. Whatever's going on, it is definitely *not* just about intellectual property rights."

CHAPTER 88

"HERE IT is." Steven jabbed his finger at a spot in the island's Yellow Pages.

"Really?" Nathan asked. "I didn't think it would be that easy."

Jenna jumped in. "Well, now that we've found what appears to be a private airfield, we should head on over there, right?"

The other three were silent. The thought of running into Slater and his team again suddenly poured cold water on their plan. It was a moment before anyone spoke.

"Look," Jenna began, "they've probably left the island already. With the police showing up at Dr. Byers's house, this thing is much more in the public eye now. They'd want to be well away from that. I think we should be fine."

It was the word 'should' that stood out to the rest and gave them pause.

"Yeah," offered Steven, "we'll be fine. Let's get a cab."

They initially thought of stopping the cab a short distance away from the airfield. But during the ride over, Randi pointed out how that might arouse suspicion with the driver, and he might then feel obliged to raise an alarm bell or two. While they agreed, it was still nerve-racking to have the driver drop them off right at the terminal building of the airfield. Once they had left the cab, they moved quickly into the bland, metal-clad building. There was one central counter in the outer office, and they walked up to it. Nathan rang the bell for service, and a neatly dressed man, who appeared to be in his thirties, came out of an inner office.

"May I help you?"

Nathan turned back to look at his friends. Randi urged him to go on with an expression of impatience on her face. Before turning back to the man, he noticed that Steven was missing. "We'd like to enquire about chartering a plane to fly us to New York city." Nathan realized how absurd his request must sound, but he also didn't want to couch it in uncertainty or beat around the bush.

The man looked at Nathan warily, and then glanced at the two companions standing behind him. He stopped and half stared at both Jenna and Randi. "We can arrange that," he started slowly, "but it'll be very expensive."

"Yes, that's okay," Nathan said. "How do we go about setting it up?"

"Well, we have a few charter companies here. I can help you choose one that's right for you."

"Are you some sort of travel agent?" Jenna blurted out.

"No, no," he answered, "I run the airport here, so I know all the companies. And while it is expensive, we actually get this sort of request more often than you might think. Is this for a medical emergency? Or a crisis back home, perhaps?"

Nathan ignored these questions and asked one of his own: "Is it difficult? I mean, we've never done this sort of thing before."

The man's eyes narrowed a little, and Randi sensed that Nathan had raised some suspicion. She jumped to the front, reached out, and took the man's hand in hers, clasping it tight. "We do have something of an emergency back home, and we're anxious to get back. We so appreciate your help." She finished with an extra squeeze of the man's hand and a thousand-watt smile.

Clearly disarmed and visibly flustered, the man's eyes opened wide. He blushed as he looked at Randi, smiled back at her, and then placed his other hand on top of hers.

"Yes, yes, I see. No, I can help you. Like I said, we do get this sort of thing more often than you might imagine. I can get things set up." He again looked Randi directly in the eye and gently slid his hands out of their joint clasp before turning and walking back into his inner office.

Nathan just looked at Randi, shook his head, and smiled. "By the way, where's Steve?"

"What?" Jenna asked. She looked around the office. "Where is he?" Her question had more than a touch of anxiety in it.

"I noticed he wasn't with us when I got up to the front counter," answered Nathan.

Randi chimed in as well. "I don't know where he is. He didn't say anything about going AWOL."

Jenna now started walking back toward the front door to look out the window. "Where could he be?" she asked no one in particular, looking out towards the parking lot and the runway.

"Jenna, I'm sure he's fine," Randi said, trying to use reason to calm her. "We didn't see anybody when we arrived."

Just then, the front door opened, and Steven walked in. Jenna smiled broadly and ran over to him, though her tone was scolding as she asked, "Where have you been?"

"I walked around the grounds and building to look for anyone nasty."

"Well, you could have told one of us."

"Oh yeah. Sorry about that. But the good news is there's nobody here."

"Well, that's good," Randi said. "C'mon, we've found someone to help us with a charter to get back to the States."

They moved back to the front counter, where Nathan was with the airport manager, looking over some paperwork. The man behind the counter brightened right up when he saw Randi coming back over.

They went over a few different charter companies and settled on one that looked comfortable, and more importantly, could be ready to go in two hours. A flight plan would have to be filed, and they would need to contact the local airfield in New York to notify them of their impending arrival. All the necessary notifications would be filed with the appropriate authorities. The cost was based on the type of plane and number of passengers. Nathan quipped it was "kind of like a hotel room." The total bill, including taxes was fifty-seven-thousand U.S. dollars. Sensing that if they stammered, huddled, or hesitated, more suspicion would pop up, Randi pulled out a Platinum Amex and handed it to the manager, again with an even brighter smile than she'd offered him the first time. "That will be fine," she said with as much confidence as she could muster. As he went back to process the payment, she turned to her companions. "We're gonna settle this when we get back."

The other three just raised their hands and nodded while mumbling, "Absolutely, of course, definitely."

Their processing was very low-key. All part of their "white-glove service," as the manager had stressed to Randi. He was clearly smitten with her, and she used that to their collective advantage to get things done quickly and quietly. There was not even a passport scanner. The manager explained that he would file their passport numbers with the local U.S. authorities right away. Randi looked at him and shrugged. "Don't worry. As long as it gets done eventually, we'll be okay."

The four were very surprised that everything seemed to go off without any hitches at all. Their plane was ready just when they were told it would be, and they climbed aboard. However, the airport manager did wriggle for some more time with Randi by asking her if she was coming back to the island soon, and offering to be her personal tour guide if and when she was. She enthusiastically accepted his offer of future help and hugged him before climbing on board.

"I think you have a new friend," Jenna commented after the plane's door had closed, and they were all seated.

"Hey, whatever helps us move on from here. And he wasn't bad looking. It might be nice to come back here and have a 'personal tour guide.'"

The other three all liked Randi's positivity, thinking about being back there again someday, as it meant she believed that they'd get through the rest of this ordeal alive.

CHAPTER 89

AS SLATER'S plane touched down in the U.S., his four adversaries were an hour or so out of Barbados, and about three and a half hours out of New York.

Back in Barbados, the airport manager had filed all the necessary paperwork, including the passenger manifest with the attendant passport numbers. He had emailed them over to his contact at 4:34 p.m., which was the same time in New York. As he hit send, he thought he'd be just in time to get it done by the end of the day. In the U.S., the passport numbers were immediately uploaded into the system.

Slater and his passengers got off their plane and went straight to their respective cars. Slater had instructed them that they could all go home, but that they were essentially on call. They would have to move quickly once he got the word on the timing and point of entry for Randi, Nathan, Jenna, and Steven.

Slater headed for home. Alman headed for his favorite bar. And Ben and Colin decided to try to get some answers.

CHAPTER 90

AT THIRTY-THREE thousand feet, the four traveling companions sat and talked. The full weight of what they possessed was still sinking in. They now knew that many of the major players in the pharmaceutical industry were sitting on research and discoveries that could eradicate a host of diseases and chronic conditions. Their desire to keep these from the public was based on what they *felt* was a noble premise: the industry of medicine and medical care being dependant on managing the sick instead of curing the condition.

Steven was fuming. "We have the cure for Parkinson's, MS, schizophrenia, Alzheimer's, and I don't know how many other diseases! We have to get this out!"

Ever the scientist, Randi tried to interject some reason. "What we have, Steve, is the leading results of some of the best research efforts so far in those particular areas, among others. *Are* they cures? I don't know. But we definitely have to get them back into the research lab and have people working on them again."

"What?!" Steven was flabbergasted. "C'mon, Randi, you saw what Byers's drug did to that Cowlings guy! You heard Byers say he had a cure for Parkinson's!"

"I know. I know... I'm not saying they *aren't* cures. And what's on that stick *must* be made public. But even after it gets out, there'll be tons of work to do, and the research still might not pan out. I've been in this a long time, and I know that what looks amazing today may very well be a bust tomorrow."

"You sound like you half agree with Slater and his bunch," Jenna said accusingly.

"No way, Jenna," she said, shaking her head. "No way. We've got to get this out in the public domain, and their secrecy *must* end. All those pharma bastards need to be brought down. I mean, how many people have died while they sat on this work? And all to preserve their world order? No. This *has* to come out. But at the same time, people's expectations will also have to be managed."

"Expectations?"

"Yes, Steven," Nathan said, jumping in. "Expectations. If the word gets out that cures are available for all these conditions, there will be chaos. Everyone will want them, like, yesterday. And even after research is essentially concluded, it still takes time to get drugs to market. And then we really won't know what they'll do to people on a mass scale until several years *after* they hit the market. They could start out great and then hit huge snags or flop altogether."

"Nathan's right," Randi said. "We can't just go to the papers with this. We have to make sure this information gets to people who can help, both in terms of bringing down the assholes and getting the research going again ... in a responsible way."

Steven and Jenna really didn't like hearing this, but they could also concede the point. It was not just a matter of giving what they had to a newspaper and walking away. They would need to find a strong ally to help them.

"Okay," Jenna reasoned, "if we can't just release this stuff, how do we go about it?"

"I have an idea about that," Randi began. "I know of a couple senators who have been going after Big Pharma on a number of issues over the past few years. I've met them, and based on their record, I think they'd listen to us." The other three looked at Randi, and then each other.

"It all sounds too easy," cautioned Nathan. "I mean, we land, we hike to Washington, meet these guys, and *poof*, we're done? I don't think so. Those bastards are still out there, and they're looking for us."

"They *are* looking for us," Steve said then. "All four of us together."

"Your point?"

"Nate, after we land, I think we should split up. Move in pairs. We can agree on a meeting place in Washington on a given date and time. It'll be harder for them to track us if we split up."

The other three agreed. Steven and Jenna would be one pair, and Nathan and Randi the other. They would take two days to make the short trek to

255

Washington. Each pair would head away from Washington initially and use a credit card to make a purchase. This would make it clear where they were, but it was a risk worth taking. They would also rent a car for each pair, not be shy about where they were going with the rental agency. Jenna and Steven would say they were going to Canada, and Nathan and Randi would say they were going back to Seattle. It was all designed to throw off their pursuers. Randi would contact the senators' offices and tell them just enough to get an appointment or two but not enough to entice them to go public or to phone a drug company and ask for clarification. They were comfortable with their next moves. They all felt that getting the information to Washington would result in some sort of investigation. They also felt that this way of releasing the USB would ensure their survival.

"Do you really think this will all work?" Nathan asked.

"Nate, I have no idea," Steven said. "I'm not James Bond or Jason Bourne here. I'm just playing this out as I go."

"What do you think will happen once we bring this out into the open?" Jenna asked.

"I'm not totally sure," Randi began. "I know I'll push for the research to be started up again. I'd like to see the compounds made into medications in a hurry. Then we can start clinical trials to see if they're safe, and if they work. But like Nathan said, it could take years to get them developed."

"What do you think will happen to the drug companies?"

"Oh, I don't know. I'm more concerned about therapy than business."

"It's going to have a massive impact," Steven said. "I mean, Slater was right in the sense that curing these diseases will cause major turmoil. Chaos even. Just think of our own little world." He pointed to Jenna and himself. "If we cure Alzheimer's for example, which we should, then our drug rep friends that sell Aricept, Reminyl, and Exelon will be out of their jobs. My God, just think of all the drug reps that would—or will—be affected. Without pills to sell for all these chronic conditions, they don't have jobs. What the hell are they going to do?"

"Yeah," Nathan chimed in, "even pharmacists will be hit hard. We dispense billions of pills and such for those conditions. If they can be cured quickly, then you're going to see massive upheaval and job loss in my industry. What the hell are we going to do?"

"And like Slater said," Jenna said, thinking out loud, "there are so many jobs and such tied to *all* this. It won't just affect our industry or yours, Nathan, but industries that are interconnected and interwoven because of the need for medications, and all the industries that rely on them. It will damage tax rolls. *So* many people will have to turn to different careers, won't they?"

There was an odd silence among the four of them. It lasted several seconds before Randi broke it, saying, "Tell me you're not thinking Slater is right? You think we should throw this all away?"

The others stared straight ahead, and Jenna answered first. "No, no ... at least, I don't think we're saying that. But the consequences of this *are* huge. That's all."

"Yeah. People will live longer. More disease will go in the garbage dump, and society will adjust." Randi almost spat out these words.

"Yes, of course," Steven said, "but it *will* be one hell of an adjustment."

CHAPTER 91

THE ALERT didn't come as a complete surprise, but the method of transport and the destination were both a bit of a shocker.

Slater had been home about two hours when he got a call from his government contact. His four runaways had chartered a private plane and were headed for a small regional airfield outside Manhattan. He knew it well. He knew it very well. Maybe there was some sort of cosmic anomaly that pulled them all together. Whatever the reason, he would be waiting for them at the airfield when they arrived. He had already made the necessary calls and was on his way to meet his team at the airfield.

BEN AND Colin had been interrupted in their work at the bunker, trying to find some more information on the operation, when Colin's cell phone rang. They really hadn't found anything up to that point, at least nothing they hadn't already known. But they had come up against some very tough, encrypted security measures—measures more difficult than necessary for the internal system of a pharma company. They'd never questioned an assigned task. The work they did for Alman and Slater was just an extension of what they had done in the service as government operatives. When Alman had called them five years ago to offer them jobs, they had jumped at the chance because both had their doubts as to what they were going to do post-service. This job seemed heaven sent though, a perfect fit for their particular qualifications. All that being said, they didn't like the feeling that there was something larger going on they didn't know about. At least in the service, they'd had a good handle on why they were being tasked with any operation. Their time with Matthews had been different. They couldn't quite explain it to themselves, and they couldn't articulate it to each other either. But they wanted to know more. The hair was starting to stand up on the backs of their necks, and those were survival instincts they'd developed over years spent running and participating in dangerous operations. But the call had come, and so they answered it like always, though more disgruntled this time than before.

ALMAN HAD been nursing his second beer when his phone had gone off. *Clever,* he thought upon learning the fugitives' plan. They had chartered a plane to avoid the immediate system notifications of their passports, which would have told of their return to the U.S. They had finally figured out that they were being tracked in a number of different ways. This meant it was imperative they were taken out right at the airfield. If they got away this time, they would surely set some diversions in place to throw him off. They were smart—smarter than he had given them credit for. This had to end today. He had bigger things to focus on, like collecting his "fee" to complete Slater's next bold plan.

CHAPTER 92

THE PILOT of the incoming private plane began his descent just after five o'clock. He thought the request he'd received shortly before beginning the descent was a little odd, but they were paying the freight, so he readily complied. He asked for permission to divert to the requested airfield, and once he received it, he followed air-traffic control's instructions and began to descend. The new arrival field was only minutes from the original destination.

Inside the cabin, the passengers could feel the descent beginning. They hoped by asking to divert very late in their flight, they would avoid having an arrival crew there greet them. They went over their plans again to make sure everyone was on the same page. They would buy burner phones and separate, staying in near constant contact with one another by phone every thirty minutes, reporting any run-ins with Slater and company if they could. They had asked permission of the flight crew to use their cell phone to call ahead for two cabs to be waiting for them to take them to a car-rental company in New Jersey. Everything seemed ready to go. As the plane approached the airfield, all four looked out the windows. The first person to notice the cars was Steven, perhaps because he was hypersensitive to the threat. Whatever the reason, he saw that there were three cars in a row in the parking lot ... very close to the two waiting cabs.

"That doesn't mean anything." Jenna said, trying to calm him down.

"You think?" he shot back. "Just how many flights do you think this airfield gets? Not many, I'd say. It's them. They must have found us through their government contacts. Man, they must be connected. It's them. I know it is."

"Okay," Nathan cut in, "if it is them, then what do we do?"

"Can we ask the pilot to take off and go back to our original airfield?" Randi asked. "Or can we ask that he stop the plane back on the runway, and then we jump off and run?"

"I don't think so. Both of those suggestions would raise big alarm bells. Plus, I don't think he'd do either. Shit." Steven was still looking out the window at the approaching airfield. "We may have a shot right after the plane is parked. There's no jetway here. We should just deplane and walk directly into the terminal. But what if we don't? What if we just bolt from the plane and run over to those bigger buildings over there?" He pointed to what looked like two hangar buildings about a hundred yards from the terminal.

"And what do we do once, or if, we get there?" Randi asked.

Jenna now spoke up. "We do whatever the fuck we have to do to get away! We hide, we run, and we fight if necessary. But we get away and follow our plan. I don't know about the rest of you, but *I'm* going to survive." It was the absolute conviction in her voice that emboldened them all.

The issues of their entire journey, struggle, and eventual destination might be soon resolved. But either way, they were going to see it through.

They decided to act as if they had not spotted their enemies, not tipping their hand until they got to the bottom of the plane's stairs. Then they'd make their break. The plane's wheels touched the ground, and started to taxi them to their final stop.

Inside the terminal, Slater, Alman, Colin, and Ben waited.

Outside, the cab drivers were starting their cars and driving away. Alman had casually gone up to them earlier and asked them if they had been contracted to pick up two pairs of people who were coming in on an approaching private plane. After confirming this, he explained to them that he and his friends were actually there to meet them as a surprise. The cab drivers were annoyed to the point of staying so they could collect their fare, at first, but Alman had gotten them to go away with a hundred dollars each. Easy.

Alman turned to Slater. "Just remember, this ends now. We get the information back, and this ends now. No negotiations. No hesitations. So, you make sure you grow a pair, and that we finish this." Slater just nodded grimly while looking down at the floor.

The plane approached its stopping point as the aircraft marshaller guided it to its parking spot. Through their windows, Randi and Jenna spotted Slater and Colin inside the terminal building. They were going to have to run. Their stomachs churned to the point of nausea. Jenna turned to face Nathan and Steven. "They're in there. You were right, Steve."

"Yeah, shit," he replied. "Look, we get to the bottom of the stairs and just book it for that hangar, okay? If we can make it inside, we might have a chance to lose them."

Nathan was worried. "What if we change plans? What if we just go inside and get whoever else is in there to call the police. We wait for the cops and just refuse to go with Slater and crew?"

Randi shook her head. "Remember, they'd just claim that we've stolen their intellectual property, which we actually did. And if the police then make us give it back or take it from us, we'll be dead before their investigation even begins. Our safety depends on us keeping both this information and us away from them."

"Okay, okay, but this isn't the movies where the good guys always get away. This is real, and we're ordinary people. Ordinary people die in real life all the time."

"I know, Nathan. I know, and I'm petrified as well." She put her hands on Nathan's shoulders. "But we're going to make it."

The plane came to a full stop, and the pilot popped out of the cockpit. "Enjoy the ride, folks?" All four nodded that they had.

The pilot pulled on the door handle, the hatch opened, and stairs folded down in a quiet whir, like an arm bending at the elbow. When the last step touched the ground, the four of them stood up and hesitantly moved towards the opening. The pilot stood to one side and smiled broadly at them as they approached the door one at a time. Steven was the first to emerge and immediately picked out Alman and Ben, standing inside the terminal. He glanced back at his friends with a *"here we go"* expression and stepped down the stairs. He got to the bottom and looked to his left first, and then to his right, towards the hangar destination. There wasn't anyone else around. He got down to the tarmac and waited for his friends. They all finished coming down and then the four of them stood together for a moment, on the tarmac at the base of the plane's steps, until Steven spoke up in a very matter of fact tone. "Let's go."

With that, all four of them took off as if they'd been waiting for a starter's pistol that had finally sounded.

Inside the small terminal building, Alman spat, "Shit." Then he commanded Ben and Colin to give chase, and turned to Slater. "You stay here. Get back to your car and wait. Don't let anyone see you. I'll corral them and bring them to the cars." With a nod, Slater moved away to do exactly as he was told.

The lone terminal employee lazily glanced up from his paper to watch Colin and Ben charge out of the building, followed closely by Alman. The pilot had returned to his cockpit to go over his postflight checklist and did not see a thing.

THE FOUR friends raced towards the hangar, and when they were at about the halfway point, Steven glanced behind them. Ben and Colin were about eighty yards back, and Alman had just come out of the terminal building, running hard. They'd have only seconds once they got inside—if they got inside—to either lock the door and try to bar it or just try to hide. Randi reached the hangar first and went straight for the only door she could see. Much to their glee, it opened. They tumbled inside, with Steven and Nathan literally rolling through onto the floor. Randi pushed the door closed and fumbled for a locking mechanism on the doorknob before getting it engaged, with Jenna right behind her, reaching over her shoulder to slide the deadbolt home. Just then, a loud thud from the other side of the door signaled the arrival of Ben and Colin. They banged against it several times, but it didn't open.

"Get away from the door," Steven huffed. "They may try to shoot through it."

Jenna and Randi leapt to the side just as a gunshot rang out. The impact on the other side was followed by an angry (if somewhat muffled) yell: "You idiot! It's a metal door! That ricochet could have killed us!"

All four backed away farther into the hangar as they heard Alman arrive outside and start issuing orders: "Look for a window, stupid. We'll break in through that."

The four turned to look at their surroundings. The hangar was quite dark but looked to be about the size of a football field. There was an open, cubicle type office, just to the side of the door they had just come through, that had a small window on one exterior wall. *That's where they'll get in,* they all thought. They continued looking around, and in the shadowed recesses at the back, they could make out a small plane. Thinking fast, they ran towards it.

Right at the back of the building was a scaffold-like structure that looked something like a rocket gantry, missing its rocket. At the top was a boom that extended across the entire building, was secured to the wall at the opposite end, and had a clamping device hanging from it. Beyond the small plane they'd run to, they spotted three other planes, two smaller than the first and one larger. There was also a forklift and a golf cart sitting idle. The only other door appeared to be a large double set that looked big enough to allow planes to be moved in and serviced inside the hangar. They knew they weren't going to be able to open that door, so they'd need to get back to where they'd started in order to get back out of the hangar. They were all standing on the other side of the small plane in the middle of the hangar, when suddenly, the sound of breaking glass snapped them to attention. Turning towards the office, they saw Ben smashing the rest of the glass from the window. He was going to be able to climb through for sure.

Jenna whispered, "It will take them a moment to get in. We should break into pairs now."

"No," Randi countered. "In here, we've got to stay together. We *have* to get back to the front door to get out. So, we've got to stay close."

"Okay, I agree," Steven added. "Anyone got any idea of how we do that?"

Randi looked around. "It's quite dark down this end, so for now, let's head further back and stay out of sight."

The four of them quickly headed down to the end of the hangar, furthest from the office, disappearing into the hangar's blackness, one by one.

IN THE office, Ben had finished smashing the window and was helping Colin climb through it. Once inside, he moved to the front door and let the others in. Finally, the three stood inside the darkened hangar and looked into its shadowy depths.

Affiliation

They couldn't make out much, their eyes having yet to fully adjust from the brightness of outside. Alman looked around for a light panel but couldn't find one. "There must be a way to turn on the lights in here," he muttered.

Colin and Ben stared into the inky black space, and realised that they could see the faint outline of a plane. "We'll move inside and start looking," Ben said to Alman. "It's the only way our eyes will ever adjust to this."

"Okay, good. I'll stay here and keep looking for the lights."

Ben and Colin started in, guns drawn. Moving slowly as their eyes began to adjust, they reached the plane, parked near the middle of the hangar, and saw that its door was open. Ben pointed at it with his gun, and Colin readied himself to climb in.

FROM THE far end of the hangar, the other four watched this happening, Ben and Colin little more than faint, silhouetted outlines against the pale light from the front-office window.

"Okay," whispered Randi, "opening the door to lure them inside that one bought us a little time. Good thinking, Steve, but what now?"

Steven looked around the dark hangar. The three other planes and other equipment gave them some cover but not much. They were at the far end of the hangar, about fifty yards from the small plane Ben and Colin had just climbed into, which was roughly centered in the width of the space. Looking past it to his left, Steven could *just* make out the far wall. It might give them a chance.

"What if we move to that far side wall and start inching our way back? As they move into the main part of the hangar, they'll be checking planes and around the equipment. If we move slowly and quietly, they probably won't see us in the shadows there. We can probably make it back to the other side and then get out." Steven looked at his three friends and shrugged his shoulders.

There was a moment's pause and then Jenna said, "Look, it just might work. If we move quietly but quickly, while they're focused on checking the planes and the equipment, they'll have no reason to even look at the wall."

There was another pause, and then Randi nodded. "Okay, let's do it."

"One of us," Nathan said, "will have to constantly look back to see if they're still working on the planes and equipment. And as we move closer to the office, the lights from the outside will slowly expose us more and more."

Nathan was right. One half of the hangar was in near complete darkness, and that was their half. As they moved more towards the lighted half, they would be more and more visible, as if coming out of a thick fog as it gets thinner and thinner.

"It doesn't matter," Steven said. "It's our only option."

They could see images of Ben and Colin moving inside the small plane, and then saw them climb out and begin to move deeper into the hangar. This was their cue to start moving towards the far wall, which they quickly did.

BACK IN the office, Alman had continued to look for a light panel for the hangar. He found the switch for the office lights, and flipped it on, and then looked towards the door Randi and the others had tumbled through. He thought he could see a box beside the door and wondered if it could be a main switch for the hangar lights.

BEN AND Colin climbed down the small plane's stairs and looked deeper into the rest of the hangar. Their eyes were adjusting now, and they could make out the forms of three other planes. They moved towards the closest to check it out.

"Okay," Ben whispered. "We'll go to each one and check them out one at a time."

"Yeah, okay," Colin whispered back, "but what if they're not *in* the planes?"

"Then we keep looking."

"But as we search the planes, they could be slipping away in this darkness. Maybe I should just search through the hangar as you search the planes."

"Yeah, okay."

ALONG THE far side wall, the four had inched towards the center of the hangar, and the light was becoming more and more problematic, making them feel more and more exposed. But they kept inching along, passing the small plane in the hangar's centre. Steven had volunteered to stay at the back and keep an eye on Ben and Colin. In front of him were Nathan and Jenna, and Randi was in the lead. In a few more yards, they knew they'd be visible to anyone who happened to glance in their direction. They watched as Alman moved towards the door they'd come in through, focussing on that area, and had yet to look in their direction at all. Behind them, Ben was checking the second of the three other planes, and Colin had just accidentally kicked over a toolbox and let out a muffled "Shit! Son of a bitch" as his shin suffered the brunt of the trauma.

Alman was now at the door, looking like he was trying to open a box on the wall beside it, but the four friends kept inching along. As long as his back stayed towards them, they knew they could keep moving undetected. But then they heard a faint click, followed by a buzz, and a row of lights at the far end, where the four friends had been only moments earlier, flickered and then started glowing a solid, muted white that was growing steadily brighter as the system warmed up.

The friends looked up at the lights behind them, and then back at Alman. He was still focused on the lights, looking up at them instead in their direction. He flicked another switch. Another humming sound and another row of lights snapped on, flickering for a second, and then staying solid. Alman continued to look up at them. Steven nudged Jenna to keep moving and to nudge the others. With his attention focused on the lights, Alman still hadn't noticed them. So, petrified or not, they kept moving.

Alman flicked a third switch, and the next row of lights came on. The glow of the first row was already growing brightly. He could now make out the back wall of the hangar through an ever-thinning veil of shadow. Things were brightening up. "I should have this place totally light in a few seconds!" he shouted, hoping to both alert Colin and Ben and scare the other four.

The friends had kept moving and were only a few yards from the office, the low dividing wall of which jutted out into the hangar. If they could just get to it, they would at least have some cover from Alman, though not from Ben and Colin. Still, one thing at a time.

ALMAN TURNED to face the rest of the hangar and just missed spotting them in his peripheral vision before they reached cover, ducked down, and continued creeping towards the edge of it. Randi peered around the corner. Alman was moving slowly towards the small plane in the middle of the hangar now, his head pivoting right and left, and he would have seen them if he'd started this even ten seconds earlier. Unfortunately for him, they were already behind him.

The hangar was completely lit now, its overhead lights as bright as small suns. They could see Colin and Ben moving between the equipment and planes. The four of them stayed crouched down, glued to the dividing wall even though it offered no real cover from that direction. Randi peered around the corner again, assessing their next move.

"The door is about fifteen feet away," she whispered. "Too far. I say we make a break for it and jump out the same window they came through. If we keep low, the office walls should keep us hidden."

The others looked at her, then each other, and then at their pursuers. A silent, *"yeah, whatever"* expression was exchanged between them, and then they started to move, with Randi in the lead, making their way silently to the window wall and then looking back into the hangar.

"Okay, let's go," Steven said as soon as they were in place.

Randi went through first. Then Steven helped Jenna through, and just as she hit the ground outside, Steven and Nathan heard the faint but distinctive ringing of a phone. A cell phone. They looked back into the hangar and could see Alman, standing by the small plane in the middle of the hangar, raise his phone slowly to his ear and listen for a moment. Then he turned his gaze directly towards the office, spotting two of his remaining adversaries still standing at the window and quickly raise his other hand, pointing something at them.

"Gun!" Steven blurted out, and he and Nathan both jumped back. They felt the heat of the bullet zip between them and saw a hole appear in the wall as if by magic, followed by the sound of the retort. He looked at Nathan. "Go!"

Nathan jumped—or more accurately, dove—headfirst through the window. Steven followed close on his heels, even as he felt something burn past his ear. He hit the ground outside and rolled, and then Jenna was helping him up, even as Randi was helping Nathan. She pointed towards the parking lot, and they took off at a sprint.

Without slowing, Steven glanced over at the actual terminal and saw Slater looking out the window towards them. He had a cell phone pressed to his ear.

CHAPTER 93

THEY REACHED the parking lot at breakneck speed without catching any additional sightings of Slater, and slammed into the back of first in a row of parked cars. Steven turned and looked back towards the hangar. Ben had just come around the outside corner and rejoined Colin and Alman.

"We've got to move fast," Steven said, aware that the three men chasing them had already crossed almost half the distance separating them. "Are any of these car doors unlocked? We need to see if any have the keys inside. C'mon!" The friends split up a bit and started frantically checking doors. No keys were visible in the first or second car Steven came to, but when he got to the third, a large black Cadillac, he saw that it was running. In the same moment, he saw Slater emerge from the terminal building at a run, heading straight for them.

"Over here!" Steven shouted to the others. "Get over here! We've got to go now!"

"Wait!" Slater called out. "We can work this out, young man! No one will get hurt! I promise."

A chorus of "Screw you!" rang out from the frightened four, as Steven climbed in the driver's side and the others started scrambling in as well. A shot rang out, and they instinctively ducked, but nothing happened either to the car or to them. Alman and his crew were getting closer and closer.

Steven threw the Cadillac into reverse and floored the accelerator, then quickly stopped, spun the wheel around hard, shifted into "drive," and took off with the tires screeching. In his rear-view mirror, he saw the three gunmen stop and take aim at their car.

"Get down!" he yelled as he swerved the car to the right, and then the left, as more gunshots rang out. Still, none hit the car, and Steven kept glancing back. Slater and his three hitmen were climbing into one of the remaining cars to give chase, so he sped out of the terminal grounds and onto what appeared to be a secondary highway.

Nathan looked over at Steven from the passenger seat. "Where are we going?"

"How the hell should I know? I don't even know where we are!"

In the back seat, Jenna and Randi were looking out the rear window.

"Do you see them?" Jenna asked.

"No, I don't. But they're coming... That's for sure."

BACK IN the trailing car, Slater was looking at this cell phone. He had connected to the GPS device in his Cadillac, in which the four fugitives were currently fleeing, and was calmly relaying information to Alman as to where it was going. They might be out of sight for the moment, but the device was tracking them nicely.

"When do you want to take them?" Alman asked.

"Ideally, when they stop for something, but failing that, we may have to choose a deserted stretch and try to knock them off the road." He shrugged and shook his head. "That's more your department."

"How much gas was in your car?"

"I'm not too sure. Close to a full tank."

"They can go a long way on a full tank."

"Maybe we should close in now."

Without waiting for another word, Alman pressed down on his accelerator.

UP AHEAD in the Cadillac, Randi was typing something furiously into her cell phone.

"What are you doing, Randi?" asked Jenna.

"I'm trying to send a message to a couple of friends in Washington."

"Your senator friends?"

"You got it."

"Will they help?"

"I think so. Like I told you guys, they've been looking into pharma-company practices for years. I just hope their staffers give them this message as quickly as we'd like."

"Oh shit," Nathan said as he turned to look back.

"What is it?" Steven asked.

"I think that's them coming up fast behind us!"

Steven looked in his mirror, and sure enough, he could see the town car that the others had jumped into back at the airport, and it was closing in on them.

Nathan shook his head. "They sure found us fast! There must be a GPS system in this thing that's letting them track us!"

"That's just great." Steven rolled his eyes. "In the last few days, I've been threatened and chased, had a friend die, been shot at, and now I'm apparently in a high-speed car chase. Only they don't teach you how to *drive* a car chase when you're just a drug rep."

Jenna leaned over to the front seat. "Consider this on-the-job training. Now drive."

Steven put his foot down hard, and the Cadillac responded immediately with full acceleration, widening its lead on the pursuing car, which quickly increased its speed to keep up.

"Okay," Steven said, "so now we're going crazy fast, but just where are we going?"

"OnStar!" Randi exclaimed suddenly. "All these fancy, fat-cat cars have real-person help systems on board! If not OnStar, then something like it!"

Nathan half turned his head. "You want to get us directions to a nice restaurant?"

"No," Randi said in an impatient, scolding tone. "We can get directions to the interstate that will take us to Washington!"

Steven looked over at Nathan and smiled. "That's why *she's* the scientist."

Nathan began frantically searching the dashboard for a button that looked like it might connect them to someone, then started touching the display screen and looking at the different icons.

Jenna pointed and said, "That one maybe? Or that one?"

Steven glanced at this speedometer. They were driving close to a hundred miles an hour, and he was coming up fast on a car doing the posted fifty-five.

"Hang on everyone." The others looked up as they quickly closed in on the car in front of them.

Steven swung the wheel to the right, steering the Cadillac onto the shoulder, its back end fishtailed a bit, making their stomachs do a little backflip, and then straightened it out. He quickly got them around and past the slower car, and then steered back onto the highway. In his mirror, he saw the other car doing the same maneuver.

Finally, Nathan located the icon that would connect them to the car's help service and tapped it.

"This is OnStar help service. How may I help you, Mr. Slater?"

Nathan and Steven looked at each other, each waiting for the other to be William Slater.

"Mr. Slater? How may I help? Is everything okay?"

Jenna suddenly poked Steven in the back and his voice almost jumped out of him. "Yes! Yes, this is William Slater. I'd like directions to the nearest interstate that will take me to Washington. I've got a meeting there." He finished by shrugging his shoulders at his friends.

The help service answered immediately. "Certainly, sir. I'm happy to help with that."

CHAPTER 94

IN THE office of Senator Tom Hickey, an aide was staring at a computer screen.

"Having a fun time today?" a young woman asked him.

"Oh, loads, Paula. Just loads. I love screening the senator's emails. Maybe the president will send one."

That would be highly unlikely. For the past several years, Senator Hickey had been on something of a crusade, looking into the practices of Big Pharma with his partner Senator Brock Randall. The president currently occupying the White House was very pro Big Pharma, having accepted millions in campaign donations from them. He was also a Republican—a party that, historically, had always been firmly on the side the pharmaceutical companies.

Senators Hickey and Randal, both Democrats, had examined dozens of cases against pharmaceutical companies relating to marketing abuse, scientific fabrications, the cover-up of bad data, coercion, and the bullying of FDA officials, just to name a few. They had stumbled into the crusade by way of a constituent whose daughter had been diagnosed with schizophrenia when she was twenty-two years old. She'd been started on the antipsychotic medication Zyprexa, which was indicated for schizophrenia and other related psychotic disorders. The treating psychiatrist had followed the recommendations on dosing listed on the company's product monograph, which stated there was a chance of a "small gain in weight." On average, the weight gain, as noted in the monograph, was seven to nine kilograms or sixteen to twenty pounds. The psychiatrist had counseled his patient and her family that, with proper diet and continued exercise, the weight gain would be minimal.

The had drug worked. The daughter's psychotic symptoms had disappeared. She no longer heard voices. She no longer hallucinated. Her thought process, once garbled and jumbled, became clearer. Her feelings of persecution abated. Prior to taking Zyprexa, her mood had been flat, but after being on the medication for several weeks, her mood had brightened. So, initially, things were quite good. However, the company's claims on weight gain had been misleading and grossly underreported as per the product monograph. She had not gained sixteen to twenty pounds. In six months on Zyprexa, she'd gained ninety-seven pounds.

She'd gone from being a fit and athletic beauty, at 117 pounds and five-foot-two-inches tall, to a bloated, unhealthy, and miserably depressed woman at 214 pounds. In six months. And the weight gain showed no signs of stopping, or even slowing, either. She begged to get off the medication, and then quit on her own only to become floridly psychotic within weeks. So, she went back on the pills and continued to gain weight. Not only that but other metabolic issues arose. Her cholesterol was wildly out of control. Her sugar levels put her in the diabetic range. More pills followed, to try to control all the metabolic issues, but as the weight went up, her mood, once brightened, began to decline again. Her persona became blunted. She lost interest in many things that used to give her pleasure. Her mother had told the senators that her daughter seemed to become a little more depressed with each pound she gained, with her motivation to exercise at all decreasing with each increase. And with each new pill that was added to her regimen, she just sank further and further down. Then one day, she'd come down the stairs for breakfast cheerful, positive, and smiling, with vigor in her step and seeming to exude positivity. Her mother had been thrilled.

She and her husband had decided right then and there to book a fun "coming out" trip to Hawaii to celebrate. They had a great week in Honolulu, returned home, and the day after getting back, the mum had gone shopping. It was a quarter past eleven in the morning when she returned home and called for her daughter but didn't get an answer. So, she went to the daughter's room, but she wasn't there. When she'd come in, she had noticed that the door to the basement was ajar, so she went downstairs, and found her daughter hanging from a beam. She had killed herself. The note she'd left behind was all-too-brief: "I can't weight for death."

The mother had been arguing with the treating psychiatrist and the drug company ever since her daughter had started gaining the weight. While her daughter had been alive, the mum had phoned the drug company to try and get some answers on the true nature of the weight gain caused by Zyprexa. Was the drug *causing* her daughter's weight gain? The only answer she received referred her back to the product monograph. Could the weight gain be alleviated in some way? She got the same answer. The company's standard and repeated response was to refer back to the monograph and encourage her to encourage her daughter to exercise more. What about the blunted personality? Was it a sign the drug was no longer working? Refer back to the monograph. Though they admitted that they were unsure of Zyprexa's exact mechanism of action, it *had* been approved by the FDA for her daughter's condition, and as such, she should refer back to the product monograph.

The mum really got no answers but the company's stonewalling. She then heard about Senators Hickey and Randal looking into pharmaceutical companies and finally convinced them to give her an appointment. It was during this appointment that the mum's passion and anguish came together to convince the two senators to start digging even deeper. They also promised her that all the resources of their office would be committed to finding out more. Over the next several months, the senators looked deeper and deeper and realized just how out of control Big Pharma had truly become. Yes, their medications helped people. But their behavior and practices when confronted with alarming news about one of their meds was (in itself) alarming. They found that some of the marketing and sales practices displayed by the pharma companies was plainly unethical.

In the case of Zyprexa, the senators had taken notes and followed the many lawsuits that had been filed against Zyprexa's maker, Eli Lilly, by multiple American states. The suits centered around the marketing of the drug and how the company had downplayed the serious weight-gain issue. There were several successfully prosecuted lawsuits completed against them. The financial damages had been in the hundreds of millions of dollars. Yet that drug company and others soldiered on. Buoyed by billions in the bank and a consumer need for the "quick-fix" pill, they pressed forward, but the senators were not going to give up. It was their crusade now.

And it was during the course of this journey that they had come across a scientist named Randi Thilwell, an outspoken critic of the influence of

Big Pharma and how it exerted undue influence over the research of chemical compounds.

As such, the aide who'd been looking at the computer screen perked up somewhat when an email from a Randi Thilwell appeared in Senator Hickey's inbox. The senator had a priority list of email senders, and Randi was on it. He was to be personally informed of any messages she sent him. The aide opened the message and read it: *Tom, must speak. Have information about Big Pharma. You must see it. It's huge. Please get back. RT.*

"Hey, Paula, I think we may have something here. Would you please call the senator?"

CHAPTER 95

THE CHASE on the secondary highway had changed in dramatic fashion. Over the last few minutes, in the Cadillac, Steven had noticed that the pursuing car had backed off. So, he'd slowed down to the speed limit to avoid any police interest, and the following car had slowed to match. It was now less of a high-speed chase and more of a slow-speed tailing or monitoring. Steven and the others knew they were being followed and by whom. The followers knew who they were after and were keeping them in sight. Neither side wanted to push the issue further at the moment, or at least, so it seemed. The four being followed certainly didn't want to stop and provoke a confrontation, and the followers appeared to be happy just following.

"Why don't they come after us? Why are they just following?"

"I don't know, Jenna, I don't know. If we were going any slower, this would be O.J. 2.0," Steven replied with a frustrated smirk.

"I guess we just keep running along," Nathan offered with a shrug.

IN THE pursuing car, Slater had been working the phone. He had called his government contact and was trying to arrange an interception by some federal agents at some future point down the road. He had tried to frame it as a concerned CEO, trying to peacefully retrieve some intellectual property, but his government contact had been very reluctant to commit federal agents to a car chase on any kind of highway. It was one thing to quietly detain some people at an airport. It was quite another to get involved in what could potentially become a dangerous confrontation on the road. If any injuries or worse occurred, then no amount of trying would cover it up. Slater had become exasperated and made a silent note to curtail his contributions to this particular department in the future.

"Why don't we just move in and take them ASAP?" Alman was growing impatient. In his view, they could simply move on the car, and so they should. When the time was right, with no other cars around, he would execute the same maneuver used by law enforcement agencies to get a vehicle to stop or run it off the road. Then his two men could take out the four fleeing people in the Cadillac, retrieve Thilwell's cell phone, and then move on.

Up ahead, the Cadillac veered onto an exit ramp and continued, turning onto I-95 South.

"I know where they're going," said Slater. "They're headed to Washington."

CHAPTER 96

SENATOR HICKEY burst through the door to his office and found Paula, his aide. "What's this all about? I was in a pretty important committee meeting."

"I'm sorry, Senator, but Eric just read an email that just came for you. It was from Dr. Randi Thilwell. We thought you would like to see it right away."

"Randi sent me a message? That's it? So, what's the big deal? She and I have communicated in the past."

"I know that, Senator. But it was her wording on this one that struck us as odd. And her..." She was struggling to find the word. "Her..."

"Her what?"

"Her ... tone, I guess. Or the tone of her message. It seemed excited and scared at the same time. You have to see it."

CHAPTER 97

INSIDE THE Cadillac, the four friends were silent. None of them could make sense of what was happening. They didn't appear to be in any imminent danger, yet they weren't being left alone either. They were now on an interstate heading south toward Washington. Randi's email had not been answered, but they were confident they'd hear back. Just as Nathan was about to speak, Randi's cell phone rang. All four jumped, and the car swerved to the right for a moment before Steven quickly corrected it.

"Is it the senator?" Jenna asked.

"No, it's Slater," Randi replied. She looked at her three companions, and then answered on the third ring.

"Hello?"

"Dr. Thilwell, how are you?" Slater's tone was saccharin sweet.

"How the hell do you think I am? How do you think we all are? You assholes want us dead. You tried to kill us, and now you're just staying back there ... menacing us."

"Dr. Thilwell, calm down. My associate acted hastily back at the airfield. We don't want you dead. We just want our property back. That's all. You give us all you have, and we'll call it a day. I have to tell you; I'm tired of this chase. It's time to go home, don't you think?"

Randi paused and looked around the car. Slater's voice was convincing, almost soothing. Going home sounded nice. But then she remembered Alex and Miguel. She put her phone on speaker before answering him.

"Go home? Is that what you said? Did Alex and Miguel get to go home? You son of a bitch."

"Those were unfortunate accidents. We ... *I* did not mean for that to happen. Rest assured; their families will be taken care of. You have my word.

Now, let's stop this nonsense. You can pull into the busiest place you want. Nothing will happen to you. Turn over to me everything you have of ours, and then go on your way."

"Really. We can 'go on our way'? You're going to just let us go, knowing what we know? You'd let us go public?"

"Absolutely. Think about it. You'd have no proof. You could whistle blow until the cows come home, and we'd politely reject your assertions. You may think holding onto that USB information and the files protects you, but it doesn't. Quite the opposite. You're in danger *because* you're holding onto what you have. In fact, I encourage you to go public with what you know. Then if anything happened to *any* of you, after that, it would raise many suspicions, and you know we wouldn't want that. You can secure your own safety, and the safety of your friends, by giving us our property and moving on with your lives. You might know what you know but you wouldn't be a threat."

Randi looked at Nathan and Jenna. Their faces were a collage of conflict. Could this be genuine? If they gave up the USB information and the files, they would have no proof. And without it, even were they to go public, their story would be so wild, so fantastically unlikely, that who would ever believe them? Investigations need a basis of credibility to even get started. And even if one did get started, the Big Pharma companies would just shut it down, and it would become just another wild conspiracy theory It would be a pharmaceutical industry Sasquatch. The equivalent of a car that runs on water.

Nathan pointed at the phone and drew his hand across his throat.

Randi looked down at the phone. "I'm going to put you on hold for a minute."

"JUST WHAT the hell are you doing?" Alman demanded, looking over at Slater.

"Relax. I'm negotiating. It's one of the many skills I've honed over the years. If they accept my offer, we get our property back, and it ends here. We can still pursue our other ideas, but they'll be eunuchs. Accusers with no proof."

"And you think that's foolproof?"

"Absolutely. In fact, it came to me before they even turned towards Washington. That's why I had you back off the chase. A one- or two-car crash on a busy highway would have raised too many questions, and too many suspicions, especially if one or more of them were left dead or injured. I'd reasoned that they would likely turn towards Washington, given Dr. Thilwell's public consultations with certain elected officials there. I even know the two senators they're going to see, and while they don't like the pharmaceutical industry, they're politicians. They don't like being publicly embarrassed. If they accept my offer and still go see the senators, nothing will happen because they've got no proof. If the senators decide to investigate, we'll gladly comply with any requests and then give them just what we want them to have. And nothing will happen. The point being, we'll be back in control."

"And what if they've already sent the information to another computer?"

"Relax. Before we let them go, you can do a search, or whatever, to see if they've done just that. If it's clean, we move on. If not, we have them give us everything back, and go get the other devices, and *then* we move on. Listen, it's not like they're not used to this. This isn't some movie. They're ordinary people trapped in an extraordinary set of circumstances, and I think they want a way out. Wouldn't you if you were them?"

IN THE Cadillac, Randi removed the hold on the call and said, "Slater, are you there?"

"Absolutely."

"So, we've been talking up here and want to know how can we trust you. I mean, you've been trying to kill us for days. You killed Miguel and Alex. You're obviously capable of anything."

"I know it seems that way, but I've *only* been trying to get our property back. What happened in Barbados was horrible and regrettable. We didn't mean to harm anyone, let alone kill Dr. Byers and Miguel. As I said, that was regrettable. I should have broached this much sooner, and I'm sorry. But you *can* trust me. You can pick the place where we stop. Make it very public. I implore you. Only myself and my associate will approach. You give us the information, and we'll part company. Have you forwarded it along to anyone or anything else?"

"I sent it to my office computer."

"Yes, I suspected you would. I will make sure your office computer is seized."

"How on earth can you do that?"

"I'm sure you've guessed by now that we are very plugged in, and we are thorough as well."

"But what about the work? You're hiding cures for diseases that are a plague to millions. How can you... How can *we* just let them die?"

"We've talked about that. We have kept those compounds a secret for very sound reasons." Slater was feeling annoyed but forcefully calmed himself. "Dr. Thilwell, the work will continue. The industry *wants* to help people, but we *must* do it in a manner that is *sustainable*, not only for us but for society as a whole. We'll continue to work on the compounds you have in order to come up with medications that keep the diseases and symptoms at bay as long as one takes their pills over the course of their lifetime. You can even help us! Join a research team and work to help us, yourself, *and* other people."

"You'd allow me to join a research team?"

"Of course!" Slater enthused. Sensing that he had them, he pressed on. "You can join Matthews as a lead researcher in any therapeutic area of your interest."

"What about my friends here?"

"They can go back to their jobs, and their lives, and we can put this ugly episode behind us."

Randi looked at her friends, who nodded their agreement. "Okay, you've got a deal. We'll look up a place using your fancy OnStar system and call you back. Agreed?"

"Agreed. And I just want to reiterate how sorry I am for all of this. I look forward to working with you in the future."

"Yeah, sure. I'll phone back soon."

In the Cadillac, Jenna looked at Randi. "I hope we're doing the right thing."

IN THE town car, Alman looked at Slater. "I hope we're doing the right thing."

CHAPTER 98

STEVEN KEPT driving while Nathan talked to the OnStar woman about upcoming towns, cities, and other destination points. They wanted someplace public with easy access off the highway. They also wanted a very direct route. No quiet roads or secluded areas. Slater could be lying. Speed and a direct line of escape were key to their survival.

"What do we have so far, Nate?"

"Well, there's a place about half an hour ahead—an outlet mall just outside of the first exit for Washington. That might work well."

"Actually," Randi chimed in from the back, "that would be perfect. Let's use that."

"Okay." Steven nodded. "Phone Slater."

SLATER CLICKED his phone shut, after speaking with Randi, and looked at Alman. "They're going to pull into an outlet mall about thirty minutes ahead. You see? It's working out well. Just as I planned."

"Yeah ... and what if they change their minds?"

"They won't."

"I still say we take them out, even if we get the information back."

"I agree. Just do it *after* they've gone back to their lives."

"So, you were lying to them all along?"

"As I told you, I was negotiating. And sometimes you hold things back in a negotiation."

"Why didn't you tell me this before?"

"You may have made an offhand comment or even a sound that might have tipped them off. It's best, during negotiations, to have the real information known to only the most important individuals."

That was a clear shot across Alman's bow, with Slater reasserting his dominance, but Alman just accepted it. He had a hundred-million-dollar payout coming, so it really didn't matter.

THE CARS sped along the interstate. In the Cadillac, the occupants were nervous and scared, talking about what was about to happen and making sure that each of them knew what to do. Nathan would hang back and watch for any suspicious activity. If he saw something odd before they were ready, he'd sound the car horn so the other three could scatter. They had decided to have Jenna, Steven, and Randi move towards Slater, just to have an extra set of eyes to watch for anything out of the ordinary that Nathan might miss from his vantage point.

"We're coming up to the exit," Steven called out.

"Okay," Jenna said. "Does everyone know what to do?" There were nods all around. "Randi, is everything set?" Randi looked up from her cell phone and nodded.

Nathan nodded too. "Okay. So, I guess we're good to go."

IN THE town car, Alman signaled that the exit was coming up. Slater acknowledged this and confirmed with Colin and Ben in the back seat. "Just follow them in. Don't do anything aggressive." He looked at Alman then and spoke to all three. "We've finally got them. I'll be glad to get back to New York tonight."

Alman held his tongue, though he wasn't quite as confident of their success.

STEVEN STEERED their car onto the exit ramp, and as they climbed, they could see the outlet mall. One right turn and they'd be within half a mile of it. The pursuing car followed but did not close the distance as the Cadillac approached the entrance to the mall and turned in. It was busy. The parking lot was nearly full, and there were people everywhere, walking to and from their cars. It was a very public place indeed.

"Okay," Steven started, "where is this going to happen?"

The others looked around the lot. Randi spotted a row that had a few empty spaces and pointed towards it. "Over there. That's enough room, I think." The cars crept towards a small island of space in the sea of cars.

Steven pulled into a parking spot and immediately got out, motioning for the other car to park in a spot about eight spaces away. He wanted a little distance between them. The other car rolled slowly by them and parked as directed. Colin and Ben were looking straight ahead, their gaze never even flinching sideways. *It's like that scene in Jaws,* Steven thought, *where they see the shark for the first time.*

The doors of the other car opened. Slater got out of the passenger door and stood facing them for the second time. Alman got out next and moved around the vehicle to join Slater. They looked at each other and then back towards the four friends. Slater even smiled and gave them a small wave before buttoning his coat and taking a few steps towards Steven, who had now been joined by Jenna and Randi, standing about four parking spaces ahead of where Nathan was sitting in the Cadillac, watching out for trouble.

The four would argue later about what they'd heard first. It could have been the multiple car doors opening, the screech of tires, or the shouts of 'FREEZE!' It doesn't really matter though. Just as Slater and Alman stepped towards the Cadillac, two cars pulled into their row and came to a screeching stop. Four doors seemed to open simultaneously, just as two more cars pulled in, each from a different direction, boxing everyone between them as eight men brandishing guns descended on the rendezvous.

Slater spun from side to side with his eyes as big as saucers, whereas Alman looked around and simply smiled. *Figures,* he thought.

Colin and Ben moved slowly from their car, emerging with their hands in the air. Two of the armed men moved swiftly in and secured them.

Steven, Jenna, and Randi were startled by the speed at which it all took place.

"Are you alright, Randi?" Senator Tom Hickey asked them as he came running up from one of the newly arrived vehicles. "Are you all alright? Where's your other friend?"

Randi looked at him, and for reasons unbeknownst to her at that moment, began to cry. "I'm fine. We're fine ... I think. Nathan's in our car over there." Then she flung her arms around the senator in a giant hug.

Steven looked around at the scene and then at Jenna. She was smiling broadly. Back in the Cadillac, Nathan was sitting with his head resting on his forearms, which were resting on the dashboard. Steven looked again at Jenna then and impulsively moved towards her, opening his arms wide. To his delight (and some surprise), she jumped into his embrace.

"I think we're all fine," she said then ... to no one and everyone at the same time.

CHAPTER 99

"JUST WHAT the hell is going on?" Slater thundered in response to the scene unfolding all around him.

"Well, Mr. Slater, this is called the end of the line for you and your friends," Senator Hickey answered.

"Now just a minute, Senator. These four people stole some very sensitive, proprietary information from my company. We're just here to get it back. That's all."

"Mr. Slater, I have no doubt that you'd be far from done with these people once they'd handed over their information. I'm sure you'd kill them just like you've done to others."

"Kill? Senator, I'm in the pharmaceutical business! I do not kill people, nor do I have them killed."

"Oh really?" The senator pulled his cell phone from his pocket and motioned for Slater to step closer. He pushed a couple of buttons, and Slater's and Randi's voices suddenly filled the air, replaying their phone conversation from when they'd still been traveling on the interstate. Slater could be heard acknowledging the murders of Byers and Miguel, as well as his assertion about the importance of maintaining the secrecy of the information that could be found on the USB. Slater looked at Randi.

"I didn't trust you," she began. "The reason I put you on hold is that Nathan noticed that Tom here was texting me." She gestured towards at the senator. "I called him, he answered, and we told him everything. Then I conferenced him in on our next conversation. It wasn't my idea to tape it. I guess Tom did that on his own." She looked at him and smiled. "Nice move, by the way."

Slater looked around. The agents had already pulled Colin and Ben to one of the cars and were helping them into the back seat. Alman was also being escorted to a waiting car. Then an agent moved towards Slater and asked him to follow him to another one.

Slater sputtered with rage, "I-I am the CEO of the b-biggest pharmaceutical company in the world! I do *not* get arrested! I—"

"Mr. Slater," said Senator Hickey, interrupting his rant, "you are about to enter a world where you are no longer in control, which I'm sure will be like the twilight zone for you. So, while it may be difficult for you to contemplate such an idea ... you should get used to it. Now get in the car."

Slater looked at the senator, then at the federal agent about to escort him into custody, and was just beginning to move towards the indicated car when Jenna stepped in front of him, staring at him for several long seconds before she spoke.

"You had my sister killed. You killed Miguel and Dr. Byers. You've killed countless other people by withholding the information on that stick. You're going to go to jail, and I'm going to be there to watch. I wanted you to know that." Tears were streaming down her face. Slater made a motion as though he were going to say something, but Steven stepped forward and put his hands on Jenna's shoulders, locking his gaze on Slater's face and effectively silencing him before he could even start to respond. Looking down, the CEO said nothing and moved towards his assigned car.

Steven turned to the senator then. "Thank you. Thank you so much."

"Well, you're welcome. But I'm afraid the excitement's not over for you four. Not by a longshot. You're going to have to come with us back to Washington and provide detailed statements about everything you've learned and witnessed. As well, if what you say is true regarding this Big Pharma cover-up, there'll be investigations, hearings, and media coverage the likes of which we haven't seen since Watergate." All four looked at him. "All I'm saying is ... be careful what you wish for because you will all be seeing a ton of Washington over the next several weeks if not months or years."

Randi looked at her three friends. "I like Washington. It's a nice town."

"I've never been," said Jenna. "Heck, I'm Canadian."

"We can do the museums," Steven offered.

Nathan stepped forward and looked at the senator. "You'll put us up in a decent hotel, right?"

The senator's eyes grew wide. Then he smiled and took a step back. "I think we can meet your needs."

EPILOGUE

IT HAD been two years since Nathan, Randi, Jenna, and Steven strode into the senate committee room to give their testimony. They'd had lawyers in tow, as well as many supporters in the audience, and were fully armed with the information they'd retained by way of Miguel's guile, cunning, and sacrifice, as well as the measured contrition and sacrifice of Dr. Byers. They testified and answered questions for two days. Some on the senate panel tried to torpedo them as nothing more than troublemakers and lawbreakers, but most of the examining board were fair and impartial.

The friends had assumed that going public would basically mean that their lives would be over, but to their surprise, they were living under the protection of the Whistleblower Act. The very public nature of their disclosure and testimony was keeping their safety of absolute paramount importance to the Affiliation as well. If any of them—or all of them—wound up dead, it would all but confirm that their information and accusations had been true.

Of course, after their testimony was finished, it had been the Affiliation's turn. They'd struggled to slip, slide, and deny the truth, and had cut Slater loose right from the start, claiming that he was a rogue individual who had acted totally on his own. He had misused the resources available to him as Matthews's CEO to go on an unhinged crime spree. No one in the Affiliation had possessed any knowledge of what he was doing (of course), and so he should go to jail. They fired back at the whistleblowers and the lead senator, Tom Hickey. They stated that the information on the USB stick and the files were being misrepresented and taken out of context. *Of course*, they wanted to cure disease, but caution was their buzzword. They did not want to unduly raise expectations, and ultimately, hope, only to have both crushed when the compound did not pan out.

Affiliation

And the Affiliation? It was nothing more than a collegial collaboration for the open sharing of scientific knowledge. The extreme nature of CEO payouts? Those were in line with current industry and corporate practice. The spyware embedded in the computers of independent researchers? This was simply to protect their intellectual property and incredibly significant investments. It was a high-risk, high-reward business, after all, so they were well within their rights to use those measures to protect themselves and their shareholders. The spyware and GPS monitoring of employees? Nothing more than what many other industries do to monitor the overall health and compliance of employees. After all, many of the employees of pharmaceutical companies work from their homes. They do not punch a clock that makes sure they arrive and actually do their work. These small measures protected against fraud and ensured that employees and their companies complied with internal and external regulations. The political contributions listed were legal, although even the committee members agreed that they were excessive. And what about the payouts to all those scientists? Just rewarding, challenging work and phenomenal contributions to science and research. All their arguments seemed logical, valid, and at least somewhat believable. Their lawyers were well prepared, and the CEOs who represented the Affiliation were well chosen. They were folksy at times, serious at other times, and always excellent, articulate spokespeople.

On the first two days of Big Pharma testimony, the whistleblowers had been a little disheartened. Then day three had arrived, and the committee turned its attention to the "termination list."

The CEOs began by stating that it was not a "termination list" but a sincere attempt to compile a list of scientists who had tragically passed. This was done to both honor the individuals and to make sure that they or their families were not contacted regarding their research, thus upsetting remaining family members. Again, this seemed logical, and some fear was felt that it might actually work. Then two surprise witnesses came forward just prior to the start of day four.

Two stern individuals walked into the committee room to tell everyone what they had done for the Affiliation. Their testimony led to the truth coming out, and finally brought everything crashing down. It also led to multiple indictments and the complete exposure of horrible wrongdoing by the Affiliation. But it was still extremely hard on all four of the friends—Jenna especially—to see Colin and Ben seat themselves at the witness table and recount the things they had done on behalf of their employers. It was their testimony that truly began the unraveling of the Affiliation. By coming forward, Colin and Ben had hoped to be able to cut a deal and stay alive—and possibly even stay out of jail.

But Slater hadn't been wrong about one thing: When it all came out, and the Affiliation came crashing down, the shockwaves that swept through the pharmaceutical industry were brutal. Stock prices plummeted right along with many executive careers. The phrase "cures kill profits" became synonymous with evil and deceit. There were fears that the entire pharmaceutical industry would collapse, but Senator Hickey—now the very famous face of the investigation—was able to allay those fears.

"Of course, these companies must keep going! The medications they provide are *essential*. In many ways, pharmaceutical companies are as important to people as heat, water, and electricity. In many cases, they are the de facto utility companies of people's lives. Perhaps, if the people running these companies had realized that they were sitting in a position of trust for people and patients alike, this would never have happened. Still, if there was a scandal at a utility company, we would not shut off people's heat, water, and electricity. We'd do just as we're doing here: investigate, and where necessary, punish the people who actually broke the law. And then we'd make corrections to ensure something like that never happened again."

From the depths of scandal came new reforms. After the committee had rendered its findings, all pharma research moving forward would be subject to random audits, much like drug testing in the world of sport. Pharmaceutical companies would now have to contribute a significant portion of before-tax profit to an independent board, which would distribute it to worthy research efforts. Research was to be judged in terms of the good it could bring to people, not by how much money it might make for its producers. This had the effect of providing more balance between private- and public-controlled research. CEO payouts were also stopped in favor of simple severance rules that governed all working people.

Randi was offered the job of heading up the new federal body that would determine which research efforts were worthy of funding, but she declined, opting instead to lead the team that would be continuing Dr. Byers's work. Even without her input though, the first research dollars from the new publicly controlled research fund would go towards the study and development of the very compounds that Slater had been so determined to retrieve and keep hidden.

Finally, once everything had ended, the four were given compensation under the Whistleblower Act, with which they made sure that Miguel's family was taken care of, just as Slater had promised them (in bad faith). They also started a bursary program in Miguel's name to help teens from poorer homes attend university.

And as for the cures themselves, some were developed quickly once science got ahold of the information previously in the Affiliation's sole possession. Parkinson's was the first disease from the USB list to become curable. Then a cure was realized for Alzheimer's, schizophrenia, and ALS, among several others. A few of the compounds didn't pan out at all, and some are still being worked on and developed. Many of the cures were tougher to develop but did eventually come to fruition, and as more of them did, scientific researchers were able to turn their attention to new areas of study. And while the stock market definitely experienced a crash, it began to rebound quickly as soon as new and rewarding products started being developed. In the end, despite the dire predictions of Slater and far too many others like him, the healthcare industry and society in general went on largely unchanged except for the better.

IN THE two years that had passed since the hearings, Jenna and Steven had often talked about paranoia and greed, working to process how they could warp people so badly that it had led to the creation of the Affiliation and unbridled secrecy, as well as the fact that, if not for greed and paranoia keeping the development of the compounds they'd stumbled onto from unfolding naturally, countless people who had died for lack of a cure would not have, and many others would have lived far better lives than they had.

They weren't talking about that today though. Instead, Jenna and Steven were walking along a ridge line in Kananaskis Country. It was a spot Jenna knew well and had introduced Steven to months earlier. He had come to love it just as much as she did. Holding hands, they walked slowly, enjoying the sound of fallen leaves crunching under their feet. They looked up at the brilliant blue sky often—almost as often as they looked at each other.

Thanks to the ordeal that had thrown them together, they had become friends. Of course, in the weeks and months that had followed their testimony, they had moved back to their respective homes in Seattle and Calgary, but even then, they'd connected (at least) three times a week, either over the phone or with FaceTime. Their early conversations had lasted only minutes but soon began to stretch into far more in-depth and lengthy chats. Soon, both found themselves thinking about the other as they prepared for bed, and still thinking of them when they woke up.

Then, one sunny day, Jenna had looked out her window and been thrilled to see Steven climbing out of a cab, right in front of her house, without any warning—holding a suitcase. She'd watched as he'd strolled up her front walkway, and met him in the threshold of her front door, where he'd asked her if they could be more than friends.

And now they were holding hands, on a beautiful fall day, and walking together in the mountains along a ridge they both loved.

Steven's cell phone buzzed, signalling that a text message had just come in. After getting an encouraging nod from Jenna, he pulled it out of his pocket and checked it.

"It's Nathan."

"What's he want? Is he upset we didn't include this glorious hike on *his* visit?"

He smiled at her. "No. He wants to know if he can barbecue steak for dinner."

As Jenna and Steven looked at each other, the shared affection in their gaze warmed them both from deep inside.

This was normal. And their lives would stay that way from now on.

"Well, text him back," she said with a smile. "Tell him we'll be home by six."

THE END

Printed in Canada